Scottish Borders Library Service

3 4144 0075 5374 2

D0298339

WITHDRAWN

22/7

DEAD MAN'S HAND

Dead Man's Hand

♥ ♣ ♦ ♠

Edited by Otto Penzler

Introduction by Howard Lederer

Quercus

First published in Great Britain in 2007 by

Quercus Plc
21 Bloomsbury Square
London
WC1A 2NS

Foreword copyright © 2007 by Otto Penzler
Compilation copyright © 2007 by Otto Penzler
Introduction copyright © 2007 by Howard Lederer

'Missing the Morning Bus' by Lorenzo Carcaterra. Copyright © 2007 by Lorenzo Carcaterra.
'Pitch Black' by Christopher Coake. Copyright © 2007 by Christopher Coake.
'One Dollar Jackpot' by Michael Connelly. Copyright © 2007 by Michael Connelly.
'Bump' by Jeffrey Deaver. Copyright © 2007 by Jeffrey Deaver.
'Poker and Shooter' by Sue DeNymme. Copyright © 2007 by Sue DeNymme.
'Deal Me In' by Parnell Hall. Copyright © 2007 by Parnell Hall.
'The Stake' by Sam Hill. Copyright © 2007 by Sam Hill.
'The Monks of the Abby Victoria' by Rupert Holmes. Copyright © 2007 by Rupert Holmes.
'A Friendly Little Game' by John Lescroart. Copyright © 2007 by Lescroart Corporation.
'Hardly Knew Her' by Laura Lippman. Copyright © 2007 by Laura Lippman.
'The Uncertainty Principle' by Eric Van Lustbader. Copyright © 2007 by Eric Van Lustbader.
'In the Eyes of Children' by Alexander McCall Smith. Copyright © 2007 by Alexander
McCall Smith.
'Mister In-Between' by Walter Mosley. Copyright © 2007 by Walter Mosley.
'Strip Poker' by Joyce Carol Oates. Copyright © 2007 by The Ontario Review Inc.
'The Eastvale Ladies' Poker Circle' by Peter Robinson. Copyright © 2007 by Peter Robinson.

The moral right of Otto Penzler to be identified as the author of this work has been
asserted in accordance with the Copyright, Designs and Patents Act, 1988.

All rights reserved. No part of this publication may be reproduced or transmitted in any form
or by any means, electronic or mechanical, including photocopy, recording, or any information
storage and retrieval system, without permission in writing from the publisher.

A CIP catalogue reference for this book is available from the British Library.

ISBN (HB) 1 84724 112 3
ISBN-13 978 1 84724 112 2
ISBN (TPB) 1 84724 113 1
ISBN-13 978 1 84724 113 9

This book is a work of fiction. Names, characters, businesses, organizations, places and
events are either the product of the author's imagination or are used fictitiously.
Any resemblance to actual persons, living or dead, events or locales is entirely coincidental.

10 9 8 7 6 5 4 3 2 1

Designed and typeset in Minion by Lindsay Nash
Printed and bound in Great Britain by Clays Ltd, St Ives plc.

THIS IS FOR MY FELLOW GAMESMEN:

Joe DeBlasio
Douglas Madeley
Todd Parsons
Robert Passikoff
Jerry Schmetterer
Monte Wasch
and, in loving memory,
John Burgoyne

SCOTTISH BORDERS LIBRARY SERVICE	
00755374	
Bertrams	12.11.07
	£14.99

WITHDRAWN

♠

Contents

WITHDRAWN

Foreword

T HE BIGGEST SURPRISE about putting together a collection of stories combining poker and crime is that it has not been done before now. If ever a subject begged to be associated with crime it is gambling, and if you think poker doesn't involve gambling, you are seven years old and think it's fun to play for matchsticks.

For most of my long life, I have played a little poker and always considered it a participatory form of entertainment and pleasure, unlike, say, horse racing, which is best enjoyed as a spectator sport. I don't know about you, but I'd be reluctant to climb aboard one of those seven-foot high, half-ton beasts as it careers along at a thousand miles an hour... at least.

Poker is a game that seems at its best when played with friends who laugh at your witty repartee, as you laugh at theirs. There has to be some money involved, of course – enough to hurt a little if you lose, enough to add some spring to your step if you win, but not enough to change your life forever in either direction.

I have played in a monthly game for about twenty years, making me one of the newcomers among a group that started nearly fifty years ago. Players have come and gone, of course. Of the originals, two have died, one moved to Florida (which is the same thing), one to California, and a few have merely drifted away. Some friends of the core players joined for a while and dropped out, to be replaced by newcomers like me. It's a friendly game with most of the guys (and it's all guys, whether by design or happenstance or custom) taking turns as host, the biggest change being that, somehow, beer has been abandoned in favor of Diet Coke and ice water.

With minor variations, this is how I've always known the game of poker in my mind's eye. We're not that different from the players who sit around the table in *The Odd Couple*. One will bet on every hand, no matter what he's been dealt. Another is more interested in telling stories and listening to them than in playing. A member of the game for about thirty years still asks, at least once a night, if a full house beats a straight. One deals as if each card had a different and peculiar shape, inevitably dropping cards to the floor and dealing some face up when they should be down, and vice-versa. Still another bets each hand – no, each card, in seven card stud – as if his son's college education depended on it. One plays so badly that, if he says he can't make it to the game, we offer to have a limousine pick him up.

Like so many other elements of life with which I was once familiar and comfortable, poker has changed. Twenty years ago, if someone had been invited, not to play poker but to watch it, he would have asked to be shot instead as a more humane method of execution than being tortured to death.

Today, of course, telecasts of big money poker are ubiquitous, hugely popular and, admittedly, addictive. The great players, those with mountain spring water instead of blood and a giant ball-bearing in the place where others have a heart, used to ply their skills clandestinely, slipping into a town, cleaning out the local hot-shots, and skedaddling before they realized they had been taken by a professional card sharp. Now, they are like rock stars, though they wear clean clothes and take baths. Even occasional tele-vised poker viewers recognize Johnny Moneymaker, Annie Duke, Howard Lederer, Johnny Chan, Phil Hellmuth and Amarillo Slim.

There is a lot of money involved in the World Series of Poker and other televised events, and there are high stakes games in Las Vegas, various Indian casinos, and in the back rooms of bars across the country. And the total gambled in these venues is dwarfed by the staggering sums wagered on internet poker, which is like crack for compulsive gamblers. Where a lot of money is involved, can crime ever be far behind? In the case of poker specifically and gambling in general, defining crime is as easy and sensible as drawing to an inside straight.

In what must be regarded as Orwellian doublespeak or the height of cynicism, there are laws on the books of every state that make it a crime to gamble for money. There are far more venues in which it is permitted to place a wager in Las Vegas than in New York, for example, where it's a lot easier than in Utah, where it's pretty much outlawed. OK, you figure, while you may not agree with the law, or like it, you understand the concept, which is to protect those who can least afford to lose their hard-earned food and rent money. While those who see it as a form of moral depravity may be a trifle zealous, federal and state regulations against alcohol (at one time) and drugs (currently) and cigarettes (imminently) were also passed in what is perceived as the common good.

Ah, but there is a lot of money involved, so some clever politicians, in consort with those who stood to gain, made an occasional exception. It was horse racing in some states. Bingo and charity 'gambling nights' received some exemptions. Certain cities like Las Vegas, then New Jersey (and can the rest of the country be far behind) licensed gambling casinos. Perhaps the most pernicious exceptions are the state run lotteries, which spend fortunes advertising. The odds of winning the big prize are astronomical, but it's not very expensive to buy a ticket, or two or three, every week, year after year, so the poor plunk down their precious dollars as TV, radio and newspaper advertising exhorts them to play again and again. 'Hey, you never know.' Lotteries are a tax on the stupid. The greedy politicians who promote it, wanting always more and more tax revenue, smirk at how cleverly they got away with it. Off-track betting parlors fall into a similar sewer of moral cynicism. Many years ago, when I worked in the sports department of the *New York Daily News*, I bet (oh, the shame, the shame) on sports and horse racing. I knew my bookie, who used his profits to send two kids to Notre Dame, and who talked me out of a couple of bets that were beyond my means. He was at risk of being arrested at any moment of any day. The OTB emporium two blocks away flourished as subway and television advertising pimped the glories of betting – just so long as it was with a state-run gambling enterprise.

How, then, are these state-run gambling establishments worse than the Mafia and other hoodlums who make gambling opportunities available to those who want it? OK, I'll concede that the governor won't knock on your door in the middle of the night and break your arms and legs, but then the crooked noses don't broadcast commercials telling you what a great idea it is to put the rent money on your lucky number, either.

Poker is quite a different kettle of fish from playing a number or putting down twenty bucks on some horse running in a $6,000 claiming race at a distant race track, of course. A poker player relies on getting some good cards, without doubt, but also on knowing what to do with them. Understanding a little about the odds, trying to keep track of which cards have been played, reading your opponents' faces and body language, makes it a test of skill, as well as nerve. Those smart dudes (and dudesses) on ESPN (and virtually every other channel, it seems) winning hundreds of thousands, or even millions, at Texas Hold 'Em, don't become legends because they're lucky, although that is an element of poker, as it is in life, that should never be discounted.

There are some smart dudes (and, yes, dudesses) on the following pages and, as in real life, some excruciatingly stupid ones. There are some you wish could be in your regular poker game, and some you pray will never ask to be dealt in. The writers who brought them to life are among the most distinguished of their era – the Moneymaker, Duke, Lederer, Chan, Hellmuth and Amarillo Slim of the mystery writing world.

You've already tossed in your ante, so enjoy the game.

Otto Penzler
December 2006
New York City

♠

Introduction

FOR WELL OVER 150 YEARS, poker has been America's table game of choice. The mere mention of the game would conjure images of Mississippi riverboat gamblers, cowboys willing to shoot a man if he thought his opponent had an ace up his sleeve, and brazen Vegas hustlers drinking whisky and smoking cigars while using marked cards to take off the unsuspecting.

While there may be a little truth to these bygone notions, poker has become inextricably woven into the fabric of the American experience. The game has been played by American presidents and Supreme Court justices. Grandmothers teach their grandchildren how to play on the kitchen table (I'm betting on grandma). Friends use it as an excuse to get together each week to drink a few beers, curse their bad luck, and, most important, strengthen the bonds of friendship that can be so fragile. Ten years ago, the *New York Times* reported that fifty million Americans played the game on at least a monthly basis.

With all this in mind, one shouldn't be amazed that the game has become such a popular form of television programming. In 2003 the World Poker Tour brought hole-card cameras and high pro-duction values to televised poker. Later in that year, the aptly named Chris Moneymaker, a Tennessee accountant, turned a $40 online entry into a seat at the $10,000 buy-in main event of the

World Series of Poker, where he beat 839 of the best poker players in the world to become world champion while pocketing $2.5 million. These two events combined to make poker an overnight media sensation.

Of course, within a few months, those same media were already predicting that the poker fad was bound to fizzle in, at most, a year. They failed to realize that poker never gets old. Playing and watching the game will always fascinate because it is more about the people you are playing with than the cards you are dealt. Poker is simply a vehicle that facilitates human connection. Two office mates might learn more about each other in a single evening of spirited poker play than they would in a year of shared meetings and tepid hellos at work. Long before 2003, poker had already worked its way into our language. Colorful, often-used phrases such as blue chip, bottom dollar, pass the buck, above board and square deal, can trace their origins to poker. A game that has so firmly entrenched itself in a culture's psyche is not likely to burn out anytime soon.

Poker has even spawned a rich tradition of non-fiction. Al Alvarez's *The Biggest Game in Town* is a classic, and more recent books like Jim McManus's *Positively Fifth Street* and Michael Craig's *The Professor, the Banker and the Suicide King* point towards a bright future in the poker non-fiction category. However, poker fiction, until now, has been nearly non-existent.

With this in mind, Otto Penzler assembled a staggering array of crime novelists and asked each of them to weave the great game of poker into an original short story. John Lescroart writes a story about how the memories of a father's home poker game still haunt the son many years after his death. Rupert Holmes tells a tale of a poker game that is more than it appears. Eric Van Lustbader shows how the game can form the basis for a unique father/daughter relationship. Walter Mosley examines how the game of poker can provide a unique platform for non-verbal communication. And Sam Hill writes of a poker pro coming to grips with his own mortality; both physically and professionally. These are just a small sampling of the stories you will find inside the collection.

There were few rules for each writer. How they used the game to further the narrative was entirely up to them. And the results prove that poker fiction can consist of much more than the typical tale full of poker cheats and con men. Clearly, each author has had a different experience with the game, and that experience comes shining through in unique ways in each story. Poker's varied forms and attributes are all utilized differently by each author. *Dead Man's Hand* ultimately ends up creating a mosaic of the game that will, hopefully, change how fiction writers use the game in the future. It's a fresh approach that was a long time coming.

Whether you are a poker enthusiast, a crime novel aficionado or both, curl up with this collection of exciting single sitting stories and you will be rewarded with an array of bluffs, gut shots and surprise river cards. Enjoy!

Howard Lederer
January 2007

SCOTTISH BORDERS COUNCIL

LIBRARY &
INFORMATION SERVICES

♠ Mister In-Between

Walter Mosley

'YOU CAN CALL ME MASTER,' I said to the white man behind the broad ivory colored desk. The stretch of 59th Street known as Central Park South lay far beneath his windows. The street was filled with toy-sized yellow cabs and tiny noonday strollers.

'Come again?' Clive Ford said, bristling in his oversized chair.

'That's my name – Master Vincent. My mother christened me so that no man could insult me without lowering his own head.'

'Is there something else they call you?' Ford asked.

I eased into the wide-bottomed, walnut client's chair and crossed my legs. I didn't like Ford. He had watery eyes and was short and fat with stubble on his chin. I felt that a man, despite his liabilities, should make the most of himself. And appearance was the easiest blemish to cover.

When I looked in the bathroom mirror I didn't see a handsome or even a good-looking man. Tall and gawky, more gray than brown-skinned, I had big ears and an over-broad nose. But at least I wore nice suits that made me look filled out and hats that partly hid the insult of my *Dumbo* lobes.

'Call me Mister In-Between,' I said. 'It fits my nature and my vocation.'

'Your what?'

'Job.'

'Oh. Yes. That's why you're here isn't it?' I wondered how a man like Clive Ford got to be the vice president of some big corporation when he looked like a warthog and didn't even know simple, everyday words.

'I have a friend who needs a favour,' Ford said.

'What friend?'

'That's not important.'

'To whom?'

'Say what?' Ford asked.

'To whom is the identity of your friend unimportant?'

'You don't need to know his name,' Ford said showing irritation at my continued impertinence.

I shrugged.

'My friend is owed a great deal of money by a man who wants to pay but who also needs his anonymity.'

'Now that's a big word,' I said gazing out of the high window down across Central Park. It was a beautiful sunny office and a lovely summer's day.

'All we need is for you to attend a private poker game in Brooklyn Heights – and win.'

'I can play but I can't promise to win.' I put my hands on the arms of the chair indicating that it was time to go.

'Game is fixed. You use this…' he threw down two tight bundles of what looked to me to be a hundred hundred-dollar bills each, '…and when the night is over you take either ten thousand dollars or ten per cent of the winnings, whatever's more. You don't have to worry about the game being fixed, my client will repay any losses by the other players.'

I settled back into the chair. I'd promised Felicia a trip in October and my funds were low. There was my emergency cash but that was inviolate. Then again, I'd have to look long and hard to find another woman like Felicia. She didn't mind my odd hours or sporadic, sometimes days-long, absences.

'I trust you, Baby,' she'd say in her high voice, 'but you got to treat me right.'

'How's the game fixed?' I asked Clive Ford.

'By an expert,' Ford said. 'All you have to do is play and bet heavy if you have more than two of a kind.'

'Deuces?'

'If its three twos in your hand you're gonna win – probably.'

'How much?'

'No less than a hundred grand.'

I didn't like it. But the ugly man was referred by Crow, and Crow was as good an agent as you could have. Still, Clive Ford was ugly and didn't care who knew it. If that was what he was like on the surface, what might there be hidden underneath?

'Why don't you exercise?' I asked him unable to keep the disgust out of my tone.

'What?'

'Why don't you go to a gym? You got something wrong with your legs?'

'What the hell does that have to do with the game tonight? Bernardi told me that you were professional.'

'I carry things,' I said, 'from one set of hands to another. I deliver but I don't work for just anybody.'

'My references are good. Play the game, take your winnings, and bring them back to me tomorrow.'

'What if I lose?'

'You won't.'

I hesitated a moment past the comfort zone of a normal conversation.

'Besides,' Ford said, 'you're covered by Bernardi. He's the one I go to if anything goes wrong.'

I had never met Bobo Bernardi. He was an ex-professional wrestler who had gone into the private delivery business. He only contacted me through Crow. Crow had a one room office on 146th

Street near Malcolm X. That office was the highway onramp that led from Harlem to the rest of the world.

'Take this job as a gift,' Crow had whispered over the phone. 'It's the best payin' gig you evah gonna get.'

Ten thousand dollars was a good payday and cash was the cleanest package to carry. It wasn't like prescription drugs or stolen property; it wasn't like counterfeiters' product or stock-market tips that couldn't be trusted to electronic media. Real money was clean; something the cops could question but they could not, legally, confiscate.

'We're not talkin' counterfeit here are we, Mr Ford?'

'Clean American currency... Master.'

I knew then that Ford was no fool. He saw my vain spot as soon as I told him my name.

We spent the next forty minutes going through the details of the pickup.

Pickup, drop-off; these were the two terms that bound my world, the bookends of my entire professional life. If an FBI agent wanted to speak to a prostitute he'd gotten fond of I would deliver the Valentine. If an informant deep within a criminal organization needed a line out I was his connection.

With Crow as the router, Mr In-Between was the express mail system for a dozen and more shadow worlds. There was nothing that I wouldn't move except for slaves, the condemned, and terrorist communiqués.

'I'm not an assassin or an assassin's helper,' I told my intern, Mike Peron, a youngish New Yorker of Peruvian descent.

'But what if it was a message to some CIA guy in Cuba to wipe out somebody down there?' Mike asked.

'No. Once you open that door then anything, and everything, goes.'

Mike nodded once and filed the information away. He would make a good bagman one day.

*

I had a loft apartment in Tribeca that didn't require rent. I'd once done a favour for the landlord, Joe Moorland, which had earned me a lifetime get-out-of-rent-free card.

The ceilings were eighteen feet high looming over three thousand square feet of mostly empty space.

I like space. One of my favorite pastimes is to stare out over the empty bamboo floor of my home. At the front corner of the loft I walled off four hundred square feet for an office. This was where Mike and I worked. We could gaze out of the fourth floor window onto Greenwich Street and discuss the best ways to go about a problem; not that I had any difficulty forming strategies. It's just that sometimes I needed an extra pair of hands and it was always good to see how someone else would go about getting from point a to point b.

And Mike had other qualities. He spoke Spanish and street, and he was small with a New World Indian look about him. Nobody would ever suspect him on a sophisticated run.

'Why you gonna take this job?' Mike asked that afternoon as three fire engines blared past on the street below.

'It's good money and Crow asked me to do it.'

'But you're like a shill.'

'Crow says it's not like that.'

'When I'm'a meet this Crow?'

'When you learn to speak proper English,' I said.

'I know how to talk.'

'Good. Now all you have to do is implement that knowledge and the windows of the world will open for you.'

Mike glared at me but he didn't argue. He knew that I was the doorway to his dreams of dignity, wealth, and respect. He didn't even have a high school diploma when I found him hustling for nickels in east New York. Now he'd earned his GED and no one had stabbed him in over two and half years.

'You got that address?' I asked him.

'Yeah.'

'Check it out and follow procedure.'

'If there's trouble ahead?'

'Blue cell,' I said, and I gave him the new number.

I had three pay-as-you-go cellphones, each one of a different primary color. I changed the number on one of these phones every month. When I'd make a change I'd tell Mike which one to call.

After Mike left on his errand I went into my apartment and lay down on the chaise longue I'd bought from my psychoanalyst at the end of six years of deep therapy. I'd spent five days a week on that brown, backless sofa. I bought it for eighteen thousand dollars telling my analyst, Dr Myra Golden, that I'd use it when I felt the need to tap into my unconscious mind.

I closed my eyes thinking about Clive Ford and his mission.

The more I thought the more I worried that the whole thing was a mistake. Pickup, drop-off – that was my mantra. This poker playing lay outside my area of expertise. But Crow had asked and ten thousand dollars was heavy cash for a day's work.

The red phone made the sound of Zen bells in the distance.

'Hello.'

'Hey, Baby, how you doin'?'

'Felicia.'

'You know it make me dizzy when you say my name like that, Master,' Felicia said.

'I told you that you don't have to call me that, girl.'

'How can I help it,' she said in a serious tone, 'when I know every time I say it your dick gets hard?'

'That's only when I'm looking at you, Baby.'

'Is it hard right now?'

'Why are you calling me?' I asked allowing her question to seek its own reply.

'I want a steak and to see if we can do sumpin'.'

*

Felicia was twenty-three, fifteen years my junior. She was a large woman from Bedford-Stuyvesant. Felicia had worked part way out of the hood. A junior cashier at a grocery store in the Village, she was the least likely girlfriend I could imagine.

One day I was buying chicken breasts and broccoli at her register and she asked, 'You cook for yourself?'

I said yes as I looked up, falling into her eyes. Her reply was that she'd be off at nine and that I could buy her dinner if I was there.

'I got a job tonight, Baby,' I told Felicia.

'A job or another girlfriend?'

'A job. A job so good that we can go to Hawaii for a week on your vacation.'

'Really?'

'No lie.'

Felicia had a very large butt. I'd always liked skinny women. But somehow I found myself waiting for her at nine and we've been together since.

I stretched out on the psychiatrist's couch after that first night of deep passionate sex with Felicia; lying there I could hear Dr Golden saying, *go with it*, which was odd because Golden had never given me one word of advice in fourteen hundred and forty hours of therapy.

'What is it you do again?' Felicia asked.

She had posed that question many times and I always gave the same answer, 'I'm an assistant to a guy who hangs out on a corner up in Harlem. I help him and he gives me advice.'

'Oh. Can he give you the night off? I got a itch that I want you to scratch… wit' yo' tongue.'

My chest throbbed and I wanted to say 'I love you', but stifled the urge. I did not understand this feeling Felicia brought out in me. She was undereducated and used crude language, she was completely unsophisticated but still when she looked at me I wanted to get down on my knees and thank God, even though

I had been an atheist since the age of eight after seeing my parents brutally murdered.

'I have to go, Felicia. I need to get ready for the job.'

'I might have to go see my old boyfriend then,' she speculated.

'I've told you before, honey, if you need another man just leave. You don't even need to tell me that you're gone.'

'Don't be like that, Daddy. I'm just playin' wit' you. You don't have to get all serious an' shit.'

'You're wrong, girl. I am serious, very serious.'

'OK. We see each other tomorrow night then. All right?'

'As long as you're not with your old boyfriend. What was his name? Hatton, George Hatton.'

'You remembah that?'

'I remember everything.'

The game was to be held on the top floor of a private brownstone on Montague Street near the water, in the Heights. I arrived at eleven forty-five in order to be there for the first hand to be dealt at midnight. I was met at the door by two big men armed with electronic wands.

'Excuse me, Mr Vincent,' the sandy haired one said, 'but we have to make sure you're clean.'

They took my blue cellphone, removed the battery, and put them both in a box. They also searched my wallet, made me take off my jacket so they could feel through the fabric, and asked me if I wore glasses. They even checked my eyes with a flashlight to see if I had contacts.

I didn't mind the search. This was high-stakes poker. Someone would be a fool not to cheat if they could.

There was a small elevator that went to the fourth floor gambling room. I was met at the top by a red-haired white girl, no more than nineteen, dressed in a full length satin yellow evening dress. The gown looked a little too new, making her seem as though she was a child playing dressing-up.

'Welcome, Mr Vincent. I'm Marla. You're the last to arrive.' She took me by the arm. 'Let me show you to your place at the table.'

The young woman walked me five steps to the plush red six-sided table. The second I got there I started thinking about how to turn back time. Four of the five men were a Who's Who of the real New York underworld.

Marla introduced me but I already knew the four.

'Faust Littleman,' the girl said.

He was the heroin connection between Afghanistan and Baltimore. He lived in New York for the restaurants and to stymie police intervention in his business. Crow had gotten an offer from Faust for me to make regular deliveries but my agent demurred telling Littleman, 'We're mailmen, not drug dealers.'

'Welcome, Mr Vincent,' Littleman said without a smile or even a nod.

'Brian Mettgang,' Marla said.

He was a powerful Hollywood producer who'd gotten his start in extreme pornography. It was rumoured that he'd still provide a snuff film for the right amount of cash.

I had worked for Mettgang's company but never met the boss.

I was also introduced to Tommy Arland, the infamous West Side Hit Man, Jamaica Jim, a one-time enforcer who now ran the mid-town numbers racket, and a man named Mr Wisteria.

Wisteria wore a dark, dark red suit – a colour that I had never seen in men's dress clothes. He also wore a buff-coloured, short-brimmed hat. He had the kind of mouth that often smiled but never laughed. 'Mr Vincent,' the bird-boned, middle-aged white man piped. 'Welcome to our little game.'

'Thank you,' I said wishing that I were somewhere else. I chided myself again for not asking who else would be playing. This company was serious business. I'd have walked out if not for my longtime friend and mentor, Crow.

Crow must have known what was coming down, I told myself over and over.

I took my seat, managing to look calm.

'I'm the last one here?' I asked. 'I can't remember the last time that happened.'

'We're playing five card draw,' Jamaica Jim said, 'nothing wild. The deal shifts from man to man to the left and the limit to the pot is five thousand dollars unless all active players agree to raise it. If you have at least five you can't get busted.'

Marla placed a new deck by my right hand.

I tore the tight plastic wrapper from the box wondering who it was that had fixed the game. The men I knew of were all unlikely to do something like this, at least not in person. That left Wisteria.

'Where you from, Mr Wisteria?' I asked while shuffling the deck under the watchful eyes of my fellow players.

'Beloit, Wisconsin,' he said in his mild Milquetoast voice.

'Wisconsin,' I mused. 'Dairy farms and mountains of snow.'

Wisteria smiled and nodded. 'My family owns a dairy out there. They make three and half per cent of the butter used in the Midwest.'

He was the one, I thought. Everything about him seemed a fabrication. Even his pale gaze was faraway, deceptive.

The stares from everyone else were intense. Their eyes were bright challenges daring anyone to defeat them.

Each man had a drawer filled with a few hundred chips at their station; the four denominations ranged from $100 to $100,000. Each man had different colour chips: red, blue, yellow, green, violet, and orange.

I threw out an orange chip and dealt the cards. The rest of the players followed my ante.

'How's Pete Morgan doin'?' big black Jamaica Jim asked.

Peter François Morgan was the man that Ford got to invite me to the game. I knew various facts about him but we weren't supposed to be close friends. I didn't need to know much.

'He's OK. Dolly had another kid, girl I think. Anyway he sends his best. He's in Miami right now.'

'Peter Morgan?' Mr Wisteria asked. His voice could have been a satyr's reed, a barely audible, almost impossible sound coming from a deep wood.

'He suggested Vincent for the game,' Faust Littleman said. The drug-dealer's face was puffy. He had a highway map of blue veins under the almost yellow skin of his nose.

'What do you do for a living, Mr Vincent?' Littleman asked.

'I work for stockbrokers,' I said as I dealt.

'You are a stockbroker?'

'No. I just do research for a few clients.'

'Oh.'

There was an air of tension in the room. Only Wisteria was immune to the atmosphere. His nimble little fingers flipped among his cards. Everyone else seemed to think long and hard about their decisions.

I had two queens.

Fold if you have nothing, Clive Ford had told me. *Stay for the ride on everything else. If you don't have at least three of a kind after the draw then fold. If you get three or more then play to the limit.*

'Check,' said Faust Littleman. The drug dealer looked up defiantly as if daring anyone to question him.

'I'll bet a thousand,' Jim said throwing in a green coloured chip.

'I'll see that,' Tommy Arland, the assassin added.

I looked at the killer noting that he was as nondescript a white man as I had ever met. Not tall or particularly strong-looking, he wouldn't show up on anyone's radar unless they knew him. He could be the cheat at the table; anyone could.

Mettgang met the thousand dollar limit. Wisteria and Littleman folded.

I called the bet and threw down three cards. When I dealt again I still had only two queens and folded.

'Nice of you to lose the first hand you dealt, Mr Vincent,'

Wisteria said in an odd, but still mild tone. 'Otherwise we might have to kill you.'

'Good luck always follows bad,' I said optimistically.

'Amen,' Wisteria said and, unaccountably, I felt a chill.

I lost the next two hands because I didn't have anything. I had three fives on the fourth hand but Wisteria beat me with a diamond flush.

It wasn't until the sixth hand that I had something worth while. Three tens backed up by an ace and a jack. Littleman and Arland battled me over that hand. I took in eight thousand four hundred when they finally folded.

All the while I felt the gaze of Wisteria upon me.

The men were true gamblers. They spoke very little and showed almost no emotion. Now and then Marla would bring a drink to someone. Mettgang and Wisteria each left once to go to the toilet.

At three fifteen in the morning I got dealt three nines by Jamaica Jim. I only drew one card which gave me a pair of fives to go with my nines.

There was no logic to my manufactured luck, no mechanism that I could see that gave me an edge. No one dealer gave me my winning hands.

I cleaned up with the full house. Sixty-one thousand dollars in a single hand of poker. That put me over the top. One hundred twenty-seven thousand, eight hundred dollars.

Tommy Arland was the big loser in that hand. He had two pair, sixes and eights. I wondered if he was the one paying me off. But I couldn't tell. All the men had on their poker faces. We spoke less at that table than I did to the harried counterman at the deli where I get my pastrami on rye during lunch hour on Tuesdays and Fridays.

Soon after my big win Wisteria yawned. Jamaica Jim stretched and said, 'I t'ink it's time we go.'

And the game was over.

While the others went downstairs to gather their things I sat alone at the red table with Marla as she counted one thousand two hundred and seventy-eight one hundred dollar bills. She counted my winnings three times and then put the cash into a cute little briefcase no larger than a woman's purse.

'Do you have a roll of nickels in your bank there?' I asked her.

She reached down into the safe under the table and came out with a two dollar plastic roll.

I handed her three hundred dollar bills and said, 'Keep the change.'

By the time I got downstairs everyone was gone except for the sandy-haired man who had apologized for searching me. He gave me back my phone and I wished him well.

I had walked half a block from the house when someone shouted, 'Hey you!'

By the time I had turned around the three men were almost upon me. Not one of them was particularly tall but they were all sturdy, built for the hurting trade.

As I said, I'm tall but not bulky or extremely strong. I will go one on one with anybody, though, because I will hurt you if I can get at you. But three men at once was beyond my physical limits.

'Gimme the case,' the leader, a blocky white guy with a squashed face, commanded.

I heard a tiny motor rev in the distance. It was little more than the sound of a mosquito in your ear at night.

'What did you say?' I asked as if I really hadn't understood.

'Gimme the fuckin' case,' the man said.

He moved ahead of his friends and reached for me. I responded by striking him on the temple with the side of my right fist, in which I held the roll of nickels. I hit him very hard. He grunted in a high tone like a pig caught in a fence. I hit him in the same spot again before his friends registered the attack.

The engine in the distance got louder.

The other two men, one black and one brown, came at me then.

The one on the left brandished a knife while the black man on the right was holding a pistol down at his side.

As they came forward I took a long step back. They had to go around the prone body of their unconscious boss. This gave me a six to eight second reprieve. It doesn't sound like much when armed men are after you and all you have is a roll of nickels in your hand. But I had faith in that small engine in the night.

Mike Peron zipped up behind my attackers, managing to hit both of them at about fifteen miles an hour. He was thrown from his motorbike but I moved in quickly clubbing the muggers with my coin reinforced hand. After I was certain that the muggers were incapacitated I helped Mike up and together we rode away into the night.

I got off in Manhattan at five-thirty and went to a 24-hour diner on 6th Avenue in the Village. I drank some coffee and then drank some more. I ordered a waffle with cooked apples and whipped cream and downed two more cups of coffee. I didn't read the newspaper or make small talk with the waitress. I didn't do anything but think about what had happened.

Anyone at that table could have set me up. Clive Ford or Bobo Bernardi could have been behind the mugging. It wouldn't have been Crow. It's not that I'm above suspecting my mentor but Crow was the one who told me about having backup on a job that felt hinky. Crow would have had someone in reserve to come in on the chance that Mike was in the wings.

Someone had fixed the game but it didn't make sense that he would have tried to rob me. After all I was going to turn the money over to his agent, Clive Ford.

It was rare for Mr In-Between to get double-crossed. It was almost always a straight-forward kind of business.

At six-fifteen I called a number.

'Speak to me,' answered a whispery voice.

'Somebody tried to hijack me, Crow,' I said.

'Who did?'

'I don't know. Three guys were waiting for me. If it wasn't for Mike I might be dead by now.'

'Damn.'

Silence fell on the payphone line for a full two minutes.

'You think it's Ford?' Crow hissed.

'I don't like him but then again I don't know.'

'If it was him then it's over now anyway. You still got the money?'

'Yes, I do.'

'How much?'

'One twenty-seven plus the twenty he gave me.'

'Take out your percentage and put the rest in my box. I'll call Bernardi and see what's what.'

'OK.'

'And you know the drill, right?' Crow added.

The drill was not to go anywhere that someone in our world might see me or be able to find me. Not my apartment. Not Crow's office.

'Oh, yeah,' I said. 'I know.'

The fact that he felt the need to remind me showed how seriously my mentor took this business.

I went to Bailey's Bank on 42nd Street where Crow and I shared a safe deposit box. In a private room I removed my twelve thousand five hundred dollars (accounting for the three hundred I'd tipped Marla) and put the rest in storage. Then I went to the Metropolitan Museum of Art and studied the South American and African exhibits.

I love history because the past belongs to all of us. The saga of the human race is a kind of cultural socialism that even the richest people cannot control or truly possess. I like thinking about the past when the present is impinging on me. It makes me feel untouchable.

I was waiting for Felicia at six when she got off work and we went to her apartment off Flatbush Avenue in Brooklyn. Her mother and sister came over because they had not met me before and we ordered barbecue from a delivery place – Winston's Memphis Belle BBQ.

Felicia's mother, Helen, was the image of the woman that Felicia would become in sixteen years. She was one year older and forty pounds heavier than I. Her face was the same as Felicia's and her laugh was the same too. Bunny, Felicia's sister, had a whole other father. His genes had made her slight and light skinned. Bunny was a very pretty girl and she gave me looks that might have been seen by Felicia as flirtatious but Bunny never let her sister see.

'Yeah,' Helen was saying that evening, 'me an' Bunny thought that Feel was makin' up her boyfriend. I mean what a successful businessman be doin' hooked up with some wide-bottomed dark-skinned girl from Bed-Stuy?'

'I just looked at her,' I said draping my arm on Felicia's shoulders, 'and that was it. She said to come by later and I believe I would have fought Mike Tyson to be there.'

Helen and Bunny were stunned by my naked passion. Felicia leaned over and kissed my neck. She whispered in my ear, 'I'm'a do it right tonight, Master.'

And even though I was deeply troubled I was still thrilled by the connection Felicia made with my soul.

She kissed my neck again and my mind flashed. It was like a flicker, a phenomenon that Myra Golden called 'the precursor to my intuition.' I was about to come to some deep understanding when my blue phone made the sound of migrating geese passing overhead.

'Hold on,' I said answering the phone as I stood.

I took the phone into Felicia's bedroom and said, 'Go on.'

'Clive Ford fell off the top'a his office buildin',' Crow hissed. 'Cops lookin' for everybody been to his office in the last three days.'

'Damn. What about Bobo?'

'He told me that he washes his hands of it. The money's ours.'

'What's happening, Crow?'

'I'm sorry, man,' Crow said. 'The way Clive laid it out to me nobody was getting ripped off.'

My intuition kicked in then and I realized that all the men at that table were in on the fix. I said this to Crow.

'Most of them anyway,' he said ominously.

'What should I do?' I asked.

'Find a hole and stay in it till the smoke clears.'

Even the fear of death did not weaken the ardour I felt for Felicia Torres. I strained over her grunting like an old man passing a stone. I held her so tightly that she had to ask me to let up.

The next morning at a coffee shop I was reading the *Post* because that was the only paper they had. Terrorists in England had invented an exploding iPod and a movie star of some renown got divorced from one guy and married another in a single day.

On page three I read that James 'Jamaica Jim' Rolleyman had been found hanged in his apartment near 48th Street and 9th Avenue. The police said that the death was suspicious. There was no note and no warning that he might have committed suicide.

Wild geese cried out while I was reading the article.

'Hello?'

'Hey, man,' Mike Peron said. 'You read the paper?'

'You got family in Peru still, Mikey?'

'Some.'

'Go for a visit. Two weeks should do it. I'll pay.'

'What about you?'

'I'm going to catch up on my reading.'

I went to the diner's toilet, counted out fifty one-hundred-dollar bills, and wrapped them in a paper towel. I folded the paper to make a pretty secure envelope. Then I went to the reading room of the main branch of the New York Public Library.

In the north-west corner of the reading room, on any day that the library was open, from eight in the morning till closing time, you could find Nelson 'The Dean' Koslowski. He was always reading a book and usually flanked by two women. For the past year these posts had been held by Minna Olson and Arianna Tey.

The way they were seated you couldn't get very close to Nelson and so you had to start a discussion with one of the women first.

'Hi,' I said to Minna, a thin, black woman of twenty-something years. She had a plain face but there was sensuality in her posture.

'Do I know you?' she asked, not unpleasantly.

I handed her the jury-rigged envelope and she, showing me the respect I deserved, did not open it to count out my offering. She turned to Nelson, an elderly white man of seventy-eight or -nine, and whispered something.

He looked up from his book, made a face, and nodded. Minna moved aside.

I sat down next to the old man. He was very short and wore clothes that would have been suitable for a janitor or a gardener.

'Master,' Nelson said. 'Long time.'

'As a rule I don't need to come to you for information,' I said. 'Usually two addresses will do me fine.'

'So why are you here? Do you have a message for me?'

'Clive Ford, Faust Littleman, Jamaica Jim, Tommy Arland, Brian Mettgang, and a little guy named Wisteria,' I said. 'Does that mean anything to you?'

The Dean stared at my forehead for what seemed like a very long time.

'Minna, Arianna,' he said.

The women turned their heads to regard him.

'Go get yourselves some coffee. Mr Vance and I need a few minutes alone.'

The ladies were reluctant but they knew better than to question their boss. After they were gone Nelson stared at me a while longer. The envelope with my money was nowhere to be seen.

Koslowski was a self-made man of what Crow liked to call

Nefarious Letters. The Dean knew everything that went down in the city. He never talked to the police or any other government agent and if you fooled him into giving you information for the cops he was likely to take revenge upon you, one way or the other. He had a full head of grey-blue hair and skin that sagged with the weight of all he knew. It cost five thousand dollars just to ask him a question, research on his part could run much higher.

'What's your interest?' Nelson asked me.

'Trouble,' I said simply.

'Serious trouble?'

I didn't even nod. Koslowski knew I wouldn't be there unless the guns were loaded and the crosshairs in place.

'Ford was point man for a guy named Ring,' Nelson told me.

'The assassin?'

'Littleman, Jamaica Jim, Arland, and Mettgang all worked for Wisteria.'

'Worked?' I asked. 'I saw them last night.'

'Jamaica Jim's fake suicide was in the paper. The rest of them probably won't show up any time soon.'

'And Wisteria?'

'Olaf Wisteria, I am told, suffers from a variety of mental illnesses. They all come together under the general heading of paranoia. It was said that he suspected one of his henchmen of stealing from him. For the last six months he has had them all followed, bugged, and attached at the hip with men who answer only to Olaf. They could not take a step that wasn't watched, listened to, and studied. They were never allowed to handle money unless it was their winnings at the weekly poker game.'

'He couldn't watch them that closely.'

'Have you looked into his eyes?'

I had.

'Is Ring dead too?' I asked.

'Ring, I hear, has switched loyalties.'

'Where can I find Ring?'

'I don't know.'

'I can have ten thousand here in an hour, Mr Koslowski.'

'I don't know, Master. If I did I would tell you.'

On the 5th Avenue stairs of the library I called Crow but he didn't answer. This bothered me because Crow always answered his personal line. He even took it to the hospital when he was having knee surgery. They gave him a local anesthetic and he conducted business while the doctor cut, shaved bone, and sewed.

I kept a small apartment under my mother's maiden name in Queens, not far from JFK. I went there via subway and bus. It was clean because I hired a service to come once every two weeks to dust and do whatever else was necessary.

I sat on the springy bed and went over all I knew.

Ford was an assassin's agent and Ring was the killer. The four men I had feared at the poker table were in turn frightened by Wisteria. They siphoned off their money to pay for the killing of their paranoid boss.

The fix was brilliant. Four of the five players knew when I was betting and the parameters of what I held. If they had a better hand they folded. If they didn't they bluffed. Wisteria wouldn't wise up because he would beat me at least half of the time we bet against each other.

The money came from the bank that Wisteria controlled.

But if Koslowski was right and Wisteria had such a tight rein on his men that they couldn't get a message out then how did they get in touch with Ford to make such complex plans?

Sure they could make a clandestine call from some friend's cellphone but that wouldn't be enough. No. They needed to get word to someone that would build the plan for them; someone who would understand their plight and set up the game for them.

Crow.

I sorely missed my analyst's couch but I made do with the

bouncy bed in my getaway room. Crow was the only solution to the problem. If he was aware of Wisteria and knew the men at the table he might have set up the game, setting me up as he did so. Crow knew how to leave messages anywhere. He figured out the poker game and then got word to the players how the game should go. He called Clive Ford, Ring's agent, and then pulled me in to pay the assassin's fee.

Crow knew I wouldn't willingly be party to an assassin's trade. He worked it out so that I would be paid well and Wisteria would be eliminated. He had all the bases covered except for the unheard of betrayal by Ring.

The sun set and I lay still, my eyes closed, my breath shallow. I lay there for many hours considering the next action to take.

The smartest thing would have been to take the money and run. Now that I understood Wisteria I knew enough to fear him. Crow had never once failed to answer his phone and so he was probably dead too.

I had two hundred and seventy-eight thousand dollars in savings. I couldn't take Felicia because she'd have to call her mother one day.

I was ready to run. All I needed was a few morning hours to collect my savings and get on the Path Train to a Jersey bus and I'd be gone.

Zen bells rang near midnight.

'Yeah?'

'How you, Baby?' Felicia asked.

'Fine. My business had a little backlash. But I got a hold of it.'

'You OK?'

'Uh-huh. Why you ask?'

'I 'ont know,' she said. 'I just got the feelin' you might need somebody to call and say they loved you.'

My throat caught and a pain set off in my chest. My intuitive dizziness set in and for a moment I remembered being happy. It's not that I *was* happy; I just remembered how it once felt.

'Felicia,' I said. 'Felicia, you are something else, you know that, girl?'

'I love you,' she said. 'You don't have to say it back. You don't have to do nuthin' but promise me that you will come to my house and stay here again.'

'Unless I'm dead and cold you better believe I will be there,' I said.

Three a.m. found me on a rooftop across the street from the gambling house in Brooklyn Heights. I had a high-powered pistol that doubled as a rifle in my pocket. I had tried five times to call Crow. If he hadn't answered by then I knew he never would.

And even though I had been betrayed by my mentor I still respected him and gave him the benefit of the doubt. I had worked for Crow since I was a teenager. He taught me to articulate and how to walk straight, how to dress and how to behave in the company of other men.

Unlike me, Crow was strong and powerful. Even now, in his mid-fifties, he posed a daunting figure. I looked up to him and he showed me a way.

For long minutes I stared at the gambler's house. No one came in or out but there was an odd shadow in the doorway. The longer I looked at it, the stranger it appeared.

At three-thirty I climbed down the fire-escape and crossed the street. Crow had taught me how to move silently through the noisiest terrains. I could have been a cat burglar if I wasn't a delivery specialist.

The shadow was caused by the front door to the gambling establishment being ajar. I stared at it a full thirty seconds before crossing the threshold. I locked the door behind me and located the stairs. One and a half flights up I came upon a dead white man of middle years. His head was at the bottom of the flight and his legs were above and to the side. He'd been shot in the back.

The blood pooled under him in the green carpeting.

I decided to start in the room I knew best so I went to the fourth floor and pushed the door open.

Olaf Wisteria was sitting with his back to the red gambling table smiling at me. That was when I learned that I wasn't a natural born killer. The moment a real killer had even suspected another living being he would have opened fire.

But all I did was stare at Olaf as he stared sightlessly back at me.

'I wondered when you'd get here,' a crackling voice said.

I turned quickly and lifted my gun but I knew before I could pull the trigger that it was Crow who called to me.

He was laid up in a corner with blood on his face and army jacket. I ran to him and got down on my knees.

'Motherfucker shot me three times 'fore I could get off one shot,' my mentor said. His chiselled black face seemed thinner from the strain of his wounds. 'Lucky he didn't wear a vest like me.'

'Let's get you out of here,' I told him.

'I knew you'd come,' Crow said to me. 'I knew you wouldn't let me and him take your life away.'

Two days later in a very private Bronx clinic Crow regained consciousness.

'Olaf had a lover,' Crow told me when the nurse left us alone. 'Her name was Connie and she was a friend.'

'He kill her?'

'Yeah. I didn't know it until Jamaica Jim told me. He said that Wisteria was going to break up everything, he was so crazy… I'm sorry, Boy. I used you but you got to know that I had no idea Ring would double-cross us.'

'Why didn't they kill him at the game themselves?' I asked.

'During the game Wisteria had men in the walls, watching.'

'In the walls?'

'He was a sick puppy,' Crow said. 'But he only had Ring with him at night. I disabled the alarm and took my chances.'

'That was Ring you killed on the stairs?'

'Uncle Sam trained me real good in Nam,' Crow said. It was the first I'd ever heard of his being in the military. 'I killed him for you, Master. I was trying to make restitution for tricking you like I did.'

'That's OK,' I said.

'It is?'

'Yeah,' I said. 'It's like my final exam.'

Crow looked at me and nodded slowly.

'Yeah,' he said. 'You can't trust anybody.'

Outside the sun was rising over the Bronx. Crow would live and I'd still work for him. Mike would come back and Felicia would thrill me in the night. And I would be a stronger man in an ever more uncertain world.

♠

Bump
Jeffery Deaver

HAT IN HAND.

There was no other way to describe it.

Aside from the flashy secretary, the middle-aged man in jeans and a sports coat was alone, surveying the glassy waiting room which overlooked Century City's Avenue of the Stars. No, not *that* one, with the footprints in concrete (that was Hollywood Boulevard, about five miles from here). This street was an ordinary office park of hotels and high-rises, near an OK shopping centre and a pretty-good TV network.

Checking out the flowers (fresh), the art (originals), the secretary (a wannabe, like nine-tenths of the other help in L.A.).

How many waiting rooms had he been in just like this, over his thirty some years in the industry? Mike O'Connor wondered.

He couldn't even begin to guess.

O'Connor was now examining a purple orchid, trying to shake the thought: Here I am begging, hat in hand.

But he couldn't.

Nor could he ditch the adjunct thought: This is your last Goddamn chance.

A faint buzz from somewhere on the woman's desk. She was blonde, and O'Connor, who tended to judge women by a very high standard, his wife, thought she was attractive enough. Though, this being Hollywood, attractive enough for *what*? was a legitimate question, and sadly the answer to that was not enough for leading roles. A pretty character actress, walk-ons. We're in the toughest business on the face of the earth, baby, he thought to her.

She put down the phone. 'He'll see you now, Mr O'Connor.' She rose to get the door for him.

'That's OK. I'll get it… Good luck.' He'd seen her reading a script.

She didn't know what he meant.

O'Connor closed the door behind him, and Aaron Felter, a fit man in his early thirties, wearing expensive slacks and a dark grey shirt without a tie, rose to greet him.

'Mike. My God, it's been two years.'

'Your dad's funeral.'

'Right.'

'How's your mom doing?'

'Scandal. She's dating! A production designer over on the Universal lot. At least he's only five years younger. But he wears an earring.'

'Give her my best.'

'Will do.'

Felter's father had been a director of photography for a time on O'Connor's TV show in the eighties. He'd been a talented man and wily… and a voice of reason in the chaotic world of weekly television.

They carried on a bit of conversation about their own families – neither particularly interested, but such was the protocol of business throughout the world.

Then because this wasn't just business, it was Hollywood, the moment soon arrived when it was OK to cut to the chase.

Felter tapped the packet of material O'Connor had sent. 'I read it, Mike. It's a real interesting concept. Tell me a little more.'

O'Connor knew the difference between *it's interesting* and *I'm interested*. But he continued to describe the proposal for a new TV series in more depth.

Michael O'Connor had been hot in the late seventies and eighties. He'd starred in several prime-time dramas – featuring a law firm, an EMT facility and, most successfully, the famous *Homicide Detail.* The show lasted for seven seasons, which was a huge success, considering that one year in the life of a TV show usually counts as dog years times two.

It had been a great time. O'Connor, a UCLA film grad, had always been serious about acting and *Homicide Detail* was cutting edge TV. It was gritty, was shot with hand-held cameras and the writers (O'Connor co-wrote scripts from time to time) weren't afraid to blow away a main character occasionally or let the bad guy get off. An LAPD detective who became a good friend of O'Connor's was the show consultant and he worked them hard to get the details right. The shows dealt with religion, abortion, race, terrorism, sex, anything. 'Cutting-edge story telling, creativity on steroids,' was *The New York Times*'s assessment of the show, and those few words meant more to O'Connor than the Emmy nomination (he lost to an actor from *Law & Order*, a thoroughly noble defeat.)

But then the series folded, and it was drought time.

He couldn't get work – not the kind of work that was inspired and challenging. His agent sent him scripts with absurd premises or were hackneyed rip-offs of his own show or sitcoms, which he had no patience or talent for. And O'Connor collected his residual cheques (and signed most of them over to the Ivy League schools his daughters attended), and kept trying to survive in a town where he'd actually heard someone say of *Richard III*, 'You mean it was a play too?'

But O'Connor was interested in more than acting. He had a vision. There's a joke in Hollywood that, when looking for a project to turn into a film or series, producers want something that's completely original and yet has been wildly successful in the past. There is, however, some truth to that irony. And for years O'Connor had it in mind to do a project that was fresh but still was rooted in television history: each week a different story, with new characters. Like TV from the 1950s and '60s: *Alfred Hitchcock Presents*, *Playhouse 90*, *The Twilight Zone*. Sometimes drama, sometimes comedy, sometimes science fiction.

He'd written a proposal and the pilot script and then shopped *Stories* all over Hollywood and to the BBC, Sky and Channel 4 in England as well – but everyone passed. The only major producer he hadn't contacted was Aaron Felter, since the man's dad and O'Connor had been friends, and he hadn't wanted to unfairly pressure him. Besides, Felter wasn't exactly in the stratosphere himself. His various production companies had backed some losing TV and film projects recently and he couldn't afford to take any risks.

Still, O'Connor was desperate.

Hence, hat in hand.

Felter nodded, listening attentively as O'Connor pitched his idea. He was good; he'd done it many times in the past year.

There was a knock and a large man, dressed similarly to Felter walked into the office without being formally admitted. His youth and the reverential look he gave to Felter told O'Connor immediately he was a production assistant – the backbone of most TV and film companies. The man, with an effeminate manner, gave a pleasant smile to O'Connor, long enough of a gaze to make him want to say, I'm straight, but thanks for the compliment.

The PA said to Felter, 'He passed.'

'He what?'

'Yep. I was beside myself.'

'He said he was in.'

'He's not in. He's out.'

The elliptical conversation – probably about an actor who'd agreed to do something but backed out at the last minute because of a better offer – continued for a few minutes. As they dealt with the emergency, O'Connor tuned out and glanced at the walls of the man's office. Like many producers' it was covered with posters. Some were of the shows that Felter had created. Others were of recent films – those starring Tom Cruise, Kate Winslet, Ethan Hawke, Tobey Maguire, Leonardo DiCaprio. And, curiously, some were of films that O'Connor remembered fondly from his childhood, the great classics like *The Guns of Navarone*, *The Dirty Dozen*, *The Magnificent Seven* and *Bullitt*.

The actor remembered that he and Felter's dad would sometimes hang out for a beer after the week's shooting for *Homicide Detail* had wrapped. Of course, they'd gossip about the shenanigans on the set but they'd also talk about their shared passion: feature films. O'Connor recalled that often young Aaron would join them, their conversations helping to plant the seeds of the boy's future career.

Felter and the bodybuilder of a production assistant concluded their discussion of the actor crisis. The producer shook his head. 'OK, find somebody else. But I'm talking one day, tops.'

'I'm on it.'

Felter grimaced. 'People make a commitment, you'd think they'd stick to it. Was it different back then?'

'Back then?'

'The *Homicide Detail* days.'

'Not really. There were good people and bad people.'

'The bad ones, fuck 'em,' Felter summarized. 'Anyway, sorry for the interruption.'

O'Connor nodded.

The producer rocked back in a sumptuous leather chair. 'I've got to be honest with you, Mike.'

Ah, one of the more-often-used rejections. O'Connor at least gave him credit for meeting with him in person to deliver the bad news; Felter had a staff of assistants, like Mr America, who could've called and left a message. He could even just have mailed back the materials. O'Connor had included a self-addressed, stamped envelope.

'We just couldn't sell episodic TV like this nowadays. We have to go with what's hot. People want reality, sitcoms, traditional drama. Look at *Arrested Development*. Brilliant. But they couldn't keep it afloat.' Another tap of O'Connor's proposal for *Stories*. 'This is ground-breaking. But to the industry now, ground-breaking means earthquake. Natural disaster. Everybody wants formula. Syndicators want formula, stations want formula, the audience too. They want a familiar team of stereotypical characters in predicable conflicts. This's been true for decades.'

'So you're saying that *The Sopranos* is just *The Honeymooners* with guns and the f word.'

Felter laughed. 'That's good. Can I use it?'

'It's yours.'

'Mike, I wish I could help you out. My dad, rest his soul, loved working on your show. He said you were a genius. But we've gotta go with the trends.'

'Trends change. Wouldn't you like to be part of a new one?'

'Not really.' Felter laughed. 'And you know why? Because I'm a coward. We're all cowards, Mike.'

O'Connor couldn't help but smile himself.

On his show, O'Connor had played a Columbo kind of cop. Sharp, nothing got by him. Mike Olson, the cop on *Homicide Detail*, wasn't a lot different from Mike O'Connor the actor. He looked Felter over carefully. 'What else?'

Felter placed his hands on his massive glass desk. 'What can I say? Come on, Mike. You're not a kid any more.'

'This is no industry for old men,' he said, paraphrasing William Butler Yeats's line from 'Sailing to Byzantium'.

In general men have a longer shelf-life than women in TV and films, but there are limits. Mike O'Connor was fifty-eight years old.

'Exactly.'

'I don't want to star. I'll play character from time to time, just for the fun of it. We'll have a new lead every week. We could get Damon or DiCaprio, Scarlett Johansson, Cate Blanchett. People like that.'

'Oh, you can?' Felter wryly responded to the enviable wish list.

'Or the youngster of the month. Up and coming talent.'

'It's brilliant, Mike. It's just not saleable.'

'Well, Aaron, I've taken up enough of your time. Thanks for seeing me. I mean that. A lot of people wouldn't have.'

They chatted a bit more about family and local sports teams and then O'Connor could see that it was time to go. Something in Felter's body language said he had another meeting to take.

They shook hands. O'Connor respected it that Felter did end the conversation with 'Let's get together some time.' When people in his position said that to people in O'Connor's, the lunch dates were invariably cancelled at the last minute.

O'Connor was at the door when he heard Felter say, 'Hey, Mike. Hold on a minute.'

The actor turned and noted the producer was looking at him closely with furrowed brows: O'Connor's flop of greying blond hair, the broad shoulders, trim hips. Like most professional actors – whether working or not – Mike O'Connor stayed in shape.

'Something just occurred to me. Take a pew again.' Nodding at the chair.

O'Connor sat and observed a curious smile on Felter's face. His eyes were sparkling.

'I've got an idea.'

'Which is?'

'You're might not like it at first. But there's a method to my madness.'

'Sanity hasn't worked for me, Aaron. I'll listen to madness.'

'You play poker?'

'Of course I play poker.'

O'Connor and Diane were sitting on the patio of their house in the hills off Beverly Glen, the winding road connecting West Hollywood and Beverly Hills to the San Fernando Valley. It was a pleasant house, but modest. They'd lived here for years and he couldn't imagine another abode.

He sipped the wine he'd brought them both out from the kitchen.

'Thanks, lover,' she said. Diane, petite, feisty and wry, was a real estate broker, and she and O'Connor had been together for thirty years, with never an affair between them, a testament to the fact that not all Hollywood marriages are doomed.

She poured more wine.

The patio overlooked a pleasant valley – now tinted blue at dusk. Directly beneath them was a gorgeous house. Occasionally film crews would disappear inside, the shades would be drawn, then the crews would emerge five hours later. This part of California was the number-one producer of pornography in the world.

'So, here's what Felter's proposing,' he told her. 'Celebrity poker.'

'OK,' Diane said dubiously. 'Go on.' Her voice was yawning.

'No, no. I was sceptical at first too. But listen to this. It's apparently a big deal. For one thing it airs during Sweeps Week.'

The week during which the networks presented the shows with the biggest draw to suck up the viewership rating points.

'Really?'

'And it's live.'

'Live TV?'

'Yep.' O'Connor went on to explain the premise of *Go For Broke*.

'So it's *live*, sleazy reality TV. What makes it any different?'

'Have some more wine' was O'Connor's answer.

'Oh-oh.'

O'Connor explained that what set *Go For Broke* apart from typical celebrity poker shows was that on this one the contestants would be playing with their own money. Real money. Not for charity contributions, like the usual celeb gambling programmes.

'*What?*'

'Aaron's view is that reality TV isn't real at all. Nobody's got anything to lose. *Survivor*, *Fear Factor*... there's really no risk. The people who climb walls or walk on girders're tethered and they've got spotters everywhere. And eating worms isn't going to kill you.'

Savvy businesswoman Diane O'Connor said, 'Get back to the "our own money" part.'

'The stakes are a quarter million. We come in with that.'

'Bullshit.'

'Nope. It's true. And we play with cash on the table. No chips. Like riverboat gamblers.'

'And the networks're behind it?'

'Huge. The ad budget alone's twenty-five million. National print, TV, radio, transit ads… everything. The time slot for the first show is after *Central Park West* and on Thursday it's right after *Hostage*.'

CPW was the hottest comedy since *Friends*, and *Hostage* was the season's biggest crime drama, a show like *24*.

'OK, it's big. And we can probably get our hands on the money, but we can't afford for you to lose it, Mike. And even if you win, OK, you make a million dollars. We could do that in a couple of years in the real estate market. So, what's in it for you?'

'Oh, it's not about the money. It has nothing to do with that.'

'Then what's it about?'

'The bump.'

'The bump? What is that? A Hollywoodism?'

'Of course,' he said. 'Why use a dozen words to express yourself exactly when you can use a buzzword?'

He explained to his wife, in a slightly censored fashion, what Aaron Felter had told him earlier: 'Mike, buddy, a bump is a leg-up. It's getting recognized on the media radar. It's grabbing the limelight. A bump means you're fuckable. A bump gets your name in *Daily Variety*. You haven't had a bump for years. You need one.'

O'Connor had asked Felter, 'So you're saying that if I'm in this game, I get a bump?'

'No, I'm saying if you *win* the game, you get a bump. Will it get you a housekeeping deal at a studio? I don't know. But it'll open doors. And I'll tell you if you win, I promise I'll take your proposal for *Stories* to the people I've got deals with. Again, am I promising they'll greenlight it? No, but it'll get me in the front door.'

He now said to Diane, 'All the contestants're like me. At a certain level, but not where we want to be. They're from a cross section of entertainment industries, music, acting, stand-up comedy.'

The woman considered this for a long time, looking over the blue hills, the porn house, the pale evening stars. 'This is really your last chance to get *Stories* on, isn't it?'

'I'd say that's right.'

Then, to his disappointment Diane was shaking her head and rising, walking into the kitchen. He was upset, but he'd never think of doing anything that went against his wife's deepest wishes. He loved her. And, more important, he trusted her. O'Connor was a craggy guy, big and tough-looking. In *Homicide Detail* his character, Detective Mike Olson, was of course identical to Mike O'Connor; emotionally he was the antithesis of the actor. And he resolved that, seeing Diane's reaction, he'd call Felter immediately and back out.

She returned a moment later with a new bottle of Sonoma Chardonnay.

'You don't want me to do it, do you?' he asked.

'I'll answer that with one question.'

Where would they get the money, what about the girls' tuition, would they have to hit their retirement funds?

But, it turned out, she was curious about something else: she asked, 'Does a full house beat a flush?'

'Uhm, well...' He frowned.

Diane withdrew from her pocket something she'd apparently collected when she'd gone into the kitchen for the wine: a deck of Rider playing cards. 'I can see you need some practice, son.'

And cracked the wrapper on the deck.

The bar was on Melrose, one of those streets in West Hollywood where you can see celebs and people who want to be celebs and people who, whether they're celebs or not, are just absolutely fucking beautiful.

Sammy Ralston was checking some of them out now – the women at least – and looking for starlets. He watched a lot of TV.

He watched now in his small place in Glendale. And he'd watched a lot Inside too, though the Chicano inmates dictated what you saw, which during the day was mostly Spanish-language soaps, which weren't so bad, 'cause you got a lot of tits, but at night they watched weird shows he couldn't figure out. (Though everybody watched *CSI*, which he had a soft-spot for, seeing as how it was physical evidence – from one of his cigarettes – that landed him inside in the first place after the B & E at a Best Buy warehouse.)

He looked up and saw Jake walk through the door, shaved head, inked forearms. Huge. A biker. He wore a leather jacket with *Oakland* on the back. Say no more. He stood above Ralston. Way above. 'Why'd you get a table?'

'I don't know. I just did.'

'Because you wanted some faggot chicken wings, or what?'

'I don't know. I just did.' The repetition was edgy. Ralston was small but he didn't put up with much shit.

Jake shrugged. They moved to the bar. Jake ordered a whisky, double, which meant he'd been here before and knew they were small pours.

He drank half the glass down, looked around and said in a soft voice, 'Normally I wouldn't fuck around with a stranger but I'm in a bind. I've got a thing going down and my man – nigger out of Bakersfield – had to get the fuck out of state. Now, here's the story. Joey Fadden—'

'Sure, I know Joey.'

'I know you know Joey. Why I'm here. Lemme finish. Jesus. Joey said you were solid. And I need somebody solid, from your line of work.'

'Windows?'

'Your other line of fucking work.'

Ralston actually had two. One was washing windows. The other was breaking into houses and offices and walking off with anything saleable. People thought that people who boosted merch went for valuable things. They didn't. They went for *saleable* things. Big difference. You have to know your distribution pipeline, a fence had once told him.

'And you understand that if we can't come to an agreement here and anything goes bad later, me or one of my buddies from up north'll come visit you.'

The threat was like the fine print in a car contract. It had to be included but nobody paid it much mind.

'Yeah, yeah. Fine. Go ahead.'

'So. What it is. I heard from Joey about a month ago this TV crew did a story at Lompoc. Life in prison, some shit like that, I don't know. And the crew got this hard-on to hang with the prisoners.'

'Macho shit, sure.' Ralston'd seen this before. People from the Outside feeling this connection with people Inside.

'So Joey heard them talking about this TV poker show some asshole producer is doing. It's planned for Vegas, but in a hotel, not a real casino. And they don't use chips. They use real cash. The buy-in's supposedly two-fifty K.'

'Shit. Cash? What's the game?' Ralston loved poker.

'Fuck, I don't know. Old Maid. Or Go Fish. I don't fucking lose my money at cards. So I'm thinking, if it's not a casino, security won't be so tight. Might be something to think about.' Jake ordered another whisky. 'OK. So I check out the prison show and get some names. And one of the gaffers—'

'Yeah, what is that? I've heard of them.'

'Electrician. Can I finish? He's a biker too, from Culver City. And he's a little loose in the mouth when he's had a few, and so I get the details. First of all, this's a live show.'

'What's that mean?'

'Live? They don't record it ahead of time.'

'They do that?' Ralston thought everything was recorded.

'So it's a big surprise who wins.'

'That's not a bad idea for a show. I mean, I'd watch it.' Ralston peeled the label off his beer. It was a nervous habit. Jake noticed him and he stopped.

'Well, you can tell 'em you fucking approve, or you can shut up and listen. My point is that they'll have a mil and a half in small bills on the set. And we'll know exactly when and exactly where. So Joey speaks for you and I thought you might be interested. You want in, you get twenty points.'

'It's not a casino's money, but there'll still be armed guards.'

'Last time I looked Seven-Elevens don't have that kind of money in their fucking cash registers.'

'Guns involved, I'd be more interested for thirty.'

'I could go twenty-five.'

Sammy Ralston said he'd have to think about it.

Which meant only one thing: getting a call through to Lompoc. After he and Jake adjourned he managed to get Joey Fadden, doing three to five for GTA, hard because a weapon was involved. By virtue of the circumstances, their conversation was convoluted, but the most important sentence was a soft, 'Yeah, I know Jake. He's OK.'

Which was all Ralston needed.

And they proceeded to talk about the sports teams and how much they both lamented the name change of the San Francisco 49ers's home to 'Monster Park'.

The site of the game was the Elysium Fields Resort and Spa on the outskirts of Vegas.

On Wednesday morning, the day of the show, the contestants assembled in one of the hotel's conference rooms. It was a curious atmosphere – the typical camaraderie of fellow performers, with the added element that each one wanted to take a quarter million dollars away from the others. The mix was eclectic:

Stone T, a hip hop artist, whose real name, O'Connor learned from the bio that Felter had prepared for the press, was Emmanuel Evan Jackson. He had been a choirboy in Bethany Baptist church in South Central, had put himself through Cal State, performing at night, and then got into the L.A. rap, ska and hip hop scene. Stone was decked out like a homie from Compton or Inwood – drooping JNCO jeans, Nikes, a vast sweatshirt and bling. All of which made it jarring to hear him say things like, 'It's a true pleasure to meet you. I've admired your work for a long time.' And: 'My wife is my muse, my Aphrodite. She's the one whom I dedicate all my songs to.'

O'Connor was surprised to see Brad Kresge was one of the contestants. He was a bad boy of West Hollywood. The lean, intense-eyed kid was a pretty good actor in small roles – never with a major lead – but it was his personal life that had made the headlines. He'd been thrown out of clubs for fighting, had several DUI arrests, and he'd even done short time in L.A. County jail for busting up a hotel room as well as the two security guards who'd come to see what the fuss was about. He seemed cheerful enough at the moment, though, and was attentive to the emaciated blonde hanging on his arm – despite the fact that Aaron Felter had asked that the contestants attend this preliminary meeting alone, without partners or spouses.

Kresge was unfocused and O'Connor wondered if he was stoned. He wore his hat backward and the sleeves of his wrinkled shirt rolled up, revealing a tat that started with a gothic letter F. The rest of the word disappeared underneath the sleeve but nobody doubted what the remaining letters were.

Sandra Glickman was the only woman in the game. She was a stand-up comic from New York originally and who lived out here now. She worked the Laugh Factory and Caroline's and appeared occasionally on Comedy Central. O'Connor had seen her once or twice on TV. Her routines were crude and funny ('Hey, you guys out there'll be interested to know I'm bisexual; buy me something and I'll have sex with you.'). O'Connor was surprised to learn that she'd gone to Harvard on a full scholarship and had a master's degree in advanced math. She'd started doing the comedy thing as a lark before she settled down to teach math or science. That had been six years ago, and comedy had won over academia.

Charles Bingham was a familiar face from TV and movies, though few people knew his name. Extremely tanned, fit, in his early sixties, he wore a blue blazer and tan slacks, dress shirt and tie. His dyed blonde hair was parted perfectly down the side and it was a fifty-fifty chance that the coif was a piece, O'Connor estimated. Bingham was a solid character player, and the character was almost always the same: the older ex-husband of the leading lady, the co-worker or brother of the leading man, a petty officer in a war movie – and usually one of the first to get killed in battle.

He'd been born Charles Brziesneski, the rumour was. But so what? O'Connor's own first name was still legally Maurice.

The big surprise in the crowd was Dillon McKennah. The handsome, thirty-something was a big-screen actor. He'd be the one real star at the table. He'd been nominated for an Oscar for his role in a Spielberg film, and everybody was surprised he'd lost. He'd been called the New James Dean. But his career had faltered. He'd made some bad choices recently: lacklustre teen comedies and a truly terrible horror film – in which gore and a crashing soundtrack substituted, poorly, for suspense. Even on his most depressed days, O'Connor could look at himself in the mirror and say that he'd never taken on a script he didn't respect. McKennah mentioned that he was working on a new project, though he gave no details. But every actor in Hollywood was engaged in a 'new project', just like every writer had a script 'in development'.

They drank coffee, ate from the luxurious spread of breakfast delicacies and chatted, generally playing type: Stone T was hip. Sandra cracked jokes. Bingham smiled vacantly, stiff and polite, Kresge was loud. McKennah was Matt Damon in *Good Will Hunting*. And O'Connor was the strong silent sort.

As the conversation continued, O'Connor was surprised to find how lucky he was to be here. Apparently, when word went out about *Go For Broke*, close to five thousand people had contacted Aaron Felter's office, either directly or through their agents.

Everybody wanted the bump.

Now, the door of the conference room swung open and Aaron Felter entered.

'OK, all, how you doing? Hey, Sandy caught your act on Sunset this weekend.'

The woman comic gave him a thumbs up. 'Were you the heckler?'

'Like I'd spar against you? Am I fucking nuts?'

'Yo, Aaron, can we drink?' asked Brad Kresge. 'On the set, I mean. I play better that way.'

'You can do whatever you want,' Felter told him. 'But you break any cameras – or any heads – you pay for 'em.'

'Fucking funny.'

When coffee cups were refilled and the bagel table raided again, Felter sat on the edge of the table in the front of the room. 'Now, folks. Today's the day. I want to run through the plan. First, let's talk about the game itself.' He asked a young man into the room. The slim guy was the professional dealer Felter had flown in from Atlantic City. He sat down at the table and – after awing them with his incredible dexterity – went through protocol and rules of the game they'd be playing, Texas Hold 'Em.

This was one of the simplest of all poker games (selected, O'Connor guessed, not because of the contestants, but because of the audience, so they could follow the play). There was no ante; the players to the dealer's left would place blind bets before the deal – a small blind and a large – to create a pot. Each player then was dealt two 'hole' cards, which nobody else could see, and then placed bets or folded, based on those cards.

Then came the 'flop': three community, or 'board', cards dealt face up in the middle of the table. Betting commenced again and two more community cards are dealt face up making five. Traditional rules of poker apply to the betting process: checking – choosing not to bet – as well as seeing, raising or calling someone at the showdown.

When that occurs, players use their two hole cards plus any three of the five face-up board cards to make the best hand they can.

'Now, one thing we're not doing,' Felter announced. 'No hidden cameras.'

Most televised poker shows feature small cameras that allow the audience and commentators to see each player's hole cards. The systems were tightly controlled and the games usually recorded ahead of time so there was no risk of using that information to cheat in real time, but that wasn't Felter's concern. A born showman, he wanted the tension of live drama: 'What's the excitement if the audience knows what everybody's hand is? I want people at home to be on the edge of their seats. Hell, I want them to fall *off* their seats.'

'Now remember, you're live. Don't pick your nose or grab your crotch.'

'Can I grab somebody else's crotch?' Glickman asked.

McKennah and, despite the blonde on his arm, Kresge, raised their hands.

Everyone laughed.

'And,' Felter continued, 'you'll be miked, so if you whisper, "Fuck me", we'll bleep it but your mother's going to know you said something naughty. Now, I want laughs and sighs, and banter. We'll have three cameras on close-ups and medium angles and one camera on top showing the board. No sunglasses.' This was directed to Brad Kresge, who was always wearing them. 'I want expression. Cry, look exasperated, laugh, get pissed off. This is a poker game but first and foremost it's TV! I want the audience engaged… Any questions?'

There were none, and the contestants dispersed.

On his way to join Diane for a swim before the show, Mike O'Connor was trying to recall what was familiar about Felter's speech.

Then he remembered: it was out of some gladiator film, when the man who was in charge gave his before-the-games pep talk, reminding the warriors that though most of them were about to die, they should go out and put on the best show they could.

*

Sammy Ralston and Jake were in a bar up the street from Elysium Fields Spa.

Jesus, it was hot.

'Why Nevada?' Ralston asked. 'Why the desert? They oughta put casinos where the weather's nicer.' Ralston was sweating like crazy. Jake wasn't. Big guy like that and he wasn't sweating. What was that about?

The biker said, 'If the weather's nice people stay outside and don't gamble. If the weather's shitty, they stay inside and do. That's not rocket science.'

Oh. Made sense.

Ralston fed a quarter into the minislot at the end of the bar, and Jake looked at him like, you want to throw your money away, go ahead. He lost. He fed another quarter in and lost again.

The two men had spent the last few days checking out the Elysium Fields. It was one of those places that dated from the fifties and was pretty nice, but also sort of shabby. It reminded Ralston of his grandmother's apartment's décor in Paramus, New Jersey. A lot of yellows, a lot of mirrors that looked like they had bad skin conditions, a lot of fading white statuettes.

Jake, with his tats and biker physique, stood out big time, so he'd done most of the behind-the-scenes information gathering, from press releases and a few discreet calls to his union contact on the studio backlot. He'd learned that the TV show would be shot in the grand ballroom. At the beginning of the show, armed guards would give each player a suitcase containing his buy-in, which would sit on a table behind his chair. He'd take what he needed from it to play.

'Gotta be a big suitcase, I'd guess.'

'No. Two-fifty takes up shit. If it's in twenties or bigger.'

'Oh.' Ralston supposed Jake would know this. The most he himself had ever boosted in cash was about $2,000. But that was in quarters and he pulled his back out, schlepping it from the arcade to his car.

After the initial episode tonight was over, the money went back in the suitcases of the players who hadn't gone bust. The guards would take it to the hotel's safe for the night.

As for the surveillance of the Elysium Fields, Ralston had done most of that. He had his window washing truck and his gear here, so he was virtually invisible. All contractors are. He'd learned that the ballroom was in a separate building. The guards would have to wheel the money down a service walk about sixty feet or so to get to the safe. Ralston had found that the walk was lined with tall plants, a perfect place to hide to jump out and surprise the guards. They'd overpower, cuff and duct tape them, grab the suitcases and flee to the opposite lot.

He and Jake discussed it, and they decided to act tonight, after the first round of games; tomorrow, after the finale, there'd be more people around and they couldn't be sure if the money would be returned to the safe.

The plan sounded OK to both men, but Jake said, 'I think we need some kind of, you know, distraction. These security people around here. They're pros. They're going to be looking everywhere.'

Ralston suggested setting off some explosion on the grounds. Blow up a car or pull the fire alarm.

But Jake didn't like that. 'Fuck, as soon as anybody hears that, they'll know something's going down, and the money'll have guards all over it.' Then the biker blinked and nodded. 'Hey, you noticed people getting married around here a lot?'

'Yeah, I guess.'

'And everybody getting their pictures taken?'

Ralston caught on. 'All those flashes, yeah. You mean, blind 'em somehow with a camera?'

Jake nodded. 'But we walk up with a camera, the guards'd freak.'

'How about we get one of those flashes you see at weddings. The remote ones.'

'Yeah. On tripods.'

'Yeah.' We get one of those, set it up about halfway along the walk.

When they're nearby we flash it. They'll be totally fucking blinded. We come up from behind. They won't fucking know what hit them. I like it. Think we can find something like that around here?'

'Probably.'

The men paid for their beers and stepped out into the heat.

'Oh, one thing?'

'Yeah?' Jake grunted.

'What about… you know.'

'No, I don't fucking know until you tell me.'

'A piece. I don't have a piece.'

Jake laughed. 'I'm curious. You ever used one?'

'Fuck, yes.' In fact, no, he'd never fired a gun, not on a job. But he was pissed that Jake seemed to be laughing at him about it.

When they were in the window-washing truck, Jake grabbed his canvas backpack from behind the seat. He opened it up for Ralston to see. There were three pistols inside.

'Take your pick.'

Ralston chose the revolver. It had fewer moving parts and levers and things on the side. With this one he wouldn't have to ask Jake how it worked.

The banquet hall where *Go For Broke* was being shot was huge and it was completely packed.

The place was also decked out like every TV set that Mike O'Connor had ever been on: a very small portion – what the camera saw – was sleek and fashionably decorated. The rest was a mess: scaffolding, bleachers, cameras, wires, lights. It looked like a factory.

The contestants had finished with hair and makeup (except Kresge: 'You get me the way I am, leave me the fuck alone.') and the sound man had wired them – mikes to their chests and plugs to their ears. They were presently in the green room, making small talk. O'Connor noted the costumes. Sandra Glickman was low-cut and glittery, Kresge was still in his hat-backward, show-the-tats mode. Stone T was subdued South Central and had gotten Felter's

OK to wear Ali G goggles, not nearly as dark as sunglasses; you could get a good look at his eyes (for the 'drama' when he won a big pot or ended up busted, presumably). Charles Bingham was in another blazer and razor-creased grey slacks. He wore a tie but an ascot wouldn't've been out of place. Dillon McKennah wore the de rigueur costume of youthful West Hollywood, an untucked striped blue and white shirt over a black T-shirt and tan chinos. His hair was spiked up in a fringe above his handsome face.

O'Connor had been dressed by Diane in 'older man sexy'. Black sport coat, white T-shirt, jeans and cowboy boots. 'Gunfight at the OK corral,' she'd whispered and kissed him for luck. 'Go break a thumb.'

The production assistant – not the big gay fellow from L.A., but a young nervous brunette – stood in the green room's doorway, clutching a clipboard, a massive radio on her hip. She listened to the voice of the director from the control room and kept glancing at her watch.

Television was timed to the tenth of a second.

Suddenly she stiffened. 'All right, everybody, please. We're on in three.' She then rounded them up like cattle and headed them to the assembly point.

There, O'Connor looked at the monitor, showing what the viewers around the country would be seeing: splashy graphics and some brash music. Then the camera settled on a handsome young man – dressed similarly to Dillon McKennah – sitting at a desk, like a sports commentator. Beside him was an African-American in a suit and a skinny white guy in a cowboy outfit.

'Good evening, I'm Lyle Westerbrook, your host for *Go For Broke*. Two exciting days of no-holds-barred poker. And joining me here are Andy Brock, three times winner of the World Championship of Poker in Atlantic City. Welcome, Andy.'

'Good to see you, Lyle.'

'And Pete Bronsky, a professional gambler from Dallas and the man who wrote *Making a Living at Cards*. Hi, Pete.'

'Back at you, Lyle.'

'This is reality TV at its most real. You are watching live, on location, six individuals who aren't playing for prestige, they aren't playing for a charity of their choice. They're playing with their own hard cash. Somebody's going to lose big – a quarter of a million dollars. And somebody's going to win – maybe as much as six times that. One and a half million dollars is going to be at play tonight. You gentlemen must know the excitement of what our contestants are feeling.'

'Oh, you bet I do, Lyle...'

O'Connor tuned out of the banter, realizing that this was, in fact, the big time. Millions of people would be watching them, and, more important, dozens of network and studio execs would be watching the ratings.

The bump...

'And now, let's meet our contestants...'

They went out in alphabetical order, as the announcer made a few comments about them and their careers. O'Connor caught Diane's eye – she was in the front row – when the applause erupted at the mention of *Homicide Detail* and the character of Det. Mike Olson. Though when, like the rest of the players, he said a few words to Lyle and mentioned the phrase, 'Save it for the judge', one of his signature lines from the series, not many people laughed, which told him that the *APPLAUSE* sign had prompted people to cheer when the name of his show was mentioned.

Welcome to the world of TV.

Then they were all seated around the table, security guards brought in the cash, which had been wire transferred to a local bank yesterday. The audience murmured when the guards, rather dramatically, opened the cases and set them behind each player on a low table. (Was there an illuminated sign that urged, 'SOUND AWED'?) The guards stood back, hands near their guns, scanning the audience from behind sunglasses.

O'Connor tried not to laugh.

The dealer explained the rules again – for the audience – then with cameras hovering, sweat already dripping, the room went utterly silent. Cards were shuffled and the cut offered and accepted. The dealer nodded to O'Connor, to his immediate left. He pushed the small blind bet out onto the table. One thousand dollars.

For the big blind, Kresge splashed the table, tossing the money out carelessly – very bad form. Chugging a beer, he grinned as the dealer straightened it.

The game began, erratic at first, with nobody winning or losing in big, dramatic hands. Kresge bet hard and took some bad losses but then pulled back. Sandy Glickman, with the quick mind of a natural comedian (and mathematician), seemed to be calculating the odds before each bet. She increased her winnings slowly. Stone T was a middle-of-the-road player, suffering some losses, and caught some wins, as did McKennah. Neither seemed like natural players. O'Connor played conservatively and continually reminded himself of the basic poker strategy he'd picked up over the years – and that Diane had helped drill into him in the last few weeks:

It's all right to fold up front. You don't have to play every hand.

Bluff rarely, if at all. Bluffing should be used appropriately and only against certain players in limited circumstances. Many professional players go for months at a time without bluffing.

Fold if you think you're going to lose no matter how much you've already put into the pot.

Always watch the cards. Texas Hold 'Em is played with a single fifty-two card deck and only seven cards are known to any one player: his two and the five community cards. Unlike counting cards at blackjack or baccarat, knowing those seven won't give you great insights into what the others have. But knowing the board, you can roughly calculate the odds of whether someone else has a hand that beats yours.

Most important in poker, of course, is to watch the people playing against you. Some gamblers believe in tells – gestures or expressions that suggest what people have as their hole cards.

O'Connor didn't believe that there were obvious tells, like scratching your eye when you had a high pair in the hole. But he did know that people respond consistently to stimuli – he'd learned this not from his limited experience as a card player but as an empathic actor. For instance he'd noticed that Stone T's face grew still when he had a good, though not necessarily a winning, hand. File those facts away and be aware of them.

The game progressed, with Glickman and McKennah up slightly, Kresge, Stone and O'Connor were down a bit. Bingham was the big loser so far. On the whole O'Connor was pleased with his performance. He was playing a solid game.

They took a commercial break and Felter walked out, dispensing water and telling everybody how pleased he was – and how favourable the initial responses were. He walked off stage and they heard the voice of God.

'Now, back to the million-dollar action,' the commentator said. Then silence. O'Connor and the others couldn't hear anything else from the host or the pros in the control booth; he wondered how they were critiquing the performances.

A new deal. The blind bets were made and the dealer offered the cut. Then the hole cards were dealt.

Shit.

O'Connor hoped he hadn't muttered that out loud. (His mother *was* watching.)

He had a 'hammer.' This was the worst hole cards dealt anyone could have, an unsuited two and a seven. You can't make a straight – you're allowed only three cards from the board – and there was no chance of a flush. There was a miraculous possibility for a full house but at best it would be sevens and twos, a very low one.

He stayed in for one round of betting but Bingham and Glickman started raising each other. Kresge folded, spitting out a word that O'Connor knew the standards and practices people would bleep (even 'live' shows had a few seconds' delay to allow for things like that).

McKennah folded and then O'Connor did too. He was mentally counting the money he had left – about $220,000 – when he realized that something was going on at the table. Bingham, Glickman and Stone were engaged in battle. He sensed that Stone didn't have great cards but was already in for close to a hundred thousand. Glickman was less raucous than earlier, which told him that she might have a solid hand, and Bingham tried to appear neutral. He fondled the lapel of his blazer.

The community cards were the jack of spades, king of diamonds, three of clubs, seven of clubs, six of hearts.

'Ma'am?' the dealer asked Glickman.

'Seventy-five thousand,' she raised, sighing, 'think of all the eyeliner that'd buy.'

The audience laughed. In her routines she was known for excessive makeup.

Stone sighed too. And folded.

Bingham snuck a peek at his cards again. This was a bad tell. It meant that you were double checking to verify that you had one of the better hands, like a straight or flush. Then he looked over his money. His suitcase was empty and he had only about sixty thousand on the table.

'All in,' he said. Under standard rules of poker he could call with less than the raise, but couldn't win more than what he'd put into the pot.

O'Connor saw the older man's hands descend to his slacks; he wiped his sweaty palms. His face was still.

All eyes were on the cards.

O'Connor was sitting forward. Who won? What were the cards?

And the announcer said, 'And we'll be right back, folks, for the conclusion of this exciting day in Las Vegas.'

Agony. The next five minutes were agony.

The cards remained face down on the table, the contestants chatted, sipped water. Kresge told a filthy joke to Glickman, who was subdued, for a change, and did nothing but smile distantly. If she lost this hand she wouldn't go bust, but she'd be way behind. If Bingham lost, he'd be heading home.

No money, no bump.

Both Glickman and Bingham kept smiles on their faces, but you could see the tension they felt. Their overturned cards sat in front of them. The waiting was torture for O'Connor – and he had nothing to lose.

After an interminable few minutes during which beer, cars and consulting services were hawked to millions of people around the country, the action returned to the table.

The dealer said, 'Ma'am, you've been called. Would you please show your cards?'

She turned her two over, and her jack and ten joined another jack and two more tens on the board for a full house.

Bingham smiled stoically. 'Ah.' He displayed the ace-high flush. She'd beaten him with one hand better than his.

He rose and gave her a kiss. Then shook the others' hands.

The protocol, Aaron Felter had told them, was that anyone who went bust had to rise and leave.

Head off down the Walk of Shame, O'Connor dubbed it.

Departing this way seemed a bit ignominious, but this wasn't just poker, of course; it was the hybrid of poker on television.

I want drama…

The security guard displayed his empty suitcase to the table and the camera – more drama – and then deposited it in a specially built trash can.

The audience applauded furiously as Sandy raked in her cash.

After a commercial break and the ceremonial opening of a fresh deck of cards, the play continued. The remaining players were warmed up now and the betting grew more furious. On the sixth hand of this segment, Glickman, O'Connor and McKennah all folded and Stone T went one on one with Kresge.

Then the rapper made a bad mistake. He tried to bluff.

O'Connor knew you couldn't bluff against people like Kresge – in poker or in real life. People who trash hotel rooms and smack their girlfriends don't have anything to lose. They kept raising hard, and O'Connor could see that Stone was breaking the rule he himself had been reciting to himself all night: Don't stay in, just because you've already spent money.

Stone pushed in all his remaining stake – nearly eighty thousand – a cool smile on his lips, terror in his eyes, through Da Ali G lenses.

Kresge took his time finishing a light beer and then, with a sour smile, called the rapper.

Stone's two-pair hand was annihilated by an ace-high full house.

One more contestant was gone.

There was time on tonight's show for one more hand and it was during this round that divine retribution, in the form of Mike O'Connor, was visited upon Brad Kresge.

It was really too bad, O'Connor reflected from the vantage point of someone who happened to have the best hand he'd ever had in poker: a straight flush, jack high. As the betting progressed and Glickman and McKennah dropped out, O'Connor assumed the same mannerisms he'd witnessed in Stone T when the rapper was bluffing.

You're an actor, he told himself; so *act*.

Kresge was buzzed from the beer and kept raising, intent on bankrupting the old guy. The odds were minuscule that Kresge had a better hand than this, so it seemed almost unfair to drive him out of the game so easily. But O'Connor had always treated acting as a serious profession and was offended by Kresge's ego and his childish behaviour, which demeaned the business. Especially after seeing the sneer on his face when he knocked Stone T out of the game, O'Connor wanted the punk gone.

Which happened all of ten seconds later.

Kresge went all in, and O'Connor turned the hole cards, his eyes boring into Kresge's, as if saying: When *I* stay in a hotel, kid, I clean it up before I leave.

The audience applauded, as if the good gunslinger had just beat the hell out of the bad one.

Kresge grinned, finished his beer and took O'Connor's hand, trying for a vice grip, which didn't work, given O'Connor's workout regimen. The kid then sauntered off, down the Walk of Shame, as if he could actually set fire to a quarter million dollars and have more fun.

Then the theme music came up and the host announced the winnings for the night: McKennah had $490,000. Glickman had $505,000. Mike O'Connor was the night's big winner with $515,000. Now, the control room mike went live to them and the poker experts took the stage to talk a bit about how the game had gone. The three remaining contestants chatted with them and Lyle for a few minutes.

Then, the theme once again and the red eyes on the cameras went dark.

The show was over for the night.

Exhausted and sweating, O'Connor said goodnight to the other players, the host and the experts. Aaron Felter joined them. He was excited about the initial ratings, which were apparently even better than he'd hoped. Diane joined them. They all made plans to have dinner together in the resort's dining room. O'Connor suggested that those who'd lost join them too, but Felter said they were being taken out to the best restaurant in the city by an assistant.

O'Connor understood. It was important to keep the buzz going. And losers don't figure in that.

Diane said she'd meet them in the bar in twenty minutes; she wanted to call the girls. She headed off to the room and Felter went to talk to the line producer, while O'Connor and McKennah signed some autographs.

'Hey, buy you a beer?' McKennah asked.

O'Connor said sure and they started through the huge hall as the assistants took care of the equipment. TV and movies are as much about lights and electronics and computers as they are about acting.

The two security guards were assembling the suitcases of money.

He didn't have his bump, not yet, he reflected.

On the other hand, he was a quarter-million dollars richer.

Nothing wrong with that.

'Where's the bar?'

McKennah looked around. 'The main building. I think that's a shortcut. There's a walkway there.'

'Let's do it. I need a drink. Man, do I need a drink.'

Sammy Ralston felt the pistol, hot and heavy, in his back waistband. He was standing in the bushes in dark coveralls spearing trash and slipping it into a garbage bag.

On the other side of the walkway, behind other bushes, waited big Jake. The plan was that when the guards wheeling the money from the ballroom to the motel safe were halfway down the walkway, Ralston would hit the switch and flash the powerful photographer's light, which was set up at eye level. They'd tried it earlier. The flash was so bright it had blinded him, even in the well-lit hotel room, for a good ten, twenty seconds.

After the burst of light, Ralston and Jake would race up behind them, cuff the guards, then wrap duct tape around their mouths. With the suitcases of money, the men would return to the stolen van, parked thirty feet away, around the corner of the banquet facility. They'd drive a few miles away to Ralston's window-washing truck, then head back to California.

Ralston looked at his watch. The show was over and the guards would be packing up the money now.

But where were they? It seemed to be taking a lot of time. Were they coming this way, after all?

He glanced towards the door, then he saw it open.

Except that, no, it wasn't the guards at all. It was just a couple of men. A younger one in a striped shirt and an older one in a T-shirt, jeans and sports coat. They were walking along the path slowly, talking and laughing.

What the fuck were they doing here?

Oh, no… Behind them the door opened again, and the guards – two of them, big and armed, of course – were wheeling the cart containing the cash suitcases along the path.

Shit. The two men in front were screwing everything up.

How was he going to handle it?

He crouched in the bushes, pulling the pistol from his pocket.

'Gotta say, man. I loved your show.'

'*Homicide Detail*? Thanks.'

'Classic TV. Righteous.'

'We had fun making it. That's the important thing. You interested in television?'

'Probably features for now.'

Meaning, O'Connor supposed, after a successful career he could 'retire' to the small screen. Well, some people had done it. Others, like O'Connor, thought TV was a medium totally separate from feature films, but just as valid.

'I saw *Town House*,' O'Connor offered.

'That piece of crap?'

O'Connor shrugged. He said sincerely, 'You did a good job. It was a tough role. The writing wasn't so hot.'

McKennah laughed. 'Most of the script was like: "SFX: Groaning as if the house itself is trying to cry for help." And "FX: blood pouring down the stairs, slippery mess. Stacey falls and is swept away." I thought it would be more like traditional horror. *The Exorcist. The Omen. Don't Look Now.* Or Howard Hawks's *The Thing.* Nineteen fifty-one and it still scares the piss out of me. Brilliant.'

They both agreed the recent British zombie movie, *The 28th Day,* was one of the creepiest things ever filmed.

'You mentioned a new project. What's it about?' O'Connor asked.

'A caper. Sort of *The Italian Job* meets *Ocean's Eleven*. Wahlberg kind of thing. Pulling the money together now. You know how that goes… How 'bout you?'

'TV probably. A new series.'

If I get my bump, O'Connor thought.

McKennah nodded behind him. 'That was pretty bizarre. Celebrity poker.'

'Beats *Survivor*. I don't dive off any platforms or eat anything too low on the food chain.'

'That Sandy, she's one hot chick. I'm glad she's still with us.'

McKennah wore no wedding ring; nor did Sandra Glickman. O'Connor wished them the best, though he knew that two-career relationships in Hollywood were sort of like hammer at Texas Hold 'Em – not impossible to win with, you needed luck and a lot of careful forethought.

'Oh, watch it there.' McKennah pointed to a thick wire on the sidewalk. It was curled and O'Connor had nearly caught his foot. The young actor paused and squinted at it.

O'Connor glanced at him.

McKennah explained that he was concerned about paparazzi. How they'd stalk you, even lay booby traps to catch you in embarrassing situations.

O'Connor laughed. 'Not a problem I've had for a while.'

'Damn, look.' McKennah gave a sour laugh. He walked to what the wire was attached to, a photographer's light, set up on a short tripod halfway along the path. Angrily he unplugged it and looked around. 'Some goddamn photog's around here somewhere.'

'Maybe it's part of the show.'

'Then Aaron should've told us.'

'True.'

'Oh, there're some guards.' He nodded at the security detail with the money, behind them. 'I'll tell them. Sometimes I get a little paranoid, I have to admit. But there are some crazy fucking people out there, you know.'

'Tell me about it.'

Ralston had to do something fast.

The two men had spotted the photoflash and, it seemed, had unplugged it.

And the guards were only about fifty feet behind.

What the hell could he do?

Without the flash there was no way they'd surprise the guards.

He glanced towards Jake but the biker was hiding behind thick bushes and seemed not to have seen. And the two men were just standing beside the lights, talking and now – fuck it – waiting for the guards. Assholes.

This was their last chance. Only seconds remained. Then an idea occurred to Ralston.

Hostage.

He'd grab one of the men at gunpoint and draw the guards' attention while Jake came up behind them.

No, better than that, he'd grab one and wound the other – leg or shoulder. That would show he meant business. The security guards'd drop their guns. Jake could cuff and tape them and the two men would flee. Everybody would be so busy caring for the wounded man, he and Jake could get to their truck before anybody realized which way they'd gone.

He pulled on the ski mask and, taking a deep breath, stepped fast out of the bushes, lifting the barrel toward the older of the two men, the one in the T-shirt and jacket, who gazed at him in astonishment. He aimed at the man's knee and started to pull the trigger.

O'Connor gasped, seeing the small man materialize from the bushes and aim a gun at him.

He'd never had a real gun pointed toward him – only fake ones on the set of the TV shows – and his initial reaction was to cringe and raise a protective hand.

As if that would do any good.

'No, wait!' he shouted involuntarily.

But just as the man was about to shoot, there came a flash of motion from his right, accompanied by a grunting gasp.

Dillon McKennah leapt forward and, with his left hand, expertly twisted away the pistol. With his right he delivered a stunning blow to the assailant, sending him staggering back, cradling his wrist. McKennah then moved in again and flipped the man to his belly, and knelt on his back, calling for the guards. The gesture seemed a perfect karate move from an action-adventure film.

O'Connor, still too stunned to feel afraid, glanced back at the sound of footsteps running towards the parking lot. 'There's another one too! That way!'

But the guards remained on the sidewalk, drawing their guns. One stayed with the money, looking around. The other ran forward, calling into his microphone. In less than ten seconds the walkway was filled with security guards and Las Vegas cops too, who were apparently stationed in the motel for the show.

Two officers jogged in the direction O'Connor indicated he'd heard fleeing footsteps.

The assailant's ski mask was off, revealing an emaciated little man in his forties, eyes wide with fear and dismay.

O'Connor watched a phalanx of guards, surrounding the money from *Go For Broke*, wheeling the cart fast into the motel. Yet more guards arrived.

The officers who'd gone after the footsteps reported that they'd seen no one, though a couple reported a big man had jumped into a van and sped off. 'Dark, that's about all they could tell. You gentlemen all right?'

O'Connor nodded. McKennah was ashen faced. 'Fine, yeah. But oh, man I can't believe that. I just reacted.'

'You've got your moves down,' O'Connor told him.

'Tae Kwon Do. I just do it for a sport. I never thought I'd actually use it.'

'I'm glad you did. All I could see was that guy's eyes and I think he was about to pull the trigger.'

Diane came running out – word had spread quickly – and she hugged her husband and asked how he was.

'Fine. I'm fine. Just… I'm not even shaken. Not yet. It all happened so fast.'

A police captain arrived and supervised the arrest. When he was apprised of the circumstances the sombre man shook his head. 'Gives a new meaning to the term "reality TV", wouldn't you say? Now, let's get your statements taken.'

Shaken, Aaron Felter walked into the bar and found O'Connor and Diane, McKennah and Glickman. He ordered a club soda.

'Jesus. How are you all?'

For a man who'd almost been shot, O'Connor admitted he was doing pretty well.

'It was my idea to use cash. I thought it'd play better. Man, this's my fault.'

'You can hardly blame yourself for some wacko, Aaron. Who was he?'

'Some punk from L.A., apparently. Got a history of petty theft, the captain tells me. He had a partner but he got away.'

They talked about the incident and O'Connor recounted McKennah's martial arts skills. The young actor seemed embarrassed. He repeated, 'I just reacted.'

Felter said, 'I've got to say. I'm sure this fucked you up some, pardon my French,' he said, glancing at the women.

'I'm so offended,' Sandra Glickman said, frowning, 'you motherfucking cocksucker.'

They all laughed.

Felter continued, 'Are you cool going ahead with the show?'

McKennah and Glickman said they were. O'Connor said, 'Of course,' but then he caught something in the producer's eyes. 'That's not really what you're asking, is it, Aaron?'

A laugh. 'OK. What I want to know is: if we go ahead with the show tomorrow, how are people going to react? I want your honest opinions. Should we give it some time to calm down? The dust to settle?'

'Which people?' McKennah asked. 'The audience?'

'Exactly. Are they going to think it's in bad taste. I mean somebody could've gotten hurt bad.'

O'Connor laughed. 'Excuse me, Aaron, but when have you ever known a TV show to fail because it's in poor taste?'

Aaron Felter pointed his finger at the man.

'Score one for the old guy' was the message in his eyes.

The Thursday finale of *Go For Broke* began with a description of the events of last night. But since *Entertainment Tonight* and every other quasi news programme in the universe had covered the story, it made little sense to rehash the facts.

Besides, there was poker to be played.

With the same fanfare as yesterday – and *five* sunglasses-clad guards nearby – the play among the last three contestants began.

They played for some time without any significant changes in their positions. Then O'Connor got his first good hole deal of the night. An ace and jack, both spades.

The betting began. O'Connor played it cautious, though, checking at first then matching the other bets or raising slightly.

The flop cards were another ace, a jack and a two, all varied suits.

Betting continued, with both Glickman and McKennah now raising significantly. Though he was uneasy, O'Connor kept a faint smile on his face as he matched the hundred thousand bet by McKennah.

The fourth card, or the 'turn', went face up smoothly onto the table under the dealer's skilful hands. It was another two.

Glickman eyed both of her opponents' piles of cash. But then she held back, checking. Which could mean a weak hand or was a brilliant strategy if she had a really strong one.

When the bet came to McKennah he bet fifty thousand.

O'Connor raised another fifty. Glickman hesitated and then matched the hundred with a brassy laugh.

The final card went down, the fifth, or 'river' card. It was an eight. This meant nothing to O'Connor. His hand was set. Two pair, aces and jacks. It was a fair hand for Texas Hold 'em, but hardly a guaranteed winner.

But they'd be thinking he had a full house, aces and twos, or maybe even a four of a kind – in twos.

They, of course, could have powerful hands as well.

Then Glickman made her move. She pushed everything she had left into the middle of the table.

After a moment of debate McKennah folded.

O'Connor glanced into the brash comedian's eyes, took a deep breath, and called her, counting out the money to match the bet.

If he lost he'd've had about fifty thousand to call his own, and his time on *Go For Broke* would be over.

Sandy Glickman gave a wry smile. She slid her cards, face down into the mush – the pile of discards. She said, for the microphone, 'Not many people know when I'm bluffing. You've got a good eye.' The brassy woman delivered another message to him when she leaned forward to embrace him, whispering: 'You fucked me and you didn't even buy me dinner.'

But she gave him a warm kiss and a wink before she headed off down the Walk of Shame.

About twenty minutes remained for the confrontation between the last two players, O'Connor with $623,000, McKennah with $877,000.

The young actor, to the dealer's left, slid in the small blind, ten thousand, and O'Connor counted out the big blind, twenty.

As the dealer shuffled expertly the two men glanced at each other. O'Connor's eyes conveyed a message. You're an OK kid, and you saved my hide yesterday, but this is poker and I wouldn't be honest to myself, to you or the game, if I pulled back.

The faint glistening in McKennah's eyes said that he acknowledged the message. And said much the same in return.

It's showdown time. Let's go for the bump.

The deals continued for a time, with neither of them winning or losing big. McKennah tried a bluff and lost. O'Connor tried a big move with three of a kind and got knocked out by a flush, which he should've seen coming.

A commercial break and then, with minutes enough for only one hand, the game resumed. The new deck of cards was shuffled, the cut offered. McKennah put in the small blind bet. He chose twenty-five thousand, and O'Connor himself put in fifty.

Then the deal began.

O'Connor was astonished to glance at his hole cards and see he'd gotten a pair of aces.

This was the best hand to get in Texas Hold 'Em.

McKennah glanced at his own cards without emotion. And bet a modest, under the circumstances, fifty thousand.

Careful not to give away his pleasure at the hole cards, O'Connor pushed in the same amount. He was tempted to raise, but decided not to. He had a good chance to win but it was still early and he didn't want to move too fast.

The dealer burned the top card – slid it aside – and then dealt the flop. First, a two of hearts, then the four of hearts and then the ace of spades.

Suddenly O'Connor had three of a kind, with the other two board cards yet to come.

McKennah bet fifty thousand. At this point, because he himself had upped the bet, it wouldn't frighten the younger player off for O'Connor to raise him. He saw the fifty and raised by another fifty.

Murmurs from the crowd.

McKennah hesitated and added the amount to see.

The turn card, the fourth one, wasn't helpful to O'Connor, the six of hearts. Perhaps it was useless to McKennah as well. He checked.

O'Connor noted the hesitation of the man's betting and concluded he had a fair, but unspectacular hand. Afraid to drive him to fold, he bet only fifty thousand again, which McKennah matched.

They looked at each other over the sea of money as the fifth card, the river, slid out.

It was an ace.

As delighted as O'Connor was, he regretted that this amazing hand – four of a kind – hadn't come when more people were in play. It was obvious that McKennah had a functional hand at best and that there'd be a limit to how much O'Connor could raise before he folded. If McKennah folded now the younger actor would still have enough in his bankroll to be declared the winner.

'Sir, the bet is to you.'

He'd have to handle it carefully. Too much the man would fold, and he'd lose.

Too little and the man would simply call, and O'Connor would still come in number two.

He bought time. 'Check.' He rapped the table with his knuckles.

A ripple through the audience. Why was he doing that? He'd seem so confident before.

McKennah looked him over closely. Then said, 'Five hundred thousand.'

And pushed the bills out.

The crowd gasped.

Bluff, O'Connor thought instantly. The only thing McKennah could have that would beat O'Connor was a straight flush. But, as Diane had made him learn over the past several weeks, the odds of O'Connor's winning under these circumstances would be eighty per cent, the odds of McKennah were less than twenty.

Still, O'Connor was painfully aware that he could fold now and walk away having won close to a quarter million in cash. He'd lose the bump but maybe he could use that to bankroll a production company of his own and get *Stories* produced independently.

O'Connor looked up from the money to McKennah.

He said, 'All in,' pushing every penny of his into the huge pile of cash on the table, nearly a million and a half dollars.

'Gentlemen, please show your cards.'

O'Connor turned over his two aces. The crowd erupted in applause.

And they then fell completely silent when McKennah turned over the modest three and five of hearts to reveal his winning straight flush.

O'Connor let out a slow breath, closed his eyes momentarily and smiled.

He stood and, before taking the Walk of Shame, shook the hand of the man who'd just won himself one hell of a bump, not to mention more than a million dollars.

The weeks that followed the airing of *Go For Broke* were not the best of Mike O'Connor's life.

The loss of a quarter million dollars hurt more than he wanted to admit.

More troubling he thought he'd get *some* publicity. But in fact there was virtually none whatsoever. Oh, he got some phone calls. But they mostly were about the foiled robbery attempt and Dillon McKennah's rescue. He finally stopped returning the reporters' calls.

His pilot for *Stories* was now completely dead and nobody was the least interested in hiring him for anything other than things like Viagra or Cialis commercials.

'I can't do it, honey,' he said to Diane.

And she'd laughed, saying, 'It wouldn't be truth-in-advertising anyway, not with you.'

And so he puttered around the house, painted the guest room. Played a little golf.

He even considered helping Diane sell real estate. He sat around the house and watched TV and movies from Net Flix and On Demand.

And then one day, several weeks after the poker show, he happened to be playing couch potato and watching a World War II adventure film from the sixties. O'Connor had seen it when it first came out, when he was just a boy. He'd loved it then, and he'd loved it the times he'd seen it in the intervening years.

But now he realized there was something about it he'd missed. He sat up and remained riveted throughout the film.

Fascinating.

Long after the movie was over he continued to sit and think about it. He realized that he could identify with the people in the movie. They were driven and they were desperate.

He remembered a line from *Homicide Detail*. It had stuck with him all these years. His character, tough, rule-bending Detective Olson, had said to his sergeant, 'The man's desperate. And you know what desperation does – it turns you into a hero or it turns you into a villain. Don't ever forget that.'

Mike O'Connor rose from the couch and headed to his closet.

'Hey, Mike. How you doing? I'm sorry it didn't work out. That last hand. Phew. That was a cliff hanger.'

'I saw the ratings.' O'Connor said to Aaron Felter.

'They weren't bad.'

Not bad? No, O'Connor thought, they were over-the-top amazing. They were close to OJ confessing on *Oprah*, with Dr Phil pitching in the psychobabble.

'So.' Silence rolled along for a moment. 'What're you up to next?'

Felter was pleased to see him but his attitude said that a deal was a deal. This was true in Hollywood just as much as on Wall Street. O'Connor had taken a chance and lost, and the rules of business meant that his and the producer's arrangement was now concluded.

'Taking some time off. Rewriting a bit of *Stories*.'

'Ah. Good. You know what goes around comes around.'

O'Connor wasn't sure that it did. Or even what the hell the phrase meant. But he smiled and nodded.

Silence, during which the producer was, of course, wondering what exactly O'Connor *was* doing here.

So the actor got right down to it.

'Let me ask you a question, Aaron. You like old movies, right? Like your dad and I used to talk about.'

Another pause. Felter glanced at the spotless glass frames of his posters covering the walls. 'Sure. Who doesn't?'

A lot of people didn't, O'Connor was thinking; they liked modern films. Oh, there was nothing wrong with that. In fifty years people would be treasuring some of today's movies the way O'Connor treasured films like *Bonnie and Clyde, M*A*S*H* or *Shane*.

Every generation ought to like its own darlings best.

'You know, I was thinking about *Go For Broke*. And guess what it reminded me of?'

'Couldn't tell you.'

'A movie I just saw on TV.'

'Really? About a poker showdown? An old Western?'

'No. *The Guns of Navarone*.' He nodded at the poster to O'Connor's right.

'*Go For Broke* reminded you of that?'

'And that's not all. It also reminded me of *The Magnificent Seven, The Wild Bunch, Dirty Dozen, Top Gun, Saving Private Ryan, Alien*... in fact, a lot of films... action films.'

'I don't follow, Mike.'

'Well, think about... what was the word you used when we were talking about *Stories*? "Formula". You start with a group of diverse heroes and send 'em on a mission. One by one they're eliminated before the big third-act scene. Like the *Guns of Navarone*. It's a great film, by the way.'

'One of the best,' Felter agreed uncertainly.

'Group of intrepid commandos. Eliminated one by one... but in a certain order, of course: sort of in reverse order of their youth or sex appeal. The stiff white guy's often the first to go – say, Anthony

Quayle in *Navarone*. Or Robert Vaughn in *The Magnificent Seven*. Next we lose the minorities. Yaphet Kotto in *Alien*. Then the hotheaded young kid is bound to go. James Darren. Shouldn't he have ducked when he was facing down the Nazi with the machine gun? I would have. But, no, he just kept going till he was dead.

'That brings us to women. If they're not the leads, they better be careful, Tyne Daily in one of the Dirty Harry films. And even if they survive, it's usually so they can hang on the arm of the man who wins the showdown. And who does that bring us to finally? The main opponents? The older white guy versus the enthusiastic young white guy. Tom Cruise versus Nicholson. Denzel versus Gene Hackman. Clint Eastwood versus Lee van Cleef. DiCaprio versus all the first-class passengers on *Titanic*.

'Kind of like the contestants on the show. Stodgy white guy, minority, hot headed youth, the woman… Bingham, Stone, Kresge, Sandy. And after they were gone, who was left? Old me versus young Dillon McKennah.'

'I think you're pissed off about something, Mike. Why don't you just tell me?'

'The game was rigged, Aaron. I know it. You wrote your quote "reality" show like it was a classic Hollywood western or war movie. You knew how it was going to come out from the beginning. You followed the formula perfectly.'

'And why the fuck would I do that?'

'Because I think you're trying to get a movie financing package going with Dillon McKennah. That caper film he was talking about. He'd shot himself in the foot with *Town House* and that other crap he appeared in. He needed a bump – for both of you.'

Felter was speechless for a moment. Then he looked down. 'We talked about a few things, that's all, Dillon and me. Hell, you and *I* talked about *Stories*. That's my business. Oh, come on, Mike. Don't embarrass yourself. It was a fucking piss-ant reality show. There was no guarantee of a bump.'

'But it did get Dillon a bump. A big one. And you know why?

Because of the robbery. The more I thought about it, the more I realized that was a classic Act Two reversal – according to the *formula* of scriptwriting. You know how that works. Big plot twist three-quarters of the way through. *Guns of Navarone*? The young Greek girl, Gia Scala, the supposed patriot, turns out to be the traitor. She destroys the detonators. How're the commandos going to blow up the German guns now? We're sitting on the edge of our seats, wondering.'

'What does that have to do with anything?'

'The robbery, Aaron. The *attempted* robbery. It was all set up too. You arranged the whole thing... that's what made it more than boring reality TV. My God, you even added a dash of *COPS*. You got the attempt and Dillon's Steven Seagal karate moves on security camera and that night it was on YouTube and every network in the country. TV at its best. You think there wasn't a human being in the country wasn't going to turn on the second episode of *Go For Broke* and watch Dillon and me slug it out?'

'I don't know what—'

O'Connor held up a hand. 'Now, don't embarrass *yourself*, Aaron. On the set of *Homicide Detail*, we had an advisor, a real cop in the LAPD. He's retired now but we're still good buddies. I talked to him and told him I had a problem. I needed to know some facts about the case. He made some calls. First of all, the gun that Sammy Ralston had? It was a fake gun. From a studio property department. The sort they use on TV sets, the sort I carried for seven years. Second, turns out that his phone records show Ralston called a prisoner, Joey Fadden, in Lompoc prison a few weeks ago. The same prisoner that you interviewed as part of that series you shot on California prisons last year. I think you paid Joey to get Ralston's name... ah, ah, ah, let me finish. Gets better. Third, Ralston keeps talking about this mysterious biker named Jake who put the whole thing together and nobody knows about.'

'Jake.'

'I dug up my fake shield from the TV show and went to the bar on Melrose where Ralston said he met with Jake. I had a mug shot with me.'

'A—'

'From *Variety*. It was a picture of you and your assistant. The big one. The bartender recognized him. You got him to play the role of Jake, costume, fake tats, the whole thing… I just walked past his office, by the way. There're posters on *his* wall too. One of them's *Brokeback Mountain*. Staring Jake Gyllenhaal. *Jake*. Think about it.'

Felter said nothing but his expression was essentially: Shit.

'Dillon knew about the set up. He knew about the fake gun. That's why he took on a guy who was armed. He wasn't in any danger. It was all planned. All planned for the bump.'

O'Connor shook his head. 'I should've guessed before. I mean, the final hand, Aaron? You know how most poker games end: two guys half-comatose from lack of sleep, and one beats the other with three sixes over a pair of threes. A four-of-a-kind versus a straight flush? That only happens in the movies. That's not real life.'

'How could I rig the game?'

'Because you hired a sleight of hand artist as the dealer. You saw his card tricks when we met him… I ran him down. And I checked the tapes. There were no close ups of his hands. I've got his name and address. Oh, and I also got the phone number of the gaming commission in Nevada.'

The man closed his eyes. Maybe he was thinking of excuses and explanations.

O'Connor almost hoped he'd say something. Which would give the actor a chance to throw out his famous tag line from the old TV series. *Save it for the judge.*

But Felter didn't try to excuse himself. He looked across the desk, as if it were a poker table, and he said, 'So where do we go from here?'

'To put it in terms of television, Aaron,' Mike O'Connor said, pulling several thick envelopes out of his briefcase, 'let's make a deal.'

♠

In the Eyes of Children
Alexander McCall Smith

'OVER THERE,' she said. 'Look over there.'

The girl standing at the rail on the starboard side of the ship gazed out over the flat water. The sea was so bright, so calm, that it seemed one might dive in and swim the last few miles that separated them from the shore of the island. But distances at sea were deceptive; she knew that, as Miss Hart had told them earlier.

'The problem, boys and girls,' she had explained, 'is that there are no reference points. The sea is just one big expanse of... well, expanse and so you can't really tell how far one point is from another.'

'Unless you're a sailor,' said one of the boys. 'Like that man up on the bridge there. He can tell.'

They had glanced up from the deck in which they had been standing and looked at the officer standing just outside the bridge, his binoculars trained on something out to port, something that none of them could see.

'They look so silly in those uniforms,' one of the girls whispered. 'Those stupid shorts. Their knees must get sunburned.'

'Like your shoulders,' said a boy. 'Look. Disgusting. Your skin's peeling off.'

But now, a few days later, there were no boys on deck to make that sort of remark, just Alice, who was fifteen and her slightly older friend, Rachel. They were standing together, shaded by the shadow of the ship's superstructure, watching the island drawing closer. This was Grand Cayman, the third island that the cruise had called at, and the smallest. They would go ashore – there was a turtle farm they would visit, and shops, of course.

It was a school party, consisting of just over twenty children. Apart from one or two younger children who were travelling with their parents, the members of the school party were the only young people on the ship; everybody else, it seemed to the children themselves, seemed to be in their forties or above. 'Ancient,' said one of the boys. 'An ancient ship full of ancient people.'

And he was right, or almost right, about the ship, which was coming up for its final cruise and which was already booked in at the shipbreakers. But in spite of the shabbiness of the fittings, the scuffed carpets and the chipped paint on the railings, the company was making a brave effort. There was a full programme of events – dances, talks on the islands, competitions and the like – and the cabins were clean and reasonably comfortable. Or at least they were comfortable for most of the passengers; the school party had been given a generous discount in return for occupying two large, stuffy cabins which had previously been allocated to crew, and these were distinctly Spartan in their atmosphere. The girls occupied the slightly better of the two cabins, where at least there were portholes on one side; the boys' cabin, with its line of bunks stacked three high, was on the inside, with no natural light. It was a bad place to be if one was sea-sick, which some of the boys were for the first few days out of Southampton as the ship ploughed through an oily Atlantic roll.

There were two teachers in charge of the party; one, Miss Hart, who looked after the girls, and her male colleague, Mr Gordon. Miss Hart was thirty four, a tall, slim woman with a rather attractive high cheekboned face. Both she and Mr Gordon were Scottish, as were the children. Mr Gordon was a small worried-looking man who taught chemistry, and who had only once been out of the country before, some years earlier, when he had fulfilled a lifelong ambition to go to the Oktoberfest in Munich. He had taken pictures at the beer festival events, and had stuck these into a large photo album he bought on his return to Edinburgh. He was divorced, and had not remarried; Miss Hart had never found a husband and, she predicted, never would. 'I have had my admirers,' she would say, and would look away, as if remembering something precious. But these admirers had come to nothing, and her friends assumed that their admiration had probably been unexpressed and certainly never acted upon.

Both teachers had felt some hesitation in accepting the request to accompany the school cruise. Being responsible for twenty children on a school trip, even for one day, to a museum or gallery, was daunting enough, but to be responsible for twenty children on a three week cruise to the Caribbean would be enough to destroy all peace of mind. But they had both accepted the duty for good enough reasons; Miss Hart because she wanted to please the school principal, whom she worshipped and for whom she would do virtually anything; Mr Gordon because he was bored and wanted to get away from his dingy home in a dull street in Edinburgh. The Caribbean was light; it was music; it was the wider world; and the prospect of these things would compensate for the anxieties of supervising the teenagers. And they were rather nice children anyway – the well-behaved offspring of serious-minded Edinburgh families; not tearaways or delinquents; respectable children, if one could use such a term about any teenagers.

It was Alice who first noticed that Miss Hart had attracted the attention of an admirer.

'You know what I saw?' she said to Rachel. 'I saw old Hart being chatted up by a man. I swear I did!'

'No! Impossible!'

'I did! I really did.'

Rachel's scepticism was replaced by interest. 'Where? On deck?'

Alice shook her head. 'No, it was in that lounge. You know, the one with the red chairs. She was standing near the door and this man was talking to her, really close, and he took her by the arm, just here, and held her, as if he was pinching her or something.'

'Who was he? What sort of man would go for old Hart?'

Alice was able to provide some information. 'He plays in the band. He's the one who plays the trombone. The tall one.'

Rachel thought about this. She had noticed the trombonist, had noticed his face, which was animated, lively. There was something in his eyes, something bright and mischievous, which made one notice him. He was an unlikely friend for Miss Hart, she thought; very unlikely.

'And then,' Alice continued. 'Then something else.' She paused, watching with pleasure the growth of her friend's interest. She liked having information which other people did not have; it gave one power. 'Then, when I went back there half an hour later, she was sitting with him and some of his friends around a table at the end of that room. They had pulled the table out a bit and there were three men there. Three men and Miss H. And guess what they were doing? Go on, guess.'

Rachel shrugged. 'Drinking?'

Alice shook her head. 'No. Playing cards.'

Rachel was not impressed. 'So? So what? People play cards. There are all those people who play bridge. Even when we're in port they still sit there, playing bridge. Haven't you noticed?'

'But this wasn't bridge they were playing,' Alice said. 'This was poker! And they were betting. I saw it.'

Rachel giggled. 'No! Betting! Old Hart?'

Miss Hart had not wanted to play poker, at least at the beginning. She had noticed the trombonist when the band had been playing on the upper deck shortly after they had left Nassau. Whenever the ship left a port, the band assembled on deck and played a medley of suitable tunes; in this case, *Yellow Bird*, *Jamaica Farewell* (not entirely appropriate, but close enough), and other tunes of a Caribbean nature. The percussionist had replaced his normal drums with steel ones, and Miss Hart had been struck by the infectious nature of the music, by its jauntiness. *I am in the Caribbean*, she thought. *I am far away from home. Anything can happen.*

She had noticed the trombonist looking at her, and had blushed when their eyes had met. She had looked away, but when she had looked up again he was still staring at her, with those bright, amused eyes. She drifted away, confused, and walked to the other end of the deck. There she watched a private yacht sailing behind the ship, its bowsprit pitching with the waves, pointing one moment at the sky, another moment down into the trough of the waves. Why had he been looking at her? She was not used to the gaze of men; she was one of those women who imagined that men she did not know, strangers, would not look at her. Yet although she was surprised, she was not displeased. He was a striking-looking man, about her age, or perhaps slightly older, and there was about him that glamour, that vague whiff of danger that surrounds the jazz musician.

She saw him again the following day, out on deck. He was dressed in one of the colourful open-necked shirts that he wore when he played in the band; it was a sort of uniform, she decided, like the white uniforms that the ship's officers wore. He noticed her, said something to the man he was talking to, and walked across the deck to greet her. She stopped where she was, uncertain what to do. She blushed.

He said, 'I'm Geoff. I hope you enjoyed the music yesterday. Bill likes to get going on the steel drums.'

'It was very nice.' She realized, as she spoke, how trite she sounded. Very nice; as if she had been at a concert at home, in one of those douce concert halls.

'Good,' he said. He looked at her quizzically, as if trying to fathom something. 'Come and have a drink through there.' He nodded in the direction of the bar. 'Allow me to buy you one.'

She looked about her, almost in panic. There were one or two of the teenagers at the other end of the deck; they were absorbed in themselves, as all adolescents are; they would not see her going into the bar with him. But did she want to?

'Come on,' he said. 'I'll introduce you to my friends.'

There was something disarming in his manner, and she found herself agreeing. And what harm was there anyway? People made new friends on cruises; it was not the normal, quotidian world; it was different at sea.

They went inside, where he introduced her to his two friends. Tom, he said. Bill. Tom was the band's pianist; Bill had played the steel drums the day before. They stood up as she came to the table and shook hands. She saw that Bill looked at Geoff, that he caught his eye, and that something passed between them; a quizzical glance.

They talked for a while. She found their company pleasant, their wit sharp. Bill did an imitation of the captain's voice. The captain was an Irishman, from the north of Ireland, and he talked in such a way as to give the final word of each sentence a strong emphasis. Everything he said sounded like a threat or warning. 'That's how he got ahead at sea,' said Bill. 'There are lots of threats and warnings at sea. He had the voice for it.'

She found herself laughing, and when Tom suggested that they play cards, she said that she thought it would be a good idea.

'Poker?'

'I don't know how to play,' she said. 'But I suppose I could learn.'

'Of course you could,' said Tom. 'You're a teacher, after all.'

She wondered how he knew that, but then realized immediately that they would have seen her trailing about with the teenagers; it was so obvious. *And I look like a teacher*, she said to herself. *I can't get away from that.*

She played poker with them the next day, and the day after that. They played for small amounts of money, then for slightly larger sums, but still not very much.

'It's the challenge of the game,' said Geoff. 'Not the money.'

Geoff paid attention to her and his manner was flirtatious. He asked her to join him for a drink after the band had finished playing one evening, and she accepted. She waited for him in the bar, feeling as nervous as a teenager on the first date. He came up to her and kissed her lightly on the cheek. He had bay-rum on his cheeks and it was the smell of the islands, of where they were.

'We're going to have a game tonight,' he said. 'In Bill's cabin. Would you like to join us?'

She hesitated. It would not do for her to go to a man's cabin, but they would all be there and so that made it all right. She accepted.

'Good,' said Geoff.

They called in at Kingston the next day. The children were due to go ashore and she and Mr Gordon had to be vigilant.

'This place can be a bit dangerous,' he said. 'We'll have to watch the kids like hawks.'

She had nodded, but she did not say anything. He noticed this; she had been rather quiet all that day and he wondered whether there was anything wrong. Women were like that, he thought; they can be moody, and there would be no point in trying to find out what was wrong.

The group visited a plantation and saw an exhibition about the use of slave labour. Mr Gordon shook his head; he found it difficult to believe that his people had done this.

'But it wasn't just us,' said Miss Hart. 'Everybody did it. The Arabs were the big slave-traders. The Africans themselves suffered slavery at the hands of their own people. Everybody.'

'But it still makes me feel bad,' Mr Gordon said.

They moved out of the room in which the exhibition was mounted. The vegetation around the building was lush and green; sea-grape trees, cane, creepers. They stood under a tree while he smoked a cigarette. She did not like the smell of smoke, but that was not the reason why, as she stood there, she started to sob.

He was no good with displays of emotion, especially feminine ones. He dropped his cigarette. 'Elspeth,' he said, 'what on earth is wrong? Are you all right?'

She did not reply immediately, and he stood there awkwardly. He wondered whether he should put an arm about her shoulder, to comfort her, but he felt inhibited. He could not touch her, a colleague.

She had not intended to tell him, but she found herself compelled to do so. She had to tell somebody, and there was nobody else. 'I have been humiliated,' she said. 'Humiliated.'

He was puzzled. 'I don't understand.'

She took a handkerchief out of her pocket. He noticed that it had embroidery on the corner: a palm tree and the initial E. There had been handkerchiefs like that for sale on Grand Cayman; a fat woman in a blue-checked dress had tried to sell him one.

'I have been very foolish,' she said. 'It is my own fault. I have had my money taken away from me. All of it.'

He drew in his breath. 'Your money? You've been robbed?'

'In a way,' she said.

She told him, and he listened in astonishment, as did one of the boys, who had gone out of the building on the other side and was standing behind a half-open door on the veranda. He stood there, unseen, hearing everything that was said between the teachers.

The ship stayed in Kingston for a day longer. As it left, she stood on the deck with a group of the teenagers. Alice was there, as was Rachel.

'I liked Jamaica, Miss Hart,' said Alice. 'Did you?'

'Yes,' she said. 'I enjoyed it.'

There was silence. The band had not been on deck; now the members appeared and took up their places. She did not want to look; she wanted to move away, so that she would not see him. But she could not detach herself from the children; so she glanced quickly in the band's direction. There was no trombonist.

Alice and Rachel were looking at her. They had noticed her anxious glances.

'We don't like to see you unhappy,' said Alice. 'We really don't. So that man has been punished.'

She caught her breath. How could they possibly have known? And what did they mean by being punished?

'I don't know what you're talking about,' she said. 'Please explain yourselves.'

'The boys helped us,' said Alice. 'You don't have to worry.'

She stood completely still. Children.

♠

One Dollar Jackpot
Michael Connelly

T HE CALL CAME IN after the usual killing hours. Bosch
checked the clock as he rolled to the side of the bed and sat
up. It was 5.45 a.m. and that was late for a murder call.

It was Lieutenant Larry Gandle with the news.

'Harry, you and Ignacio are up. Pacific is turning over a case to
us. Female, thirty-eight years of age, name of Tracey Blitzstein. She
got shot to death this morning in her car. One in the head. She was
parked in her own driveway.'

The name sounded slightly familiar but Bosch couldn't immediately place it.

'Who is she and why are we getting it?'

'She's sort of a TV star. She plays poker. Uses the name Tracey
Blitz. Her husband plays too, I'm told. So if you watch that sort of
thing on cable then you've probably seen her a few times. She gets
profiled. They use her on the commercials. She was good looking
and apparently the best thing the female species had to offer in the
arena of professional poker.'

Bosch nodded. He only watched poker on TV when he had
insomnia and the World Series of Poker reruns were on ESPN. He
knew it was popular. But that wasn't why he knew the name Tracey
Blitz. Years earlier the name would come up from time to time

with his ex-wife, who also played poker for a living. Eleanor Wish, his ex, had always called the world of professional poker a men's club and maintained that no woman would ever win the World Series. She said a woman named Tracey Blitz had the skills and reads to win poker's greatest tournament but the men would simply never allow it. They would subconsciously pool their testosterone, if needed, and gang up and eliminate her if she ever got to the final table. It was about dominance of the species, Eleanor Wish said.

Now Tracey Blitz would never get the chance to win the big one. She had been eliminated from competition in a different and more permanent manner.

Bosch asked Gandle for the location of the crime scene and was given an address in Venice on the canals.

'What else, Lieutenant?' Bosch asked. 'We got any witnesses?'

'Not yet – we're not even an hour into this. I'm told the husband was home asleep. He woke up and came out and found her in the car. He saw no suspect or getaway vehicle.'

'Where is the husband?'

'I told them to take him downtown to Parker Center.'

'Who is he? You said he's a player, too?'

'Yeah, just not at the same level as his wife. His name is David Blitzstein.'

Bosch thought about things, his mind becoming sharper as he left sleep behind and concentrated on what he was being told.

'Is it just going to be me and Ignacio?' he asked, referring to his partner.

'You guys are lead. I'll bring in Reggie Sauer and he can coordinate from Parker Center and baby-sit the husband till you get in there. You also have the Pacific team for as long as you need them.'

Bosch nodded. That wouldn't be much help. Usually when divisional detectives were replaced by Homicide Special there was resentment. It was hard to get them to hang in and help.

'You got any names from Pacific?'

'Just one.'

Gandle gave him the name and cell number of the lead Pacific Division detective who had gotten the first call out at 5.01 that morning. Bosch was impressed that decisions were made quickly and he was now on the case less than an hour into it. That was a good sign. He told the lieutenant he would be in touch as the case progressed and then hung up. He immediately called Ignacio Ferras, woke him from a sound sleep and got him moving. Ferras lived more than an hour from Venice and Bosch told him to waste no time.

He then called the Pacific detective whose name Gandle had given him. Kimber Gunn picked up the call quickly and Bosch identified himself and explained he had just been tapped to take over her case. He apologized but said he was just following orders. The transfer of the case wasn't news to her but Bosch always liked to tread lightly in such situations. He had never worked with Gunn before and she surprised him. She offered her help and said she was awaiting his direction.

'I could use the help,' Bosch responded. 'I'm probably a half hour from the crime scene and my partner lives out in Diamond Bar. He'll be even longer.'

'Diamond Bar? You might want to redirect him. He's closer to Commerce than to Venice.'

'Commerce? Why Commerce?'

'According to the vic's husband, she spent the night playing poker at the card casino in Commerce. He said she called when she was leaving and told him she had won big.'

'Did he say how much?'

'He said she won more than six thousand dollars cash. My partner and I, well…'

'Well, what?'

'We don't want to jump your case but we were thinking that it looks a lot like a follow home from the casino.'

Bosch thought about that for a few seconds before responding.

'Tell you what, let me call my partner and send him that way, then I'll get right back to you.'

He closed the phone and called Ferras, who had not left his home yet. Bosch told him what he had just learned and instructed him to drive to the casino in Commerce and begin his part of the investigation there. He then called Gunn back.

'What else did the victim's husband say, Detective Gunn?'

'He said he fell back asleep after she called. He then woke up when she pulled into the driveway – she's got a tricked-out Mustang with glass pipes. It makes some noise. He was lying in bed and he heard her kill the engine but then she never came inside the house. He waited a few minutes and then came out to check. He found her in the car dead. He didn't see anybody and didn't see any vehicles. That was it. You can call me Kim, by the way.'

'OK, Kim. Anybody put the husband through the box?'

'My partner. No record.'

'What about ATF?'

'We checked that, too. He owns no firearms. Neither did she.'

Bosch was holding the phone in the crook of his neck while buttoning his shirt.

'Anybody swab him?'

'You mean GSR? We figured that was a call you should make. The husband's cooperating. We didn't want to mess with that.'

She was right in waiting for Bosch to make the call. Conducting a gunshot residue test to determine if a person had fired a weapon had become trickier and stickier in recent years. It was in a legal gray area and choices made now by detectives would be questioned and reviewed repeatedly down the line by supervisors, reporters, prosecutors, defense lawyers, judges and juries.

The issue at hand was that such testing put the subject on clear notice that he was a suspect. Therefore, he should be treated as a suspect – advised of his constitutional rights and given the opportunity to seek legal counsel. This put a chilling effect on cooperation.

Additionally, a recent directive from the District Attorney's office concluded that GSR testing was an invasive evidence gathering technique that should only come voluntarily or after a search warrant had been approved by a judge, another move that would clearly put an individual on notice that he was a suspect. So gone were the days when a detective could casually tell an individual of interest to submit to GSR testing as a routine part of an investigation. A GSR test was now an indisputable means of tagging someone as It.

As Gunn had explained, David Blitzstein was cooperative at the moment. It was too early in the investigation to tag him as It.

'OK, we'll hold that till later,' Bosch said. 'Where's your partner?'

'He's driving Blitzstein downtown. He'll come back after.'

'What's his name?'

'Glenn Simmons.'

Bosch didn't know him. So far he didn't know anybody on the case and that was a rub. So much of the work came down to personalities and relationships. It always helped to already know people.

'Forensics at the scene yet?' he asked.

'They just rolled in. I'll keep an eye on things till you're here.'

Bosch checked his watch. It was now six a.m. and he knew his promise of being there in a half hour was a stretch. He'd have to stop on the way to get coffee.

'Better yet,' he said, 'why don't you knock on doors before we start losing people to work and school and the day. See if anybody saw or heard anything.'

He almost heard her nod over the phone.

'I've got a number of the neighbours already standing in the street here watching,' Gunn said. 'Shouldn't be too hard to scare up some wits.'

'Good,' Bosch said. 'I'll see you soon.'

The crime scene was already a hive of activity by the time Bosch got there. He parked half a block down the street and as he approached on foot he got his bearings. He realized that the houses on the left side of the street backed up against one of the Venice canals while those on the right, smaller and older, did not. This resulted in the houses on the left being quite a bit more valuable than those on the right. It created an economic division on the same street. The residents on the left had money, their houses newer, bigger and in better condition than those right across the street. The house where Tracey Blitzstein had lived was one of the canal houses. As he approached the glowing lights set up by Forensics around a black hardtop Mustang, a woman stepped away from the gathering and approached him. She wore navy slacks and a black turtleneck sweater. She had a badge clipped to her belt and introduced herself as Kim Gunn. Bosch handed her the extra coffee he had brought and she was almost gleeful about receiving it. She seemed very young to be a homicide detective, even in a divisional squad. This told Bosch that she was good at it or politically connected – or both.

'You've got to be a cop's kid,' Bosch said.

'Why's that?'

'I was told your full name is Kimber Gunn. Only a cop would name a kid that.'

She smiled and nodded. Kimber was the name of a company that manufactured firearms, in particular the tactical pistols used by specialty squads in law enforcement.

'You got me,' she said. 'My father was in LAPD SWAT in the seventies. But I got it better than he did. His name is Tommy Gunn.'

Bosch nodded. He remembered the name from when he first came on the department and was in patrol.

'I heard of him back then. I didn't know him, though.'

'Well, I've heard of you. So I guess that makes us even.'

'You've heard of me?'

'From my friend Kiz Rider. We go to BPO meetings together.'

Bosch nodded. Rider was his former partner, now working out of the office of the chief of police. She was also recently elected president of the Black Police Officers Association, a group that monitored the racial equality of hiring and firing as well as promotions and demotions in the department.

'I miss working with her and I don't say that about too many people,' Bosch said.

'Well, she says the same about you. You want to take a look at the crime scene now?'

'Yes, I do.'

They started walking toward the lights and the waiting Mustang.

'Did you get anything from the neighbours yet?' Bosch asked.

Gunn nodded.

'No shortage of witnesses,' she said. 'When David Blitzstein started yelling in the street, he woke up the neighbourhood. I had the best of the lot taken to the station to give formal statements.'

'Anybody hear the gun?'

'Uh uh.'

Bosch stopped and looked at her.

'Nobody?'

'Nobody we've found – and that includes Blitzstein himself. I've been up and down the street and nobody heard a gunshot. Everybody heard the guy screaming and plenty of them looked out their windows and saw him standing in the street. Nobody heard or saw a gun. Nobody heard or saw the getaway vehicle, either.'

'You mean if there was one.'

'If there was one.'

Bosch started back towards the Mustang but then stopped again.

'What was your take on the husband?' he asked.

'Like I said, he's been nothing but cooperative so far. You thinking the husband?'

'At the moment I'm thinking everybody. What was this guy wearing when he was in the middle of the street yelling for help?'

'Blue jeans. No shirt, no shoes.'

'Any blood on him?'

'Not that I saw.'

Bosch's phone buzzed. It was his partner.

'Harry, I've been talking to the manager of the card room. He said Tracey Blitz won a lot of money last night.'

'How much is a lot?'

'She cashed in sixty-four hundred in chips.'

That jibed with what David Blitzstein had told Kimber Gunn.

'Do they have cameras in the parking lot?' Bosch asked.

'Hold on.'

Ferras put his hand over the phone and Bosch heard a muffled back and forth conversation. Then Ferras came back on the line.

'There are cameras,' Ferras reported. 'He's going to let me see if she was followed out of the lot.'

'Good. Let me know.'

Bosch hung up.

'That was my partner at the casino,' he told Gunn. 'He confirmed she won sixty-four hundred dollars last night. He'll check the cameras to see if she was followed when she left.'

Gunn nodded.

'Let's go take a look at the victim,' Bosch said.

Bosch silently studied the murder scene for several minutes, trying to take in the nuances of motivation. Tracey Blitzstein had a contact wound on the left side of her head just above the ear. There was an explosive exit wound encompassing much of her upper right cheek. Her body sat behind the steering wheel of the Mustang, held in place by the seat belt and shoulder strap. She was killed before she had made a move to get out of the car.

Her small clutch purse was lying unzipped on her lap. Her head was turned slightly to the right and down, her chin on her chest. There was blood spatter and brain material on the dashboard, steering wheel and passenger side seat and door. But little blood had dripped from the wounds down onto her clothes or purse. Death had come instantly, the heart getting no chance to pump blood from the wounds.

Bosch noted that the Mustang's windows were all intact. The fatal shot had been fired through the driver's open door. Bosch drove a Mustang himself. He knew that when the car's transmission was placed in drive the doors automatically locked. This meant that the shooter didn't open the door. The victim did. She had likely stopped the car, killed the engine and then opened the door to get out before taking off the seat belt. It was when she opened the door that the killer approached, most likely from behind the car, and fired the fatal shot into her brain from a position slightly behind her. She probably never saw her killer or knew what was coming.

Bosch noticed a yellow evidence marker on the passenger side door. There was a padded armrest with a hole in it. The yellow tags were used to mark locations of ballistic evidence. He knew that the slug that had killed Tracey Blitzstein had been stopped by the car door.

Bosch saw another yellow marker on the front hood of the car. It marked the location of a bullet casing that had been found in the crack between the hood and the car's front right fender. It was most likely the shell ejected from the killer's gun. Bullet casings were usually ejected from the gun's chamber in an arc to the right rear of the weapon. This was by design because almost all automatics were manufactured for right-handed shooters and a right-rear ejection arc would take the casing away from the shooter.

But a shell could easily be redirected forward after rebounding off another object. And if a left-hander was firing the weapon, that object could be the shooter himself. Bosch was left handed and had personal experience with this – one-time a red hot shell hit him in the eye after being ejected during range practice. He knew that, depending on the shooter's stance and how the weapon was held, the possibility in this case was that the ejected shell hit the shooter and then caromed forward – possibly to land on the front hood of the car the killer had just fired into.

Bosch nodded to himself. He had a hunch that he was looking for a left-handed shooter.

'What is it?' Gunn asked.

'Nothing yet. Just a theory.'

An assistant coroner named Puneet Pram was working the scene along with a forensics team from the LAPD's Scientific Investigation Division. While some coroners kept up a running commentary of what they were doing and seeing at a crime scene, Pram was a very quiet worker. Bosch had been at murder scenes with him before and knew that he would not be getting a lot from him until the autopsy. Donald Dussein, the head of the forensics team, was another matter. He was a known character in the department. Known by a variety of nicknames ranging from Donald Duck to D-Squared, he was usually overly forthcoming – to the point of bending facts into theory and confusing his role at a crime scene. Bosch had worked with him as well and knew he would have to rein him in and keep him on point.

And it wasn't long into Dussein's initial briefing that Bosch had to do just that.

'Couple things first,' Dussein said. 'The contact wound to the head. Neat and very clean. Too clean if you ask me.'

'All right, then I'm asking you,' Bosch said. 'What do you mean by too clean?'

'Well, Harry, I've seen a lot of these in my time. And this has the look of a hitter's work. I'm talking about a contract killer. You have the illicit world of gambling and money in which this victim traversed and then a hit like this and it all adds—'

'Hold on a second there, Double D. How about you stick to forensics and we'll do the detective work, OK? I need facts from you, not theories. Now, what about the contact wound is too clean for you? What are you trying to say?'

Chastened, Dussein nodded.

'The burn pattern is too small,' he said. 'You see, normally, you put the muzzle up to the side of somebody's head and pull the trigger, you get a three to five inch burn in the hair and on the skin. The hot gases coming out of the barrel spread and burn. You follow?'

'We follow,' Bosch said.

'OK, well, we've got no burn here. We've got a contact wound but we've got no burn. No gases and you know what that means.'

Bosch nodded. He did know. It meant that the weapon used to kill Tracey Blitzstein was likely equipped with a sound suppressor – a silencer that would have re-channelled the sound of the shot. In doing so it would have re-channelled the explosion of hot gases as well. It would have sent them backward through the baffles of the snap-on device towards the shooter, leaving the victim's hair unburned except in the immediate area of the wound.

'It would explain why none of the witnesses heard the shot,' he said.

Dussein nodded.

'What are you saying, the shooter used a silencer?' Gunn asked.

'That's what I'm saying,' Dussein said. He gestured toward the body. 'There is no burn. This is a contact wound with no burn. I'm telling you, the shooter used a suppressor.'

Bosch nodded. He decided it might be best to move on to the rest of the review.

'OK,' he said. 'Let's talk about ballistics.'

Dussein nodded, ready to move on himself.

'We got lucky there,' he said. 'The slug impacted in the padding of the door and we recovered it in good shape. We also have the casing recovered from the front of the vehicle. A forty calibre federal. Between the slug and the shell we will be able to match it to a weapon. You just need to find the weapon.'

Bosch nodded.

'I'm wondering how the shell ended up on the front hood,' he said.

'That's a good question,' Dussein said. 'You want to hear my theory?'

'How about I tell you mine?'

Bosch moved to the open door of the Mustang and reached in with his left hand, stopping a half foot from the victim's head.

'I'm thinking the shooter was possibly left-handed. In this position the shell could have bounced off his body and then ricocheted forward over the roof to the front hood.'

'My theory exactly.'

Dussein beamed. Bosch just nodded.

'What about the purse?' he asked. 'Can we have that yet?'

'Give me five more minutes and then it's yours,' Dussein replied.

Bosch nodded again and stepped back away from the car. He signalled Gunn outside the grouping so they could confer privately.

'Tell me again what the witnesses said about the husband when they saw him in the street?'

'They said he was in the middle of the street screaming for help, yelling things like call the cops and call for an ambulance. The man who lives across the street was the next on scene and checked on the victim. He saw that there was no hope and took the husband back over to his place. He was sitting on the porch with him when police arrived on scene.'

Gunn pointed across the street to the old craftsman with a porch running its entire length.

'The neighbour gave him some clothes, too,' she added. 'A T-shirt and a pair of sandals. Blitzstein never went back into his own house before we shipped him downtown.'

'OK, good. Let's just make sure nobody goes into the house until we get a search warrant.'

He looked around the crime scene. Gunn took a step closer and spoke in a lower voice.

'You really like him for this, don't you? The husband. I wish I knew what I was missing.'

Bosch shook his head.

'I don't know. You're probably not missing anything. Things just don't seem right to me. Do you know if David Blitzstein is left-handed or right-handed?'

'I don't know. Do you want me to call my partner? He's probably still delivering him. He could ask.'

'No, that would tip him off. Let that go for now. Until we…'

He didn't finish. *Until we what?* He didn't know yet.

'What doesn't seem right about the scene?' Gunn said, pressing him. 'Teach me something.'

'Just a feeling, that's all. The door was locked on that car when she pulled in. I know, I have a Mustang and the doors automatically lock.'

'OK, it was locked, but she opened it.'

Bosch shook his head.

'That's what I don't see. I know this kind of woman. I was married to one. Someone like her, somebody who moves in a man's world, somebody who plays cards all night and wins big… somebody who knows the dangers that comes with all of that… I don't see her swinging that door open before she takes off the seatbelt. She wouldn't open that door until she was ready to move.'

Gunn digested Bosch's ramble and nodded.

'But she would open it for someone she trusted,' she said.

Bosch pointed a finger at her like a gun and nodded his head.

'Only one problem with that scenario,' she said. 'Where's the gun? I've got about a dozen witnesses who saw Blitzstein in the middle of the street in his blue jeans and nothing else.'

Bosch was ready for that argument.

'The gun could be anywhere. It could be in the house or the canal behind the house. It doesn't matter because the gun and the gunshot do not set the time of the killing. The witnesses didn't look at their windows because they heard a shot. They looked because Blitzstein was out there screaming in the street.'

Bosch saw recognition flare in Gunn's eyes.

'You're saying he had time to get rid of the gun because nobody knows how long it was between when she was capped with the silencer and when he went into the street and started waking up the neighborhood.'

Bosch nodded.

'That's the other thing. Him going into the street and yelling for help – like he wanted the neighbours to see him. I don't know, if that was my wife in that car with her brains all over the place… I don't think I'd end up in the middle of the street with no blood on me. I don't see that at all.'

His phone started to buzz and he started digging it out of his pocket.

'See if Dussein's done with the purse,' he said. 'I've got a guy at Parker Center waiting to go to work. I'll get him on the search warrant for the house.'

'You got it.'

Bosch opened his phone. It was Ignacio Ferras.

'Harry, I've looked at all the tapes from the casino's entrance area and the parking lot. It looks to me like she had a follower.'

Bosch felt a sudden pause. A follower would completely contradict the theory he had just spun with Gunn.

'Are you sure, Ignacio?'

'Well, nothing's for sure but I have her on tape leaving the casino with a security escort. The guy walked her out to her car. He then stood in the lot until she pulled out. Everything was copasetic. But then in thirty second intervals two more cars pulled out and headed in the same direction she did. Towards the freeway entrance down the block.'

'Two cars…'

'Yeah, two.'

'OK, but aren't cars pulling in and out of there at a regular clip? Even in the middle of the night? And probably most of the cars that leave go to the freeway, right?'

'Yeah, they do. At all hours – the casino's open twenty-four hours. But after I saw these two cars follow her out, I went back through the tapes to trace the drivers. I found one of them came out a couple minutes before the victim. He got in his car and took a little time before pulling out. I think he was smoking. That allowed the victim to leave first.'

'OK, and what about the second car?'

'That's the thing, Harry. I couldn't find anybody walking out of the casino that connects with that car. Not at first. So I had to go all the way back an hour to find the guy. He left an hour before the victim and he sat out there in his car waiting for her.'

Bosch started to pace in the street as all of this registered.

'Did you also look at the tapes from inside the casino for this guy?' he asked.

'I did. And the guy wasn't playing, Harry. He was just watching. He was walking around, acting like he was a player but he never actually played. He was watching the tables and in the last hour he was watching her play. The victim. He zeroed in on her, then he left and waited for her in the parking lot.'

Bosch nodded slowly. He was seeing the case turning completely in a new direction. Kimber Gunn walked up to him then but he held up a finger so he could finish the call.

'Ignacio, did you get plates off the cars that left after Tracey Blitzstein?'

'Yeah, we got the plates on the tape. The first car was registered to a Douglas Pennington of Beverly Hills. The second car's registered to a Charles Turnbull of Hollywood.'

Beverly Hills and Hollywood were on the west side, same as Venice. If Pennington and Turnbull were heading home from the casino in Commerce they would have gone in the same direction as Tracey Blitzstein. That was explainable – at least as far as Pennington went. But Turnbull's activity in the casino and then his waiting in the parking lot for an hour wasn't – yet.

'And you put them through the box?' Bosch asked his partner.

'Yeah, both clean. I mean, Turnbull's got a lot of parking and moving violations but that's it.'

Bosch looked into Gunn's eyes while he tried to think about what to do. Her eyebrows were raised. He could tell she sensed a change in the winds of the investigation.

'Harry, what do you want me to do?' Ferras asked.

'Head to Parker Center. I'm going to put Sauer on a search

warrant for the victim's house. Hopefully, he'll have it signed and ready to go by the time you get there. Pick it up and come out here to the scene. We'll figure out things then.'

'What about Turnbull?'

'Give me his address. I'm going to take a run by there now.'

After he finished the call and hung up, Gunn spoke first.

'I checked the purse. The money's gone. What's happening?'

'You have a company car here?'

'Yeah, I've got a piece-of-shit cruiser from the barn at Pacific.'

'Good. You drive. I'll tell you what's happening on the way. Everything I just told you – that we talked about, it all just went down the tubes.'

The address Ferras had given Bosch for the home of Charles Turnbull led to a brick apartment building on Franklin. On the way there Bosch had filled Gunn in on what Ferras had come up with at the casino in Commerce.

They had no background on Turnbull other than what Ferras had given them but when they got to the entrance of the apartment building another new dimension was added. Next to the button for apartment 4B it said *Turnbull Investigations*. Before pushing the button Bosch called Jim Sauer at Parker Center and asked him to run the name Charles Turnbull through the state corporations and licensing computer. A few minutes later he hung up.

'He's held a PI license for sixteen years,' he told Gunn. 'Before that he was a Santa Monica cop.'

Bosch pushed the button next to Turnbull Investigations. After getting no response he pushed it two more times, each time longer than the time before. He had opened his phone again and was asking directory assistance for a number for Turnbull when a sleepy and annoyed voice sounded from the speaker above the entrance buttons.

'*Whaaat* is it?'

Bosch stepped close to the speaker.

'Mr Turnbull?'

'What? It's eight o'clock in the morning!'

'LAPD, Mr Turnbull. We need to speak to you.'

'About what?'

'It's an emergency situation, sir, involving one of your clients. Can we come up?'

'Which client?'

'Can we come up?'

There was no response for five seconds and then there was a buzzing sound and the entrance door was electronically unlocked. They took the elevator up to the fourth floor and on the way Bosch unsnapped the safety strap on his holster. Gunn did the same.

'That a Kimber?' Bosch asked.

'Yeah, the Ultra Carry.'

Bosch nodded. It was the same weapon he carried.

'Good gun. Never jams.'

'I hope we don't have to find out.'

When they stepped out of the elevator there was a man standing in the hallway in blue jeans and a white T-shirt. He wore a ragged bathrobe over the ensemble which hid much of his belt line and anything he might have hidden in it. He was in bare feet and his dark brown hair was sticking straight up on one side. He had been asleep.

'Turnbull?' Bosch asked, while using his right hand to show the man his badge.

'What's this about?' the man asked.

'Not in the hallway. Can we come in, Mr Turnbull?'

'Whatever.'

He pointed them towards the open door to apartment B but Bosch signalled him to go in first. Bosch wanted to keep Turnbull in front of him and in sight at all times.

'Have a seat if you can find a spot,' Turnbull said as they entered. 'Coffee?'

'I could use some,' Bosch said.

'Thank you,' said Gunn.

They both remained standing. The apartment had furnishings of a contemporary design but it was cluttered with Turnbull's work. There were files stacked on the coffee table and spread on a couch. It was clear that the living room was the nexus of his practice.

Bosch followed him to the kitchen alcove, again so he could keep a visual on him. Turnbull spoke as he filled a glass coffee pot with water.

'Which client is in the shit?' Turnbull asked.

'What do you mean?'

'You said there was an emergency. So which client is in the shit?'

Bosch decided to roll with things.

'David Blitzstein,' he said.

Turnbull was about to pour the water into the coffee brewer but paused with the glass pot held above it. He shook his head.

'Don't know that name,' he said. 'Not my client.'

'Really? You were working for him last night,' Bosch said.

Turnbull smiled.

'You've got your facts wrong, Detective.'

Turnbull poured the water into the brewer and set the pot underneath it.

'You own a weapon, Mr Turnbull? You know I can find out with one phone call.'

'You probably already have. Yes, I own a weapon but I almost never carry it. It's ancient. From my days with the cops. A thirty-eight calibre Smith & Wesson. A wheel gun. No cop would use one today.'

A revolver. No ejection of shells. It was the wrong calibre and wrong kind of gun for the Blitzstein killing.

'We'll check to make sure. You want to show it to me?'

Turnbull leaned back against a counter in the kitchen and folded his arms in a gesture of frustration.

'Sure, I'll show it to you, just as soon as the bank down the street opens up at nine because it's in a safe deposit box. Like I told you,

I rarely use the thing. Now you guys are either seriously running down the wrong alley or I am missing something right in front of my face. I don't know any David Blitzstein. I don't know what you're talking about.'

Bosch instinctively believed him. He also believed that something was wrong. They were indeed down the wrong alley. He decided to try the direct approach.

'All right, let's stop dancing. You were at the casino in Commerce last night. Why?'

Turnbull raised his eyebrows. It was the first thing that made sense to him.

'I was working. But not for or against David Blitzstein.'

'Then let's start with who hired you?'

'A lawyer named Robert Suggs. I do a lot of work for him. He's a divorce lawyer.'

'All right, then what were you doing?'

'I was watching an individual for another individual, a client of Bob Suggs.'

Bosch nodded that he understood.

'Mr Turnbull. I think we have made a mistake here but we need to be sure. The individual you were watching, what was his name?'

'I would have to call Suggs before I could reveal that.'

'Was it Douglas Pennington of Brentwood?'

Bosch saw the tell in Turnbull's eyes. The name was familiar to him.

'I can't say,' Turnbull said.

'You just did,' Bosch said. 'Look, I understand your position. I spent two years working a private ticket myself and I know how that is. But we're working a homicide here. So let's find a middle ground where you can help us and help yourself by being done with us. Let's forget names. We'll go with individuals. Tell us what you can about the case you were working last night.'

Coffee started dripping into the pot and its smell began to

pervade the apartment. It kicked off a craving in Bosch. The charge from his first cup of the day was dead and gone.

'An individual hired my employer to begin the marital dissolution process. Only this individual's husband doesn't know about it yet. We're in what we call the hunting and gathering stage. She tells us that she thinks her husband's got a girlfriend on the side. Once or twice a week he stays out almost all night, telling her he's playing poker. She's noticed that the bank account has been dropping eight to ten grand a month with withdrawals he has made.'

'So you were tailing him last night,' Bosch said.

Turnbull nodded

'That's correct.'

'And it turned out he actually was playing poker.'

'Correct again.'

'How much did he lose?'

'About two grand. He played at a high stakes table and a woman cleaned him out. In a way, the wife turned out to be right. He gave his money to another woman.'

Turnbull smiled and then snapped his fingers and pointed at Bosch.

'Blitz. I heard the woman who was cleaning up at that table was called Blitz. Is she the homicide?'

He turned towards a cabinet but kept his eyes on Bosch. He opened it and pulled out three cups. He set them on the counter next to the coffee maker.

'Yeah, she's the one,' Bosch said.

'She left at the same time as my guy and so the cameras in the parking lot gave you the idea that I was tailing her, not him.'

'Something like that.'

Turnbull hit a switch on the brewer and pulled out the glass pot. He poured three cups and asked if anybody wanted sugar or powdered cream. There were no takers.

'Of course,' he said. 'You're cops.'

Bosch drank from the cup he was given and the coffee was strong and hot, just like he wanted it. He relaxed a bit. Turnbull was a dead end as far as being a suspect but he could still be useful as a witness.

'You went out to the parking lot about an hour ahead of your subject,' he said. 'How come?'

'Because I was tired of acting like I belonged in there. I had to start playing or I had to get out of there. I don't play poker. No interest. So I went out and sat in my car.'

'See anything unusual out there?'

'No, just people coming and going.'

'What about the woman when she came out? Did you see her?'

'I saw her. My guy had already come out and he was sitting in his car smoking and trying to cool down after dropping all that money. So then she came out with a security guy. I thought that was a good move. She was probably carrying a lot of dough after the way she was playing. She was cleaning everybody out. Not just my guy.'

Bosch nodded.

'Then what?'

'Then nothing. I was watching because my guy was in his car and thought maybe if there was something going on I was going to see it right there. But she got in her car and left. Then my guy left and I followed him.'

'Nothing else with her in the parking lot.'

'Not in the parking lot, no.'

'Meaning…?'

'Well, I don't know if it means anything at all. But I was on the job once, a long, long time ago, and I know you guys want everything about everything. So I'll give you everything. On the freeway she almost lost control of her car.'

'How so?'

'I'm not really sure but I think she was doing something, maybe she dropped something or she was reaching for something, and it made her swerve out of her lane and then back into it. She looked like she was drunk driving but she wasn't drunk. When I was watching her in the card room she was drinking bottled water only.'

'Was it a cellphone? Was she looking down while driving?'

'I don't think so. Not a cellphone. I probably would have seen the light. Anyway, when she swerved I was right behind her so I lit her up with my brights to see if she was all right. I didn't see any phone. She was sort of bent over like she had dropped something down by the bottom of the door. She sat up when I hit her with the brights. She looked back at me in the rear view and I turned them off.'

Bosch thought about this for a few minutes, wondering what Tracey Blitzstein had been doing. He then realized that maybe she had made the same mistake he had just made, mistaking Turnbull for a follower, and was hiding the money she had won under the seat as a precaution against robbery.

'Do you think she saw you leaving the casino lot?' he asked.

'I don't know. She could have.'

'Is there a chance she could have thought you were following her? Or a chance that she thought the guy you were following was following her?'

Turnbull drank some coffee and thought over his answer before voicing it.

'If she thought anybody was following her it would have been me. We were all going the same way but my guy got ahead of her. So if she was checking the mirrors she would have seen me. If I had won that kind of money I would've been checking my mirrors.'

Bosch nodded and thought about everything for a few moments.

'When exactly did she make that swerve between the lanes?' he then asked.

'Almost as soon as we got up on the freeway. Like I said, my guy got ahead of the both of us. So I dropped behind her and was kind of using her car to shield myself from my guy – in case *he* was watching the mirrors. So she might've easily thought I was on her instead of him.'

Turnbull poured more coffee into his cup and then offered the glass pot to Bosch and Gunn but both passed on the refill.

'I just remembered something,' Turnbull said. 'Something that goes with her thinking I was following her.'

'What was it?' Bosch asked.

'About ten minutes after she did the swerve she kind of made an evasive manoeuvre. At the time I thought maybe she'd fallen asleep and almost missed her exit, but now I see it. She was trying to see if she had a tail.'

'What exactly did she do?'

'We were on the ten going west, right? Well, we were coming up on La Cienega and at the last moment she all of a sudden cut across two lanes to go down the exit.'

'You mean like she was trying to see if somebody would follow her down the ramp?'

'Yeah, like if we would make the same cut across the freeway as her. It was a good move. It would reveal a tail or lose a tail, either way.'

Bosch nodded and looked at Gunn to see if she had anything to add or ask but she remained silent.

'Did you see her again after that?' Bosch asked.

'No, not after that,' Turnbull said. 'She was gone in the night.'

In more ways than one, Bosch thought. He ended the interview. He needed to get away from Turnbull to make a call.

'Mr Turnbull, we're sorry to have gotten you up after you worked all night,' he said. 'But you've helped us and we appreciate it.'

Turnbull raised his hands like his efforts were minimal.

'I'm just glad I'm no longer a suspect,' Turnbull said. 'Good luck catching the bad guy.'

Bosch put his empty cup on the counter.

'Thanks for the coffee, too.'

Bosch pulled his phone as soon as they were out of the building and heading back to the car. He called his partner.

'It's me,' he said. 'Are you at the scene yet?'

'Just got here. I've got the search warrant for the house.'

'Good. But before you go in I want you to get with Dussein, the forensics guy.'

'OK.'

'Tell him to pull the interior of the Mustang apart if he has to but I think the missing money is still in it somewhere.'

'You mean it wasn't a follow home?'

'I don't know what it was yet but when she was driving home I think she thought she was being followed. I think she hid the money in the car somewhere, somewhere within reach while driving. Maybe just under the seat but I would assume Dussein already looked there.'

'OK, I'm on it.'

'Call me back if you get something.'

Bosch closed the phone. He didn't speak until they were back in the car.

'I think we're back to the husband,' he said. 'What Turnbull told us reinforces the theory. If she was scared or thought she might've been followed she wouldn't have swung the door open until she was ready to make a quick move to the house. She thought it was safe.'

Gunn nodded. 'I forgot to tell you something about the purse,' she said.

'The victim's purse? What about it?'

'She had a small can of pepper spray in it. She never took it out.'

Bosch thought about this for a moment and saw how it fit with the current theory.

'Again, if she thought she had been followed, and even if she believed she had lost the follower with her manoeuvre on the freeway, she wouldn't have opened that door and left the pepper spray in her purse unless she felt safe.'

'Unless someone was there to make her feel safe.'

'Her husband. Maybe he was holding the gun in plain sight and she thought it was for her protection. She opened the door and he turned it on her.'

Gunn nodded like she believed the scenario but then she played devil's advocate.

'But we can't prove any of that. We don't have anything. No gun, no motive. Even if we find the money in the car it's not going to matter. It doesn't preclude a follow home and we won't be able to charge him.'

'Then it's an eight by eight case.'

'What's that mean?'

'It means it's going to come down to what happens in that eight by eight room at Parker Center. We go talk to him and wait for him to make a mistake.'

'He's a professional poker player, remember?'

'Yeah, I remember.'

It took them half an hour to get from Hollywood to Parker Center downtown because of the morning rush hour. In the third floor Robbery-Homicide Division office Bosch watched David Blitzstein through one way glass for five minutes as he readied himself for the interview. Blitzstein didn't look like a man mourning the murder of his wife. He reminded Bosch more of a caged tiger. He was pacing. There was little space for this with the table and two chairs taking up most of the interview room, but Blitzstein was moving from one wall to the opposite wall, repeatedly going back and forth. Each time his pattern brought him within inches of the one-way glass – mirrored on his side – and each time that he stared into his own eyes he was also unknowingly staring into Bosch's eyes on the other side.

'OK,' Bosch finally said. 'I'm ready.'

He handed his cellphone to Gunn.

'Keep this. If my partner calls with news, come in and say the captain's on the phone.'

'Got it.'

They went into the detective bureau and Bosch filled two foam cups with coffee. He put four packs of sugar into one and took them both to the interview room. He entered and put the over-sugared coffee down on one side of the table in the centre while he sat on the other side with the other.

'Why don't you sit down, Mr Blitzstein?' he said. 'Have some coffee. It's going to be a long day for you.'

Blitzstein came over and sat down.

'Thank you,' he said. 'Who are you? What's going on with my wife?'

'My name's Harry Bosch. I've been assigned as lead detective on your wife's case. I am very sorry for your loss. I am sorry to keep you waiting but hope to get you out of here as soon as possible so that you can be with your family and begin to make arrangements for your wife.'

Blitzstein nodded his thanks. He picked up his coffee cup and sipped from it. His face soured at the taste but he didn't complain. This was good. Bosch wanted him to keep drinking. He was hoping to push him into a sugar rush. People often mistook a sugar high for clarity of thought. Bosch knew the truth was that the rush made them take chances and they made mistakes.

Blitzstein put the cup down and Bosch noticed he had used his left hand. There was the first mistake.

'I just need to go over things once more before we get you out of here,' Bosch said.

'I told everything I know to that black girl.'

'You mean Detective Gunn? Well, that was sort of preliminary. Before I was assigned. I need to hear some things for myself. Plus we now have the advantage of having studied the crime scene and talked to the witnesses.'

Blitzstein's eyebrows shot up momentarily and he tried to cover by bringing the cup up and gulping down more coffee. But Bosch now had one of his tells and he registered it accordingly.

'Wow, that's hot!' he exclaimed. 'You mean there are witnesses?'

'We'll get to the witnesses in a few minutes,' Bosch said. 'First I want to hear your version of events again. This way I have it directly from you instead of second hand through Detective Gunn. This way it's not coloured by anything anybody else has said or claimed to have seen.'

'What do you mean, "claimed to have seen"?'

'Just a turn of phrase, Mr Blitzstein,' Bosch said.

Blitzstein blew out his breath in exasperation and started recounting the same story he had told Gunn two hours earlier. He threw in no new details and left nothing out from his first accounting. This was unusual. True stories evolve as details are remembered and others are forgotten. A false story, one that has been rehearsed in the mind, usually remains constant. Bosch knew all of this and felt his suspicion of Blitzstein was moving onto more solid ground.

'So how soon were you to the car after the shot?'

'I don't know because I didn't hear it. But I don't think it was too long. I had heard her pull in. I waited and when she didn't come into the house I went out to see what was wrong.'

'So if somebody said they thought you were already at the car when the shot was fired would they be wrong?'

'What? Right at the… no way, I wasn't right there when the shot was fired. I didn't even see who did it. What are you trying to say?'

Bosch shook his head. 'I'm not trying to say anything. I'm trying to get as clear a picture of what happened as I can. As you can imagine, we get conflicting views. People say different things. I had a partner once who said if you put twenty people in a room and a naked man ran through it, you'd get twelve people who would say he was white, seven who would say he was black and at least one who would claim it was a woman.'

Blitzstein didn't even smile.

'Tell you what,' Bosch said. 'Why don't you tell me your theory on what happened out there?'

Blitzsteen didn't even have to think about it.

'Simple. She was followed home. She won a lot of money and somebody from that casino followed her home and killed her for it.'

Bosch nodded like it all fit.

'How do you know that she won a lot of money?'

'Because she told me when she called me from the cage to tell me she was coming home.'

'What cage?'

'The cash cage. She was cashing in her chips and they let her use the phone because she's a regular. She forgot her cellphone last night. She called me and said she was driving home.'

'Was she scared carrying all of that cash?'

'Not really. She won more often than she lost and knew to take precautions.'

'Did she carry a weapon?'

'No. Actually... I think she had like a little can of mace in her purse.'

Bosch nodded.

'We found that. But that's it, just the pepper spray?'

'Far as I know.'

'OK, then what about you? Did you play down there? Did you ever go with her?'

'I used to. But not in about a year.'

'How come?'

'I'm sort of banned from that casino. There was a misunderstanding last year.'

Bosch drank some more coffee and wondered if he should pursue this or if it was a misdirection Blitzstein was hoping he would pursue. He decided to proceed with caution.

'What was the misunderstanding?'

'It's got nothing to do with this.'

'If it has to do with that card room in Commerce then it does have something to do with this. If you want to help me find your wife's killer then you have to answer my questions and let me decide what matters and what is important. What was the misunderstanding?'

'All right, I'll tell you if you have to know. They accused me of cheating and there's nothing I could do to defend myself. I wasn't cheating and it's their interpretation against my word. End of story. They kicked me out and won't let me back in. Banned for life.'

'But they didn't have a problem with your wife still coming?'

Blitzstein shook his head angrily.

'Of course not. She's a draw, man. She brings business in over there. When she's playing you get all these guys coming out of the woodwork to play against the girl from the world series and the ESPN commercials. They all want to kick her ass. It's a guy thing. It's like marking their turf, coming in her face. It's the same with all the women on the tour.'

Bosch was silent for a moment. This was no misdirection by Blitzstein. Bosch was beginning to see at least part of the motivation for murder. Blitzstein knew that if the murder of his wife – a well liked and well known player – was attributed to a follow home from the casino in Commerce then the card room would take a major public relations hit that could impact its business and reputation. As if on cue to these thoughts, Blitzstein's bile boiled up and added further to Bosch's understanding of the crime.

'You know what?' he said. 'If this thing turns out to be a follow home I am going to sue their asses over there. It will be the biggest goddamn jackpot I ever rake in.'

Bosch simply nodded, hoping Blitzstein would say more. But he may have realized he had already said too much. He turned quiet and Bosch started off in a new direction.

'How would you describe your relationship with your wife?'

'How do you mean?'

'You know, were you happy with each other, was it getting boring, were you upset that she was a poker celebrity and you weren't?'

Bosch stared pointedly at him while he said the last part. Blitzstein reacted immediately.

'We were fine. We were still in love and I didn't give a shit about who was a celebrity and who wasn't. You know what poker comes down to? Twenty per cent skill and eighty per cent luck. Some people are more skilled than others but luck is always the thing.'

Again Bosch waited a few moments to see if he would say more but he didn't. Bosch continued.

'All right, so the card room in Commerce is off limits. Where then do you play? The Hustler or the card room at the Hollywood track?'

'Nope, I don't play anywhere. They're all together on this. You get banned one place and they put your picture on the wall every place else. It's fucking unconstitutional but nothing I can do anything about.'

'So you play private games?'

'When I can get them, yeah. Meantime, I was my wife's manager.'

Bosch thought about his ex-wife and the stories she told about private games, the personal items, car keys and *guns* that would sometimes go into the pots.

'You ever win anything besides money at those private games?'

'What are you talking about?'

'My ex-wife is a player – you might even know her. Eleanor Wish?'

Blitzstein hesitated and then nodded.

'Yeah, I remember her. I think Tracey told me she was in Hong Kong or Macau these days. I was even thinking of heading over there to check out the casinoes.'

Bosch saw an opening and headed toward it.

'When did you start thinking about that?'

'What?'

'Moving to Hong Kong or Macau.'

'Don't put words in my mouth, man. I said I was thinking of going over there to check it out, not move there. Why would I think of moving there?'

'Because you were banned here. Did the ban extend to Las Vegas? Maybe you were thinking of pulling up stakes.'

'Look, man, it's none of your business. I wasn't thinking about moving anywhere. We have a house here and I was happy. A lot of things were happening for Trace and I was managing her career. I don't need to defend myself to you.'

Bosch raised his hands in a back off gesture.

'You certainly don't. Anyway, back to what I was asking about. Yes, my ex-wife does play in Macau. She likes it. Anyway, she used to tell me about these private games she played when she was over here. She said you could win anything sometimes. It was like owning a pawnshop. People would throw in jewellery, cars, guns. You ever won any stuff like that?'

Blitzstein looked at Bosch for a long moment, his eyes going through a slow burn from cold to hot.

'Fuck you, Detective Bosch. I want a lawyer.'

'What's wrong?'

'Nothing's wrong except for you trying to fuck me in the ass. I want a goddamn phone and I want to call a lawyer.'

Bosch leaned back in his seat.

'You know once you say that we're done. I can't talk to you and I can't help you. You sure you want—'

'Help me? Yeah, help me into a prison cell for something I didn't do. Fuck you. Get me the phone. We're done here.'

Bosch drummed his fingers on the table for a moment and then nodded.

'All right, we'll do it your way. I'll go get you the phone.'

He slowly got up, giving Blitzstein a last chance to change his mind, then left the room when he didn't.

Gunn met him in the hallway.

'Well, you got close,' she said. 'You convinced me – or rather, he convinced me – but I still don't think we have enough to charge him.'

'Maybe not. Has my partner called?'

'Oh, shit! Your phone! Where is it? I… I think I left it out there on your desk when we got the coffee.'

They walked out to the squad room and Bosch grabbed his

phone. He'd missed three calls from Ferras while he was in the interview room with Blitzstein. He quickly called back.

'Harry, where you been?'

'In an interview. You got something?'

'Jackpot, man. We got it all.'

'Tell me.'

'You were right. The driver side door has a secret compartment. The armrest unsnaps from the door and opens up. The latch was hidden behind the speaker grill in the door.'

'What did you find?'

'We found the money, the gun, a workout shirt and gloves. It's all there. The gun's got a suppressor on it, too. A homemade job. There was also a bracelet in the compartment she must've put in there. It's from when she won a qualifying tournament for the World Series of Poker in oh-four.'

Bosch looked at Gunn. He was annoyed. It was all information he could've used before Blitzstein shut things down and called for a lawyer. He turned away and went back to Ferras.

'Did you run the gun yet?'

'Yeah, just did. It's a dead end. It was reported stolen nine months ago by the original owner in Long Beach. A gun dealer named Kermit Lodge. Said it was stolen off a table at a gun show in Pomono.'

Bosch knew it wasn't a dead end. If they found a link between the gun's original owner and Blitzstein then the dead end could become an integral piece of evidence. But that was for later. He asked Ferras about the workout shirt and the gloves.

'It's a long sleeve plastic pullover. You know, for like sweating and losing weight.'

'And the gloves?'

'Just your basic work gloves. They look new. There's blowback on the shirt and the gloves. The thing is, Harry, the shooter knew about the secret compartment. He shot her then dumped the gun, the shirt and the gloves in the compartment. The husband, Harry.'

He shot her, hid everything in the compartment and then started calling for help.'

'Yeah, now we just have to prove it. He just lawyered up.'

Ferras didn't respond and in the silence Bosch thought of something. One last thing to attempt.

'What kind of work gloves are they? Leather, plastic, cotton?'

'Cotton.'

Bosch felt a small spark of hope. The gloves and the shirt had been worn by the killer so that he would avoid getting blowback – blood, brains and gunshot residue – on his body. But blowback came in all sizes – including microscopic – and cotton was porous.

'OK, I want you to leave the scene,' Bosch said. 'Go down to Long Beach and pick up the gun dealer. Bring him up here to RHD.'

'Pick him up for what?'

'Just tell him he reported the theft of a weapon and that we've recovered it and need him to come downtown to identify it. Keep him in the dark. Just get him down here.'

'OK, I'm on it.'

'Good.'

Bosch closed the phone.

'What did they get?' Gunn asked.

'Everything.'

He updated her on the phone call and she was immediately apologetic about forgetting about his phone. She knew he could have used the information about the secret compartment to press Gunn. It seemed obvious that he would have known about the compartment in his wife's car, yet he never mentioned it when discussing the precautions she took.

'Don't worry about it,' Bosch said. 'It's done.'

'Then what's the next move?'

Bosch didn't answer at first. He pulled his fold of cash out of his pocket. He had three one dollar bills. He studied these and asked Gunn if she had any ones. She pulled out some cash and held out two ones.

Bosch chose one of Gunn's dollars and gave her one of his in exchange. He then put the dollars in one pocket and returned his cash fold to the other.

'OK,' he said. 'Now we'll see what kind of a poker player David Blitzstein is.'

Bosch walked back into the interview room and put his cellphone down on the table in front of Blitzstein.

'There's the phone,' he said. 'But since you are calling an attorney I need to read you your constitutional rights and make sure you have a full understanding of them. It's procedure.'

'Then let's get it on,' Blitzstein said. 'I want to make the call.'

Bosch pulled out a business card and sat down at the interview table across from Blitzstein. The card had the rights advisory on the back side. He read it out loud, then had Blitzstein read it and sign it as well. He watched as the suspect signed it with his left hand.

Bosch pushed the phone across the table to him.

'Who you going to call?' Bosch asked.

This seemed to give Blitzstein pause.

'I don't know,' he said. 'I don't know any criminal defense attorneys.'

Bosch looked up at the ceiling as if considering it.

'Let see... Johnny Cochran's dead. And Maury Swann's in jail. There's Dan Daly and Roger Mills. Those are good guys. There's also Mickey Haller. I hear he's back in business.'

'Haller. I've heard of him. He's on TV a lot so he must be good.'

Bosch shrugged.

Blitzstein clicked a button on the phone and then punched in 411. He asked the directory assistance operator for Haller's number. He then hung up without a thank you and punched in Haller's number. Someone answered and transferred him. There was a long silence before Blitzstein had the lawyer of his choice on the line. After a few minutes of short-sentence discussion he clicked off the phone.

'He's on the way,' Blitzstein said. 'He'll get me out of here.'

'That shows a lot of confidence in somebody you've never met,' Bosch said.

'I have to have confidence in somebody. You people are trying to pin this on me.'

'We look for evidence and it takes us where it takes us. We aren't looking to pin anything on anybody – unless they deserve it.'

'Got it.'

'Anyway, that's all I'm saying. You asked for a lawyer and we can't talk about the case any more. Those are the rules.'

'Damn right. You can leave now.'

'Not quite. I have to stay with you until your lawyer gets here. Those are the rules too. We've had a few people hurt themselves after we leave them alone. Then they try to blame us.'

'You know, that's not a bad idea. Maybe I should pop myself in the eye and say you did it.'

'You try that and I'll make sure you file the report from the hospital.'

They sat in uncomfortable silence for a long three minutes after that. Bosch studied Blitzstein and waited for the right moment. Finally, he began.

'You want more coffee?'

'No, it tasted like oil.'

Bosch nodded and let another thirty seconds go by.

'When did you start playing poker?'

Blitzstein shrugged.

'When I was a kid. My old man was a beer drunk who played with his drinking buddies in the garage a couple nights a week. I used to watch and he'd let me take his hand when he went to take a leak.'

'Starting early like that, you must've played a lot of games over the years.'

'Too many to remember.'

'I never played against my wife. Did you ever play against Tracey?'

'We tried to avoid it. Me and Trace knew each other too well. We knew the tells.'

Bosch nodded. 'I always wanted to go head to head against a pro,' he said. 'What do you say?'

Blitzstein shook his head in confusion. 'What are you talking about?'

Bosch leaned forward across the table while pulling his money out of his pocket. 'You ever play liar's poker?'

Blitzstein made a dismissive gesture with his left hand. 'Not since I was about thirteen.'

Bosch held up the bill he had traded Gunn for. He folded it in his hand so Blitzstein would be unable to read the serial number.

'Five sixes,' he said.

The object of liar's poker was to predict the total number of specific letters or numbers in the serial numbers of all dollar bills in the game. If Blitzstein took the bait it would be a total coming from only two bills. Five sixes was a high bid.

Blitzstein shook his head. 'I don't play with amateurs.'

'With all those card rooms cutting you out, I would say that was all you had left to play with. Six sixes.'

'Jesus,' Blitzstein said in an exasperated tone.

'Come on, Mr Pro. What've you got?'

'I've got an hour in this room with you and I think you're going to drive me nuts.'

'Then I guess I win by default.'

Bosch started putting his money away. Blitzstein leaned forward.

'Just hold on, boy.'

He reached into the pocket of his jeans and pulled out his cash. He found a dollar bill and crunched it in his fist.

'You bid six sixes? Then I call without even looking. I know you're bluffing. You've got a major tell.'

'Yeah, what is that?'

'You look away at the precise moment you should stare unflinchingly at your opponent.'

'Is that right?'

Blitzstein dropped his bill on the table and Bosch did likewise. Bosch had five sixes in his serial number. He carefully opened Blitzstein's bill and it had one six. Bosch took both bills off the table.

He held Blitzstein's up and smiled.

'I'm going to frame this!'

He put it into his shirt pocket, shoved his winning dollar bill into his pants pocket and smiled.

'Now I can tell people I beat a poker pro.'

'Yeah, I hope it makes you happy.'

This time Bosch stared unflinchingly at his opponent. And he saw Blitzstein's tell. A quick moment where his confidence deserted him and he wondered if he had just stepped into a trap.

'It does make me happy,' Bosch said. 'Very happy.'

Bosch and Gunn walked into the Forensics lab on the fourth floor and asked the counter woman if a lab rat named Ronald Cantor was working. They were in luck. Cantor was in the lab and they were buzzed through the gate.

Cantor was a SEM jockey. His job was to analyze collected evidence with a scanning electron microscope. The normal wait time for this particular analysis ranged from four to six months. But there were unofficial ways around this. Lab rats were given morning, lunch and afternoon breaks. What they did on those breaks was up to them. It was personal time. If they wanted, for example, they could take cases out of order and put the evidence on the SEM lens. It was all about the incentives to do so.

Ronald Cantor had an ongoing incentive when it came to Bosch. Five years earlier Bosch had solved the murder of his nine-year-old niece, who had been snatched from her front yard in Laurel Canyon by a man who asked her for help finding a lost dog. Though devastated by the loss of the young girl, the Cantor family was always grateful to Bosch, primarily because he not only solved the case but also saved them the agony of going through a trial. During the killer's capture, Bosch had shot the man to death during a struggle for control of Bosch's gun. Ever since that day Bosch was gold when it came to getting case time on the scanning electron microscope.

'Ronnie, how are you?' Bosch said as he approached.

'Doing good, Harry. This your new partner?'

'For the day, you could say. Detective Gunn, this is Ronnie Cantor, SEM expert. Have you taken your morning break yet, Ronnie?'

'No, just beginning to think about some hot chocolate, actually.'

'Well, I gotta little thing here I was hoping you'd take a look at real quick. We got a guy down in one of our rooms and we need to pull the trigger on him in the next hour. Keep him or kick him loose. You could help us out while I went down and got the hot chocolate.'

Cantor swivelled on his stool away from the lab table where he was working and looked directly at Bosch.

'What have you got?' he asked.

With two fingers Bosch pulled Blitzstein's dollar bill out of his shirt pocket and held it out.

'Shit?' Cantor said. 'You've been carrying it in your pocket?'

'Just a couple minutes. It's been in our suspect's pocket and he just handled it. I'm looking for anything and everything. GSR, blood, anything. We think he killed his wife this morning but we're having a hard time making the jump from thinking to knowing. He's got a big time lawyer heading our way as we speak.'

Cantor grabbed a pair of tweezers off the lab table and used them to take the dollar bill from Bosch.

'Can you do it?' Bosch urged.

'Yes, I can do it. But the prospect of contamination is very high.'

'It's unofficial. If you find something we'll make the arrest and do it all over again according to protocol.'

'All right then.'

'Good, Ronnie. I'll go get the hot chocolate and be right back.'

Gunn offered to make the hot chocolate run but Bosch told her to stay in the lab and watch Cantor work. He said she might learn something. Going for hot chocolate wouldn't teach her a thing.

Bosch was gone fifteen minutes and when he came back with two black coffees and one hot chocolate, Cantor said he was finished analyzing the one dollar bill.

He put the foam cup containing his drink off to the side and gave his report. He spoke without inflection, using the tone and words he employed when testifying in court.

'SEM analysis shows quantifiable amounts of primer, powder, projectile material and the products of their combustion. While the amounts identified in this analysis are low, I would be confident in testifying that the last person to handle this currency had recently discharged a firearm.'

Bosch felt a stab of excitement go through his chest. For a moment he visualized the scene of Tracey Blitzstein sitting dead in her car. He nodded to himself. Her killer wouldn't get away with it.

'Thank you, Ronnie,' he said.

'I'm not finished,' Cantor said. 'Further analysis reveals microscopic particles of blood in the material being examined as well.'

Bosch held up his coffee cup to Cantor.

'Cheers, man. We gotta go hook this guy up.'

Bosch and Gunn quickly left the lab. While they waited for the elevator they talked about what needed to be done next. First, they would officially charge David Blitzstein with murder and put a no bail hold on him. Mickey Haller would not be getting him out today. That was for sure. Second, they would seek another search warrant allowing them to use adhesive tape discs and chemically treated swabs to collect gunshot residue from the suspect's hands and arm. They would additionally ask the judge to allow for a luminol test which would reveal microscopic blood spatter on the suspect's body as well.

Relief showed in their faces. They felt good about where things stood with Blitzstein. Less than four hours into the investigation they were about to make the arrest.

'That was smooth,' Gunn said. 'You were smooth, Harry. Kiz Rider was right about you.'

'Yeah? What did she say?'

'She told me to never to play poker with you.'

Bosch smiled. The elevator opened and they got on.

♠

Strip Poker

Joyce Carol Oates

T HAT DAY AT WOLF'S HEAD LAKE! Nobody ever knew.
Of my family, I mean. Not even Daddy. I did not tell Daddy.

It was late August. Humid-hot August. At the lake you'd see these giant thunderhead clouds edging across the sky like a mouth closing over and in the mountains, streaks of heat lightning that appear and disappear so swiftly you can't be sure that you have actually seen them. For kids my age nothing much to do except swim – unless you liked fishing, which I did not – or 'boating' – but we didn't own a boat – and the only place to swim for us was on the far side of the lake at the crowded public beach since the lake on our side was choked with seaweed so slimy and disgusting only young boys could swim through it. That day we're over at the beach swimming, trying to dive from the diving board at the end of the concrete pier, but we're not very good at diving, mostly we're just jumping from the high board (twelve feet, that's high for us), seeing who can jump the most times, climb the ladder dripping wet, run out on the board and grab your nose, shut your eyes, and jump, reckless and panicky and thrilled, striking the water and propelling beneath and your long hair in a pony tail trailing up, bubbles released from your dazed lips, closest thing to dying – is it? Except sometimes you'd hit the water wrong, slapped hard as if in rebuke by the lake's surface that looks like it should be soft, red welts across my back, murky water up my nose so my head was water-logged, ears ringing and I'm dazed and dizzy staggering around like a drunk girl, all of us loud-laughing and attracting disapproving stares. And there comes my mother telling me to stop before I drown myself or injure myself, trying not to sound angry as she's feeling, and Momma makes this gesture – oh, this is mortifying! – makes me hate her! – with her hands to suggest that I might injure my chest, my breasts, jumping into the water like that, as if I give a damn about my breasts, or anything about my body, or if I do, if I am anxious about my body, this is not the place, the public beach at Wolf's Head Lake on an afternoon in August, for Momma to scold me. I'm a tall lanky-lean girl almost fourteen years old with small-boned wrists and ankles, deep-set dark eyes and a thin curvy mouth that gets me into trouble, the things I say, or mumble inaudibly, my ashy-blond hair is in a pony tail straggling like a wet rat's tail down my bony vertebrae, except for this pony tail you'd think that I might be a boy and I hoped to God that I would remain this way forever, nothing so disgusting as a grown woman in a swimsuit, a fleshy woman like Momma and her women friends that men, adult men, actually looked at like there was something glamorous and sexy about them.

Momma is glaring at me, speaking my full, formal name Annislee, which means that she is disgusted with me, saying she's driving back to the cottage now and I'd better come with her and Jacky, and I'm stubborn shaking my head no, I am not ready to leave the beach where it's still sunny and maybe will not storm and anyway my bicycle is at the beach, I'd biked to the beach that morning so I'd have to bike back. And Momma says all right, Annislee, but if it starts storming you're out of luck. Like she hopes it will storm, just to punish me. But Momma goes away, and leaves me. All this while I've been feeling kind of excited and angry – and sad – why I've been jumping from the high board not giving a damn if I do hurt myself – this fiery wildness coming over me sometimes: *Why should I care if I hurt myself, if I drown!* Missing my father who isn't living with us right now in Strykersville and resenting that my closest cousin Gracie Stearns went away for the weekend to Lake Placid in the Adirondacks staying with a new friend of hers from Christian Youth, a girl I hardly knew, people at Lake Placid are likely to be rich not like at Wolf's Head Lake where the cottages are small and crowded together and the boats at the marina are nothing special. All this day I've been feeling mean thinking how could I hurt Gracie's feelings when she came back, our last week at the lake before Labor Day and I wouldn't have time to spend with Gracie, maybe.

This guy I met. Wants me to go out with him. He's got a boat, wants to teach me to water-ski.

There was no guy. The boys I went swimming with, hung out with were my age, or younger. Older kids at Wolf's Head, I scarcely knew. Older guys, I was scared of. Mostly.

At the lake we stayed with my mother's brother Tyrone and his family. Momma and my younger brother Jacky and me. Uncle Tyrone's cottage which wasn't on the lake but a hike through the woods and a haze of mosquitoes and gnats and the lake offshore choked with seaweed and cattails and I wasn't comfortable sleeping three to a room, Momma and Jacky and me, anxious about my privacy, but Wolf's Head Lake was something to look forward to, as Momma was always saying now that my father was out of the picture.

Out of the picture. I hate such a way of speaking. Like Momma can't bring herself to say exactly what the situation is so it's vague and fading like an old Polaroid where you can't make out people's faces that have started to blur. As if my father wasn't watching over his family somehow or anyway knowing of our whereabouts every day of our lives you can bet!

Him and Momma, they were still married. I was sure of that. The time Daddy said, I will lay down my life for you, Irene. And the kids. Just tell me, if ever you wish it.

Momma doesn't even know how true that statement is. Momma will never know.

There was a time when I was seven, Daddy had to go away. And Momma got excitable then. We were cautioned by Momma's family not to upset her. Not to make loud noises playing and not to get up at night to use the bathroom if we could help it, Jacky and me, because Momma had trouble sleeping and we'd wake her and might scare her; Momma kept a knife under her pillow in case somebody broke into the house, sometimes it was a hammer she kept by her bed, but never any kind of gun for Momma hated guns, she'd seen her own brother killed in a hunting accident, she made Daddy keep his guns over at his brother's house, his two rifles and his shotgun and the hand-gun called a revolver with a long mean-looking barrel he'd won in a poker game in the U.S. Army stationed in Korea at a time when I had not yet been born, that made me feel shivery, sickish, for my parents did not know me then and did not know of me and did not miss me. And if they had not married each other, it would be that they would never miss me.

So we were told not to upset Momma. It is a scary thing to see your mother cry. Either you run away (like Jacky) or you do something to make your mother cry more (like me). Just to show that it's you your mother is crying about and not something else.

"'Anns'lee" – what kind of name's that?'

This older guy must be in his late twenties named Deek – what sounds like 'Deek' – oily-dark spiky haircut and scruffy whiskers and on his right forearm a tattoo of a leaping black panther so it's like him and me are instantly bonded 'cause I am wearing over my swimsuit a Cougars T-shirt (Strykersville High's mascot is a 'cougar') a similar big cat leaping and snarling. Just the look of this Deek is scary and riveting to me, him and his buddies, all of them older guys and strangers to me hanging out at the marina pier, where I've drifted to instead of heading back to the cottage where Momma expects me.

I'm embarrassed telling Deek that 'Annislee' is some weird name derived from a Norwegian name, my mother's grandmother was Norwegian, from Oslo, but Deek isn't hearing this, not a guy who listens to details nor are his beer-drinking buddies with big sunburnt faces and big wide grins like they've been partying a long time already and it isn't even suppertime. Deek is near-about a full head taller than me, bare-legged in swim trunks and a Harley-Davidson T-shirt, winking at me like there's a joke between us – or am I, so much younger than he is, the joke? – asking how I'd like to ride in his speedboat across the lake? – how'd I like to play poker with him and his buddies? I tell Deek that I don't know how to play poker and Deek says, 'Li'l babe, we can teach you.' Tapping my wrist with his forefinger like it's a secret code between us.

Li'l babe. Turns out that Deek is Rick Diekenfeld, owns the flashy white ten-foot speedboat with red letters painted on the hull *HOT LI'L BABE* you'd see roaring around Wolf's Head Lake raising choppy waves in its wake to roil up individuals in slower boats, fishermen in stodgy rowboats like my uncle Tyrone yelling after *Hot Li'l Babe* shaking his fist but *Hot Li'l Babe* with Rick Diekenfeld just roars on away. There's other girls hanging out with these guys I am trying to determine if they are the guys' girlfriends but I guess they are not. Seems like they just met at the Lake Inn Marina Café where you have to be twenty-one to sit by the outdoor bar. These girls in two-piece swimsuits fleshy as Momma spilling out of their bikini tops. And the guys in T-shirts and swim trunks or shorts, flip-flops on their big feet, and the names they call one another are harsh and staccato as cartoon-names: sounding like 'Heins', 'Jax', 'Croke'. And there's 'Deek' who seems to like me, pronouncing and mispronouncing my name *Anns'lee* running the tip of his tongue around his lips, asking again how'd I like to come for a ride in his speedboat, quick before the storm starts, how's about it? Deek has held out his Coors can for me to sip out of which is daring, if we get caught, I'm underage by eight years, but nobody's noticing. Lukewarm beer that makes me sputter and cough, a fizzy sensation up inside my nose provoking a sneeze-giggle, which Deek seems to find funny, and something about me he finds funny, so I'm thinking *What the hell.* I'm thinking, Daddy isn't here, I am not even sure where Daddy is. And Gracie isn't here. This will be something to tell Gracie.

This guy I met. These guys. Riding on the lake, and they taught me to play poker.

So we pile into *Hot Li'l Babe*, these four big guys and me. There's lots of people around at the marina, nothing to worry about I am thinking. Or maybe I am not thinking. Momma says *Annislee for God's sake where is your mind?* Well, it looked like – I thought – these other girls were getting into the speedboat, too, but they changed their minds saying the clouds were looking too threatening, what if you're struck by lightning the girls are saying with shivery little giggles, in fact there's only just heat lightning (which is harmless – isn't it?) 'way off in the distance beyond Mount Hammer miles from the lake so I'm thinking *What the hell, I am not afraid.*

'Hang on, Anns'lee. Here we go.'

This wild thumping ride out onto the lake, full throttle taking off from the marina and the looks on the faces of boaters coming in – a family in an outboard boat, a fisherman in a rowboat – register such alarm, it's hilarious. Everything seems hilarious, like in a speeded-up film where nothing can go seriously wrong, nobody can get hurt. Deek steers *Hot Li'l Babe* with one hand, drinking Coors from the other, I'm hanging onto my seat crowded between two of the guys (Jax? Croke? or is this big guy panting beside me Heins?) trying not to shriek with fear, in fact I am not afraid, am I? – can't get my breath the wind is coming so fierce and there's a smell of gasoline in the boat and in the pit of my stomach that sickish-excited sensation you get on the downward plunge of a roller coaster. Overhead it's a surprise, the sky is darkening fast, the giant mouth is about closed over the sun, and the way the thunderclouds are ridged, and ribbed, makes me think of the inside of a mouth, a certain kind of dog that has a purplish-black mouth, oh

God. Just these few minutes, there's nobody else on Wolf's Head Lake that I can see. That boat engine is roaring so hard, these guys are so loud, a beer can I've been gripping has spilled lukewarm beer onto my bare legs, can't catch my breath telling myself *You are not going to die don't be stupid, you are not important enough to die.* Telling myself that Daddy is close by watching over me for didn't Daddy once say *My little girl is going to live a long, long time that is a promise.*

To a man like Daddy, and maybe Deek, is given a certain power: to snuff out a life, as you might (if you were feeling mean, and nobody watching) grinding a broken-winged butterfly that's flailing beneath your foot, or to allow that life to continue.

'Made it! Fuckin' made it! Record time!' Deek is crowing like a rooster, we're across the lake and OK. Deek cuts the motor bringing the speedboat to dock, it's a clumsy-shaped boat it seems now banging against the dock, Deek has to loop a nylon rope over one of the posts cursing Fuck! fuck! fuck! he's having so much trouble, finally Heins helps him and they manage to tie up the boat, we're in an inlet here in some part of Wolf's Head Lake that isn't familiar to me, short stubby pier with rotted pilings, mostly outboard-motor and rowboats docked here. Getting out of the boat, I need to be helped by one of the guys, slipped and fell, hit my knee, one of my sandals falling off, and the guy, Croke is the name they call him, big-shouldered in a T-shirt, thick hairs like a pelt on his arms and the backs of his hands, and a gap-tooth grin in a sunburnt wedge-face sprouting dark whiskers on his jaws, grabs my elbow, hauls me up onto the dock, 'There ya go, li'l dude, ya OK?' Greeny-grey eyes on me, in that instant he's being nice, kindly, like I'm a kid sister, somebody to be watched over, and I'm grateful for this, almost I'd want to cry when people are nice to me, that I can't believe I deserve because I am not a nice girl – am I? *Damn I don't care. Why should I care.* The fact is, these new friends of mine are smiling at me calling me Anns'lee, Anns'lee… honey, c'mon with us, next thing I know the five of us are swarming into a convenience store at the end of the dock, Otto's Beer & Bait, where Momma has stopped sometimes but which direction it is to Uncle Tyrone's cottage, and how far it is, I could not say. The guys are getting six-packs of Coors and Black Horse Ale and Deek tells me to get some 'eats' so I select giant bags of taco chips, Ritz crackers and CheezWhip and at the deli counter some cellophane-wrapped ham sandwiches and dill pickles. Out of the freezer a six-pack of chocolate ice cream bars, I'm leaning over and the frost-mist lifts into my warm face so cool it makes my eyes mist over so one of the guys, I think it's Jax, pokes his finger toward my eye meaning to wipe away a tear, I guess, saying 'Hey li'l dude you OK?' This guy is so tall, my head hardly comes to his shoulder. Maybe he works at the quarry, those guys are all so big, muscular and going to fat, the quarry at Sparta was where my father was working, last time I'd heard. Up front at the cashier's counter there is this bleach-hair bulldog-woman older than Momma staring at the five of us taking up so much space in the cramped aisles not cracking a smile though the guys are joking with her calling her Ma'am trying to be friendly. A thought cuts into me like a blade *This woman knows me, she will call Momma.* How I feel about this possibility, I'm not sure. (Do I want to be here, with these guys? Is this maybe a mistake? But girls hook up with guys at Wolf's Head Lake, that is what you do at Wolf's Head Lake isn't it? What people talk about back at school, next month? And Labor Day in another week.) The cashier-woman doesn't seem to know me only just regards me with cold curious eyes, a girl my age, young even for high school, with these guys who must be ten, fifteen years older, guys who've been drinking beer for hours (you can tell: you can smell beer on their breaths, their reddened eyes are combustible) speaking to the girl in a kind of sly-teasing way but not a mean way so I'm feeling a stab of something like pride, maybe it is even sexual pride, my flat boy-body and dark eyes and curvy mouth and my thick ashy-blond hair springing from a low forehead like my Daddy's prone to brooding. *Anns'lee* is like music in these guys' mouths, this name that has made me cringe since first grade.

Hearing *Anns'lee-honey, Anns-lee-babe* makes me grateful now. Deek tugs my pony-tail and praises the 'eats' I've brought to the counter and pays for everything with a credit card.

Next we hike through a marshy pine woods, clouds of mosquitoes, gnats, those fat black flies that bite before a thunderstorm. A sultry wind is blowing up yet the sun is still shining, rifts in black clouds hot and fiery so you think there might not be a storm, the clouds might be blown away. In the woods are scattered cottages linked by a rutted lane. Loud voices, kids shouting. Bathing suits and towels hanging on drooping clothes lines. Most of the cottages are small like my uncle Tyrone's with shingleboard siding or fake pine or maple, crowded close together, but Deek's uncle's cottage is at the end of the lane with nothing beyond but trees, bushes grown close against the cottage so neighbours can't see into the windows. Deek tries the front door but it's locked, dumps his groceries on the porch and goes around to the back of the cottage to jimmy off a window screen, Heins is excited asking what the hell is Deek doing, doesn't he have a key for the cottage? – 'This is "breaking and entering"', Heins says, but Deek only laughs saying, 'Din't I tell you this is my uncle's fuckin' place I'm welcome in, any fuckin' time.'

When Deek gets the screen off the window he turns to me, grabs me around my middle and lifts me like you'd lift a small child not a girl weighing eighty pounds and five feet three which is tall for my age, saying for me to crawl inside, and open the door, I am a better fit through the window than he is. Deek's fingers on me are so hard almost I can't catch my breath, squirming to get free like a captured bird but a bird so scared it isn't going to struggle much, and next thing I know Deek has shoved me through the window with a grunt, head-first I'm falling, might've broken my neck except I'm able to grab hold of something, scrambling up on my hands and knees panting like a dog and my heart pounding fast as the guys are cheering behind me and the skin of my buttocks, inside the puckered fabric of my swimsuit bottom, is tingling from the palms of Deek's hard hands shoving me.

It's no problem opening the front door of the cottage, just a Yale lock, the guys come whooping and laughing inside dropping six-packs and groceries on a dingy counter. Seems like more than four of them in this small room. It's one of those cottages that is mostly just a single room with two small rooms at the back for sleeping. In the main room are mismatched pieces of furniture, a rickety formica-topped kitchen table, chairs with torn seats, against a wall a narrow kitchen counter, a tiny sink and a tiny two-burner gas stove, cupboards and one of those half-sized refrigerators you have to stoop to reach into. Smells here of cooking, old grease, plain old grime. Looks like it hasn't been cleaned or even swept for months, there are cobwebs everywhere, dust-balls and husks of dead insects on the floorboards, ants on the sticky formica-topped table and on the counter, tiny black ants that move in columns like soldiers. Deek is looking through a stack of magazines on an end table, whistling through his teeth and laughing: 'Oh, man. Sweet Jesus.' The guys crowd around Deek looking at the magazines while I'm ignoring them removing the groceries from the bags, wiping down the sticky formica-topped table and counters with wetted paper towels, trying to get rid of the ants. Damn nasty ants! And the smell in here. The way the guys are carrying on over the magazines, crude things they are saying, I'm edgy, embarrassed. Deek sees me, the hot flush in my cheeks, laughs and says, 'C'mere, Anns'lee. Look here,' but Jax says quick and sharp, 'This ain't for her, Deek. Fuck off.' Deek is laughing at me saying not to be looking so mean but I'm turned away sullen and uneasy not smiling back at him saying maybe I don't want to play poker after all, my mother is probably wondering where I am, I can walk back to our cottage, I won't need a ride. Deek says OK li'l babe, dumping the magazines into a trash can and one of the guys has opened a Coors for me, icy-cold from Otto's Beer & Bait. They are trying to be nice now so I'm thinking maybe I will stay for a while, learn to play poker, it's nowhere near dark. Nothing waiting for me at the cottage except helping Momma and my aunt prepare supper and if it's raining just TV till we go to bed. Here I'm entrusted with setting out food for these big hulking hungry guys, there's a feeling like an indoor picnic, finding paper plates in the cupboard, a plastic bowl to empty chips into, unwrapping the mashed-looking ham sandwiches, the storm hasn't started yet, maybe there won't even be a storm, the thunder is still far away in the mountains. I'm thinking that Deek really likes me, the way he looks at me, smiles. It's a special smile like a wink, for me. Pushing me through the window *He touched me! He touched me there – did he?*

I won't need many beers to become giddy-drunk.

That buzzing sensation in the head when your thoughts come rushing past like crazed bats you can't be sure even you've seen, blink and they're gone.

Deek says: name of the game is five-card draw.

Deek says: poker isn't hard, is it? Not for a smart girl like me.

Hard to tell if Deek is teasing or serious. These first few games, I seem to be doing well. Deek's chair is close beside mine so that he can oversee my cards as well as his own. Like we're a 'team' Deek says. Telling me the values of the cards which isn't so different from gin rummy, euchre and Truth (which is the card game my friends and I play). 'Royal flush' – 'straight flush' – 'flush' – 'five-of-a-kind hand' (when the joker is wild) and it is all logical to me, common sense I'm thinking, except maybe I'm not remembering, Deek talks so fast and there's so much happening each time cards are dealt. In the third game Deek nudges me to 'raise' with three eights, two kings, Deek whispers in my ear this is a 'full house' – I think that's what he has said, 'full house' – and the cards are strong enough to win the pot: fifteen dollars! This is amazing to me, I'm laughing like a little kid being tickled and the guys are saying how fast I am catching on. Heins says, li'l dude is gonna pull in all our money, wait and see.

Deek has been the one to 'stake' me, these early games. Five one-dollar bills Deek has given me.

In his chair close beside mine, Deek is looming over me twice my size breathing his hot beer-breath against the side of my face, hairs on his tattoo-arm making the hairs on my arm stir when his arm brushes near. Like we are young kids whispering and conspiring together. I am thinking that poker isn't so hard except you have to keep on betting and if you don't stay in the game you have to 'fold' and if you 'fold' you can't win no matter the cards in your hand and so you have to think really hard, try to figure out the cards the other players have, and if they are serious 'raising' the bet, or only just bluffing. Deek says that's the point of poker, bluffing out the other guy, seeing can you bullshit him, or he's going to bullshit you.

'Doesn't it matter what your actual cards are?' I ask Deek, if they are high or low. Deek says sort of scornfully like this is a damn dumb question he will answer because he likes me, 'Sure it matters but not so much's how you play what you're dealt. What you do with the fuckin' cards you are dealt, that's poker.'

Through the beer-buzz in my brain comes these words *What you do with what you're dealt. That's poker.*

These first few games when good cards come to me, or Deek tells me how to play them it's like riding in the speedboat across the choppy lake gripping my seat squealing and breathless and the boat thump-thump-thumping through the waves like nothing could stop it ever, such a good feeling, a sensation in my stomach that is almost unbearable, Deek casting his sidelong glance at me, stroking his whiskery jaws saying OK Anns'lee-honey: you are on your own now. A flashing card-shuffle in Heins's fingers and the cards flicked out and I'm fumbling my cards blinking and trying to figure out what they mean, the guys keep opening cans of Coors for me, could be I am drunk and not knowing it, biting my lower lip and laughing, God damn I am clumsy dropping a card (an ace!) that Croke can see, and the guys are waiting for me, seems like I've lost the thread of what is going on so Deek nudges me saying you have to bet, Anns'lee, or fold. I'm frowning and moving my lips like a first-grader trying to read, what's it mean – ace of hearts and ace of spades and four of diamonds and four of clubs and a nine of clubs, should I get rid of the nine, I guess I should get rid of the nine, my thoughts seem to be coming in slow motion now as I toss down the four of clubs, no! take it back it's the nine of clubs I don't want, Heins deals a replacement card to me and I fumble turning it over, my face falls it's a nine of spades, I'm disappointed, should I be disappointed? The guys are trying to be patient with me. I am itchy and sweaty inside the Cougars T-shirt, and my swimsuit beneath, halter-top with straps that tie around the neck and puckered-fabric bottom, still damp from the lake, and my pony tail straggling down my back still damp too, Momma says we should shower and shampoo our hair after swimming in that lake water there's 'impurities' in it – sewage draining from some of the cottages – diesel fuel leaked into the lake from motorboats – some people, Uncle Tyrone says, no better than pigs. Must be, the guys are waiting for me to make a decision (but what decision should I be making? I've forgotten), Deek leans over to take hold of the nape of my neck gripping me the way you'd grip a dog to shake it a little, reprimand it, 'C'mon babe, you in or out?' and I try to ease away from him, I think it's meant as a joke, and not some kind of threat, and Heins says, 'She's just a kid, Deek. Why'd you want to play with a kid,' and Deek turns on him, 'Fuck you, Heinie! Anns'lee and me, we're a *team*.'

This is warming to me, to hear. *Team, we are a team.* So I say I'm *in*, toss another bill onto the pile. Croke mulls over his cards, decides to fold, Jax folds, Heins raises like he means to provoke Deek, by now my bladder is pinching so hard, I have to pee again, itchy and nervous uncertain what to do, guess I will 'fold' now, should I 'fold'? – a single dollar-bill left of all my winnings. The winning hand is Heins's though maybe in fact Heins's cards are weaker than my 'two pair' but damn it's too late, I'm out. I folded, and I lost. Could cry, my winnings are gone so fast, it's like the dollar-bills Deek staked me were my own, now gone. A childish hurt opens in me like an old, soft wound.

'Too bad, li'l dude. This is poker.'

The guys laugh at me, I'm wanting to think fondly. The way you'd laugh at a pouting child who doesn't have a clue what is going on around her.

Outside, the sky is mostly clouds. But a hot steamy sun shining through. This smell in the air, it's like there is a lightning-storm somewhere else.

Heins is dealing. Heins says, Cut, babe. Somehow, I'm betting my last dollar-bill. Something tells me I am going to win this time – win all my money back! – but the cards are confusing to me, can't remember what Deek was telling me, 'straight' – 'flush' – 'full house' – 'two pair' – I'm staring at my cards, king of hearts, ten of hearts, eight of hearts, five of diamonds and two of diamonds, get rid of the two of diamonds that's a low card – should I? – or is this a mistake? – the replacement card Heins deals me is a six of spades, I'm disappointed, ohhh damn, in my confusion thinking that the black spade brings down the value of the red cards, that's how it looks to me, so my last dollar-bill is taken from me when I'm too scared to bet and say instead 'fold' – laying down my cards, and Jax peers at them, saying, Shit, babe, you coulda done better. Anyway I am relieved to be out of the game needing to use the bathroom bad, swaying on my feet (bare feet? where are my sandals?), the floor is sticky against the bottoms of my feet, feels like it's tilting, I'm losing my balance falling into somebody's lap but manage to get to the bathroom and shut the door behind me feeling so strange like on a roller coaster where I'd be frightened except everything seems funny to me, even losing my dollar-bills, *my* dollar-bills you'd think I had brought with me to the poker game, only just makes me laugh. In the murky mirror above the cruddy sink there's my face dazed and sunburnt and my eyes (that Momma says are my father's eyes, hazel-dark-brown, beautiful eyes but you can't trust them) are threaded with blood, that's a little scary but still I can't stop laughing. These guys like me, the way Deek looks at me, pulls my pony-tail, slaps at my rear maybe I am a pretty girl after all.

Giggling leaning to the mirror, pursing my lips so they get wrinkly kissing my mirror-lips whispering *Anns'lee-honey! Li'l dude!* nobody has ever called me before.

'I will tell Gracie. Nobody else.'

Thinking how I loved it when Daddy tickled me, when I was a little girl. Daddy spreading his big fingers and 'walking' – pretending they were 'daddy-long-legs' – come to tickle me, making me kick and squeal with laughter. I was seven, in second grade, when Daddy went away up to Follette, and the woman from Herkimer County Family Services asked did your father ever hurt you, Annislee? – and I said No! He did not. Daddy did not. You would think that when you answered such a question that would be the end of it but repeatedly the question would be asked as if to trick you. Asking did your daddy hurt you or your brother or your mother, try to remember Annislee, and I was angry saying in a sharp voice like a fingernail scraped on a blackboard *No Daddy did not.*

'Hey Anns'lee: din't fall in, did you?'

One of the guys rapping on the door, making the latch-key rattle.

At the table the guys are devouring ham sandwiches in two-three bites. Big fistfuls of chips. Cans of Black Horse Ale opened and the ale-smell is sharp and acrid. Heins is shuffling cards, pushes them across the table for me to cut. Am I still in this game? With no dollar-bill to toss into the pot? They're asking where am I staying at the lake and I tell them. Where do I live and I tell them: Strykersville, which is about twelve miles to the south. Is your family with you at Wolf's Head, Deek asks me, and I tell him yes: except for my father who isn't here. Deek asks where is my father, and I hesitate not wanting to tell him that I am not sure. Last I knew, Daddy was living in Sparta but he's one to move around some. Not liking to be tied down Momma says.

Croke asks do I have any brothers? – his greeny-grey eyes on me in a way that's kindly, I think. I say yes, Jacky who's nine years old and a damn pain in the neck.

(Why'd I say this? To make the guys laugh? You'd think that I don't love my little brother but truly I do.)

Seems like the guys want me back in their game, Deek is allowing me to put up my Cougars T-shirt 'for collateral'. Since washing my face I'm feeling more clear-headed – I think! – wanting to win back the dollar-bills I've lost. Maybe this is how gamblers get started, you are desperate to win back what you've lost for there is a kind of shame in losing.

But the cards don't come, now. Or anyway, I can't make sense of them. Like adding up a column of numbers in math class, you lose your way and have to begin again. Like multiplying numbers you can do it without thinking but if you stop to think, you can't. Staring at these new cards, nine of hearts, nine of clubs, king of spades, queen of spades, four of diamonds. I get rid of the four of diamonds and I'm excited, my replacement card is a jack of spades, but my eyes are playing tricks on me, what looks like spades is actually clubs, after raising my bet I see that it's clubs and I've made a mistake staring and blinking at the cards in my hands that are kind of shaky like I have never seen a poker hand before. Around the table the guys are playing like before, loud, funny-rude, maybe there's some tension among them, I can't figure because I am too distracted by the cards and how I am losing now, nothing I do is right now, but why? When Croke wins the hand Deek mutters, Shi-it, you God-damn fuckin' asshole, but smiling like this is a joke, a kindly-intended remark like between brothers. I'm trying to make sense of the hand: why'd Croke win? why's this a 'winning' hand? what's a 'full house'? wondering if the guys are cheating on me, how'd I know? The guys are laughing at me saying, 'Hey babe be a good sport, this is poker.'

Croke says, '*My* T-shirt, now!' Pulls the Cougars T-shirt off over my head, impatient with how slow I am trying to pull it off, there's a panicked moment when I feel the guys' eyes swerve onto me, my halter top, my small breasts the size of plums, anxious now like undressing in front of strangers but I am trying to laugh it's OK –

isn't it? – just a game. This is poker Deek says, this is Wolf's Head Lake in August, the kinds of wild things you hear about back at school, wish you'd been part of. And now I am.

In just my swimsuit now, and barefoot. Feeling kind of shivery, dizzy. Picked out the swimsuit myself at Sears so can't blame Momma it's like a kid's sun suit, too young for me: bright yellow puckered material, a halter top that ties around my neck and a matching bottom and both of them kind of tight and itchy and damp-smelling from the lake. Croke is clowning with the T-shirt wrapped around his head like a turban saying that li'l babe owes him one more thing: 'This is strip poker, honey. You raised that bet, didn't you? There's two damn bets here. My T-shirt, and now some-thing else.'

Croke is teasing, is he? All the guys are teasing? The way they are looking at me, at my halter top, I'm starting to giggle, can't stop giggling, like being examined by the doctor, icy-cold stethoscope against my chest, and I'm half-naked trembling on the edge of an examination table, so scared my teeth start chattering and the doctor gives up disgusted, calls for Momma to come in. Jax is say-ing, 'She's drunk, we better sober her up and get her out of here.'

Right away I mumble *I am not drunk!* which makes the guys laugh.

Deek says leaning over me, brushing my arm with his to make the hairs stir, 'Thass a cute li'l swimsuit, Anns'lee. You're a hot li'l babe, eh?'

Jax says, disgusted, 'She's just a kid. Ain't even in high school I bet.'

Deek says, 'Shit she ain't. How old're you, Anns'lee?'

Eighteen, I tell him. Can't stop laughing, wanting to hide my face in my hands. Thirty-eight! (Thirty-eight is Momma's age, so *old.*)

Jax says, 'I told you: she's wasted. No way she's more'n fifteen.'

Deek says, 'Fifteen is hot. This is a hot li'l babe.'

Heins says, 'Want the cops to bust us? Asshole.'

Deek says, 'How's that gonna happen? This li'l honey is my girl.'

My girl is such a warm thing to say. *My girl my girl* nobody has ever said to me except my daddy till now.

'Strip, li'l dude! C'mon.'

'Got to be a good sport, Anns'lee. That's poker.'

Deek is teasing me but he's serious, too. And Croke.

'*I'll* strip. Lookit me.'

Deek yanks off his T-shirt that's grimy at the neck, suddenly he's bare-chested, coarse black hairs like a pelt over his chest that is hard-muscled but at the waist band of his swim trunks his flesh is bunchy and flabby. Shi-it, Croke says, loud like a cross between yawning and yodelling, with a flourish yanking off his T-shirt baring his heavy, beefy, pimple-pocked chest like a TV wrestler, Croke's chest is covered with hairs like slick seaweed, and oily with sweat. There's a strong smell of underarms. Jax and Heins make crude comments. I'm saying that I don't want to play poker any more I guess, I want to go home now, need to get home where my mother is waiting for me, and Croke says, bringing his fist down hard on the table like he's drunk, 'Not a chance, babe. Ain't goin' anywhere till you pay up.'

Deek says, 'When you won the pot we paid up, din't we? Now you got to pay, Anns'lee. That's poker.'

In just my swimsuit what can I do? Can't take off the halter-top but for sure can't take off the bottom.

My sandals! Maybe the guys would let me substitute my sandals.

Except: I don't see my sandals, on the messy floor.

Maybe I lost them in the other room? climbing through the window?

The guys are pounding the table: 'Strip! Anns'lee's got to strip! Top or bottom, you owe us. That's poker.'

Deek is practically on top of me. Not just his underarms smell but his oily-spiky hair that's cut mini-hawk style. Big yellow crooked teeth, breath in my face like fumes. Deek is saying, like you'd talk to a young child, or some animal like a dog that needs to be cajoled, 'Take off your top, li'l dude, thass all, thass a damn cute li'l top, show us your cute li'l boobies, you ain't got nothin' we ain't see already, wanta bet?' All this while I'm hunched over trying to shield my front with my arms, but my arms are so thin, and Deek is pressing so close, slides his arm round my shoulders and I'm on my feet panicked trying to run to the door but Croke grabs me like it's a game we are playing, or him and Deek are playing, like football, Anns'lee is the football, captured. Croke's big fingers tear at the halter straps, Croke manages to untie the straps and pulls off the halter, Ohhhh lookit! – the guys are whistling and stamping their feet teasing, taunting like dogs circling a wounded rabbit and I'm panicked like a rabbit trying to laugh, to show this is just a joke, I know it's a joke, but I'm desperate to get away from them, stumbling to the bathroom, the only place I can get to, shutting the door behind me, fumbling to latch the door, had a glimpse before I shut it of Croke (I'd thought was my friend) with the halter-top on his head, tying the straps beneath his chin like a bonnet.

Somewhere not too far away Momma is looking at the clock fretting and fuming where is that girl! – where the hell has Annislee got to this time!

They wouldn't hurt me – would they?

They like me – don't they?

How long I am crouched in the bathroom in terror of the guys breaking in, how long I am shivering and trembling like a trapped rabbit, I won't know afterwards and even at the time what is happening is rushing past like a drunken scene glimpsed from a speeding car or boat on the lake. My right breast is throbbing with pain, must've been that Croke squeezed it, an ugly yellowish-purple bruise is taking shape.

Croke, I'd thought liked me. Helping me out of the boat.

Back in grade school already we'd begun to hear stories of what guys can do to girls if they want to hurt them though we had not understood why. And sometimes the girls are beaten, strangled, left for dead, it isn't known why.

'Hey: Anns'lee.'

There's a rap on the plywood door. I'm not going to open it.

One of the guys rattling the door so hard, the latch-key slips open. It's Jax leaning in, seeing me crouched against the wall so frightened my teeth are chattering, says, like he's embarrassed, 'Here's the swim top, nobody's gonna hurt you.'

I'm too scared to reach up and take the halter top from him. Jax shoves it at me muttering, 'Put the damn thing on.'

Jax shuts the door. With trembling fingers I refasten the top.

Avoiding my reflection in the mirror. That greasy smudge where I'd kissed my own lips.

When I emerge from the bathroom, stiff and numbed, my eyes blinking back tears, the guys are still at the table, still drinking. Seems like they're between poker games. Or maybe they're through with poker for the night. Their eyes swerve onto me in that way that reminds me of excited dogs. Deek says, 'Li'l dude! There you are. C'mon back sit on Deek's lap, eh? You're my girl.'

A glint like gasoline in Deek's bloodshot eyes and a way his big teeth are bared in a grin without warmth or mirth warns me that I am still in danger. Through the plywood door I'd heard Deek mutter what sounded like *ain't done with her yet, so don't fuck with me.*

Outside, all I can see of the early-evening sky is massive bruise-coloured clouds. Still there is heat-lightning 'way in the distance.

'Here y'are, Anns'lee. Shouldna been so scared.'

Croke tosses the Cougars T-shirt at me. I'm so grateful for the shirt smelly from where Croke has wiped his sweaty face with it, I'm stammering Thank you!

There is a break in what the guys are doing, I can feel it. Or maybe they've been waiting for Anns'lee to emerge from the bathroom uncertain what they would do with me, or if they would do anything with me: like turning a card, possibly. It just might be the card that makes you win big or it might be the card that assures you will lose. It might be a card that will mean nothing in your life. Or everything. It might even be a card you won't need to request, the card will come flying at you.

Now I'm wearing my Cougars T-shirt over my swimsuit top again, I am not feeling so exposed. It's a baggy shirt, coming down practically to my thighs.

I will pretend I haven't heard Deek. How he's staring at me with a loose wet smile running the tip of his tongue around his lips.

Things a guy can do. You don't want to know.

My heart is beating hard hidden inside the T-shirt, my voice is calm-sounding telling the guys: 'There's other kinds of stripping not just taking off clothes. There's this card game we play called Truth – you ever heard of Truth?'

'Truth? Some kid's game? No.'

I'm a little distance from the nearest of them, who happens to be Heins. The way I'm standing is to let them know that I am not going to make a run for the front door as I tried to do earlier, I am not panicked now, or desperate. I am smiling at them, the way a girl might. I am trying to smile. The heat pumping off these guys is a sex-heat so palpable you can feel it yards away. Like the charged air before a storm. I don't want to think it's the dogs' instinct to lunge, tear with their teeth, they can't help.

I tell the guys maybe we can play Truth: 'It's a little like poker except you don't bet money, instead of paying a bet you pay in 'truth'. There's high cards and low cards and a joker that's wild. If you lose you reveal a truth about yourself that nobody else knows.'

Nobody seems very interested in learning this game, I can see. Deek says disdainfully, 'How'd you know what a person said was true? Any old bullshit, how'd you know?'

'You would want to tell the truth – wouldn't you? If it was the right time.'

Croke says, '*You* tell us, li'l dude. Make up for how you been acting, like you're scared of us.'

Quickly I say, 'I'm not scared of you! I love being here, coming across the lake on Deek's boat… There's nobody I know has a boat like Deek's.'

At this, Deek smiles. Then the smile freezes.

'You bullshittin' me, babe? Wantin' a ride back acrost the lake, that's it?'

No! I'm smiling at Deek keeping my distance from him. Between us there is Heins, slouched at the table, idly shuffling the pack of cards. I tell Deek I wouldn't lie ever, not to him and his friends I would tell only the truth, that is 'stripping' the soul.

Jax shoves a chair out for me, beside him at the table. So I sit down. There's a little distance between Deek and me. One of the guys has opened an ale for me, I will pretend to sip.

I'm not drunk now – am I?

Drawing a deep breath. This truth I have to reveal.

'…two years ago this August, my father was driving back with me from his cousin's place down in Cattaraugus, this town called Salamanca on the Allegany River. It was just him and me, not my mother or my brother Jacky. Driving back to Strykersville from Salamanca and Daddy wants to stop at a tavern in this place outside Java. Daddy was living away from us then, like he does now, and this was my weekend to be with him. At the tavern that was on a lake where people had rowboats and canoes Daddy bought me some root beer and french fries and I was sitting at a picnic table while Daddy was inside at the bar. There were kids in the park, people were grilling hamburgers and steaks, some girls playing badminton asked me if I'd like to play with them so I did but after a while they went away and I was by myself and thought that I would walk around the lake, it wasn't a big lake like Wolf's Head and I thought that if I walked fast I would get back before Daddy came out of the tavern. But the path around the lake wasn't always right beside the lake and was sort of overgrown so I wasn't sure if I should keep going or turn back. I was worried that Daddy would come out of the tavern before I got back and see I wasn't there and be anxious. These years he'd been away, at Follette, he'd got so he worried about things more, like his family, he said, he'd had a lot of time to think…'

Deek interrupts: 'Follette? That's where your father was?'

'Yes.'

Not like I am ashamed just this is a fact: Daddy served four years of a nine-year sentence for 'aggravated assault' and was released on parole for 'good behaviour' when I was eleven years old. Follette is the men's maximum security prison up north at the Canadian border, the facility in the New York State prison system where nobody wants to go.

The guys' eyes are on me now. The guys are listening and I continue with the story which is a true story I have never told any living soul before this evening.

'...so I'm hoping that I am not lost, I'm on a kind of woodchip trail and there's a parking lot nearby and a restroom, I'm thinking that I can use the women's room, except out of the little building there comes this man zipping up his trousers and he's seeing me, he's in these rumpled old clothes and his face is boiled-looking and hair sticking up around his head, older than my daddy I think, and he's coming right at me, saying "H'lo honey, are you alone 'way out here?" and I tell him no, my daddy is right close by, so he looks at the parking lot but there's no cars there, but he says, "Well! Too bad, this time!" – I think that's what he said, he might've been talking to himself, I wasn't listening and walked away fast. And I waited for him to go away and I thought he did and I went inside the women's room that was hard to see in, there wasn't any light and the sun was about setting, and I'm inside one of the toilet stalls, and there's a scratching noise, and this guy, it must be this guy, has followed me into the women's room! where a man is not ever supposed to be! He's poking a tree branch beneath the stall door, to scare me, saying, "Li'l girl, d'you need help? need help in there? wiping your li'l bottom? I can wipe, and I can lick. I'm real good at that." I'm so scared, I am crying. I tell the man go away please go away and leave me alone, my daddy is waiting for me, and he's laughing telling me the kinds of things he was going to do to me, things he'd done to girls that the girls had "liked real well" and nobody would know not even my daddy. But there was a car pulling up outside, and a woman comes into the restroom with a little girl so the man runs out and when I come outside he's gone or anyway I think he's gone. The woman says to me, "Was that man bothering you? D'you want a ride with me?" and I said no, I was going back to my daddy's car and would wait for him there. Why I told the woman this, I don't know. I thought that the man was gone. I headed back to the tavern the way I'd been coming, now the sun is setting, it's getting dark. I'm walking fast, and I'm running, and there's the man with the boiled-looking face almost I don't see him squatting by the path, he's got a rope in his hands, a rope maybe two feet long stretched between his hands he's holding up for me to see, so I'm panicked and run the other way, back to the parking lot, and the man calls after me, "Li'l girl! Don't be afraid li'l girl your daddy sent me for you!" Things like that he was saying. I found a place to hide by some picnic tables, and for a long time, maybe twenty minutes, the man is looking for me calling "Li'l girl," he knows that I am there somewhere, but it's getting dark, and then there's headlights, a car is bumping up a lane into the parking lot, and I can't believe it, it's my daddy. Just taking a chance he'd find me, Daddy would say afterward, that I'd be on this side of the lake, he'd asked people if they had seen me and somebody had and he'd come to the right place, at just the right time. He caught sight of the man with the boiled face, I told Daddy how he'd been following me, and saying things to me, wanting to tie me up with a rope, and Daddy runs after him and catches him, the man is limping and can't hardly run at all, and Daddy starts hitting him with his fists, not even saying anything but real quiet, Daddy does things real quiet, it's the man who is crying out, begging for Daddy to stop but Daddy can't stop, Daddy won't stop until it's over... Daddy says, when a man uses his fists it's "self-defence". Fists or feet, nobody can dispute "self-defence". Use a "deadly weapon" – like a tyre iron – like Daddy used fighting another man in Strykersville, that got him arrested and sent to Follette – and you're in serious trouble but just your fists and your feet, no. What Daddy did to that man who'd wanted to tie me up and hurt me, I didn't see. I did not see. I heard it, or some of it. But I did not see. And afterward Daddy dragged him to a ravine, where there'd be water at some times of the year but was dry now, and pushed him over, and I did not see that, either. And Daddy comes back to me excited and breathing hard and his knuckles are skinned and bleeding but Daddy doesn't hardly notice he grabs me, and hugs me, and kisses me, Daddy is so happy that I am safe. "You never saw a thing, honey. Did you," and I told Daddy no, I did not, and that was the truth.'

Listening to my story the guys have gotten quiet. Even Deek is sitting very still listening to me. The look in his face, like he's waiting to laugh at me, bare his glistening teeth at me in a mock-grin, is gone. Fresh-opened cans of Black Horse Ale on the table, the guys have not been drinking. Must be, they are waiting for me to continue. But my story is over.

Hadn't known how it would end. Because I had not told it before. Even to myself though it is a true story, I wouldn't have known that I had the words for it. But you always have words for a true story, I think.

I am not going to tell Deek, Jax, Croke, Heins how there was never any article in any newspaper that I saw about the man with the boiled-looking face if he'd been found in Java State Park in that ravine. What was left of that man, if anything was left. Or maybe he'd gotten all right again, next morning crawled out of the ravine and limped away. That is a possibility. I didn't see, and Daddy never spoke of it afterward. Daddy drove us back to Strykersville that night, it was past midnight when we got home and Momma was waiting up watching TV and if she'd meant to be angry with Daddy for keeping me out so late, by the time we got to the house she was feeling different, and kissed us both, saw that I was looking fever-ish and said *Annislee, go to bed right now, it's hours past your bedtime.* That night, Daddy stayed with Momma.

Off and on then Daddy stayed with us then that fall something happened between him and Momma so Daddy moved out, that's when he began working at the stone quarry at Sparta. But Sparta is only about fifty miles from Strykersville and Daddy and Momma are still married, I think. *Till death do us part* Daddy believes and in her heart Momma does, too.

I'm smiling at these guys crowded at the battered old table in Deek's uncle's cottage, so close I can see their eyes, and the irises of their eyes, and as far into their souls as I need to see. Saying, 'I feel lucky, I'd like to try poker again, a few hands. I think I'm catching on now.'

♠

The Stake

Sam Hill

A WOMAN PULLING a clattering roll-aboard eyed them in prim disapproval. The younger man took a defiant drag on his cigarette and spoke, the cautious tone of a stranger careful not to overstep, 'Waiting on my limo. Do you live in Chicago?'

'Minneapolis,' the fat man in the silver suit said, 'but I'm on my way to a new job in Miami. I've spent a lot of time in Chicago, though. I love Chicago.' *People in Chicago and Atlanta and Dallas always want to be told that.*

'Yeah?' said the young man. 'What do you do that brings you to Chicago so much?'

The fat man sized him up, seeing the watermelon-coloured knit shirt from a famous golf resort, expensive Louis Vuitton travel bag, and cheap synthetic goody bag with the drug company logo on the side. 'I'm a professional poker player.' He noted the quick intake of breath, and pegged the man as one of the new breed that watches poker on TV and dreams of winning a seat at one of the big tournaments. He stuck out his hand, 'Shiny Sarkisian.'

The other man stared at him. 'Shiny?'

'Yeah,' laughed the heavy man, 'Shiny. I always been a little heavy and I got this oily Mediterranean-skin thing going. It's always hot in poker rooms so I sweat a lot. A player named Dolly Brunson started calling me Shiny, and it stuck.'

The young man stared back, mouth hanging open. 'Doyle Brunson gave you a nickname? *The* Doyle Brunson?'

Shiny laughed, dropped his cigarette and ground it with his toe. 'I only know one Dolly Brunson.' Shiny lit another cigarette, smiled, and waited.

The young man with the sparse brown hair did not disappoint. 'Marc Weinberg. I play some poker, too. Online, that sort of stuff.' Shiny nodded. Weinberg tried again, 'I don't recognize your name. Do you play any tournaments?'

Sarkisian shook his head. 'Cash game guy.'

'And that's how you know Brunson?' Weinberg said.

'Sure,' Shiny laughed. 'Forty years ago, bunch of us rode around in this old green Cadillac playing in the back rooms of bars and Elks Lodges. Half the time somebody would get mad about the whole thing and one of us would say he had to go pee. Then he'd sneak out to start up the car, and bring it around front so the rest of us could come high tailing it out and dive right through the windows and take off with those other guys chasing out the door after us. That was back before Dolly was a TV star.'

Weinberg laughed at the image. 'Wow. They ever catch you?'

'Not very often, thank goodness,' Shiny shook his head and laughed again. 'I was a little thinner then and could run pretty good for a chubby kid, so I never had to worry about fighting. Not much of a runner any more, though.' He patted his large stomach, and casually let his right arm extend, and saw Weinberg glance at the Rolex that rode there. He then carefully raised his left arm, the one with the cigarette, and read the time from his battered old Timex. 5.32 p.m.

Weinberg watched, fascinated, and asked the inevitable question, 'I don't want to be nosy, but why do you wear two watches?'

Shiny put the cigarette in the corner of his mouth, squinted to keep the smoke out of his eyes, and stuck out his wrist, pulling up his sleeve to show the Rolex with the diamond chips. 'I won it off Johnny Chan.' *Almost the truth. He'd won this watch from Stu Ungar,* but you couldn't count on Weinberg knowing who Stuey was. But he'd know Chan from that *Rounders* movie and from TV. And anyway, until Thursday, there had been another Rolex on his arm that he really had won from Chan. Hell, at one time he'd worn four watches on that arm – Ungar, Chan, Nguyen, and Brunson, in his view the four best poker players of all time, in that order, and he'd won their watches. But that was before – before Margie's cancer, before the Indian casinos, before he starting being so tired all the time.

Weinberg stared in amazement. 'You won it off Johnny Chan?' He looked up, suddenly straight-faced, and Shiny wondered if he'd played it too strong. 'Are you bullshitting me?' he asked in a lower tone.

Shiny shrugged, 'I don't know you, guy, got no reason to bullshit you.'

Marc turned and looked for his limo, and Shiny wondered if he'd lost him. Weinberg turned back, smiled, 'Sorry, didn't mean to be like that. But man, Dolly Brunson, Johnny Chan. Those are my idols, man.'

Of course they are, Shiny thought, but didn't say. Instead, he pretended to change the subject. 'So what do you do, Marc?'

'Cardiologist,' the man answered apologetically. He held up the hand with the cigarette and waved it towards Shiny, 'I know, I know. Picked up the habit in school and have never been able to shake it.'

Shiny nodded, a nod that could mean anything the man wanted it to mean.

'Well, Shiny, you here for a few days?'

'Just tonight,' Shiny responded, 'Got a daughter that goes to school here. Flying out tomorrow early.' He willed his heartbeat to slow down. He'd made his play, now he waited for the other man to decide whether to fold or call.

Marc hesitated, looked out at the far kerb where the limos were lined up, and did not see the placard he wanted. When he finally spoke, he tried to be nonchalant about it. 'You know we have a game some Friday nights, pretty serious game, actually.'

'How serious?' Shiny asked.

'Hundred, two for the blinds,' the man answered.

'That's serious,' Shiny agreed. A little luck and you could win ten or even twenty thousand at a game like that. He thought about Miranda.

'I'd invite you, but the guys would probably kill me. A pro like you would clean us all out in about thirty minutes, I'd guess,' Marc laughed.

'That's not really the way it works,' Shiny lied.

'Why not?' asked the doctor, curious.

'Lots of reasons. Run of the cards. Fact everybody now plays Texas Hold 'Em and it makes the odds easier to keep track of. Used to be dealer called the game, and it was Hold 'Em, then it was Stud or Hi Lo, and every game has different odds. Hard to keep track of. And of course everybody knows more now from watching the big tournaments on television.'

'But can't you just read us? Tells, and all that?'

'Some,' Shiny admitted, 'but I'm not like Forrest or one of those guys. You sneeze across a crowded room and they can tell you the fourth digit of your Social Security number and the name of your third grade teacher. They're spooky.'

'So how do you win?' Marc persisted.

'I got a real good memory and I understand things like playing position and betting. There are four different ways to win in no limit.' *It used to drive Pops crazy, the way Shiny always insisted on giving them fair warning – showing them the watches, telling them the Cadillac story, making sure they knew exactly what they were up against. You're way too nice a guy, Shiny, he'd say. They'll find out soon enough.*

Marc stared at Shiny, and Shiny watched him talk himself into it, the way bad players always sold themselves on a dubious call. He waited patiently for the cardiologist to scribble his cell number and an address on the back of a business card and hand it to Shiny, then watched as he scrambled across the six lanes of traffic and into the back seat of limo 7765. The window rolled down halfway, and the doctor stuck his head out, 'Nine o'clock.'

Shiny smiled, nodded and waved as the limo pulled away. The act of raising his arm above his shoulder left him breathless, and he had to lean against the glass shelter to regain his breath before going inside to the bank of telephones. *Lucky to find a phone. No one uses pay phones any more except in airports. Everybody's got a cellphone. Bet somewhere there's a homeless guy with a cellphone.* From his wallet, he fished out a calling card some airline had given him, and made two calls, the first to Miami.

'Pete Sarkisian,' the voice on the other end answered.

'Pete, this is Shiny, checking in,' the fat man said.

'You're what?' answered the voice carefully.

'Checking in. What's wrong with that?'

'Just that you haven't checked in since you left for Vietnam. What's the matter? Did you miss the plane?'

'I made the plane,' Shiny said, trying to insert a hint of indignation into his voice. 'I'm in Chicago. I'll be in Miami at eleven forty eight tomorrow.'

Pete was quiet. 'Please be here, Shiny. This is a cruise ship, it ain't gonna wait. You ain't here and you can kiss this thing goodbye. You're supposed to be here already, helping me set up. You know that.'

'I'll be there, Pete. I promise,' said Shiny. 'I appreciate what you're doing for me.'

Pete's voice was warm, but careful. 'This is a great opportunity for you, Shiny. Teach the cruisers to play a little poker, lose a hand every once in a while, let them buy you drinks while you spin a few stories. Smoke duty-free cigarettes. Meet some women. This works out, it could turn into a permanent gig for you, 401K, health insurance, the whole enchilada. I know you got reservations about this, Shiny, but sometimes you got to do what it takes to get over, you know?'

'Sure, Petey, sure. This is gonna be great.' He hesitated, then continued. 'Pete, I was wondering, you being the pit boss and all, you think there's any chance you could wire me sort of an advance. I thought maybe I could give Miranda something to help her out, you know?' He waited, listening to the heavy silence coming from Miami.

When Pete replied, the warmth was gone from his voice. 'Shiny, don't do this to me. Just get down here.' He hung up.

Shiny shrugged philosophically, and placed another call. An operator came on the line and told him the area code had changed to 773, then put him through.

'Rackaroo,' the voice on the other end of the line mumbled.

'Let me speak to Malek, please,' Shiny said.

'Ain't no Malek here,' said the voice and hung up.

Shiny called again, and this time spoke as soon as the phone was answered, 'Listen to me, playa, when Malek finds out you hung up on Shiny the Shark, he's going to stuff your bee-bees through your grills. He's at the first table up front on the left, and you know it, now hand him the damn phone.' *Grills. When did teeth become grills?* He stopped, out of breath, and held the phone away from his face so the other man could not hear him panting. There was a clatter as someone laid the phone on the counter, and a moment later it was picked up.

'Shiny, Shiny, Shiny,' a pleasant voice laughed. 'What's with this hard ass stuff? You're supposed to be the nicest guy in poker. This stupid nigger you bluffed is about six foot twelve and weighs half a ton. You two ever meet up, you might wished you had'na spoke like that.'

'Nah. I still outweigh him,' Shiny laughed.

'What you so cheery about?' Malek replied. 'I thought you was dead, man. Somebody said something about your heart or something.'

'That's why I sound happy, because I ain't dead,' Shiny said, watching his own rubber smile in the shiny metal of the payphone.

'Yet. You ain't dead yet,' Malek laughed. 'Wait till you see this nigger.'

'I got business, Malek,' Shiny said.

'Well then, Uncle Shiny, come on down. You know where I stay,' Malek laughed. 'And spend the time in the cab thinking about how you gonna talk my boy DZ out of pulling your little fat arms off.' He laughed again and hung up.

The Rack and Ruin was a classic pool hall, on Montrose at Broadway, cool and dark with three long rows of tables running up towards a plywood counter with a glass-fronted cooler behind it, a coffee pot with a poisonous-looking black brew, and a crock pot that Shiny knew from previous visits held hot dogs. Four black trays of balls rested on the counter in a neat line. Shiny noticed the old tin ashtrays had been taken down off the walls, and over the brackets that had held them hung neatly lettered signs that said, 'No smoking'. He wondered if the back room was non-smoking now. Shiny patted the pack of Newports in his pocket. *Casinos were the last place left.*

The hall was empty except for three Latino kids playing Cutthroat at a table in the back, a Filipino guy practicing alone by the window, and four men stalking around Malek's table, squinting and gesturing at an orange ball. A giant young black man looming behind the counter scowled at Shiny as he walked in.

One of the four men at the front table was Malek, young, very dark and immaculately dressed. He looked away from the game, smiled at Shiny, and arched his eyebrows toward the counter. 'That's DZ, Shiny. I told you he was big,' he laughed. A melodious tinkle of a laugh. Shiny nodded, walked over to the counter and stuck out his hand. DZ stared at it for a moment, shook his head in disgust, and snatched a towel off a small hook and began polishing the balls in the first tray.

Shiny shrugged, turned and walked past Malek's table towards a row of elevated chairs at the back. He heaved himself onto one, and rested his hands on his knees, pursing his lips and sucking in a long stream of air, the way the doctor had told him to. Malek scampered up beside him.

'So Shiny, what brings you to my little corner of the world?' Malek asked pleasantly, although Shiny had known Malek his whole life and knew he wasn't really a pleasant man. Malek did not wait for Shiny to answer, but spoke again, 'You got no idea how many Shiny stories I heard growing up, man, from Pops.'

'I need a little stake, Malek. Got a game,' Shiny wheezed. 'Standard deal. Fifties on the ups, and I'm responsible for the down.'

Malek nodded, 'I can go for that, Shiny, but how much you talking about here?'

'Twenty would do it,' he answered carefully.

Malek laughed. 'Don't got it. Well, I don't got it here. I got it all right, but not here,' He fished around in his pocket and pulled out a wad of cash wrapped in a blue rubber band. 'See what you can do with this.' He tossed it at Shiny, who trapped it on his stomach.

Shiny fanned it expertly. 'There's maybe six or seven here, Malek. This is a bigger game than that. With a good stake, I can pick up four or five pots betting. Can't do that if I'm on the short stack.'

Malek shook his head, laughed again. 'Pops used to tell me all Shiny the Shark ever needed was a chip and a chair. Well, you got a chip and a chair, so now go win us some money.' He slapped Shiny on the shoulder lightly. 'How many days this game going for? When should I expect to see you back here?'

'It's a friendly,' Shiny said. He looked at the Timex. 7.13. 'Figure me for two, three a.m. Does that work?'

Malek laughed, 'Sure it works. I'm 'bout to head down the street for a little nap, should be back about eleven or so. You know, my sort of business don't really get going until late.'

Shiny pulled up his sleeve and started to unsnap the Ungar watch, but Malek reached out and laid his fingers on the dial. 'Don't give me that old style bling, Shiny, nobody wants that stuff. You keep it. I don't do that collateral stuff no more, anyways. I keep it simple. You not back by breakfast and my boy DZ will settle up for me. Di-rectly, so to speak.'

Shiny hesitated, and Malek continued, 'And anyway, I know you ain't going to win a bunch of money and skip town. Shiny don't do stuff like that.'

Shiny smiled and nodded, worked his way down off the chair. Malek called out to the man at the counter, 'Hey, DZ, bring the Sclade around and give my man a ride up to Loyola. He's got family up that way.' Malek beamed at Shiny, who stared back expressionless. Shiny fingered the money.

'Was that a threat, Malek?' Shiny asked carefully.

Malek shook his head, still smiling. 'Don't be so sensitive man. Just go win us some money. Go on, now.' He made a gesture with his hands like the one Shiny's grandfather employed to chase pigeons off Brooklyn park benches.

Miranda already had a table at Vege-Thai when he arrived. She leapt from her seat and bounded towards him the instant he pulled the door open, ensnaring him so tightly in her long arms that he could barely breathe. And he pulled her in as tightly as he could, closing his eyes and smelling the shampoo in her dark brown hair. They stood, rocking back and forth, smiling, until interrupted by a busboy with a full tray.

At the table, they sat across from each other, uneaten spring rolls on a small rectangular dish between them. He thought she was too thin and was probably smoking too much to keep her weight down, and gestured toward the rolls. She picked one up, took a micro-nibble, and placed it on her plate. He wondered about boys but knew not to ask. 'So how you doing, baby?' Shiny asked. 'How's school? The dancing? You getting by OK?'

She answered non-specifically, as grown children do, and tried to deflect the conversation back toward him. To Minnesota. To the doctor. To Miami. He dodged most of the questions, not giving specifics, as parents of grown children do.

'Yeah, I think I'm going to like this new job,' Shiny answered. He couldn't stop looking at her, smiling.

Miranda laughed, a loud hoot at odds with her small, elegant dancer physique. Just like her mother, Shiny thought. A wave of loneliness washed over Shiny so cold and deep that he thought it would never pass. He closed his eyes for a minute. A diner at the table next to them turned. When he opened his eyes his daughter was watching him, a worried smile on her face. He forced a grin, 'What's that cackle for?'

Miranda asked, 'How many jobs have you had, Dad? Like, ever?'

Shiny pondered and answered seriously, 'Does the Army count?'

Miranda hooted again, and shook her head. 'No.'

'Then this would make one,' he said, holding up a finger. They laughed together. They talked about Miami, then Margie, then school, then Margie again.

At the end of the meal, Shiny pulled the five crisp hundred dollar bills from his wallet he'd gotten hocking the Johnny Chan watch. 'Here.' He slid them across the table.

She looked down at the money but did not pick it up. 'You're a sweetie, but I'm doing OK, really. They're talking about finding some scholarship or grant or something to help me finish up.' He read the lie, and it hurt him. He thought about her face when he brought her the money from the game tonight, and the secret excited him.

Shiny pulled the wad Malek had given him from his pocket. He waved it toward her. 'Really honey, I'm flush. Got into a good game just before I got on the plane. That money is for you.'

She stared at him, then smiled and picked up the money, 'Thanks, Dad. This will help so much.' They drank their coffee silently, and as they stood to part, she said, 'I wish you could stay.'

Shiny nodded, 'Me, too, baby, but my plane's in a couple of hours, and Uncle Pete is meeting me at the airport, so I better get moving. You know how it is with security and all that.' They held each other on the sidewalk for a long time. Finally, Shiny pried himself loose. 'You got to get going, Kiddo,' he said, 'and I do too. Hey, I'll bring you down for a cruise or something in a couple of months when I get settled. How does that sound?' She grinned, and waved furiously as she weaved backwards down the street toward the El.

The game was in a smaller mansion in a suburb called Winnetka, immaculate streets and lawns so perfect that Shiny reckoned the maids here probably had porcelain caps on their teeth. In addition to Shiny, there were six poker players and a blond woman dealer moonlighting from the casino in Joliet. She wore her work uniform of white shirt, black pants and a vest. The players were Marc, another doctor named Bill who owned the house, a landscaper named Dave, two lawyers and a kid named London.

Marc threw his arm over London's shoulders and introduced him to the professional, 'This is our ringer, Shiny. London here is a sophomore at MIT, but he's already competed in a couple of WPT events.' The kid eyed Shiny speculatively, half-smirk on his face. Shiny extended his hand, and the kid shook it with his fingers. He was tall and thin, and his Oxford shirt and khakis made him look very young. He waited for Shiny to sit before selecting a chair to his right.

At the end of the first hour, there were three winners. Doctor Bill played carelessly but got a run of cards. He had increased his chip pile by three thousand or so. Shiny had nursed a series of marginal hands to add a few hundred. London was up ten thousand, mostly at the expense of Marc. Shiny felt himself tiring, and wanted a cigarette.

The woman dealt them each two cards, then patted the felt in front of London, telling him it was his play. Three seats to London's left, Marc threw his cards into the center in disgust.

'Please wait your turn, sir,' the dealer said.

'Please shut the fuck up,' Marc snapped. The dealer coloured. Bill opened his mouth to say something, then closed it. The rest of the players exchanged glances, looking to the dealer for a sign she wanted them to intervene. She stared at the cards noncommittally and they stayed silent.

Shiny turned up the corners of his cards, and saw red. He pulled the cards closer, and peeked again. A six and a seven of diamonds. He laid the cards flat on the cloth. London moved first, limping in. Bill raised it a hundred. Shiny raised two hundred on top of Bill's raise. The button and the two blinds tossed their hands into the pot, and the bet went back to the kid.

London pulled his sunglasses down his nose and stared at Shiny. Shiny smiled back. *If Forrest can't read me, fella, I'm not that worried about you.* London pushed the glasses up, shoved in three hundred and leaned back, the smirk returning.

'Pot's right,' said the dealer, patting the cloth. The flop came, two more diamonds, a four and an eight, and a queen of clubs. London raised another hundred, and Bill called. Shiny nodded, and bumped it to four hundred. London called, and Bill dropped out.

Shiny pegged London for a pocket pair, middling, and figured London had put him on a pair as well, or maybe a big card waiting to pair up. Probably did not see the flush, yet. He smiled at the boy. London did not smile back.

The dealer turned over a queen of hearts, and the kid raised $500. Shiny stared at the cards in the middle of the table, and reran the mental film of the previous hands. This time London had pushed in the stack instantly, the first time in fourteen hands that he'd deviated from his routine, a one-thousand, two-thousand count before acting. Was he really on two pair as he represented? Or even trips – three queens maybe? Or was he bluffing? Or was the change in routine meant to make Shiny think he was bluffing? Shiny counted his stack, and pushed all but five hundred in. 'Raise seven thousand, two hundred,' he announced.

London took off his sunglasses and dropped them into his pocket. 'You trying to fill or you got something, Shiny?' Taunting him. Shiny did not answer, but smiled.

'Call,' the boy said. He counted out his chips. The other players at the table sat engrossed, trying to guess what each player had.

The dealer turned over a five of diamonds. Shiny felt his mouth go dry. He looked at London and smiled again. London counted out five hundred dollars in chips and held them ready. 'You've got to go all in, Shiny, either you're bluffing and you have to see it out, or you really did fill and you've got to protect it.' Shiny nodded, and pushed the rest of his chips in. London dropped his on top of Shiny's stack. 'What you got?' Shiny turned over the two diamonds. There was a collective gasp as the table stared at the straight flush. Shiny looked at the pile of chips. *Almost a semester's worth.*

London laughed and flipped over another queen and a five of spades. A full house. The table gasped again. 'I guess I got lucky,' the boy said.

Marc glared at him. 'He got a straight flush, London, the second best hand in the deck. How do you figure you got lucky?'

'Because I put him on a little flush, and with my hand I would have followed him home like a lost puppy. I'm lucky he didn't have a better stake to work with or I'd be down twenty grand instead of seven.'

Marc snorted, 'You had no clue he had a flush.'

'You're lucky you didn't have a pair of deuces or you'd be down seven thousand, too,' London said with a grin.

The whole table laughed. Marc turned a dark red. 'What does that mean?'

Bill raised his hand. 'It didn't mean anything, Marc. He's just a smart-ass. You were a smart-ass, too, when you were that age. He's busting your chops to get you off your game. That's all.'

'No,' said Marc, standing, 'he's been sitting here winning everything in sight, and I think it sucks. Shit-eating grin on his face. Maybe he's winning for a reason.'

London looked back at him evenly. 'I'm winning because I'm good.'

Marc stepped out from the table. 'Oh, and so the implication is I'm not? Is that what you're saying? What do you say Shiny, why do you think I'm losing? You're the guy who beat Johnny Chan.' All eyes turned toward Shiny.

'I'm not in this,' Shiny said. He continued to stack chips.

'Well I say you are in it,' Marc said. 'Give me a reason why I'm losing to this punk or I'm going to take my money back right now.'

'Oh, for Christ's sake, Marc, it's only ten grand. Hell, I'll give you the money if it's that big a deal. You're ruining a great game here, buddy,' said a sandy-haired lawyer named Brad.

Marc slapped at the man's chips, sending them skittering across the table and the floor. Brad stood up, clenching his fists, redness creeping up his throat. The dealer dropped both hands beneath the table.

'You're losing because you play bad hands and because Ray Charles could read you,' Shiny said.

'What was that?' the cardiologist responded.

'Every time you get a half-decent hand, you put your tongue up against the inside of your left cheek and hold it there. And when you bluff, which you do way too much, you drop your eyes and peek out to see if the rest of us bought it. You're one of the worst poker faces I've ever seen, and you might get by with it online, but in a real game you're just here to give away chips. He doesn't need to cheat to take your money,' Shiny said evenly, without looking up. He carefully sorted one red and two blue chips from the pile and tossed them back toward the lawyer.

Marc stared at him. 'Bullshit.' Weaker now, trying to save face.

Shiny finished with his chips and looked up. 'You playing or leaving?' Marc turned and stomped out. The kid shrugged, and studied the ceiling. Shiny looked around the table. 'I need to step out and smoke a cigarette.' *And rest. Shiny felt the tiredness and the heaviness settling in his arms.*

Shiny sat on a concrete bench beside the pool, and smoked three cigarettes in a row. He wished he had a little more stamina these days. And a better stake. He'd be way up right now if he'd had the chips to play with.

By one a.m., Shiny was down to three thousand dollars, bled dry by a succession of almost good enough hands losing to better hands that filled on the river, hands that Shiny would have won if he hadn't been playing rich men who stayed in way too long because his raises were nothing to them. The kid had gotten real hands, and had twenty-seven thousand dollars in front of him.

'Hey, Shiny,' said Brad. 'What's the secret to being a pro? Tell our prodigy here.' Lincoln fingered his sunglasses down his nose.

Shiny laughed, 'Not being afraid.'

'Afraid of losing?' Brad said.

'Or winning,' Shiny answered, staring down the kid.

London dropped his glasses and held Shiny's eyes. 'What do you do in your spare time, write fortune cookies?'

'Last round,' said Doctor Bill. 'I'm cycling tomorrow and have to get up early.' Shiny winced, calculating how much he needed to win in the next six hands to satisfy Malek. He ran the numbers. Something for Miranda was still possible, but not looking good. *A chip and a chair, though. Anything is possible as long as you have a chip and a chair.*

On the second hand, Shiny caught an ace and a king, 'Big Slick' in poker vernacular. He carefully counted his pile of chips with his eyes and waited. As the big blind, he would be the last to play. Everyone folded around, except for the boy, London, who had not glanced at his cards. He looked over at Shiny, 'How much you got there?'

Shiny told him.

'And what do you need to get right?' the boy asked.

Shiny shrugged, 'Seven all in, maybe. Why?'

'Because I'm going to put you all in, and I want to give you a chance to walk away whole. I'm offering you a thousand for the watch.'

Shiny carefully pushed up his sleeve and looked at Stuey's watch. *Ungar himself had come around the table and clicked it on Shiny's wrist. The man had been so coked out, he'd half fallen across the table as he did it, not that it took anything away from the win. Stu was the best even when he was so stoned he couldn't talk. The best.*

'Not that watch,' the kid said, 'the other one.'

One of the lawyers snorted, 'I think the Rolex is real, London, the other one is an old piece-of-crap Timex.'

London turned toward the speaker. 'You should study the game, Mr Michalak. Nobody's ever taken Shiny the Shark's Timex. I walk in any casino in the world wearing that watch, and somebody will stand up to give me a seat. Johnny Chan will walk across the room to shake my hand.'

Sarkisian felt the tiredness again, and with it the numbness in the neck and shoulder that the doctor said was the heart thing. 'Nah, I don't think so,' he said. *And waited, the trap set.*

The kid leaned forward, licked his upper lip. 'All in. I'll put all of it up. Twenty five versus the Timex. What do you say, Shiny?' He cupped his hands behind the big stacks of chips and pushed them forward a few inches.

Shiny looked at the pile. Thought about Miranda. He checked his cards again. The king and ace were still there. He laid the cards back on the table, nodded and fumbled to unstrap the watch with swollen fingers, and gave up, 'You want to help me, kid? My hands are a little slick.' He stuck out the arm with the watch. London's hands shook as he gently unstrapped the watch and laid it on top of the chips. Shiny's arm suddenly felt light, floating like a balloon without the watch to hold it down.

'But you haven't looked at your cards yet,' the lawyer said to the young man.

'It doesn't matter. From now on, it's between me and Shiny. The cards don't matter at all,' London answered.

Shiny smiled at the boy. 'You're good enough.' He flipped over his king of diamonds and the ace of spades. London turned over an ace of hearts and a queen of diamonds.

The kid smiled ruefully at the cards. 'If you'd brought twenty or thirty thousand, I'd already be home explaining to my dad how I lost his Lexus. Now I'm behind again.'

The dealer dealt two clubs, a four and a nine, and another spade

– a jack into the centre of the table. 'Looking good, Shiny,' said one of the lawyers. Shiny used his right arm to massage his left shoulder.

The dealer turned over a queen of hearts, giving London two queens against Shiny's ace high with one card left. London pumped his fists in the air, 'Yeah, baby.' There was quiet.

'What are Shiny's odds?' Bill asked the dealer.

Before she could answer, Shiny said, 'About seven per cent. Only three cards in the deck can help me.'

Shiny nodded to show the dealer he was ready, and tried to stand for the last card, tradition when you're all in and losing. The left leg refused to cooperate and he dropped back into the chair, exhausted. 'Are you OK, Shiny? You want to lie down on the sofa for a while after we get done with this hand?' said Brad.

'I'm great,' Shiny panted.

'Hey London, are you going to put your watch on the pile?' Brad asked.

'He doesn't need to,' Shiny said, 'pot's already right.'

London reached out and slowly unsnapped his watch, a stainless steel sportswatch. 'It's a Tag. I got it for high school graduation.' He dropped it on top of Shiny's Timex. 'It will make a better story this way.'

The dealer turned over the last card, a king of clubs. The colour drained from London's face. There was a perfect silence, the only sound the whirring of the overhead fan. Then Brad said, 'Bad beat, London, real bad beat.'

Shiny reached across the mountain of chips in the centre of the table, carefully picked up his Timex and strapped it on. Then just as carefully, he picked up the Tag Heuer and tossed it back to London, who caught it with two hands, surprised. 'There's your story, boy, The Shark gave you your watch back. Not many players can say that.'

Then he closed his eyes and let his hands hover over the chips, feeling their heat radiating up at him, enjoying their mass, his always temporary wealth. Wondering if this was it. The last big hand he would ever play. The last cash game. And if the ride to the airport with DZ in the Escalade would be the last time he rode out of a town in a green Cadillac leaving empty pockets and deflated egos behind him. Knowing it could well be.

He heard London stand up, thank the others for the game, and leave, but did not open his eyes. 'You OK, Shiny?' Brad asked finally.

'Sure, sure,' Shiny said, 'I'm great.'

♠

Pitch Black

Christopher Coake

1. Epics

NONE OF THIS WOULD HAVE HAPPENED if I hadn't gotten the guitar. How I came to own it is a brief, but epic, tale. You only need a few details:

Me, at sixteen, in 1987. The picture of the guitar in a battered catalogue. A summer spent out in an ag company's test field, cross-pollinating corn for minimum wage. A handful of dollars in a coffee can. Mom and Dad saying they'd pay half if I kept my grades up. Dad leaving at summer's end. Tears, recriminations, my secret shame: as I watched my father drive down our driveway and turn right towards the interstate, my mind held angry visions of the guitar – lost, I thought. Lost. My grades going in the tank. And then the blowout with Mom after she caught me and my buddy Dook smoking a joint up in the loft of the barn – the breeze blew the smoke right across the yard and into her open second-floor window. Mom in the barn in her bathrobe, screaming up: You stupid, stupid boys!

But from despair, triumph! Mom and I at counselling: She told the therapist how she felt threatened by the changes in me. The long hair, the goatee, the black T-shirts with the skeletons. That awful music she heard in my room. And then the drugs. I told her that in the wake of losing my father I just wanted to be different. That I was frustrated. That my music wasn't about Satan, that it was really just about being angry. The therapist – major dumbshit – nodded like his head was on a spring. It's important for the children of divorce to be able to express themselves fully, he said. Just as Daryl is trying to do now.

My voice trembled for the big finish: That's why I've been saving for the *guitar*.

And so that next weekend, on a Saturday morning, Mom walked into the living room and told me to get showered. We were going to Indy, she said. I grumbled – Dook wanted me to come over and hang – but she had that look. Once we were in the car, she drove me to get a hamburger, and we chatted nicely, and then afterwards she pulled into the parking lot outside IRC Music. My breathing stopped, a little.

She sat still behind the wheel. It was raining and you could smell the water and steam outside the car.

I know you haven't had much, she said. And it's going to be tight for a while. But I want you to have something that feels like *yours*. Like Dr Markham said. She gazed at the shop's windows, at the guitars hung by their necks. Her face got tight. She said, Maybe someday soon you'll write a song for me?

Her voice went up at the end, like someone was bending the note.

Yeah, Mom, I said, raspy. Sure.

She followed me inside. There were of course four other dudes in the guitar room, all of them big and hairy and tattooed. They looked at me and my mother and I could see they all knew the score. One guy towards the back was shredding a Jackson to fucking pieces, head banging, hair whipping up and down. Mom stared at him like he was killing a goat.

This one, I told her, pointing towards the wall before she lost her nerve. And, like a pussy: if it's not too much.

There it was, in the so-to-speak flesh. An Ibanez RGX. Glossy black – black headstock, black pickguard, black pointy horns. The sort of black that reflected light in a gleam but that swallowed up images. A Floyd Rose tremolo (black!), big frets and a thin neck for speed. A metal forge, that guitar.

She said, It's very pretty, isn't it?

I have to get an amp, too, I said. I knew this would surprise her, so I added: I can pay for that.

No, she said. I have a new credit card. I want you to have these things.

Seriously. She dropped a grand on me, almost but not quite crying the entire time.

I'd spent two summers looking over the catalogue picture of that Ibanez. In the meanwhile I practised on Dad's old beat-up Kay acoustic, which was shitty even if all you wanted to do was play "Johnny Crack Corn" – which I didn't. My buddy Dook had a decent bass and a piss-poor old electric whose tuners wobbled; sometimes I'd use that when we practised together. We knew a guy, Paulie, who could drum. With my new guitar and amp, we'd be a *band*. A crushing trio. Our name – we'd already decided – was going to be Pitch Black. Dook and I had already drawn up the mascot who'd be on all our album covers: a little black imp with a pitchfork. On the cover of our first album he'd be sitting on a hot chick's shoulder, grinning, the angel from the other shoulder impaled on the fork. I hadn't shown the designs to Mom.

Didn't matter. Mom paid, signed the slip. Her hand shook a little. Rock on, the ponytailed counter guy said, and I wanted to be his best friend. I reached to pick up the case and the amp – both of them wicked fucking heavy – and I nearly teared up, too. The big dude with the Jackson saw me walking out with my new axe. He grinned and flashed me the horns, but by then I was cool enough just to lift my chin a little. We were, I figured, equals.

That night I drove my new gear over to Dook's without telling him what was up. His eyes bugged out of his head when he saw the long case hanging from my hand. Dude, he said. He wailed: *Dude!*

We called Paulie and set up out in the barn. I slung that axe around my neck and watched it catch the yellow overhead light – we were in an old hayrick, where rusty tools and hooks hung abbatoirish from the rafters; we'd been banished from the house, of course, but the sound was good out there: the barn's damp old wood soaked up the sound pretty well, made metal sound chunky and wet. While we waited for Paulie I did what I'd been dreaming of for two years: I plugged in, cranked up the amp, and hit a power chord. The sound shook the air, buzzed in my head. I took that chord everywhere with the whammy bar. Dook's eyes lit up; my heart thumped. We played "War Pigs" together, slow, sludgy. Paulie appeared in the doorway towards the end, holding a snare to his chest, and watched us in awe.

We practised day and night for two months. After every practice I wiped down the Ibanez – which I had named Mephisto – and laid it carefully in its case. Some guys called their axes by girls' names, but not me. This guitar was bigger than sex. Some guys covered their axes with stickers, let them grow scratched and worn. Not me. Mephisto was an other-worldly being, and I handled it accordingly.

Was I a bad son? I was not. I wrote a little acoustic ditty, something sweet, melodic, and ran it through the clean channel, and then, because Mom cried when I played it for her, and because she asked, I had Dook help me record it to a four-track, so she could play it in her car when she drove to work.

Don't tell anyone, I told him.

But Dook liked Mom, and said, Dude, that woman made Pitch Black happen. He pulled on his cigarette and said: Do another take, and don't fuck up the last arpeggios this time.

I helped out around the house. I'd feel the old surliness in me, then think of Mom putting her credit card on the counter, and I'd snap to. Sometimes on Friday nights I'd tell the guys I'd be over late, so I could sit with Mom and watch *When Harry Met Sally* on the VCR.

I've never seen you so dedicated to something, she said, more than once. Proudly. And she'd look at me like I was just a little kid again, not a wild child with long hair and a bad goatee and sadness trailing the both of us like trash following wind through a gutter.

I felt like a new man, it's true. Before the guitar, I used to sit and listen to my headphones and not do shit. After, though, I came home from school with my heart beating hard and heavy, my fingers already flicking around in the air. I rushed to Mephisto. Tuned it, strummed it. At night I dreamed about playing. My white fingers against the black rosewood of the fretboard. The precise gleaming grid of steel strings over frets. Scales. Solos. I dreamed myself making music.

Before I got the guitar I'd never dreamed anything that didn't seem to live a thousand years away, on some icy island.

Then, two months after Mephisto came to live with me, my mother said, Daryl, I'm going to fly to California to visit your Aunt Sarah. Do you want to go?

I'd better not, I said – imagining the house to myself, imagining a whole weekend with the guitar: empty rooms, high volume. Maybe a Pitch Black rehearsal in the living room. It was getting cold outside at night, and playing in Dook's barn was getting more and more uncomfortable. I told Mom, I've got trig to study for.

My boy, she said, and kissed my head. Well, she said. Have the boys over, if you want – but no drinking, and don't play too loud. Mr Pritchett doesn't like it.

And herein lies another epic, quickly told.

We lived in an old farmhouse, miles from anything. The house sat in the middle of a vast three-acre lawn. (Which I spent my summers mowing endlessly, thank you.) To the south, east, and west were mile-wide cornfields.

Our only neighbour lived to the north, and that was Mr Pritchett. Old Billy.

His land was the same size as ours, except it was the exact opposite; our house was white, shining, clean, restored, sitting square in the middle of our expertly-mowed lawn. Billy's three acres were forested, like some fairy-tale thicket, wherein ogres kept a lair. His house crouched in the middle, barely visible, but I knew – Dook and I had sneaked up to it one afternoon, when Billy had driven his groaning pickup to town – that it was crumbling, grey from lack of paint, barely a place a man could live.

We almost never talked to Billy. He was – my mother's words – a troubled man. He'd fought in World War Two, and was, according to everyone, badly shell-shocked.

What this meant was that, every now and again, Billy would see things. And when he saw things, deep in his thicket, he'd shout at them. And then sometimes he would try to shoot them.

Once, two years before, just after we'd moved in, my father sent me out to repair the fence between our yard and Billy's. It may have been Billy's fence – no one knew for sure – but it had come apart, and my father, figuring Billy would not care for it, decided I'd spend an afternoon restringing the barbed wire and digging new postholes.

This I did, cursing and listening to Helloween on my Walkman. Then, near dusk, I looked up and screeched: because there was Old Billy on the other side of the fence, framed by the grasping trees of his woods, staring at me, and holding a rifle.

He was a squat block of a man, wearing torn overalls and unlaced boots, his hair yellow-white. He smelled like the inside of a barn – a barn where pigs live. He had binoculars slung around his neck. He held at port arms against his shoulder. It had a scope. I imagined myself in its sights.

Hello, Daryl, said Billy.

Hi there, Billy, I said. I'm just fixing the fence here. Hope you don't mind.

Billy looked down at the fence, as though surprised. Thank you kindly, he said. I was getting around to that.

Yeah, I said, no trouble.

We stared at each other.

Well Daryl, Billy said, Just thought I'd let you know. I'm going to go hunt the spirits tonight.

I probably stopped smiling. The spirits?

Yep. They been doing recon out here. I seen 'em. I know they want me, but I'd hate for 'em to come up on you or your Mama.

Yeah, I said, we don't want that.

Maybe you'd best head on to the house.

Thank you Billy, I said, and turned right then and there, abandoning the tools.

That night we listened to the gunfire from Billy's woods. We sat on the front porch – on the other side of the house from Billy's line of fire – huddled under a blanket. We listened to the shots, and then to Billy's furious, high-pitched scream:

Goddamn it! It's nineteen-eighty-two, you leave me alone!

And after that, gunshots, one after another, and a final shriek, a sound that didn't even try to become words.

The next day my father went to the sheriff.

The sheriff said, That Billy, he's a good old boy. I drive out and check on him. He takes his pills and he keeps his guns clean.

But the shooting, my father said.

As long as a man shoots on his own property, I've got no problem with him. I imagine he thinks he's protecting you.

My father protested some more, but the sheriff finally said, Fred, Old Billy's got a Silver Star and a Purple Heart. I hear he was one of the first Americans to see Dachau. His kids leave him to rot. He wants to keep fighting the war, I'm inclined to let him do it.

That was Billy. He'd told her – she often brought him vegetables from the garden – that he knew already about my guitar. He heard it some nights, he said. Daryl's a good boy, he said, But I'll be gol-darned if that music of his don't hurt my head.

Remember, she said. Low volume.

Gol-darned if I turn it up, I said, and made a face, so at least she'd leave smiling.

II. Party at Foul's

With my mother on her plane to California, on a Friday night, I called Dook and Paulie. Come over, I said. I've got the place to myself.

While waiting for them, I set up my amp in the middle of my father's old upstairs study, now bare and echoey. I slung the Ibanez's strap over my shoulder. What my mother didn't know was that when she was gone, I took the full-length mirror that hung from the inside of her closet door and leaned it against the study's wall and watched myself play: dressed in black, like my axe, my hair falling over my eyes. I sneered at myself. My stage name was going to be Lord Foul, after the villain in some fantasy novels I'd started reading but had never finished. The hero in those books was called The Unbeliever, which was cool, but not as cool as Lord Foul. I needed some pale makeup, but I hadn't had the guts to go shop for it yet.

I turned the amp up until I could feel my jawbone humming. Louder than I'd ever taken it before. Something in me was afraid of the sound I'd make. I pushed that something down. I lifted my pick and brought it down onto a perfect power chord.

The sound was almost a wind, almost a push in the back. The mirror rattled in its frame; the picture of sneering me shuddered, distorted. It was like I'd done it with my mind.

Dook arrived an hour later. I hadn't heard him. He walked up the stairs.

Dude, he said, when I'd stopped playing. Billy's shooting.

I turned off the amp and we opened the study's windows. Outside it was dusk. We listened, until we heard the pop of Billy's rifle. I waited for shouting, but it never came.

How loud was I? I asked.

Not too bad, Dook said. Then he busted out laughing. I could totally hear you from the car.

I pulled the blinds down. Just in case, I said.

Dook set up his bass, and the two of us played for a while. Paulie was late, as usual. We talked, as we often did, about how if Paulie didn't play the drums so well we'd have to kick his fucking ass. We drank a couple of beers that Dook had smuggled from his father's refrigerator.

It was ten at night when things seriously changed.

We were sitting cross-legged in the middle of the study, trying to work out a riff, when we heard a car horn from the drive near the front of the house. We crossed the hall into my room and looked out into the drive. There we saw a car we didn't recognize: a black Firebird. It pulled up next to Dook's Torino and the horn sounded again and then the doors opened and four people got out. Paulie was one of them. The other three we didn't know.

Paulie saw me at the window and held up two paper sacks that, judging from the look on his face, held liquor. Then he pointed at the other people with him. Two were girls, I could see. The other was a big man with long blond hair.

What the fuck? I said.

Got me, Dook said.

Paul shouted something. It was *Party!* Then he made metal horns in the air with both hands.

Paulie didn't go to our school. He was from Westover, which was what passed, in our parts, as a city. He went to Westover High with the gangs and the reprobates, and we didn't entirely trust him. He'd asked us, once, if we'd ever gone out cowtipping. Apart from being dumb, he was annoying and hyperactive and spent so much time assuring us he wasn't on speed that we just assumed he was.

The other people had to be Westover kids, I figured, friends of Paul's. Like any good cowtipper I knew to be afraid of them.

Dook might have had the same misgivings, but he turned to me and said, Booze and chicks, man. That rocks.

This was true.

We went downstairs. Paulie was staring through the window of the kitchen door with the same bugged-out maniac eyes he'd been practising for Pitch Black's first album cover. Then he giggled like a girl.

I opened the door. Paul held out his fist and I smacked it. Dude, he said. Party time at Foul's.

Paulie, I said. I looked past him at the others. I recognized the man, and in my head – and almost out loud – I said, Oh shit.

Dook looked past me and saw what I saw. Fuck me, he said.

I believe you gentlemen know Lars, Paul said. And this is Bethany, and this is Toni.

Lars. We knew Lars, oh yes we did. He shambled into the house, and he didn't smile at me or even look at me – he just pushed past me into the kitchen. Lars Van Der Velde, aka The Red Baron. The Baron was six foot six, maybe two-sixty. Probably all still muscle. Dressed in a black leather vest, black jeans, with studded wristbands and giant buckled boots. He was six years older than us. He'd played O-line for Westover until they kicked him off the team after an assault conviction. Then he went to juvie for pot possession. He spent several years in exile. Then he came back to Westover and started a metal band: Whorefrost. The Red Baron was the singer and rhythm guitarist. Except he didn't sing. He and his guitar *roared*, like animals in unison, the Baron's throat so sandpapered it made the air in front of his amps seem misty with blood.

Dook and Paulie and I knew this because a month before we had snuck into Whorefrost's last show of the summer, at a warehouse on the edge of Westover, after an elaborate operation to convince our parents we'd gone camping. There was no question we had to do this. The Baron had spent the first ten years of his life in Sweden, before his father came to Indy to work at Eli Lilly, and the years of his exile, too. It was common knowledge among the metalheads of Sharpe County that the Baron was part of Sweden's black metal scene; he knew, it was said, the guys in Mayhem. Mayhem! We'd heard that he'd once partied with Hellhammer himself, that he'd been allowed to touch Hellhammer's necklace, made of fragments of human skull. It was said the Baron had helped burn churches.

The metal bands of Westover – of all northern Indiana – were posers. But not Whorefrost. Everyone knew it. The warehouse crowd knew it. The Baron made them real, dangerous. We stood in the warehouse with a hundred other long-haired guys and leather chicks, all of us staring at each other with joy and terror. Then the Baron and the rest of the band stalked onstage.

Fuck you fuckers, said the Baron into his mike – the last intelligible thing he said till after the show. He spat into the crowd and then screamed and began to pummel the guitar.

Whorefrost, live, was a literal assault. The crowd started fighting the moment the bass drums started churning. I was struck in the head almost immediately and hit someone else in retaliation. My nose bled and I think my ears did too. In the big echoing warehouse I couldn't even hear the guitarists' chords; different songs were more like changes in air pressure. The Baron thrashed his guitar – a black, battered Flying V – with his bare muscled arms bulging, his legs spread, his hair stuck to the sweat on his face. He had a swastika tattooed on one bicep and the SS insignia on the other. If he'd bitten the head off a groupie – and there were groupies who would have let him – none of us would have been surprised.

The police came and shut everything down after four songs, and we were lucky we hadn't been drinking. While I was waiting to be breathalyzed I saw the Baron leering at a big beefy-necked cop. The cop stood impassively while the handcuffed Baron roared and stuck out his tongue and wagged it obscenely and growled, Piggy Piggy Piggy. They maced him and put him in the paddywagon.

And here he was. The Red *fucking* Baron stood in my kitchen. He looked angry – but then I'd never seen him look anything but angry. His hands were in the pockets of his vest, and he smelled like ten years' worth of cigarettes and booze. His eyes were red, the lids around them puffy and bleary. On his hip was a large leather knife case. A tattoo of a clawed red devil hand reached out of his collar and circled half his throat, his Adam's apple bulging just above the joint of the thumb, like Hell itself was choking him, pulling him down.

Hey Lars, I said. How's it going?

This is not a party, he said. His voice was deep and growly and had a Europe-y rubber band bounce to it. For my own safety I tried not to think of the Swedish Chef going *bork bork bork*.

I had to be cool.

Now that you guys are here, I said, it is.

The Baron sneered at me. Don't suck my dick, he said. Then: You, Paul, give me that fucking whisky.

The Baron was so impressive that for two or three minutes, even after they'd filed into the kitchen behind him, I'd neglected to check out the girls. But then I noticed what Paulie and Dook had already: that they were impressive too.

One was tall and blonde and old, by which I mean not in high school. Or maybe she was, still, at Westover, where they weren't afraid to fail the failures. She looked twenty. She was dressed in a leather jacket and leather boots and a black skirt, and her legs were in torn fishnets. Her lips were very red and a little smeary. Her hair was teased out like a firework exploding. Her breasts pushed dangerously out of her jacket. She smiled at me but not with her eyes.

Paul – so proud I thought he might rub his hands together – said, This is Bethany.

You introduced us already, she said to Paul. Her eyes flicked over him and then away. She stood by the Baron, and the Baron – who had found a steak knife in the dish drainer and was cutting at the wax seal on his bottle of whisky – casually reached down and squeezed one of her buttocks.

The other girl stood closest to me. She smiled and said Hey. Toni, I remembered. She was in boots and a skirt too, but was smaller, younger – probably younger than me and Dook. Her hair was dyed black and she had on little glasses and wore a choker.

Toni's from Alaska, Paul said.

I'm Bethany's cousin, Toni said to me, like she needed to explain her way into the house, like she'd gone somewhere cool, and not a farmhouse in the exact geographical centre of BFE.

No problem, I said. I might as well play the expansive host. Glad you could make it.

This *isn't* a fucking party, the Baron said again. Toni winced a little. Paulie stared openly at her breasts, which were, admittedly under a tight black sweater and amazing.

Paul, I said, come here for a second.

I took Paul to the living room. Behind me I heard Dook pick up the slack: Dude, we totally caught your warehouse show—

Dude, Paulie whispered, call over some guys, quick.

What the fuck, Paulie? The *Baron*?

I know I know. I was totally putting a move on Toni down at the park – and she's so fucking hot, oh my fucking *God* – and then she introduces me to her cousin, says This is my cousin Bethany and I'm like oh fuck that's the *Baron's girl.* And then the Baron's right there! And we all like talked for a while? And then I passed around a joint you know to like chill everyone out? And then I remembered your Mom's gone – right?

Fuck, I said.

So we've got to make this a party, he said.

No no no, I said. Not the Baron. Not here. Seriously. He'll torch the place when he sees how fucking hopeless we are. And we'd deserve it.

Dude. Paul did everything but grab my hand. Think about it. OK? *Tonight! Whorefrost!* with opening act Pitch Black…

I stared at him, and he stared back, nodding.

He was right. Little twerp or not, Paulie'd found an opportunity and capitalized. Whorefrost was the only metal band in the entire northern half of Indiana that had any sort of future. If the Baron chose to help us, we were made. We could either bounce around like dumbfucks in his audience or we could make a play for his stage.

I'll get on the horn, I said.

*

Another thing you should know: I didn't have many friends. I was skinny and intense and didn't like to speak much in groups. I wanted instead to stand up in front of groups and play my guitar and let my hair hide my eyes. To be sound, a force, a metal god. To that end I spent all my time inside my room, practising the guitar. Or with Dook, who I'd known since I was six, back before I knew what bravery was. I wanted groupies to pile on top of me backstage, but in the meantime I was generally too frightened of any woman not my mother to do much other than gawk. I know this isn't really unusual. But it goes a way toward explaining why, at sixteen years old, I couldn't get on the phone and summon twenty party-minded teenagers to my mother's empty house.

I tried the numbers of everyone I knew. Almost all of them were gone. It was a Friday night; they were probably all out drinking at the Westover park where Paulie'd met the Baron. The fifth number I called with trepidation; it belonged to a fat metalhead kid we all knew, who sat with us at lunch and not much else. He answered and in the background I heard Ozzy's wail. When I told him that the Baron was in my house he told me I must be as high as he was.

Dook – who knew all the same people I did, or didn't – walked into the room. I told him the score.

Dude, Dook whispered. What are we going to do?

Fuck if I know, I said. Play cards?

This was what Dook and Paulie and I usually did, when practice was over, or when we'd roused a couple of other guys from their lairs: we sat up late and played poker, usually for the same twenty bucks that changed hands week after week after week.

Dook leaned in. If you suggest cards to the Baron, he'll kill you. If I don't first.

Let's stall, I said. Say people are on the way. I'll keep trying.

Dook said, We can talk music.

That might work.

Dook glanced at the door to the kitchen and tittered. Then we joined the others.

One party, I said, coming up.

The Baron was rooting through the kitchen cabinets. He pulled out a box of saltines and opened it up and then threw a stack of crackers into his maw. He washed them down with a swig from the whisky bottle he held in his hand.

Paulie was chattering, still, about how awesome it was to have everyone around. I could have smacked him.

Bethany, who had been trying hard not to meet anyone's eyes, said to the Baron, You fucking pig. Are you gonna share the booze?

He grinned at her and spat a showerful of cracker crumbs at her. She and Toni both dodged the spray.

No, the Baron said, and cackled. He looked up at me. You. Monkey boy. He tossed me a bundle of keys, which I bobbled for a second but just managed to catch. He said, Go to the trunk and bring in the other bottles. And don't touch anything else.

Dook went with me. Once we were outside we were both struck by the silence in the air. It was us and the crickets and not much else. My house, as I've said, was a long way from anything – it got quiet out there, quiet and dark.

Shh, I said. Dook knew why. We turned to Old Billy's woods and listened. I scanned the trees for signs of his house lights – if they were off, sometimes that meant he was in his woods. I saw nothing. I looked across the yard at the dark wall of trees. For all I knew Billy was watching us through his rifle scope. I shivered, as I always did.

Dude, Dook said, reading my thoughts. Do you think Billy'd ever tell on you? Like if we *do* have a party? Would he tell your mother?

I don't know, I said. I'm not even sure what he sees.

That Toni's hot as fuck, Dook said. But Bethany…

He looked confused, like he hadn't meant to say this out loud.

She looks kind of used, I said.

Yeah, Dook said. That's it. You'd think the Baron—

I don't know, I said. I'd asked myself the same question. But then again, I said, what's he doing out here? With us?

Dook nodded and scratched his scalp.

We opened the Baron's trunk. There were no fewer than three bottles of Hardscrabble whisky in the back, in a mostly-empty box marked with the same name. A stolen case, I bet. We took the bottles out. That's when I noticed: behind the box was a guitar case, and next to it a beat-up amp. Dude, I said.

Dook looked up at the kitchen windows, where we saw the Baron gesturing with his open bottle. The open trunk hid us from sight.

Open it, Dook whispered.

I slid the case forward and flipped the latches. The inside of the case smelled awful, like cigarettes and booze, but also like vomit, or garbage. And pot. In fact, it smelled a lot like what I imagined Hell would. Dark stains covered the felt.

Dude's *so* evil, Dook said.

So was the Baron's guitar. That Flying V looked like a weapon. A used spear, blood-red and nicked. He'd carved things in it. 'The Red Baron'. 'FUCK'. '666'.

Dook closed his eyes and reached down and touched the strings. He whispered, You too, dude. Get some of this mojo.

I closed my eyes and touched the guitar. I almost expected it to burn me. But it was cold and silent. I twanged the high E, and then, sadly, we closed the case, and the trunk, and walked up to the house bearing the Baron's whisky.

We all stood drinking in the kitchen for maybe forty minutes. The Baron took the bottles from us and said, One for me, one for Bethy, one for the little kiddies. He and Bethany cackled. I poured shots for the rest of us into green plastic cups. I watched Toni drink hers, hoping she'd show the distress I was trying to hide. She drank like a pro. But she was from Alaska, where shit, I guessed, must be pretty hardcore.

We'd have been lost without Paulie. For once his motor was useful. He knew people the Baron and Bethany knew. He kept asking the Baron about bands he liked, or didn't. About guys he used to play football with. The Baron kept pounding back shots and grunting answers. Every now and again he'd ask, Where is the fucking party?

Soon, I kept saying. And he kept drinking, straight from the bottle. His second. It was amazing. And terrifying. My grandfather could drink that much, but he'd had a whole lifetime to practise.

Dook and I talked to Toni. I asked her what Alaska was like.

She sat at the kitchen table, legs crossed, her tights stretched just enough to show a ghost of white skin at her knees. Different, she said. I'm from a little town. It's called Unalakleet.

She made us say it. We did. We were both buzzed, and this took us several tries.

In Unalakleet, she told us, it was dark half the year. There were no roads in or out – to go anywhere you had to fly out, by seaplane. She slept, she said, between two Samoyed dogs, which had been bred to keep arctic people warm. The man who owned the video store was the richest person in the town. The Iditarod stopped there. The pizza delivery place brought pizzas uncooked, via snowmobile; it was too cold to bring them from the oven. She kept smiling as she told us all of this.

We're all pretty bored with each other, she said. It's always nice to come to Indiana.

First time anyone's ever said that, I said.

No! It's true. It's so warm here. Indianapolis is the biggest city I've ever seen.

What kind of music do you like? Dook asked her.

Lots of kinds. Classical, mostly. I play the harp.

Dook and I looked at each other.

Bethy sent me some of Lars's tapes, Toni said. It's sure something.

It's very pure genius, the Baron said, overhearing. Little Toni, you should learn that. We are metal gods!

We've got a band, Paulie said. Hell yeah.

Dook and I tensed. We'd of course kept taking the temperature of the conversation the whole time, waiting for the right moment to bring it up.

The Baron didn't laugh. No shit, he said. That's very fucking fascinating.

What kind of band? Toni asked.

Metal, I said.

Oh. Cool. She smiled at me. I pledged in my mind to write a ballad for her, call it "Warm at Night".

Metal, said the Baron, flat as concrete. You three. He stared at us each in turn. So what's your very evil name? he asked.

Pitch Black, Paulie said.

It was, I realized, hearing it on Paulie's lips, the worst possible name a band could ever have.

We chose it, Paulie said, because—

We're still deciding, I said.

Good thing, the Baron said. He looked at me. You must be the brains of this operation.

Guitarist, I said. Tried to laugh off the insult.

Paulie said, Lord Foul here just got a new axe. It's *awsome.*

For the first time the Baron showed a glimmer of interest in something beside the whisky and Bethany's asscheeks. He leaned at me a little. What kind?

Ibanez, I said. Not as good as... as yours, but it's nice.

It's here?

Upstairs, I said.

He drank again. Show me.

So the six of us filed up the narrow creaky stairwell. Even counting what happened later on – I don't think I've ever seen anything in my life as strange as the Red Baron thudding his way up the stairs of my house, all that creaking black leather moving past the wallpaper, which had little windmills and cows printed on it. The same stairs where I used to stage crashes with my Matchbox cars. The stairs I'd fallen down once and broken a wrist. Under the Red Baron's boots! Paulie kept nudging me in the ribs, muttering, Awesome, Awesome!

We all walked into the empty upstairs den. The Baron looked at

Mephisto on its stand, and the amp, and the chair. Then – I'd forgotten – he turned and saw the full-length mirror I'd neglected to return to my mother's room. He stared, and smiled, and I could see the insults lining up at the base of his tongue. I flushed red. But he said nothing.

He peeked past the drawn shades, into the dark. This the woodshed? he asked.

Such as it is.

It's a cool axe. Fire it up.

I wasn't bad. I really wasn't. We could make some noise, the three of us in the band, and when I was alone I could make even more. But in that moment, with the Red Baron staring me down, with beautiful Toni from cold Unalakleet standing next to Paulie and ignoring him to look me over – smiling, like I could give her something to remember – I found I could barely curl my fingers, let alone walk over to my beloved axe and pick it up and play.

But I did. I made myself.

I turned on the power. The amp hummed. I tuned for a second, my cheeks burning. I tried to remember something decent. Metallica was too obvious. Slayer too hard. Sabbath too easy. Van Halen too gay. I knew a Whorefrost riff, but if I tried that I might as well fall down on my knees and get to dick-sucking. Megadeth, maybe. 'Peace Sells'. I took a deep breath and tore into it, looked at the fretboard and not everyone else. I fumbled a couple of times but did all right, even got my hair flying a bit by the end. Then I played a bluesy solo.

I looked up. Toni smiled, Bethany smirked, Dook was opening his eyes – looking like we'd all just avoided being in a horrible car accident – and Paulie was so gleeful I wanted to hit him. The Baron smiled. A little.

Give me that thing, he said. You're hurting my poor widdle ears.

There was nothing to do but hand it over.

He slung the strap over his shoulder. The guitar perched high up on his chest, like he was some wispy English bass player. No one laughed. I thought of the back of the axe rubbing against the zipper of the Baron's leather jacket. I should have said something, but I didn't.

The Baron turned to the amp and fiddled with the knobs, dialling himself in with long practice. Struck a couple of chords that right away made me wince. No fumbling, no hesitation. His pick hand steady and fierce. He fiddled some more. Hit a monster power chord, nodded, turned the fucking thing all the way up.

Then he played. Went right for the kill – Slayer, 'Raining Blood'. My Ibanez, all at once, became a fucking chainsaw. A machine gun spitting out red death. Bethany began to do a stuttering kind of dance. Toni clapped her hands over her ears. Paul began, spastically, to air drum in the corner. Dook and I looked at each other. We looked at the Baron. His thick fingers pattered up and down the fretboard, and he never glanced at them once. His face serene, almost. No stage snarl here. Just a guy playing, and playing well.

He left Slayer and went into one of his own compositions. Bending, soaring notes. Tapping and harmonics. Riffs like lava. I glanced at Toni and she smiled, sheepishly, hands still over her ears.

I should tell you now. Nothing happened with Toni. Like a lot of things that night, any plans I had for her fell apart at the end. But she smiled, right at the moment of my humiliation, and that smile I will never forget. It was the smile I needed, kind and understanding and embarrassed, with me but not for me. We both knew I wasn't the Baron, but we both knew, too, that a girl like Toni didn't need the Baron, didn't want to be around the Baron. She went back to Alaska when it was all over and is probably up there now, in her little Unalakleet, or maybe she got out, to Anchorage or even Seattle. I hope she's married and happy. I know she remembers us. I do wonder what she thinks of me.

The Baron wrapped it up. He grabbed for a high note and shook the fucking hell of it, as fast as if he'd had the whammy bar in his hands. Then he stopped and closed his eyes and we all listened to the note hold and die.

What could we do? We clapped. The Baron didn't acknowledge us, but you could tell he felt the clapping was his due.

Fucking awesome! Paulie shouted.

The Baron looked at me. This guitar has promise, he said. It's a very good axe. Nice sustain and the pickups are hot. You keep practising. If you suck it won't be the machine's fault.

He meant it as a joke. Even cracked a little smile.

Then he said: More whisky! Paul, where's my fucking bottle?

We stood and watched the Baron drink. Except for the glugging from the bottle, there was no sound.

It was then we heard the gunshots outside. One, two, three. And following them, a shrill cry. So Old Billy *was* still up, riled, hunting the spirits. That was twice, now, that loud metal had aroused him. What did we sound like, to him? Hell's music? I remembered his glasses, his inscrutable, squashed face.

I reached behind me and turned out the light. Maybe it was a little theatrical of me, but all the same I felt safer that way.

What the fuck? the Baron said.

I explained, quickly: My neighbour, shell-shock, the ghosts of the war.

Dude's a fucking nutcase, Paulie said.

That poor guy, Toni said.

Open the window, said the Baron, eyes wide.

I should have refused, but I didn't. I opened the blind and slid open the rickety window, all the way. A half-moon shone down just enough to differentiate the darkness of Old Billy's woods from the shadowed expanse of our lawn. The crickets were shrilling, everywhere, almost sounding like overdriven high notes. Then we heard another shot, and another, and after it Old Billy yelling: *Run! Run you murdering sons of bitches!*

The war, eh? said the Baron. Which war?

World War Two, I whispered. I think he fought in Europe.

So did my grandfather, said the Baron. He was half-German. Fucking killed in battle, protecting the Aryan race.

The Baron said this with dignity and some pride. We stared at him, all of us. I remember being shocked. But what had I thought? That a guy with a Nazi tattoo – the Red fucking Baron – was just kidding?

Fuck him, the Baron said. And that was when I realized how drunk he'd been getting. Deeply and sickly drunk. His eyes narrowed to piggy slits. He snarled: Fuck him and fuck this terrible boring stupid fucking country! He drank from the bottle again and wiped his lips. Then he leaned close to the window screen. He took a deep breath and stage-roared into the night: Sieg Heil! Sieg Heil! Stupid Yank motherfucker! The thousand-year Reich will never run! Sieg Heil! We were shocked, all of us, crouched and numb and shocked. Toni held a hand to her mouth. Bethany closed her eyes, pretending, maybe, she hadn't heard. What went on in her head I never knew, not even when things were over.

There was a long silence. Then the gunshots came again, one after another. And between them Old Billy's piercing shriek.

The Baron stood. His eyes gleamed in the darkness, and he chuckled.

Slowly, without anyone suggesting it, we filed out of the den, back downstairs, into the lighted living room. The Baron was already leaving his stench behind him – the room smelled of smoke and booze.

So, he said in the kitchen. Now what? Aren't some more people supposed to come? Mr Virtuoso, where is this very excellent party?

All heads swivelled to look at me.

I made the calls, I said.

Fucking A, said the Baron. He belched. No one's coming, are they? There's no fucking party here. I'm bored. Beth, Toni, come on – fuck this place.

The Baron, swaying a bit, began to feel in his jacket pockets for his keys.

Paulie and Dook and I exchanged glances, and then all of us turned to Toni, who stared at the Baron in horror. It was ten miles to Westover, either down windy roads or along I-65, which on a weekend night was going to be packed full of cars. We – I, at least – thought of the girls' bodies, pulled bloody from the wreckage of the Baron's Firebird.

And, because I am who I am, I still imagined us on stage, still saw us on tour with Whorefrost, if only we could show the Baron, asshole that he was, a good time. Sometimes, I thought, sacrifices needed to be made. So the Baron was a fucking racist loon, and a drunk driver to boot. He could still get us where we needed to go, couldn't he?

I looked at Paulie, waited for him to say something good, but either the incident upstairs or the booze had done him in; his mouth opened and shut but nothing came out. Dook was glowering, looking at me.

Toni took the lead.

Maybe we'd better stay, she said to the Baron. You – none of us – should be driving.

Fuck that, the Baron said. I'm fine. He belched again, meaning to, waited for us to laugh, and then leered at Toni. You could see the ideas working on the surface of his mind.

Wait, he said. You like these little monkey boys? Eh?

I waited for Toni to throw us under the bus.

They're nice, Lars. Come on, it's late. Let's just crash till morning.

Fuck them. We're very gone.

Seriously, Bethany said, giving her cousin a stare that could slice rope.

I thought as fast as I could. Dook's got some weed, I said. And there's – I hesitated, thinking of my mother's private stash of vodka – there's a lot more booze here.

Dook slumped.

Yeah, he said, I got a dimebag out in my car.

Well now, said the Baron, suddenly expansive. This is a *very* different situation. So we smoke some weed, mellow out. Then what? Watch monkey boy play his guitar some more? Do each other's nails?

Paulie found himself again. Dude! he said. We could play cards.

III. What Was at Stake

This was how, some twenty minutes later, we sat around the coffee table in the living room, watching the Baron roll himself an entirely too-large joint from Dook's meagre weed. We watched the joint lit, and then passed back and forth between the Baron and Bethany. While this happened I shuffled and reshuffled a tattered old deck.

I don't want to play a stupid fucking game, the Baron said.

Come on, Lars, Toni said, singsong. Play! she cried. She was not only a little drunk – she had told us that the folks in Unalakleet, by necessity, were expert card sharks. How else to pass the long winter darkness? She'd kicked off her boots, and one of her warm stockinged feet touched about a millimeter of my left thigh.

The Baron took a drag, held it, and said, Fuck.

Come on.

On a Saturday night I'm playing a game with children.

I could see how it seemed that way. We'd all learned, to our chagrin, that we were broke. For betting I'd been reduced to emptying out the change jar I kept up in my room. Dook was, at that moment, dividing up equal piles of pennies, nickels, and dimes.

I decided it was best to keep things moving. What's our game? I asked.

Strip? Paulie asked, eyeing Toni's breasts. She sighed.

The Baron reached over – faster than a man smoking a joint had any right to move – and grabbed the front of Paulie's shirt. He then brought his fist, knuckles down, onto the top of Paulie's head. Toni let out a squeak. The Baron wore a lot of ornate rings – skulls, demon heads, that sort of thing. Paulie didn't scream – I give him that – but when the Baron released him Paulie clapped a hand to his head, eyes watering and downcast.

Little boy, the Baron said, I can see Bethany's titties without having to play cards for them. And little Toni will not show you hers. We play for money, or we do not play.

Dook – who'd looked a little excited when Paulie'd said 'strip', nodded right away. Money, sure, he said. We're ready to go.

Right on, I said.

Right on, the Baron said, Like a fucking hippie. This is not money. Get me some paper.

I gave him the message pad from beside the phone. He wrote out 'FIFTY DOLLARS' on six sheets of paper, and handed one to each of us. These are your markers, he said. Each of you sign it. The coins are our chips. Pennies are one dollar, nickels five, dimes ten.

I tried my best not give anything away with my face. Playing for real, huh? I asked.

The Baron grimaced at me. Very fucking real, monkey boy.

All right then, I said, and signed my slip.

Another thing you should know: I was, then, pretty good at poker. Mom and Dad, before the divorce, had trained me during years' worth of weekly family games. I had a natural poker face, and, thanks to Dad, I could calculate odds fairly well. He and I used to play for chores. This was why I mowed the lawn, almost every time. But I'd win against my friends more often than not, when drunkenness wasn't a factor. And, even though I was drunk *that* night – well, I also figured I wasn't quite so drunk as everyone else. I knew I was a lot more sober than the Baron, and he was the only person at the table I felt I had to impress. If not beat.

He tapped my marker, glaring at me. The others handed theirs in, with varying degrees of hesitation. Then we played.

I dealt the first hand. Basic five-card draw. My father had taught me this: use the first hands to scout people's faces. I lost the hand – I folded on nothing, chasing two pair – but not too much money with it. The deal went around the table. Paulie was his usual incomprehensible self – five card draw, sevens and sixes wild, it made no fucking sense – and even Toni stared at him with open contempt.

But I saw a few things. The Baron had good hands each time, picked up a nice little pile of change by the time the deal went to Toni.

Hold 'Em, she said. She had to explain the rules. I pretended not to know them.

I picked up the hand on a pair of jacks. Drew out Dook, who should have known better, and the Baron, who assured me I was very fucking bluffing. He had a pair of tens. He also showed me the most obvious tell in the book. A lot of players – thanks, Pop – think they have a poker face. But they only use it when they're holding something of value.

Every good hand, the Baron composed himself. When he had nothing, he relaxed, drank from his bottle. The Baron, I knew, was an amateur. If that.

Toni saw it too. I saw she saw it and she saw I saw it. We traded a glance. Otherwise Toni was made of stone.

The deal came back to me. Let's stick with Hold 'Em, I said. I smiled at Toni and repeated her line. It's the purest form of poker.

I fucking hate it, the Baron said.

We played an hour. Toni and I kept cleaning up. For the most part we avoided going head to head. But we were winning so much – we wiped out Bethany and Paulie almost immediately, and then began chipping away at the others – that I faced her down on a couple of shit hands, so at least no one could accuse us of cheating.

But then – this was Dook's deal – I pulled the last of the Baron's chips away from him. Two queens showing, and I had the other two on the deal. It was academic after that, but, as I've said, I was pretty good. I bled the Baron dry, and I'd be a liar if I said I didn't enjoy myself. He had a full house, too.

You're fucking cheating! he roared, and stood.

Bullshit, I said. I was buzzed and happy. I'm good at this. That's all.

You and that little cunt have a code, the Baron said.

Hey! Toni and I said in unison.

Bethany roused herself from a semi-nap. That's not nice, Larsy.

Fuck all of you, the Baron said. You're cheating. I know it.

Poor little baby, Bethany said, and giggled.

I'm going to piss, the Baron said, and he stalked off, boots clomping on the floorboards.

We played two more hands while he was gone, but it was mostly Toni and me exchanging a couple bucks. The sole of her foot was now pressing against my calf. It didn't occur to me to notice that the Baron was gone a long time. If I heard footsteps upstairs during those hands I might have convinced myself they were Dook's – he'd excused himself for the kitchen a while before.

The Baron came back. He sat back on the couch, smirking.

I pushed him. I couldn't help it – I grow bigger balls when I'm drinking. You want to buy back in? I asked.

He just smiled. Then Bethany put her head on his shoulder, drowsily. He grunted and closed his eyes too. I wondered if I'd have to get the couch fumigated before Mom got back from California.

Toni and I played a couple more hands. Dook and Paulie, eyelids droopy, both went into the kitchen for a side game. When they were gone Toni leaned across the table and kissed my cheek.

Hey, I whispered.

Hey yourself. She raised an eyebrow. Come on.

Where—

Upstairs. She smiled. Let's talk about our secret code.

This sort of thing, as I've explained, did not happen to me. I followed her, nearly light-headed, praising in my mind the loneliness and diminished expectations of Unalakleet, Alaska. When we were at the landing, hidden and shadowed, Toni kissed me for real. Stood on her tiptoes, put her hands in my hair.

Wow, I think I said. Toni—

Hey, she said, It is what it is. You're cute and nice and you can play the guitar and cards. She touched my cheek. I like that in a boy.

She took me by the hand and led me upstairs. We turned and tumbled into the den, pressed together. I had a boner the likes of which I have never had again. She kissed me.

Play something for me, she said, and turned on the light.

I said, I don't know if I can concentrate, but OK, and turned for my guitar.

Something was wrong. Off. I stood blinking in the new light, my blood and the booze in it rushing everywhere, and tried to focus. Everything was as we'd left it. The amp was off. The mirror from my mother's room was unbroken.

Oh no, Toni said.

I saw it too. Mephisto, my beloved guitar, was different. Wrong. I wasn't so drunk I was seeing things that weren't there. There was something *on* it.

I walked to it, knelt. On the front, on that gleaming, spotless black just below the bridge, there was now a shape: a pentagram.

I touched the shape. It had been carved into the paint. There, on the floorboards – I saw little chips of the paint and wood shavings. And, as though it was in the room with me, I saw very clearly the leather knife case on the Baron's belt.

I stood up and looked at Toni, then out the window, through my blurred reflection and into the night. I felt a number of very complicated things. Disappointment, first – who knows what Toni had in mind for me, up there, but whatever it was, was now over. She touched my shoulder, but there was no heat in it, and any of mine had been pulled down a sucking drain. Then worry – how was I going to explain this to my mother? And, too, scheming and calculation – I'd have to take the thing to a luthier, there was one in Westover – and get it repaired and repainted, and that was going to cost just about every dime I had and some I didn't.

But those concerns were secondary. They rose and faded in the face of terrible, wrenching fury.

I'd been in fights before, had gotten insulted or punched in ways that made my fists ball up and my arms pinwheel and a red curtain drop over my eyes. But this was different. *Worse.* This rage made me feel weak, made my fingers tingle, made me want to cry and scream all at once. The *fucker.* The Baron had come to my house and had insulted me and my mother and a girl I liked. He'd shown me up on the guitar. He was a fucking Nazi, for Christ's sake. And now he'd gone and desecrated my guitar. This thing I'd loved above all others.

Yes. Past tense. On top of the anger I felt grief, too.

Because I knew: I'd never love the guitar the same. I'd never pick it up and not think of the Baron. I'd never look at it with awe. I'd never think of it as a gift from my mother but, instead, as a thing I had to sneak. It was flawed. Imperfect. And why? Why? Because I'd beaten him in a game.

Because the Baron couldn't fucking play cards.

I turned for the door.

Daryl, Toni said. Wait.

I have to say something.

He's dangerous, she said. I've spent two days with him and Bethy, and he's—

I know. But I have to do something.

God. Her eyes were a little moist. Maybe it was the drink, I don't know. But I stirred her face into the mixture. Took courage from it. She liked me. I could play. I needed to avenge my axe. My honour. I had to do *something*.

We walked downstairs into the living room and stood in front of the coffee table. The Baron was awake again, just putting down the whisky bottle, empty now except for pale watery backwash. His eyes were a shining pink, and that colour was in his cheeks, too. Dook and Paulie had returned to the room, and they looked up at me and Toni, both of them lost in jealousy.

So, the Baron said to Toni. How is the party boy's very enormous wang?

Fuck you, Lars.

Little girl, he said, I'm about to wash that mouth out with piss.

My rage grew, shifted. I had no muscle, no weapon that could break through to the Baron. I looked at his bare muscled arms, at the Nazi tattoos, at the knife case. I could not fight him.

But I couldn't let things go, either.

What did you do to my guitar? I said to him. My insides felt calm, cool, floaty.

He grinned at me and hugged the bottle to himself.

I improved it! It's a very evil axe. Now it announces itself to the world!

Dook looked at my face. The blood drained from his to match mine. He stood, then went upstairs.

You're a prick, I said.

Yes! the Baron said. About time you fucking noticed. I am an evil motherfucker!

I said, my mother spent a lot of money on that guitar. She'll take it away, now.

You're a fucking pussy, the Baron said. Seriously. You want to play metal? Who the fuck cares about your fucking mother? Go run away. Live on someone's floor. Live in a goddamned car. I have. You think anyone wants you to pursue this course? No. They do not. I am *liberating* you. If there is ever going to be a Pitch Black – he snickered a little when he said it – then you are going to have to quit thinking so much about your fucking mother.

Fuck you, I said.

Fuck you, he said, mocking my pitch, the quiver in my voice. You know nothing. You think your little band is evil. You think playing loud chords and drawing skeletons is evil. He laughed. You don't know what you're doing.

Put your money where your mouth is, I said.

I do not think you mean that.

Sure I do.

Dook clattered down the stairs, his face twisted. My homeboy. He knew the stakes, now.

I want you to pay to repair the guitar, I said. I've got fifty bucks of your money already. Now give me the rest. You *owe* me.

No. He said it and then looked at me again. No! I give you strength – a gift! – and then pay you *money*? No. Go finger your vagina.

He was cutting the cards, over and over, each time looking at the card on the bottom. Like he was playing some kind of private game, barely listening.

You don't have any guts, I said. You're a coward.

He laughed and his eyes flickered up to my face.

You're not? he asked.

No.

Listen, he said. These other pussy boys are nothing. You? You're not bad on that axe. You have a brain in your head. But you *choose* to be nothing. Nothing at all. It is very fascinating to me.

He cut the deck, smiled, and showed me a queen.

A brave man would *embrace* that guitar, he said. He would not care what his mother thought. He would understand the path to greatness. The Baron looked at me sideways. He would do what is best for his band.

Let's play a hand for it, I said. You and me. A paint job or a new guitar, it's all the same to me. Five hundred bucks, all or nothing.

He said, sniggering, Don't bet what you don't have.

Actually I do have it, I said. I turned and went into my mother's room. I still felt calm. I wonder now if people who lose their lives in Vegas – who in the course of a night max out their credit cards, pawn their cars, the wedding rings off their fingers – feel the same calm I felt. I don't know. I opened my mother's closet and felt around on the top shelf. I found the old jewellery box. I lifted the lid and felt the money my mother had been squirrelling away since Dad left. I counted it in the light of the hallway. Seven hundred dollars. Her Hawaii money, she called this. Before she'd bought the guitar for me it had been much more. In my head, somehow, that made what I was doing right. I was *avenging* her. Her trust in me. Her money which had turned into something so valuable.

I reached back up onto the shelf, feeling for something else. My mother had told me about the Hawaii money. It was a matter of trust between us; I had never disturbed it.

The other thing I had discovered while snooping. Actually, I'd seen it reflected in the long mirror, the first time I'd wrestled it off her closet door.

I returned to the living room. Dook saw the cash in my hand before anyone else did, and he looked for a moment as though he might die on the spot. Dude, he said, pleading. In his eyes was the destruction of the band, the death of all our dreams, the end of me personally.

I dropped the money in the middle of the table.

One hand, I said. That's seven hundred bucks.

Oh God, Toni and Bethany said in unison.

The Baron looked at the money and pursed his lips. He shook his head.

I don't have that kind of cash, he said. He added, Not on me.

I said, That versus everything in your trunk. All of it. The whole rig.

Ridiculous. Fuck you.

I stared at him. I guess you're not man enough.

He reddened. He picked up the whisky bottle and looked at it and then set it down again, with a crash. Then he stood and bent over and swept the money up off the table in his fist.

You do not understand! he said. I do not get ordered around by little – by little stupid pussy boys! Fuck you! I *take* your money. Now you have nothing—

I wasn't stupid. I was unwise then, sure. But not dumb. Of course I knew he'd try to take the money. So I pulled my mother's little .22 pistol out of my belt and pointed it at the Baron's head.

Daryl! Toni cried.

I told him, You're going to give me your guitar. I'm going to sell it and repair mine.

Fuck you, he said, looking at the mouth of the gun. But his face had gone pale.

Come on, I said. Give your keys to Dook.

Dook could have quailed, but he didn't. He walked to the Baron and went to reach for the keys in the Baron's pocket. The Baron said, Don't you fucking dare—

I stepped forward and put the barrel of the gun against the Baron's chin.

All right, he said. All right. He looked at me, over the gun, right into my eyes.

I would like to tell you I held firm. That I gazed at him with his own strength. You see what was at stake. Not just the matter of my guitar. I took the gun out, raging; I held it to the face of another man. And he stared me down. Overcame his fear and looked me in the eyes.

And it was revealed to me, in his gaze: that while the Baron was an asshole, and maybe, just maybe, as evil as he claimed, he was not a liar.

He was right about everything. I was good at the guitar, but I was not great. And I was the best of us. Our band consisted of children pretending at something we would never be. I could steal the Baron's guitar. I could sell it and fix my own. I could shoot him dead, right here and now. But no matter what I did, there would never be a band, not the one we'd imagined.

We didn't have it in us.

He kept his steady stare on me. I looked away. I could bluff at cards, but not at this. Not at blood. We both knew it.

Without blinking the Baron reached up and took the gun from my hand. I gave it up, almost relieved. I heard a whistling in my ears. The Baron looked at the pistol in his hands, and then he did something I'd not considered. He flicked off the safety and showed it to me, one eyebrow lifted. Then he pointed the gun at my face.

Toni screamed. Shut up, the Baron said. All of you shut up and stay very still.

Incredible, you say? That somehow a night like that one produced such a scene? Me, the violence in my heart replaced by despair – and then by mortal fear? Not a minute after I first held a gun, that gun being pointed at me? It happened. It all happened. I can still feel the loosening of my bowels, still feel the sickness that rose up in me. You must know this.

The Baron pointed the gun at my head and I divided, became new. My old life was revealed as useless, a shirt too small for me; in that second, as my gaze flickered back and forth between the open mouth of the pistol and the Baron's bloodshot eyes peering at me over it, down the length of his beefy arm, I understood that everything good I would ever feel in my life had yet to happen. And I knew that, through my vanity and rage, I had just pissed all these things away. I hadn't been betting my mother's money, my guitar. The Baron was as evil as he claimed; I believed that now. I had sat down to play cards with the Devil and had finally offered up the thing he was, by nature, bound to take. Now here we were.

It seemed like an old, old song. The one I should have learned first.

Had events not taken their next turn, I would have fallen to my knees and begged. Take my guitar, I would have said. Cut off my hands. Piss on me. Do what you need to do, but leave me my life. Please, I would have said, my voice high and keening. Please. In front of my friends – in front of Toni! – I would have begged and wept.

Would he have killed me?

The Baron had it in him. I believe that, I do. He swayed drunkenly at the far end of his arm. He grinned at me. A frightened boy facing the gun in his hand. I saw again everything he'd done and said that night; it was clear to me that the Baron had said and done them all because he knew, he had always known, he could do this, now. Whenever.

Maybe he would have humiliated me. Maybe he was grinning because he thought of the possibilities.

Maybe he would have pulled the trigger and gotten in his car and driven away.

Maybe he would have kept on shooting. I don't think I am making up a recollection of his eyes quickly circling the room. Dook, Paulie, for certain. Maybe Toni and Bethany, too. And the Baron doing whatever mathematics he thought necessary.

But I did not find out what he had in mind. That's because Old Billy Pritchett shot the Baron, then, through the living room window.

IV. The Kraut

It happened like this:

The Baron said something. I can't remember what. My head rang with fear, and he opened his mouth and began to say a sentence, or even a simple word. *Go*, maybe. *Boy*, maybe. I closed my eyes and then the room exploded. I heard a *crack!* and, then, all at once: broken glass, screams, the ringing in my head exploding in volume until, for a moment, all else in the room faded into cottony silence. I thought – I remember clearly thinking – that being shot did not hurt. That it wasn't as loud as I'd expected. A little crack, almost from another room. I marvelled that the sound of my brains exploding was the same as tinkling glass and screaming. I wet myself. I thought: I've been shot and I can still feel piss on my legs.

Then hands were on my shoulders. I fell to my knees under their pressure. I opened my eyes and saw.

It was Dook, pulling me down. He kept shouting my name. The girls were crouched low, in the corner, their arms over each other's shoulders. Paulie lay face down on the floor, surrounded by glass.

And the Baron:

He sat on the floor in front of me, holding his arm, his hair falling before his eyes, his teeth clenched. Blood – the Baron was bleeding; more blood than I'd ever seen before leaked from between the fingers clamped around his arm, glistening in the light. My mother's pistol lay on the floor in front of him.

I thought, crazily, that somehow I had done this. That for all my cowardice I'd somehow shot him anyway.

But then I heard a voice, a strange one, from my left, outside the living room window. It screamed: Got you, you Kraut son of a bitch!

The Baron grunted through his teeth. He stared at me, shocked and hateful. It was then that my brain caught up with events, that I realized what must have happened.

I hissed to the Baron: Run! Hide!

Whatever the Baron thought of me, he didn't need to be told twice. He scuttled backwards, out of the living room and into the dark dining room. There he rose and lurched away. I heard his footsteps thumping up the stairs.

From outside, Billy cried: I'm coming for you! God *damn* it!

Then Billy's face peered through the window. The sill was several feet above the yard outside; Billy's head barely cleared it. His face was smudged, red with exertion. Tears or sweat streaked down his dirty cheeks. He regarded us, all of us strewn on the floor. I held my breath.

You all right there, Daryl? he asked.

I could have wept.

Yeah, I said, gasping. Yeah, Billy, I think so.

I *knew* he was in here, Billy said. I just knew it. He looked from side to side, at the broken shards of glass. Sorry about that window.

It's OK, Billy, I said.

That Kraut run off? Billy asked.

Yeah, I said.

I better come in and finish him off, I guess.

Oh Jeez, Billy, I said. I don't know. You got him pretty good.

Very quietly, Bethany started to cry in the corner.

Billy, I said, Why don't we go to the back porch. Let's talk about this.

Billy's eyes blinked behind his glasses. All right, Daryl. Then he vanished into the dark again.

Bethany crawled over to me – past Paulie, who still lay face down on the floor, shuddering – and clutched my arm. She was sobbing.

You can't let him in! she said. He'll kill Lars!

I have to try to talk to him, I said. I can talk him out of it.

Toni said, quietly, We should call the police.

Dook, I said.

Yeah, he said behind me. His voice was husky.

Call the cops, I said. I stood. I could barely feel my legs. My hands and arms felt as though, if I didn't concentrate hard, they'd spaz out all over the place. For the first time I smelled my own piss.

I made myself walk across the house. I saw little shining drops of the Baron's blood on the dining room floor. They led right to the stairs. Even Billy and his big glasses would be able to see them.

My hand shook, but I managed to open the kitchen door. I walked out onto the back porch. Billy was just coming up the steps. He was shorter than me by a foot, but wider by the same amount; he *felt* larger. He carried his rifle with the barrel pointing at a spot just in front of his feet. And he smelled. I'd caught a whiff of him before, out by the fence, but never up close, man to man, as we were now. He stank of weeks' worth of sweat, of unclean clothes and unwashed dishes, of the rotting undergrowth of his woods. I could see hairs growing out of his nose and ears, thick as clumps of weeds. It was everything I could do not to throw up. Billy smiled and held out his hand. Amazed, I shook it.

Easy there, soldier, he said. That was close, I know.

Billy, I said. I'm not a soldier. It's just me. Daryl Shepherd.

Don't sell yourself short, Billy said. That Kraut could get the drop on anyone. I know. I've been after him a good long while.

Billy looked past me, at the kitchen door.

He still in the house? Billy asked me. Is he still armed?

I couldn't remember whether the Baron had taken the pistol or not.

Billy, I said. Maybe you'd better let the police handle this.

He looked at me strangely. Son, he said, this is *France*. We *are* the police.

Billy, I said, this is Indiana. It's 1987.

His laugh was quick and wheezy and almost reassuring. More moisture ran down his cheeks, and I shivered. He was laughing and crying, all at the same time.

You're a funny one, he said, creaking. How many hostages?

This, at least, we had to make clear.

There's four in the living room, I said. Two girls, two guys. Everyone's OK.

He blinked.

And just one Kraut?

Billy, I said, I think we're all right here. You can go home—

I saw it, Billy said. That Kraut had a gun on you. Billy squinted at me. What are you hiding, son?

It was a good question. I closed my eyes, for longer than I'd planned.

I thought of the whole night, all of it. I thought of Toni kissing me – she'd never do that again. I thought of the Baron squatting in front of my guitar, grinning as he carved. The look in his eyes as he held the gun on me. I thought about the police, on their way. My mother hearing the news, from the sheriff and then from me. The blood drops on the floor. That feeling – still fluttering in me, on bat's wings – that the Baron owned me. I'd held a gun on him. He'd beaten me.

I saw all of this. And then the whole night condensed itself into two words, which I whispered:

He's upstairs.

Billy nodded.

Probably that room with the awful music, he said.

Probably, I said.

You get the hostages to the yard, Private. Leave him to me. Billy blinked and smiled. I been after this one a long while.

I walked back into the house, swallowing dust, wobbling. In the living room I said, Come on. Billy said to get out.

Bethany looked up from her hands, her streaked face eerily like Billy's.

Is he going away? she asked.

The others all looked at me. I shrank. I couldn't meet Toni's eyes.

He said get out. Come on.

Bethany stood. What about Lars?

I could only look at the floor.

Lars! she screamed. Lars!

While avoiding the sight of her I saw my mother's pistol, where it had fallen. I picked it up and stood with it in my hands. Toni and Dook saw it there. I looked at each of them and they looked back.

Then, quickly, I took the gun, and all the money from the coffee table, back to the closet in my mother's room. As I put them away I could hear my breath, harsh and rasping, and under it my heart-beat, and under that the silence of outer space.

Behind me, down the hallway, I heard screams.

Billy's voice said, It's all right. You're all safe. Go on out to the yard, now.

Don't hurt him! Bethany wailed.

Of course not, ma'am. Not if he comes peaceful. Now get.

I heard the clatter of footsteps, and Bethany's screams. I walked carefully down the hallway. Billy stood in the entrance to the stair-well, one booted foot already on the first step. He turned quickly, then saw it was me.

He saluted me, and then from his belt he drew a pistol. He put a finger to his lips.

I saluted back. And with that Billy vanished up the steps, into the shadows, quiet as a spirit.

What happened?

We huddled in the yard, all of us, next to the Baron's car. We watched the dark upper floor of the house. When I couldn't bear the staring any more I turned and looked across the yard and the cornfields beyond the yard, towards the interstate. After what seemed a wait of many, many years, I finally saw the police lights, turning onto our road, a mile off yet. And in the meantime I could see lights coming on upstairs, one by one.

I remember thinking that Billy was an old man. I thought, if Lars is smart he can take him. He's faster, stronger.

Did I have a hope, a wish? I was empty, then. I remember thinking events had grown too powerful, too confused, for me to hope for any one outcome over another.

Or maybe I did. The flashing lights turned down the county road. Half a mile away. My heart leapt.

And then we heard it, from upstairs: a brief, muffled roar. And then a gunshot. And another. And another. Through the back window we all saw the muzzle flashes, and strange, leaping shadows. Bethany screamed and screamed, and Toni and Dook had to keep her from running into the house.

The sheriff was just climbing out of his car when Billy opened the kitchen door and walked out. He was covered in blood. He sat on the top porch step and smiled at the sheriff.

Got him, he said, happily. Then he fell onto his side.

We'd forgotten: the Baron still had his knife.

V. And Now

The rest isn't that exciting. Nothing happened after that, not really. Just twenty years.

Billy died on the way to the hospital, a smile on his face. He said nothing of import to the sheriff or to the EMTs, and so the whole night became, in the end, his fault, his disaster. Quite a scandal. An old man, obviously troubled, allowed by the state and his children to keep his weapons. He'd murdered a young man. *Troubled*, the papers called the Baron.

Yes. Murder. The Baron died on the floor of the study. Billy had hit him with all three shots, all in his massive chest, and after stabbing Billy, the Baron had fallen backward, over my guitar and my amplifier. The last time I saw Mephisto, before it became state's evidence, it lay on its back in a pool of the Baron's dark crimson blood.

I will never forget that. Even then, it was beautiful.

The rest of us: we got into trouble, but nowhere near the trouble we might have. The police questioned all of us. We told the same story, each of us following the path of self-preservation. We were partying quietly, and then Billy shot the Baron. Yes, we said, the Baron liked the Nazis. Yes, he shouted hateful things at Billy's property. Yes, he'd carved the pentagram on my guitar. Billy's tracks were found all over our property. He'd circled the house for hours. Looking for the best shot, it seemed. The sheriff lectured us, all of us. We were cited for drinking, possession of marijuana, and – given the circumstances – the judge gave all of us probation.

Except Bethany. Her story was different. She was the only one of us who mentioned my mother's gun. But then, she was also the only one of us to be arrested for possession of cocaine and speed, and so her story was discounted. Not even her cousin from Alaska backed her up.

I saw Toni only once, after that night. She was on her way out of the police station in Westover, and I was on my way in. We passed right by each other. I knew by then she hadn't told. The guys in the band, sure, but her? After everything? I was with my mother. I couldn't ask her. Toni knew I couldn't. She looked me in the eye, without any expression – drawn and pale and beautiful – and not long after went back to little Unalakleet without saying goodbye.

She is, I hope – I hope – very happy.

If she is, it might be because her cousin Bethany, once clean and sober and out of jail, married a car salesman and, to this very day, lives comfortably outside of Westover with her children.

That the band broke up goes without saying. Paulie stopped calling us after the depositions. Dook didn't want to bring up the idea of another guitar, so we took up playing video games and not saying much. He kept on playing bass. We don't see much of each other now – he moved out west, to Las Vegas, and became a sound engineer. We email each other every few months, passing on news.

Me. I was grounded. Went back to therapy with my mother. She felt betrayed. I kept saying sorry, sorry, sorry.

My mother sold the house. Because of what had happened in it, she lost a lot of money. We moved to Indianapolis after that and lived in an apartment.

The only way you can repay me, she told me, is to go to college. And so I did.

Twenty years: I go to school. I am accepted by, and then graduate from, Ball State, with a degree in education. I get a job teaching sixth grade social studies and basic computer programming. On the way I date a little. Nothing serious. At my first job I make eyes with the kindergarten teacher and something happens: and then I'm in a house with a wife and a child.

Which is where I am now. In that house. My wife and child asleep upstairs. I'm in the basement rec room, strumming a little on an old acoustic I bought ten years ago at a flea market. My boy not quite as old as I was when all this happened.

When I'm alone like this I can't help but think about the Baron. I can't help but tell the story to myself, again and again. And not just what happened – but what *might* have happened. If he'd lived. If he and his band had made it.

Though he wouldn't have. Whorefrost, I know now, wasn't good. They had no future. A guy with swastika tattoos? He wasn't going to stare off the pages of guitar magazines, not here in the U.S. A guy like the Baron was bound, one way or another, for prison. Or he'd be living in a trailer park outside Westover, beating his wife and frightening his kids and the neighbours' kids. He'd be on a first-name basis with the deputies who'd have to come out there every Friday night and tell him to turn down his goddamned music. I know it.

But then again, you never know. I should have been that guy, too, and here I am. Wife, kid, decent house. Hair cut short and the Ibanez and all my old dreams long gone. I play poker with the men of my neighbourhood and we never bet worth a damn. That's understood. Someone with too many beers in him tries to pull out a hundred dollar bill, and we'll say things like, Easy now. Let's think about this.

So maybe the Baron would have made it. Maybe he would have gotten the bejeezus scared out of him that night and then pulled back – like I did – just enough to do something with himself. Maybe in an alternate universe he's on stage right now, hair flying, brutalizing the guitar and nothing else, happy and alive, his stupid random youth safely behind him.

Maybe.

Nights like this I stay awake, everyone upstairs sleeping, and here in the basement I strum and strum. I tell myself happy stories, then sad ones, and then the one that happened. Each time I fool myself into thinking I feel suspense. Each time I wonder what I'll say or do differently. With Toni. In the living room, a gun in my hands. On the back porch, with Billy, when he asks me what I'm hiding, and there's a moment where I could tell him anything.

But what I say is like Old Billy, hunting the Baron room by room. It always finds me where I'm hidden. We tussle, and I pull out my knife, but, every time, the words force themselves out of my throat.

I remember locking eyes with the Baron, a gun between us.

Upstairs, I whisper to Billy. Every time.

♠

Deal Me In
Parnell Hall

S ETH BECKMAN SAT face down at the poker table. His eyes were
wide and unblinking. His mouth was open, his nostrils were
flared, yet no breath was coming through. Mr Beckman was done
playing poker for the evening. His cards were on the table in front
of him. As were the stacks of chips in which he lay. Due to which,
the man presented at least a linguistic paradox. Mr Beckman had
not cashed in his chips because he had cashed in his chips.

In the apartment flashbulbs were going off. The medical examiner hovered, waiting for the detectives to let him at the body. He
had already pronounced the man dead. Now it would be up to him
to determine why. The froth at the mouth and slight odour of bitter
almonds pointed to cyanide. But poison was a woman's weapon.
There were no women in the game, just a bunch of good ol' boys,
who got together once a month to test their manhood at the poker
table. A cross section of Manhattan's elite who had been gambling
together over twenty years. Indeed, the game, or some variation,
had been going close to fifty, though none of the original players
remained. No Rockefellers or Carnegies, as there once were. But
there were judges, politicians, and influential businessmen, even if
Donald Trump wasn't among them. It was a prestigious game, and
an honor to be asked.

I was surprised to find Richard Rosenberg played in it. Though one of New York City's top negligence lawyers, he was still, in fact, a negligence lawyer, a profession only slightly better regarded than crack whore.

I was even more surprised to find he had asked for me. Richard usually thrived on situations like this. Ordinarily, I would have expected him to have insinuated himself into the case, interrogated all the witnesses, and coerced confessions out of at least half of them. The fact he called for backup was a shock.

The fact the police let me in was a bit of a surprise also. It turned out the cop in charge was Sergeant MacAullif. MacAullif likes my input. It gives him a chance to hone his sarcasm and irony. 'Well, well, well, Stanley Hastings. The ace PI. What brings you here?'

Here was the apartment of Adam Addington. The stock broker was either a genius or an inside trader, or some combination of the two. His Park Avenue digs probably cost more than the average Pentagon budget. In wartime. It was in his game room, around his felt-covered, octagonal oak poker table, that the crime had taken place. If it was indeed a crime, and Mr Beckman had not picked that moment to just happen to go belly up.

What brought me there was a liveried elevator operator and a uniformed cop. The fact we'd stepped straight off the elevator into the apartment was a subtle hint Mr Addington had a floor-through.

'Richard called me.'

'So I understand. Why do you suppose he did it?'

'Have you considered asking him?'

'Not without a Miranda warning. After all, the guy's a lawyer.'

'So read him his rights.'

'I'm afraid he'd cross-examine me on them.'

'Good point.'

We found Richard Rosenberg at a dining room table that seated twelve. It currently sat six, the remaining poker players who had been in the game.

Richard sprang to his feet when he saw me. A little man with an inexhaustible supply of nervous energy, Richard was always ready to bound up at a moment's notice. I was surprised to find he had the patience to sit still long enough to play poker.

'Stanley. Thank God you're here. This is a hell of a situation. There's been a murder, and I'm a suspect.'

'Oh, don't take so much credit,' said a middle-aged man with twinkling eyes and a face like the Pillsbury Dough Boy. He wore a faded Grateful Dead T-shirt. A stain on the left sleeve and a rip in the collar seemed to attest to its genuine vintage. 'We're *all* suspects. But I didn't do it, and I resent being held a prisoner in my own apartment.'

So, the Dough Boy had dough. I wondered how much was required to get away with wearing a torn T-shirt. The rest of the poker players seemed fairly well dressed.

MacAullif and I marched Richard out of earshot of the others. Amazingly, that left them still in sight. It was a very large apartment.

'OK,' MacAullif demanded, 'what's the deal?'

Richard shrugged. 'I have no idea. The guy just fell over dead.'

'I don't mean *that.*' MacAullif jerked his thumb. 'Why'd you call *him*?'

'Well, I couldn't call a lawyer. I *am* a lawyer. But I do have a vested interest in the outcome of this case. Not to disparage your investigative abilities, but you are not my investigator. You are not reporting to me what you find. Stanley, on the other hand, would lose his job if he didn't.'

'Now there's a recommendation,' I observed.

'Besides, you know him and you won't throw him out.'

'Any time you get done praising my abilities…'

'Don't be dumb. Sergeant MacAullif won't let me sit in on the interviews because I'm a quote "suspect" unquote. I need to know what's said. So I'm counting on you to listen in.'

'Assuming anyone talks,' I said. 'They have the right to remain silent, as I'm sure you pointed out.'

'Are you kidding me? With my interests at stake? I advised them all to tell everything they know.'

MacAullif cocked his head. 'You actually think I'd let him sit in on the interviews?'

'Absolutely. You guys have helped each other in the past. There's no reason not to. And these are prominent people. You want this cleaned up as quickly as possible before the commissioner gets involved. If I were you, I would look on this as a godsend.'

MacAullif sized me up. If he considered me a godsend, I wouldn't have known it.

'In return for doing me this huge favour, I'll continue to urge all my friends to spill their guts. Which can only help me, since one of them's a killer. Or you can reject this suggestion, and I'll advise all of them to clam up and hire their own lawyers.'

If it was a bluff, it was a good one. It occurred to me I wouldn't want to play poker against Richard.

'All right.' MacAullif said it with all the good grace of a tree slug.

We walked Richard back to the table. His friends greeted him like he was the waitress in a topless bar.

'So, what's it gonna be?'

'Did you ask him?'

'Yeah, did you ask him?'

'What did he say?'

'Yes, or no?'

Five men could not have looked more anxious. My god, did they all do it?

'Actually, we were discussing the other matter,' Richard said. 'You know. About Mr Beckman.'

Richard's friends didn't want to hear it.

'What's to discuss?'

'Guy has a heart attack and dies.'

'It's sad, but life goes on.'

'Yeah, life goes on.'

'So, did you ask him?'

MacAullif frowned. 'Ask me what?'

'Well,' Richard said. 'We assume you're going to keep us here a while?'

'That's your question?'

'No, I think that's a fairly safe assumption. And I know you don't want to disturb the crime scene.'

'Speaking of safe assumptions. So, whaddya want?'

'Could we get a deck of cards?'

We conducted our questioning in Adam Addington's study, which was bigger than a breadbox and smaller than your average basketball court. One wall had a floor to ceiling bookcase, which was quite something when you considered the height of the ceiling – suffice it to say one of those sliding ladders on a track went along with it. There was a mahogany desk, a large screen TV, a bar, a stereo system, and a small pool table for when Mr Addington was too busy to walk down the hall to the billiard room.

The conference table in the corner was large enough for the Green Bay Packers. It was covered with toys and knick-knacks, just in case meetings got boring.

Richard was first up. He sat on one side of the conference table. MacAullif and I sat on the other.

'All right,' Richard said. 'I'd like to remind you that anything I say could be used against me in a court of law. And while this interrogation is not being taken down, it is in the presence of a witness.'

'Thank you,' MacAullif said dryly. 'I'm glad that's taken care of. Do you intend to ask the questions too?'

'If you like.'

'Why don't you just tell us what happened. We can fill in the blanks later.'

'What happened was Seth up and died right in the middle of a rather large pot.'

'Was Seth in the pot?'

'Absolutely. He'd just raised. He threw his chips in the pot and fell flat on his face.'

'Could it have been the excitement of the hand?'

Richard made a face. 'Please.'

'You said it was a large pot.'

'That's relatively large. Not worth dying over.'

'I'll be the judge of that. What were the stakes?'

'Gonna bust us for gambling?'

'It's not a high priority.'

'That's not the answer I was looking for.'

'Cut it out. No one cares about gambling. You wanna speed this along?'

'We were playing quarter-half.'

'That's all?'

'With a dollar on the last card. Certainly not enough money to induce a heart attack.'

'What's the point?'

'What do you mean?'

'Of the game?'

'It's an old game. Been going on for over fifty years. In one or another variation. Quarter-half is actually big time. It used to be nickel-dime. Back when there was a Rockefeller playing.'

'You're kidding.'

'You think they got rich throwing their money away in card games?'

'How'd you get in the game?'

'You remember a few years back when Danny Felson died?'

'Who?'

Richard looked pained at MacAullif's ignorance. 'The musical comedy director? Guy had three Tonys. Anyway, when he died I got his seat. It was quite an honour to be asked.'

'But just an honour,' I said.

Richard frowned. 'What do you mean?'

'Well, no one's going to get rich playing quarter-half.'

'Of course. That's not the point. The thrill is playing with the big boys. The camaraderie. The associations. All financial considerations aside. Not that there aren't any. If our host threw a case my way, I could retire.'

I always have to restrain myself when Richard says things like that. The guy makes money hand over fist. He could retire tomorrow, if he wanted to.

'Who got you in the game?' MacAullif asked.

'Judge Granville put in a word for me. I appear before him a lot. He thinks I'm funny.' Richard raised his finger. 'If you quote me on that, I'll deny it. I'd hate for the old boy to have to recuse himself the next time I get a juicy malpractice case.'

'I wouldn't worry about it,' MacAullif said. 'You want to walk me through this? How long had you been playing before it happened?'

'We started around eight. Seth bit the big one at eight forty five.'

'Going around the table. Where was everyone sitting?'

'OK,' Richard said. 'Say I'm sitting here. Then Seth was sitting here.'

MacAullif raised his eyebrows. 'Next to you?'

'Yes,' Richard said ironically. 'I was sitting right next to him. Where I'd make sure to sit if I was going to do him in.'

'Where was everybody else?'

Richard snagged an ornate crystal ashtray that probably cost more than my car and placed it on the table to his right. 'Here's Seth. I'm me.' He slid one of those silver-balls-on-strings-that-swing-into-each-other doohickies to his left. 'This annoying toy is Benny – that's Benjamin Driscoll to you. He's a banker. By that I mean he owns a bank. A chain of banks, actually. Can we avoid saying which one? I wouldn't want to affect the prime lending rate.

'To his left is our host, Adam Addington. Horatio Alger story. Self-made man. Parlayed a small inheritance into a small fortune in the stock market.' Richard slid a magic 8-ball into Addington's spot.

'The hawk-faced gentleman next to him is Judge Granville.' Richard marked his place with what was either a large letter opener or a small Samurai sword. 'I wish I had a gavel.'

Richard pointed to MacAullif. 'In your seat is Dan Kingston. He's Addington's tax accountant. Like to be mine, if he could talk me into it. He's not a regular. He fills in when someone can't make it.'

MacAullif jerked his thumb at me. 'Who's in his seat?'

'No one. It's an octagonal table. We play with seven. Because there's so many games you can't play with eight. Draw, in particular, never works unless you shuffle discards. So we keep it to seven. Stanley's in the empty chair.'

'Why am I not surprised? So who's next to Stanley?'

'The rather smug gentleman is Harvey Poole. He's a pharmacologist. Has a patent on one of those Viagra knockoffs.' Richard cocked his head at us. 'Just in case you're interested. I think he also handles allergies and acid reflux.'

'And he was sitting next to the dead man?'

'Yes.'

'And no one was sitting on the other side of him?'

'Harvey's right-handed. Likes his elbow room.'

'So, assuming you didn't do it, he's the most likely suspect?'

'Don't be silly. There *is* no most likely suspect. The idea that any of us killed him is absurd. Despite all appearances, Seth probably died of natural causes.'

The doctor poked his head in right after Richard left. 'I think I got the cause of death.'

'Really? What was it?'

'This was in his throat.' The doctor produced a plastic evidence bag. In it was something that looked like it could well have been lodged in a dead man's oesophagus. A tiny, mushy, nondescript piece of god-knows-what.

'What makes you think that's the murder weapon?'

'I'm suspecting cyanide poisoning, and this was the last thing he ate. Unless I'm mistaken, it's one of these.'

The doctor held up something between his thumb and fore-finger. It was a brown, cylindrically shaped object, about a half inch in diameter and twice as long.

'What the hell is that?'

'It's a pretzel. There was a basket of them on the table.'

'He was killed with a poisoned pretzel?'

'You don't like the idea?'

'Can you put poison in a pretzel?'

'I could if I wanted to. I don't know whether it was done in this case. But it looks like cyanide, which is very fast acting. If he died from cyanide, it was something he ingested while sitting at the table. The choices are rather limited. The guy was eating pretzels and drinking Diet Coke. For my money, it wasn't in the Coke.'

'Why do you say that?'

'The pretzel in his throat. If he drank the Coke first, it would kill him before he got to the pretzel. If he ate the pretzel first, I'd expect him to chew it some before taking a sip.'

'That's assuming it was in the Diet Coke.'

'Right. So, unlikely as it might seem, it looks like that guy was killed with a pretzel.'

'You don't look happy, MacAullif,' I said as the medical examiner left.

'No kidding. How do you poison someone with a pretzel? It's like a magician forcing a card. 'Pick a pretzel, any pretzel.' How do you make sure he picks the right pretzel?'

'Maybe more than one was poisoned.'

'Then why aren't more people dead?'

'You sound disappointed, MacAullif. These aren't your favourite people?'

'Give me a break. They're out there playing cards while their friend's on his way to the morgue.'

'Evidently, he wasn't really their friend.'

'My point exactly. Say there's only one poison pretzel. Say you want this turkey to eat it. How do you get him to do that without someone seeing?'

'Maybe someone did.'

Adam Addington sat down at the table, said, 'My attorney has advised me to cooperate.'

'You consulted an attorney?' MacAullif asked.

'Of course I did. Do you think I'm stupid?'

'No, sir. I just wondered why you felt the need to do so.'

'This is my apartment.'

'That doesn't make you any more suspect.'

'Really? I would think it should. I had access to whatever it is that killed him. Unless it's something someone brought in. If you can show it's something someone brought in, I'd be very grateful.'

'So you think you'll be suspected of this crime?'

'I certainly hope not. It would spoil the whole evening.' When MacAullif didn't crack a smile, he added, 'That was a joke.'

'Better work on your delivery,' MacAullif said dryly. 'I'd still like to know why you felt the need to call a lawyer.'

'Actually, Mr Rosenberg convinced me.'

MacAullif frowned. 'Really? I was under the impression he advised everyone to cooperate.'

'Oh, he did. It's nothing he *said*. It's who he *is*. A negligence lawyer. I have money. It doesn't matter who killed him if some shyster tries to prove I was negligent. What if Seth has greedy relatives who decide to take me to the cleaners? Frankly, I wouldn't put it past them.'

'That's very interesting. You think relatives of Mr Beckman would tend to be greedy?'

'I find people in general tend to be greedy. This is a fairly nice apartment. If pictures of the crime scene wind up in the daily press, someone's going to take a look and say, 'Whoa! I'd like a piece of that!"

'So you called your lawyer?'

'I did.'

'What did he advise you?'

'He said I should cooperate with the police in every way. He said as remote a possibility as a lawsuit was, the best defense against it would be to have someone found guilty of the crime. So, how can I help you?'

'What was your relationship with the decedent?'

'I saw him at the poker games.'

'And nowhere else?'

'That's right.'

'Why not?'

'We weren't friends.'

'You didn't like him?'

'I didn't know him well.' Addington put up his hand. 'But let's not go around again. I had no wish to know him well. Seth had a rather arrogant personality, in my opinion.'

'What did he do?'

'Not much. He never did anything for his money. His family hasn't as long as anyone can remember. They just have it. But whether it comes from steel, gold, or rooking the Indians is anybody's guess.'

'Can you think of anyone who had a reason to dislike him?'

'Not in particular. But I can't think of anyone who had a reason to like him, either. Was there anything else?'

'Could you tell me what people were eating and drinking?'

'So, it was poison. Everyone's speculating poison.'

'We don't know yet. Can you help us out?'

'People were eating pretzels and drinking seltzer and Diet Coke.'

'Who brought the pretzels?'

'I did. Ever the gracious host.'

'And the drinks?'

'That's right.'

'You provided everything?'

'That I did.'

'And no one brought anything in from outside?'

'If they did, I wasn't aware of it.'

'Nothing else was served at the table except pretzels and the drinks you mentioned?'

'Yes. If he was poisoned, I provided the means. Would that be negligence?'

'Well, it wouldn't win you any medals.'

Addington nodded approvingly. '*Your* delivery is just fine.'

Dan Kingston was a nervous little man who looked as if at any moment he might be audited by the IRS. Since he was Addington's tax accountant, that could be quite a blow. The poker game might not involve big bucks, but in his line of work, fortunes could be won or lost by the simple manipulation of a decimal point.

'It's so awful,' he said, 'so awful.'

'Yes. If you could just help us straighten things out.'

'Could you hurry it up? I'd like to get back to the table.'

'I beg your pardon?'

'I'm sorry. I don't get to play all that often. Tonight's game will be short as it is.'

MacAullif rolled his eyes, shot me a look. I ignored him, said, 'So, you're not a regular in the game?'

'No. I fill in when someone can't make it.'

'That's what happened today.'

'Yes. Adam Addington called me, said, Kevin couldn't play.'

'Kevin?'

'Horowitz. The congressman. He was supposed to play, but something came up.'

'What?' I asked.

MacAullif and Dan both looked at me.

'I have no idea. Adam just said he couldn't make it, and could I fill in.'

'What time was that?' MacAullif asked.

'I don't know. Four thirty, five.'

'So, you had no idea you were going to be here until late this afternoon?'

'That's right. I didn't know till Adam called me.'

'He called you at work?'

'Yes.'

'You came right here from the office?'

'No. The game didn't start till eight. I went home and changed first.'

Dan was wearing a tweed jacket and tie. I had to wonder what he'd changed *out* of.

He got up to go.

'Could I ask a question?'

Dan looked like I'd just offered to extract his wisdom teeth without novocaine.

'This guy you filled in for today. He's not the only guy you've ever played for?'

Dan couldn't believe I'd stopped him to ask that question. MacAullif seemed to share his sentiment.

'Of course.'

'So you've filled in for other players?'

'Sure.'

'So the guy you filled in for tonight – this Kevin – you've played with him too. He's been there when you were. You know him fairly well.'

'I wouldn't go that far.'

'But you've played cards with him?'

'Yes.'

'And how did he get along with the decedent?'

Dan blinked. 'I beg your pardon?'

'They have any history? Any particular friction?'

As if explaining to a rather dull child, Dan said, 'Kevin wasn't *here*.'

'Yes, because you were. But if he had been. How would they have got along?'

'I don't think they liked each other. But nobody liked Seth much.'

'What the hell was that all about?' MacAullif demanded, when Dan was safely gone.

'Just asking the questions you overlooked.'

MacAullif made a few choice remarks such as might be heard in a rap song, suggesting I was a person of limited intelligence but impressive sexual abilities.

'You have an unpleasant man,' I explained patiently, 'killed in the presence of a bunch of guys who didn't like him. None of whom have an alibi. Wouldn't you wanna look at the lone guy who has a *perfect* alibi? Who has *arranged* to have a perfect alibi?'

MacAullif groaned. 'You've been reading murder mysteries again. Where the plot is so damn convoluted only a genius could have thought it up, and only a genius could figure it out. Real life is a little more straightforward. People kill someone because they want him dead, and their brilliant strategy for not getting caught is to say they didn't do it. Which is what we have here. There were six guys who could have committed the crime. Five, if you want to exclude Rosenberg. Which I'm sure you do, since he pays your salary.'

'I'm self employed. He hires my agency.'

'Save it for the IRS. Anyway, if you wanna come up with some theory how a guy who wasn't here managed to slip the guy a poisoned pretzel, be my guest.'

Judge Granville sat down at the table, folded his hands, and aimed his hawk-nose in our direction. The elderly jurist seemed completely at his ease. 'I'm Judge Granville. I didn't do it, and I'd be happy to assist you in putting away whoever did.'

'You have your own suspicions?' MacAullif asked.

The judge shrugged. 'I have no grounds on which to base them. Unless you'd care to put some evidence before me.'

'I really have no evidence.'

'Then go ahead and ask me.'

'Who do you think killed Seth Beckman?'

The judge grimaced. 'I didn't mean ask me that. I haven't a clue.'

'Would you care to speculate?'

'Lord, no. I hear enough of that in court. If you want to ask me anything factual, I'd be glad to answer. That I hear too little.'

'Did you like him?' I asked.

The judge frowned irritably.

'I'm not asking you for speculation,' I told him. 'Just a simple statement of fact.'

'That's not a fact. It's an opinion.'

'Whether or not you liked him may be an opinion, but that opinion is a fact.'

Judge Granville squinted his eyes, cocked his head, looked more hawk-like than ever. 'And you are?'

'Stanley Hastings. I'm a private investigator.'

'And you'd like to debate me on semantics?'

'Not really. I was hoping for a direct answer. It's not often we get a witness as evasive as you.'

The judge chuckled ironically. Shook his head. Chuckled again. 'You're a friend of Richard Rosenberg?'

'An employee, actually.'

'Do you think you're helping him here?'

'As much as you are.'

He frowned. 'Why do you say that?'

'I understand you were instrumental in getting him into the game.'

'He told you that?'

'Is it true?'

'I put a word in. Why?'

'So you're a long standing member of the poker game?'

'Yes, I am.'

'You've seen them come and go.'

'What's your point?'

'Some of whom you liked, and some of whom you disliked.'

'You're back to that?'

'Clearly it matters to you who plays in the game. You'd rather have compatible people, people you get along with.'

'So, I murdered Seth Beckman to get a seat for a more compatible member?'

'You don't think much of that theory?'

'I have the disadvantage of knowing it isn't true. So it's hard for me to assess it objectively.'

'Uh huh. And what about the congressman?'

Judge Granville frowned. 'I beg your pardon?'

'Kevin what's-his-name. The guy who isn't here tonight. Was supposed to play but cancelled. How do you feel about him?'

He looked at me for a moment, then smiled. 'Well, I must say I am impressed. Let me be sure I understand this. Are you exploring the possibility the killer was actually congressman Kevin Horowitz, who gave himself a rock-solid alibi by cancelling out at the last moment and not coming to the game?'

'What do you think of that theory?'

'I like it immensely.'

'You do?'

'Oh, yes.' The judge steepled his fingers on the table. 'It means the theory that I killed him to open up a spot for another player is no longer the stupidest idea I ever heard.'

Benjamin Driscoll came right in on the defensive. 'All right. There's no use hiding it. My wife was involved with Seth, as I'm sure everyone told you.'

'Well, that's interesting news,' MacAullif said. 'What makes you think that?'

The banker fell all over himself trying to backtrack. 'Nobody mentioned it? Then maybe it isn't true.'

'And yet you blurt it out during a murder investigation. It may not be true, but it's certainly on your mind. You might as well tell us.'

'Well, maybe they weren't involved. But he was certainly hitting on her. I guess that makes me a suspect. Which is so unfair. Kind of like getting kicked twice, you know what I mean?'

'How did the decedent know your wife?'

'That's just it. He didn't. He made a point of seeking her out.'

MacAullif frowned. 'What are you saying?'

Driscoll made a face. 'Seth and I never got along. One night we had huge disagreement over a hand. Almost came to blows. Next day he staked out my apartment building. Followed my wife. Arranged a chance encounter.'

'Now you're being paranoid.'

'Oh, yeah? You know how many "chance encounters" he arranged that month? Then, at the next game, he started dropping hints. Cryptic little insinuations. Drove me nuts.'

'What did your wife say?'

'She stopped mentioning him. When I asked, she said she hadn't seen him. Just what she would say, if there was something going on.'

'Or if she hadn't seen him,' MacAullif pointed out.

'Exactly,' Driscoll cried in exasperation. 'See what he did? Put the idea in my head, and then toyed with me. Was he *pretending* he was seeing my wife, or was he actually *doing* it? I had no way of knowing. But the son of a bitch needled me about it at the card table. Right in front of the others. You sure no one mentioned it?'

'When did this happen?'

'It was months ago. But he wouldn't let it drop. Bugged me all the time. Of course, he bugged everyone.'

'I get the impression nobody liked him.'

'I don't think anybody did.'

'Then why didn't you guys kick him out?'

Driscoll seemed shocked at the thought. 'Are you kidding? He was a regular.'

The smug pharmacologist also had a bone to pick. 'Was it poison?' Harvey Poole demanded.

MacAullif frowned. 'Why do you ask?'

'Seth keeled over and died. I thought it was a heart attack. Now I hear it's poison.'

'So, that rumour's getting around?'

'It's just a rumour?'

'Nothing's been confirmed.'

'Well, I wish people would wait before making accusations.'

'Accusations?'

'You know what I mean. People hear poison, and everyone thinks of the pharmacologist.'

'Of course,' MacAullif said.

I suppressed a smile. Clearly, *he* hadn't thought of the pharmacologist. The fact I hadn't either did not diminish my glee.

'You don't make cyanide, do you?' MacAullif asked.

'I most certainly do not.'

'Well, you say everyone is looking at you as the killer. What motive did you have?'

'Same as everybody else. I didn't like him. He was a nasty son of a bitch, and the world is better off without him.'

'Is that supposed to be refreshingly candid?' I asked.

Harvey frowned. 'It's not supposed to be anything. It's the truth. The man was unpleasant. I can't imagine that's why he was killed, but it happens to be the case.'

'Did you have any personal dealings with him?' MacAullif asked.

'None. Never saw him socially, never met him outside the poker game.'

'How about the other players?'

'I never saw them either.'

'I mean did any other of them know him socially?'

Harvey shrugged. 'I have no idea. Why don't you ask them?'

'The thought had occurred to me,' MacAullif said dryly. 'You happen to hand the decedent anything to eat or drink during the game?'

'Ah, we're back to poison. I like the way you did that, leading the conversation in another direction, and then sneaking that question in. The answer is, no, I did not.'

'You never handed him the pretzel basket?'

'I may have passed the basket. That's a far cry from giving him a pretzel.'

'You mean because he chose it himself?' I asked.

As before, Harvey resented the interruption. 'If I actually passed the basket. I have no recollection of having done so.'

'So you might have?'

'It wasn't important. No one pays attention to stuff like that when it isn't important.'

'It's important now.'

'Yes. And I don't remember. When you're playing cards you're not concentrating on the food. You're concentrating on the hand.'

'You were in the hand?'

'Damn right, I was. It was a big pot. Seth just bet, and I had him beat. Before I had a chance to raise him back, he's dead.'

'How do you know you had him beat?' MacAullif asked.

'How do I know anything? It's seven card stud. I got a flush. He's got two pair. And he's drawing dead. That means the cards he needs to improve are all gone.'

'I know what drawing dead means,' MacAullif said.

'Refresh *my* memory,' I said. 'How'd you *know* he was drawing dead?'

'He's got kings showing. And a two and an eight. Kings and eights are dead. That means we've seen them all already. They're not in the deck. They were in other people's hands. And there's only one deuce left. If he has it, which he probably does, he's got kings up. But he can't improve. His only chance of winning is if he's got a pair of god-knows-what down, catches another one, and has trips in the hole for a full house. If he's betting on that to happen, he's the type of guy I love to play cards with.'

'What about the other people in the hand?'

'They all folded. The judge was out from the beginning. The others stuck around for the sixth card, went out when Seth bet.'

'I thought he threw his money in the pot and died.'

'Yeah, but not like that. A couple of guys folded first. I was getting ready to reach for my money when he took the header.'

'Everyone folded to you?'

'Except Dan. He had garbage showing. He tends to chase too many pots. Probably had a four flush or a four straight, or was looking for trips. I think he went in before me. He wasn't going to be happy when I raised.'

'Neither was Seth Beckman,' I pointed out.

'No kidding. Believe me, if I was gonna kill him, I'd have waited until after the hand.'

'What was that all about?' MacAullif demanded, when the pharmacologist had gone out.

'That was very interesting. Of all the players, he's the first one who wanted to talk about the hand.'

'Because he had a flush.'

'Granted. And look how he played it. Guy kept track of cards right down to the last deuce. Knew that Beckman couldn't hurt him. He also had the accountant sized up. He doesn't just play the cards, he plays the man.'

'The accountant?'

'No. The druggist. He counts cards, reads personalities, probably keeps track of people's tells.'

'You mean he's good at multi-tasking?'

'Like slipping a guy a pretzel in the middle of a poker game?' I shook my head. 'I don't know. Is that all of them?'

MacAullif consulted his notes. 'Yeah, that's it. Wanna check out the crime scene?'

'Thought you'd never ask.'

The poker table was just as they had left it, with the exception of Mr Beckman, who had been cleared away. In the middle of the green felt was a messy heap of red, white, and blue chips, the thick clay ones in fashion since TV poker caught on. In front of each seat chips were stacked in piles, some large, some small. The ones that had been in front of Seth Beckman were smushed over from the gentleman lying on them. The others were neat and orderly, sorted into colours. Apparently Judge Granville and Harvey Poole were doing well. Banker Benjamin Driscoll and accountant Dan Kingston were down. Attorney Richard Rosenberg, host Adam Addington, and the dear departed Seth Beckman were close to even.

Of course, there was a large amount of chips in the centre of the table which were yet to be distributed. If the chips were Harvey Poole's, they would put him way ahead. If the chips were Dan Kingston's, they would put him close to even.

If the chips were Seth Beckman's, they weren't going to help him much.

The cards were exactly as Harvey Poole had described. Seth Beckman had two kings, an eight, and a deuce, all of different suits. Dan Kingston had queen, ten, six, five showing, with a straight or flush draw possible, as well as three of a kind or two small pair. Harvey Poole had three clubs, including one of Seth Beckman's dead kings.

All other hands were folded in front of the players.

The rest of the deck was in front of Adam Addington's chair. Evidently he'd been dealing.

'Just like he said,' MacAullif observed.

'Yeah. Wanna peek?'

'Huh?'

'At the down cards?'

I turned over the hole cards.

Seth Beckman did indeed have a deuce, giving him kings up. Dan Kingston had a pair of queens, was hoping to catch trips, which would lose to Poole's flush, assuming he had it.

He did. Harvey had two clubs in the hole, including the ace. Even if Dan Kingston had hit a flush, which he couldn't, it would have lost to Harvey's ace-king high flush.

'So,' MacAullif said. 'The druggist wins.'

'Not necessarily. Let's see what they would have caught.'

'They can't catch anything. The accountant's got nothing, and the corpse is drawing dead.'

'According to Harvey Poole. But he could be mistaken. Or lying. Killers sometimes do that.'

'Killers?'

'It doesn't hurt to check.'

It didn't help, either. Harvey Poole's hand held up. The chips were his.

I looked around. On a sidebar near the poker table was a telephone and an answering machine. I walked over, looked. There was one message. I pressed the button.

'You can't do that,' MacAullif said.

'Sorry.'

The machine played. 'Adam, this is Kevin. Something came up. I can't make it. I know it's short notice, but try Dan. He always wants to play. Oh, and catch a boat for me. See you next month.'

I looked at MacAullif.

He gave me the evil eye. 'Are you going to start that again?'

'I didn't say a word.'

'You don't have to. You hear the guy's voice on the answering machine, I can see you measuring him for handcuffs.'

'Relax, MacAullif. I don't think the congressman did it.'

'Do you know who did?'

'I got a pretty good idea.'

'Me, too. But I can't prove a thing.'

'Well, it's a poker game, isn't it?'

'So?'

'Wanna run a bluff?'

No one was happy when MacAullif and I came into the dining room to report. If anything, they seemed annoyed we were holding up their hand.

'You needn't recapitulate,' Judge Granville said. 'I know what you're going to say. You've gone over our statements. None of them were particularly useful, but you feel you're making progress. Which is a euphemism for we-haven't-got-a-clue.'

'I wasn't going to say that,' MacAullif assured him.

'Oh? Why not?'

'It isn't true. We're *not* making progress. We've made no progress at all.'

Judge Granville raised his eyebrows. 'You have *nothing*?'

'Give him a break, judge,' I protested. 'You're the one who said he has nothing. You gonna knock him for agreeing with you?'

'You're swapping words with us while there's a murderer sitting at our table,' Adam Addington said irritably. 'That is your contention, isn't it? That one of us killed him?'

'Actually, he thinks Kevin did it,' Judge Granville said ironically.

All stared at me with the contempt which a person who professed so dubious an opinion deserved.

I shrugged. 'Well, wouldn't that be nice? Better him than you, right? Wouldn't you all like to be cleared?'

Even Richard Rosenberg was having trouble swallowing that.

'Stanley? Are you *serious*?'

'I'm not ruling him in, and I'm not ruling him out. The problem is, as I'm sure you all heard, it looks like Seth was killed with a poison pretzel. And Kevin wasn't here to give it to him.'

'Isn't that rather convincing?' Judge Granville said dryly.

'It's certainly a point in his favour. We're examining possibilities here. To narrow things down, I'd like to try a little experiment.'

Judge Granville frowned suspiciously. 'What *kind* of experiment?'

'Let's play some cards.'

The six men milled around the poker table. No one sat down. I got the feeling they couldn't quite believe they were there. Which was understandable. MacAullif had to move the crime scene ribbon to let them in.

'If you would please take your seats,' I invited. 'Your original seats, of course.'

'Are you going to re-enact the crime?' Judge Granville's tone was mocking.

'I would, but we don't have Seth.'

I sat in the dead man's seat. The players sat in theirs. MacAullif stood looking on.

'OK, let's get the chips off the table. Mr Poole, you won, you take the pot.'

'Hey, wait a minute,' Dan Kingston said. 'What do you mean, *he* won?'

'He had a flush,' I explained. 'Even if you hit, you wouldn't have beat him. And you didn't hit. Go on, Harvey, take the chips.'

The pharmacologist raked in the chips, stacked them up.

'I'd love to pass around the basket of pretzels, but the cops snatched 'em up. Instead, I'm going to deal the cards.'

I picked up the deck, which was on the table in front of Beckman's seat.

'Are you going to re-deal the last hand?' Judge Granville said.

'I can't do that. I don't know what everyone had, or when they folded. I suppose I could have taken the time to work it out, but that would have been a lot of trouble. So let's do something else.'

'What?' Dan Kingston said. 'What are you going to do?'

'You ever have a deal-off at the end of the night? Everybody antes a couple of bucks, and you deal a hand of showdown to see who takes the last pot?'

'Yeah. Sure. Why?'

'I thought we'd deal a hand of showdown to see who killed Seth.'

Everyone stared at me incredulously.

'Stanley,' Richard said. 'Have you lost your mind?'

'No, but I'm low on options. And we need to get this settled. Let's play one hand of showdown for it. That's fair, isn't it? Everybody's got an equal chance. OK, here we go.'

Before anyone could protest, I dealt out the cards face up.

'Nine for Richard Rosenberg, deuce for banker Driscoll, king for our gracious host, jack for the judge, six for accountant Dan Kingston, three for Mr Poole, and an eight for the dealer.'

'Hey,' Harvey Poole said. 'You dealt yourself in.'

'Not me. I dealt Seth in. After all, he could have committed suicide.'

I wouldn't have thought their faces could have looked any more incredulous. I was wrong.

'OK,' I said. 'King is high. So far it's you, Mr Addington.'

The billionaire in the torn T-shirt looked up at MacAullif. 'Do we have to put up with this?'

'No. I can take you all downtown and we can do everything by the book.'

The men thought that over.

'Deal!' Addington snapped.

I dealt another round. 'OK, ace for Richard, queen for the banker, king gets a nine – you're no longer high, Mr Addington, ten for the judge, deuce for Mr Kingston, nine for Mr Poole, and the dealer gets a six.'

'Wait a minute,' Benjamin Driscoll said. 'Is this five card or seven card showdown?'

The others stared at him. No one could believe he'd asked.

'Seven card.' I answered with a straight face, as if it were a perfectly natural question. 'That's what you were playing, wasn't it?'

'You're certifiable,' Addington said.

'Maybe. But it's dealer's choice. And I'm the dealer. Here they come again, and, oh! Look! Judge Granville pulls into the lead with a pair of jacks. Is it possible, Your Honour, that you decided to mete out justice at the poker table?'

The judge favoured me with a superior smirk.

'Here's a five for Mr Kingston, and, ah, Mr Poole, three hearts. Possible flush. And you had a flush when Seth Beckman died.'

'So what?'

I held the deck up, didn't deal the next card. 'Well, we have a bit of a problem here. I hate to speak ill of the dead, but apparently Seth Beckman was not a nice man. Everyone here had a motive to kill him. Some more than others.'

'Come on, deal,' Driscoll said irritably. I understood his apprehension. *His* motive was better than most.

'Yes,' I agreed. 'Let's see who improves. No apparent help, no apparent help, no apparent help, no help for the judge's jacks, no apparent help.' I dealt Poole a spade. 'Off the flush. And no help for the dealer. Jacks are still high.'

'Side pot on low,' Dan Kingston quipped. He had four cards to a seven, an excellent low hand.

I pointed at the cards in front of me. They were four to an eight, not quite as good a low, but competitive. 'Seth might take you up on that. Too bad he's dead.'

I held the deck again, looked around. 'See, here's the problem. How do you force the pretzel? You can't pick it up and hand it to him. The guy reaches in the basket. Takes a pretzel or two. How do you make sure he takes the right one?'

'You can't,' Richard Rosenberg said. 'There's no way to do it. At least none I know of.'

'How about it, guys? Anyone know how to force the pretzel?'

There was no answer.

This time it was Judge Granville who said, 'Deal.'

I dealt the fifth round. 'Here we are, and, aces for Richard Rosenberg! Sorry about that. Try not to take it personally. Pair of queens for Mr Driscoll. No help for our host. Oh! Jacks and sevens for the judge!' I dealt Dan Kingston a four, giving him ace, three, four, six, seven. 'And a seven low made. You're in the wrong game. No help for the flush. And a ten high for the dealer.'

Benjamin Driscoll threw his hands in the air. 'I can't believe we're sitting here doing this!'

'That pair of queens got you nervous? Relax. Rosenberg's got aces, and the judge has jacks up. Right now you're a long shot to win.'

I paused again. 'So. We got someone who wants to give Seth Beckman a poison pretzel. How does he do that without being seen? Particularly during a big hand that Mr Beckman is in, where everyone will be looking at him? No theories? OK, let's see another card.'

I dealt the sixth card. 'No help for the aces. No help for your queens, Mr Driscoll. See, you were worried for nothing. No help for our gracious host. No help for the jacks and sevens. Low hand pairs the threes.'

'We're not playing low hand,' the banker said irritably.

I dealt a heart to Harvey Poole. 'Ah. Back on the flush. And a pair of deuces for the decedent.'

I held the deck in my hand, looked around the table. 'See, here's the thing. It's easy to poison a pretzel, next to impossible to guide it into the right hand. When you think along those lines, you're in trouble. Once you accept the assumption it couldn't be done, everything falls into place.'

They stared at me incredulously.

'OK, moment of truth. Big all or nothing card. So far the judge is in front with jacks up. Can Richard Rosenberg unseat him with aces up? No. No help for the aces. Mr Driscoll... no help for the queens.'

I swear the banker let out a sigh. 'No help for Mr Addington. No help for Judge Granville, but he's still high with jacks up.'

I dealt Dan Kingston a five. 'The seven low improves to a six low.' Dan also had three, four, five, six, seven. 'Oh! Small straight!' Dan looked sick. As if the hand actually meant anything. 'Judge, you're off the hook. Everyone's off the hook.'

I turned to Harvey Poole. 'Except you. It all comes down to you, Mr Poole. The four flush. You, who can hit a heart and win the whole thing. Just like you did when he died.'

Adam Addington frowned. 'Hey. What are you saying? Are you saying Harvey did it?'

'Well, let's think about that. The killer couldn't force the pretzel, therefore the killer didn't know who he was going to kill, therefore the killer didn't care. The killer wanted to kill someone at the table. Not anyone in particular. Just anyone at all. Does that profile fit any of the suspects?'

I turned the card over.

Ace of spades.

Busted flush.

'And we have a winner! Dan Kingston, with a small straight. Dan Kingston, who doesn't quite play in the same league, but who'd like to. Who isn't a regular, and only gets called now and then. Who needs the connections and associations this game affords, but who can't network effectively unless he's playing every month. Who needs to knock out a player, *any* player, to create a seat. I have bad news, Mr Addington. The killer is your tax accountant. I hope he finished your return.'

Dan's face had drained of colour. 'That's ridiculous. So I got a straight. It's just a stupid hand of cards.'

'That's not what proves you're guilty,' I explained. 'You left your fingerprints on the pretzel.'

'The hell I did!' Dan cried. 'You can't get fingerprints from a pretzel! I—'

Dan Kingston broke off in mid-sentence. He stared at me in horror. Then down at his cards. Then up again. He looked so crushed I almost felt sorry for him.

'No, you can't,' I told him. 'I was bluffing. But sometimes you can win with a bluff.'

MacAullif stepped forward and told Dan Kingston he had the right to remain silent. MacAullif needn't have bothered. The little accountant had nothing to say.

'So,' Judge Granville said, after MacAullif had hustled the suspect off to the hoosegow. 'All that dealing showdown was just a distraction to get Dan confused so he'd blurt out an admission.'

'Yes, and no. I wanted to get him confused, but I also wanted to accuse him of the crime. That's why I stacked the deck to let him win. Did you see his face when he caught that five? I've never seen a gambler so unhappy to catch an inside straight.'

'How'd you know he did it? Please tell me there wasn't any fingerprint.'

'Of course not. That was a bluff.'

'So, how'd you know?'

'Actually, you got me thinking in the right direction. When you suggested ironically you killed him to make way for a more harmonious player. Ridiculous, of course. But not that far from the truth. What if someone knocked out a player to create a seat?'

'That's absurd.'

'It's not absurd. It's pathetic. But understandable. Particularly when you see the guy. He's like a little kid looking through the window of a candy store, wanting to be invited to the grown-ups table.'

'You're mixing metaphors.'

'Sue me.'

As if on cue, Richard Rosenberg said, 'Come on, guys, don't give him a hard time. After all, he solved the murder.'

The others mumbled their thanks. Considering the circumstance, I couldn't help noticing a decided lack of enthusiasm.

'I don't expect you guys to be grateful, or anything, but you don't look all that happy.'

'Well,' Harvey Poole said. 'You gotta remember. We're playing with six people, what with Seth getting killed. With Dan arrested, we're down to five. That's not such a good game.'

Talk about obsessive. Of course, I could understand it. I've played poker myself.

'You're playing quarter-half?'

'Yeah.'

I pulled out my wallet. 'Deal me in.'

♠

Poker and Shooter

Sue DeNymme

*Poker & Shooter is an underground game played at a private
New England High School where a self-appointed senior Master or
Mistress invites victimized students to join 'The Secret Circle' in
order to avenge them. Using free tequila and a poker kitty as bait,
the senior lures the victim's unknowing offender into a pre-game of
Truth or Dare where the offender either reveals a shameful secret or
commits an illegal act (to be videotaped for the option of blackmail
later). Then the poker game begins and drinking rules apply. (Loser
always takes a shot; Dealer can take a shot or not; and the
Master/Mistress may randomly call shots, like it or not.) To make
the game appear fair, new members are tricked into winning five
hands of Five Card Stud. The ultimate prize is vengeance.*

NIGHT FILLED THE BOATHOUSE, smudging the space into
black except for the candle flames and what they struggled to
illuminate around the three remaining classmates: the twins and
Sharon, their third initiate. In spite of their limited experience with
the game, Daphne and her brother Piper had already begun to
crave the intoxicating feeling of superiority it provided.

Daphne leaned into the centre of the table where the candles
glowed so she could check her Rolex: three-thirty. Five Card Stud
had taken longer than planned. 'Piper?' She nodded at the Cuervo

Gold tequila bottle that gleamed in the space between them. 'Victory toast.' Her twin knew what she meant: time to punish the evil one.

Her brother picked himself up and smiled with a nod before reciting softly. '"The birds pour forth their souls in notes of rapture from a thousand throats." William Wordsworth.' As he reached to pour out the Gold, the veins bulged in his arms in the same shade of blue as the sheen on his buzz cut. Overnight, his skin had paled as the whites of his eyes brightened with red. Stubble had sprouted to camouflage his fatigue, and it all worked toward his ultimate goal of keeping people away from them by disguising their family wealth.

Open-mouthed, Sharon squinted at Daphne's brother. 'What birds? What are you talking about?' She had to be the dumbest sophomore they had ever met: suspended twice for cheating within six months, and ugly, too. Her awful teeth, honking nose and furball hair made her look like a yak. She moved her eyes back and forth as if she were seeing two heads on his neck.

'Just ignore him.' Daphne pocketed the trick deck and snapped her fingers. 'Circle, please.' It was too late for the twins to be awake, still playing and over-charged with adrenaline. Wired and clammy as grave diggers in the dew, the sounds of the creaking boathouse were intensifying everyone's paranoia. Each of them had mentioned the pylons that groaned beneath the floorboards, but Daphne had reassured them that the structure had only been erected a year before and was thus totally sound. Still, Daphne found herself grimacing in hope that the planks wouldn't cave as she took Piper's and Sharon's hands and said, 'Repeat after me, Sharon. I hereby renew my vow never to tell a soul of anything occurring here tonight.'

Sharon nodded, stumbled forward a bit, and little flames shone in her eyes as she righted herself, slurring the pledge.

'Sharon,' Daphne beamed, proud of her superior liquor tolerance, 'from this day forward, you are bound by blood to the

Secret Circle. Together we will help you pursue happiness and the welfare of our circle, and it all starts with the spoils of your victory here tonight.' She winked at her brother and raised her glass, smug in her authority. 'Congratulations, Sharon.'

Piper's diesel-coloured eyes and the sweat on his Adam's apple reflected the flickering light as he said, 'Go, Poker and Shooter!' It sounded like a sports chant.

Beneath the A-frame ceiling of the school boathouse, the three clinked their glasses as they reached into the pyramid of darkness. As Daphne toasted, she gritted her teeth, trying to make the smile look real even though she loathed herself for doing it since that was why her veneers kept chipping, and cracking a tooth meant begging her dad to pay the bill and enduring the humiliation of his power games again. The thought surged inside, shorting the buzz she'd worked so hard to get. Eyeing the glass in her hand, she assured herself that the next shot would anoint her again with that baptismal burn, restoring that sublime sensation of having swallowed the sky.

They drank and winced, then opened their mouths and breathed together like fish.

Smiling, Sharon jogged her shoulders like a kid. 'I can't believe I won,' she said. 'I always lose at poker.' Sitting on the edge of her stool, she scooped the betting money into her purse, displaying the letters on her knuckles that spelled out Cornell. It was an open tribute to him, the love of her life, the boy Christina had taken away. Nodding slowly, she unwrapped a piece of gum, popped it between her yellow teeth and chomped. 'So, what about Christina? It's an eye for an eye, right? You're not really going to help that backstabber win Homecoming Queen, are you?'

Sharon had no idea they'd been reading her cards, fixing the game for her to win, and Daphne was not about to break the spell. Daphne got off on rigging the cards and tricking the other kids into loyalty. 'Of course not.' A malicious titter escaped Daphne's lips. When they'd rowed up the river to the campus, the fog had frizzed

Sharon's copper curls into sections that snaked out like the snapping hair of Medusa, one of the Gorgons, whose face was so ugly it would turn men to stone if they looked at her, and right now Sharon seemed to be having a similar effect on Daphne. In fact, she hadn't noticed it earlier, but the blind space above felt oppressive. That and the creaking of the pylons made Daphne nervous.

'Let's go.' Daphne blew out two tapers and lifted the last one from the table, cupping the flame as she ushered Sharon and Piper out of the clubroom down the steps to the boat bays where the scent of drying varnish filled the air, then down a hall reeking with fresh paint.

A flip of the light switch and they saw the locker room with its sinks and toilets and back wall of shower stalls. She squeezed the flame from its wick before opening one of the stalls and leaning on the door.

The stench made Sharon wince and shield her nose.

Christina was slumped on the tiles in front of the toilet, all of that sparkling champagne hair now dulled and matted with puked-up bits of salad and bile spattered down to her stomach. Her skirt rode high on her thighs but for once it wasn't sexy. One of her flip-flops lay two feet away. It was hard to see if Christina's eyes were open, but Daphne was pretty sure they weren't because any conscious girl would have gotten up and left by now. The putrid fumes would have driven her off. Cornell's ring gleamed from her middle finger, a brass oval with a C in the middle. Cornell had been Sharon's boyfriend before Christina came to their school and stole him.

Daphne poked Sharon in the belly. 'Take the ring back.' A few months ago, Sharon had loved the ring as she had loved Cornell. 'You deserve it.'

'I can't,' Sharon said, eyes wide. She took the gum out of her mouth and rolled it between her fingers. 'I feel bad. I thought she just passed out. You said that, right, Piper? But Christina looks almost... dead.'

True. Christina's skin did have a whale-belly sheen, bloated and metallic, which was odd since she'd always been the best looking at school, making all the girls jealous. In fact, she was too pretty, the cold kind of pretty guys want to take and girls want to eliminate. 'What do you care? You wanted her to be punished for what she did.' Daphne looked at her brother and shrugged. 'That was the point of our game. Your problem with Christina is why we made her break in here in the first place, and if you say anything, we'll tell them you're to blame. You're the one who hated Christina. Everyone knows that.'

Sharon's forehead puckered as she stretched out her chewing gum and snapped it apart. 'Are you sure she's OK?'

Glaring, Daphne said, 'Sure, I'm sure.' Sharon had paid way too much for her hairdo. It looked more like hairballs than coiffure, but it wouldn't have helped to tell her. Sharon would always be a loser and there was no makeover for that. She decided to stay out of Sharon's hair.

Piper ran his hand back and forth over his buzzed Mohawk. 'Cornell won't want the skank if someone finds her half-naked on the library steps. Let's take her and leave her in her underwear. She'll never want to come back to this school. That's for sure.' Piper chuckled. 'We can pin a note on her jacket that says, Do Me.'

'Very poetic,' Daphne said. 'OK. What do we do with the Grand Prize then?'

'She smells so bad.' Sharon put her hand over her mouth. 'I don't know.'

'You're supposed to be happy about this, Sharon. That's why we did this for you. Christina is your prize now. Maybe you need another shot. Hair of the dog to break up the bad taste?' Daphne groped for Sharon's and Piper's hands. 'Shall we chant first? Blood on the moon, Blood on the moon.'

'Stop.' Sharon jerked away, bent down and put her ear to Christina's nostrils. 'Is she even breathing?'

'She was breathing fine before.' Piper looked at Daphne and got down on his haunches so his shorts rose over his knees. Wrestling and sculling had chiselled his quads, but he looked more like a burglar than a jock, and the image was not a good choice since he'd been arrested for breaking and entering through the school nurse's bedroom window. 'Want me to slap her? There's no way I'm giving her mouth to mouth.'

The colour of Christina's hair reminded Daphne of the amber that ancient Greeks rubbed to generate electricity. If only they could find a defibrillator, they could jolt her back to life.

'I don't like this, you guys.' Sharon stood. 'Someone should check her pulse.'

Daphne spotted a pair of polka-dotted panties by the toilet in the next stall that had to be Christina's. Kneeling in front of them, she tried to block Sharon's view and sneak them out of the bathroom before anyone else noticed because if Sharon saw, she'd probably want to tell Cornell or something. Piper could go to jail. They could all go to jail.

Her brother bent to grab Christina's wrist, feel for the pulse in her veins.

'Don't touch.' Daphne blocked his arm with her foot. 'You didn't touch her skin, did you?' She was grinding her teeth again. Her temples ached from her churning jaws.

Her brother smiled with his eyes just like he had when they were kids and he'd lie, lie, lie to their nanny. He crossed his arms and said, 'I didn't touch her.'

'You're such an idiot.' Of course he had touched her. He'd taken off her panties! Daphne shook her head. 'We have to change the whole game because of this. They can get prints off the skin.'

'I saw that on TV.' Sharon sat on her haunches next to Daphne and looked at the blonde. 'I think they use superglue.' She pulled a mobile phone out of her purse. 'I'll call for help. Maybe 911 can pump her stomach or something.'

Daphne snatched the phone. 'Put that goddamn thing away.'

'We can go to the payphone if you're scared.'

'And tell them what?' Piper snorted. 'We hazed her? You're crazy. They'll lock us up.'

Daphne took a brown paper towel from the dispenser and wiped Sharon's prints off the faucet. 'We put muscle relaxants in her tequila. Do you want to spend the rest of your life watching your back in prison?'

Sharon shook her head. 'We can tell them she agreed to take the pills. We had too much to drink and she passed out in here and that's when we called 911. She drank too much and took drugs. They can save her.' She opened her phone. 'OK?'

Daphne shook her head and held up the panties. 'That would have worked if Piper hadn't spoiled everything.' She glared at her brother. 'Will they find DNA?'

Sharon's face puckered. Her wiry locks shot in the air like antennae groping for signals, a sea anemone in shock therapy.

'No.' Piper took a step back. 'I used a condom.'

Daphne scoffed. 'What the hell were you thinking? If she wakes up now, she'll tell for sure.' She watched Christina's chest for movement, but it didn't rise or fall. No telling how long she'd been like that. They were in big trouble now.

She pictured the police at the Headmaster's office. Would they charge manslaughter or murder? Definitely rape – premeditated rape because Piper had slipped a Mickey into her booze at the beginning of the card game. They all had histories of violence and delinquency.

Burdened with the onslaught of unwanted responsibility, Daphne pushed herself up from the floor and began to plan the next move. She turned to her brother. 'Pick her up. She's not breathing.'

Sharon quickly objected. 'No way. You're not supposed to move someone like that.'

Daphne didn't want to hurt her, but it would have felt good to bop Sharon in the head. 'Listen, Sharon. Pull it together. Take a deep breath.'

'What if you killed her with those pills?'

Daphne shook her head. 'That's not what happened.' Sophomores could be so dumb. 'You're the one responsible here.'

Squeezing her fists into white knuckles Sharon said, 'This is your fault, Daphne. You set all of this up. You're the Mistress of Poker and Shooter. It was your dumb game that got us into trouble.'

The fire of betrayal stung Daphne's cheeks as she glared. 'Who do you think you are? You're new to this school, and you're just a sophomore.' Daphne was the one who used people, not the other way around. She had rigged it all for Sharon with the trick card deck in order to gain power at school, but now with Christina dead, Daphne had to revise the game. It was hers to play and preserve now that she acted as Mistress. Daphne held Sharon's gaze. 'Remember the oath you took in blood?'

Sharon looked away. Her pistachio eyes flicked around the space: at the ceiling, then the floor, anywhere it seemed but into Daphne's eyes. Finally, she fixed her eyes on the ring that gleamed on Christina's finger. 'Do what's best for the Circle? Restore harmony through the game?'

Daphne looked at her brother. 'Should we tell her?'

'The first oath.' Piper frowned. 'You don't remember the blood vow?'

Sharon opened her hand and answered. 'Not a word outside the Circle.' For a moment, she stared at the circle they'd inscribed in her palm to draw blood for the oath.

'What you hear in the Circle, what you see in the Circle, must always stay in the Circle. To break the rules is to break the Circle and risk being silenced.' The idiot had to be told again and again. 'You're linked to us now. Forever.'

'Like Knights of the Round Table,' added Piper. 'Break the vow and you're cursed.'

Sharon said, 'This is different. This is real.'

They weren't getting through. Daphne fought an impulse to kick Sharon in the stomach. She stabbed a finger into Sharon's chest. 'Remember this is all because of you, Sharon.'

Sharon's tears splashed on the tile as she crumpled and sobbed, her stomach jiggling over her jeans so that the fat smothered the gem in her navel. Not only did she need a brain transplant, but she could have used lipo, too. Extreme makeover. All the way. 'How old are you? Sixteen?'

Looking up briefly, Sharon sobbed and sniffed. 'Yeah.'

Maybe she was retarded.

She was worse than pathetic. Sharon's hysteria brought out something abysmal in Daphne, and though she knew it was wrong to want to kick the initiate in the face as she lay crying at her feet, Sharon's weakness catalyzed the predator in Daphne. It filled her with energy, and she liked the power of it.

In the long rectangular mirror, Daphne caught a glimpse of herself: a scary banshee with ratty burgundy hair and bloodshot eyes. Normally she looked like the princess in the Star Wars movies, but she had drunk off her lipstick and the eyeliner had smeared around her sockets. She was turning into Sharon, for God's sake. Quickly, she splashed water on her face and wiped the smudges away with toilet paper.

'Ugh.' Piper heaved Christina's body like fresh killed game across his shoulders: ankles to one side, wrists dangling on the other.

Daphne threw the tissue into the toilet and flushed. 'Down to Sharon's boat.' Daphne nodded and scanned the bathroom for evidence. 'Can you manage the steps?'

'Yeah. She's light as a feather.'

'Good.' Daphne wiped the sink with pink dispenser soap, then the toilet and the doors. 'Check outside, Sharon.'

Sharon hugged herself and rocked back and forth on the floor. 'It's all my fault. I just wanted Cornell so much.'

'I know. Go to the door and look outside. Make sure no one's coming.' No response. Sharon didn't even move. She and Piper couldn't have been that dumb as sophomores. There was no way everyone was created equal. She was getting on Daphne's last nerve. 'What is wrong with you? Do you want to go to jail? Get up and move.' Finally, Daphne sighed. 'All right. Don't get up. I'll check outside myself.' She walked to the window and peeked out the blinds. Every second that drew closer to dawn upped the ante of getting caught. Across the lawn near the woods by the Headmaster's cottage, an owl hooted, but the lights were still out. The mist was the only thing moving on campus. At the foot of the cliffs in the labyrinth, the fog had broken into phantoms that meandered through the boxwood as darkness fled. 'OK.' Daphne looked down at Sharon. 'Let's go.'

Piper led the girls out of the bathroom and down a hall, past a phalanx of trophies, novelties and awards, where Daphne's father smiled from a glossy 8 x 10. Once captain of the sculling team, their father had donated the boathouse to the school. Seeing his face unhinged Daphne, opening a door to the past that she had long trussed shut. She could almost feel those damn veneers popping off.

'Bet he'd return our calls if he could see us now, Daf.' Piper chuckled.

'Why now? To say he's proud of how we picked up his amazing poker skills?' She spat at his laminated eyes. 'No way he'd bail us out of jail. He never even loved us.'

Piper sighed. 'He's a fraud. Forget the jerk,' he said. 'We're in control. It's our turn to change the world.' Their childhood days were definitely over.

Daphne nodded and followed him back to the lobby and the poker table, where she stopped to stuff the candles into her back-pack with the shot glasses and the ashtray. After she downed the last of the tequila, she put the empty bottle in with the clinking shot glasses.

Suddenly, she couldn't breathe in all that darkness. Her knees felt like Silly Putty. Above, the blackness seemed to shift and the beams stretched like guillotines, four deep, about to fall on her neck.

The next thing she saw was Piper looking down, shaking her shoulders. 'What was that? I think you fainted.'

She tried to focus. 'I'm OK.'

Piper smiled and offered his hand. "'O the cunning wiles that creep in thy little heart asleep!'"

Taking his hand, Daphne finished the stanza. "'When thy little heart doth wake, then the dreadful night shall break." William Blake.' Dusting her skirt with her hands, she said, 'Pick her up. Time to blow this rat hole.'

Under a thin film of dusk, the three climbed down the boathouse stairs to the dock to untie Sharon's boat. Piper went first, taking the stairs one by one with Christina's body slung over his shoulder, an ankle in his grip as he breathed what looked like smoke. The stench of Christina's hair stained the air but the chill revitalized them as it blew off the water.

At the end of the dock where Sharon's boat waited, Piper stopped and sighed.

When he dropped his burden, the body landed in the boat with a thud, rocking it, making circles in the water that slapped back again and again.

On the surface of the river, the moon sparked in zigzags that looked like a polygraph test or maybe a heart monitor in ICU. A fish flew out of the water in a flash of silver light.

Without a word, Sharon untied the knot and tossed in the rope. Staring at the coil, she followed Piper, grabbing the side of the boat for balance until she took the seat across from him.

Daphne stepped in last, lifting her skirt to avoid the corpse. She couldn't stop looking at it, all that hair moving in a Cuervo-coloured puddle. Christina's half-open lids made her seem like a ghost, beckoning from the underworld, as if she could be revived. Arms crossed, Daphne braced herself against the lonesome chill. They had each taken blood vows to one another, but she'd never felt so alone. 'Don't start the engine,' she whispered. Her temples felt like skinless nerves. She realized her palms were sweating. 'Too noisy.' The words played again in her skull, taking on lives of their own.

Sharon looked terrified. 'What if someone comes?' She pushed off, dipping the boat to the side so that wavelets slapped back. The puddle in the boat curled Christina's hair around Daphne's toe. 'Do you two have a plan?'

'Yeah.' Piper grabbed the oar and plunged it, leaning toward the water as he stroked to propel them up river. The air felt cooler as they moved into it. 'Where to, Daf?'

Intuitively, she knew. Something primal had ignited in her soul, a sixth sense, and she projected herself up to look down on the boat like she was in some higher realm, a realm of all-knowing where she could see the shimmer of fish swimming by, the currents in the water and the people in the village waking in their beds. 'We'll lodge her body up the river by the Appalachian Trail mouth. Under the tree in the water.'

When they arrived at the trailhead, Piper put the oar in the boat. He dug a Zippo lighter out of his jeans, cupped the flame around a cigarette and sucked before spewing smoke into the stench of alcohol-drenched vomit. With the cigarette hanging from his lips, he reached down and lifted the corpse with one hand, but the head slipped and smacked against the side of the boat.

Christina seemed to be watching through her lashes.

'Jesus!' Sharon whispered with force. 'What are you doing?'

He shrugged and fumbled with the body again and finally, when he flipped it over the side, both girls flinched. Pins of icy water splashed up as Christina's head dipped under the surface.

Piper put a leg over and eased himself down, grimacing. The girls stared at the patient, rising corpse.

The eyelids had fully opened, revealing lichen green irises like the stained rose borders of the campus chapel doors. Why hadn't her parents baptized her? She would have been forgiven.

'We're going to hell for this,' Sharon said. 'We could at least tell someone she drowned so they'll give her the proper burial.'

Daphne grimaced. 'It's too late.'

Sharon opened her mouth and closed it, staring at the shell of water by the boat.

Chest deep, Piper grabbed Christina's ankle. 'Don't freak out. The animals and the water will take care my prints.' He waded the body through the river to the massive trunk that had been split by lightning and sunk years ago, then lodged the carcass under water.

Daphne lit a cigarette, gave it to Sharon and lit another for herself to smoke while she watched her brother wade to shore and back, anchoring the body with stones. Puffing while they waited, they exhaled rings that bloomed into halos that floated up to heaven. Daphne prayed there was no God.

When her brother finally came back, he splashed his sister and quoted Edgar Allan Poe. '"Resignedly beneath the sky, the melancholy waters lie."' The boat rocked as he climbed in and, like a dog, shook off spray.

'Watch it.' Sharon flicked her cigarette at his arm and watched it bounce off his bicep to the river.

Piper scooped fistfuls of water and splashed her in the face.

'Asshole.' Sharon wiped her cheeks with her shirt hem. 'It's getting light, you guys. I have to be back before my mom wakes up. What time is it?'

'"Had we but world enough, and time."' Piper looked at his diving watch. '"This coyness, lady, were no crime." Andre Marvell.'

Daphne rolled her eyes. Her head throbbed and burned. 'It's almost five. Row the boat to Sharon's house, Piper. We'll walk back after we drop her off.'

A few days later, the girls were standing catty-corner in the buffet line when they heard a teacher telling the chef that a body had risen in the river. The girls locked eyes.

Sharon whispered. 'Let's go to the Sunken Garden.'

'Good plan.' Daphne whispered and put a cupcake on her tray. 'No one goes there, and if anyone comes, we'll see them on the steps.' She eyed Sharon's loose-fitting clothes and put a cupcake on Sharon's tray. 'You're losing weight, you know. Your face looks drawn.'

Sharon huffed and followed Daphne out the French dining hall doors, across the terrace and beyond the Georgian campus buildings to a series of immaculate outdoor rooms, tennis courts, the ice rink, football field and running trail that ran alongside the service road. The footpath led them directly to the orbed gateway of the Sunken Garden, now blanketed with red roses. A central fountain spouted water from a fish's mouth in the middle of the recessed quadrangle whose sections were said to represent the four corners of paradise. Down the steps, they found a bench near a bed that filled the air with perfume.

The instant Sharon put down her tray and sat, she let the tears fall. 'I'm so scared. This game is driving me crazy.' She dabbed at the spots that kept blooming on her cotton skirt. 'You should come with me tomorrow to church. I'm going to confession.'

'Are you crazy? All we have to do is stay quiet. Don't admit anything or volunteer information. Never admit guilt. That's what Piper's lawyer tells him. Life sucks.' Daphne picked a rose and inhaled the scent. 'We just have to deal with it.' She put down the flower and said, 'They don't even know we were with Christina that night. You'll be fine.'

'Who are you, the Oracle at Delphi?' Sharon sniffed. She kept rubbing the stains but they only multiplied as more tears fell. Like the eternal labors of Sisyphus, the task seemed endless. 'What if they find something?'

'No way. It was an accident. Happens every day. Christina fell in and drowned.' Daphne nodded.

Sharon returned an empty green-eyed stare. 'So what do we do? I feel like I'm dying inside. I feel like hell.'

'You look like it. We should do your hair.' She nibbled a hangnail. 'We need manicures. And force yourself to eat something. If you start wasting away and looking like crap and crying all the time, everyone will know.'

'I won't.' Sharon shook her head. She lifted the fork and cut her chicken enchilada into little pieces, choking on the tears. 'I want to go to the river and say a prayer.' She chewed like she was eating cat litter. 'I want to see where they found Christina.'

'Are you certifiably insane?' Daphne licked a blue frosting flower off the top of her cupcake. 'We can't go there. Bad idea.'

Another bit of enchilada went into Sharon's mouth. 'Then we have to cast a spell.' She looked up at the sky as if an answer would appear in the smoky letters of a sky writer plane. 'Last year you stole frogs from the lab, right?'

Daphne frowned and bit into her cupcake. 'They never proved it was me.'

'You said it was because of your spell, that protective spell.' Sharon crossed herself in the Catholic tradition. 'Why don't we cast a spell like that so no one finds out about this? To protect ourselves?' Sharon watched her finish her cupcake. 'We could at least say a prayer for Christina. Light a candle?'

Daphne nodded. It was scary how she believed every mystical charm. If some detective asked her what happened, Sharon could actually tell the truth like some kind of idiot. 'OK. If you insist, let's go to higher ground.' She picked up the rose and waved it at the green apple on Sharon's tray. 'Are you gonna eat that?'

'I thought you wanted me to.'

'Save it.' She faked a smile. 'We'll bring it to the bluffs as an offering.'

High above the river, the air tasted like grassy topsoil and decay, but the view of the leafy hilltops and flowing river below was so exhilarating that Daphne felt she could fly away. There was something intriguing about the impulse, though she knew if she tried she would crack like a melon on the rocks. She inhaled and beamed. 'Heavenly, isn't it?'

'Heavenly.' Sharon nodded as she stepped to the edge. Her green eyes sparkled as she turned back. 'Is this where you always cast the spells?'

'Not always.' Wriggling out of the backpack, Daphne spread her jacket on the ground so she could sit and watch the idiot. She fished out her supplies: a lighter, some candles and the trick deck. 'It's a tragedy so few of us know about this, but that's why it's so nice, too.'

'Yeah. It's nice up here except for that.' Sharon pointed at a hundred-foot tree below. 'That's the Killing Tree where my cousin bled his first deer. He was so proud he brought me to see it, but I hate hunting. I was glad when they finally gave that land to the government.'

'Tax write-off?'

Sharon nodded and stepped towards Daphne, who was laying black tapers out on her jacket. 'How did you know?'

'My father does that whenever he needs a tax break. Problems of abundance.'

Sharon nodded. 'Hey. I didn't see him at the parents' picnic. How is your dad?' Daphne was grinding her teeth again and Sharon must have sensed her irritation. She changed the subject. 'Do you always use black candles for spells?'

'Only death spells.' A flicker of fear in Sharon's eyes passed as quickly as it had come. She believed all Daphne's lies about magic but nothing practical about protecting herself from jail.

'Is that why you used them at the poker game?'

'No.' Daphne stabbed three candles into the topsoil, in a triangular formation. 'That was accidental.'

'Oh.' Sharon pursed her lips, eyes watering like she was about to weep. 'Sorry.' She picked up a fallen branch and poked it into the bobbing doilies of Queen Anne's Lace that fringed the cliff. 'Don't you need like tarot cards or something occult?'

'Would you stop talking for a minute?' Stupid girl. 'Am I the Mistress here?' Sharon nodded. 'Then keep quiet. We have to clear our heads before any of this will work. Don't say anything while I sort out the altar. Got it?'

Sharon held out the apple and raised a brow at the ochre stain of rot caving in around the stem. 'Do you need this now?' Daphne glared a wall between them that stopped Sharon from breathing. 'I'm sorry,' Sharon said as she put the apple back into her pocket. 'I'm asking too many questions.'

'You're nervous.' Daphne faked a smile. 'Let's talk. Tell me how I chose my name.'

'You mean Daphne? Daughter of the river god.' Sharon nodded, eyes agleam. 'You took it from Apollo and Daphne in Mythology 101. Because of the current and the way the story seemed to juice you up. You said it gave you a charge.'

'Right. Her delight was in sport and the spoils of the chase. The river was her rapture, that and the woods.' Daphne lit the candles and said, 'Go stand by the cliff. Clear your head. Imagine the river god in the current. Just listen to the music of the water. Feel it carry you away.'

'I like the sound of water.' Sharon nodded and turned and walked to the edge. She turned back. 'But you know what? I still miss Cornell. And you won't believe this, but I miss Christina, too. I hate what we did, but at least we have each other.' Facing the gorge, she said, 'How long do I do this?'

What a moron. 'However long it takes.' Daphne rubbed her aching temples. Sharon had been a lame brain during the cover-up and now again since Christina's body had risen. Like her mythological namesake, Charon the ferryman to Hades could lead them both to hell, but Daphne was *not* going down, now or ever, and especially not because of some dumb chick named Sharon. She pictured the freak as Medusa, paddling into the underworld, and giddiness took hold. Swallowing hard, she stifled a laugh. Wouldn't the entire human gene pool improve without Sharon Hicks, Lame Brain of the Century? Daphne's future looked a lot cheerier without that imbecile in the picture. She took a step towards her.

Sharon shuffled backwards and said, 'How do you know when you're finished?' Pebbles tumbled down the cliff.

Seeing Sharon on the ledge was too much. Daphne's cheeks warmed, her stomach tingled with urgency. 'Have you been baptized?' She took a giant breath and exhaled, feeling stronger by the second as she walked towards the cliff.

'No. Why?'

'Maybe you should pray for forgiveness.'

Sharon turned around. 'What?'

'Pray.' Something surged inside and Daphne lunged.

Sharon's body betrayed her. Her back twisted. Her knees buckled. Her face morphed into a desperate shock of eyes that gave Daphne a strange sense of satisfaction as she stepped forward to watch the fall. Sharon had dropped twenty feet when the copper head smacked on something, making the body jerk before splashing down another forty feet into the eddy.

She looked a lot better under water. Her white jacket puffed out around her like wings. She wouldn't be worrying anymore.

Daphne heard something. She turned to check the staircase for any witnesses, but no one was there. Just distant thunder. Lightning charged the sky. Five counts later came the bang.

She looked up, but the heavens gave no comfort. Clouds raced past and the wind shook the trees like furies streaming down the river, the leaves shivering in gusts that moved from tree to tree. The foliage and sky were tearing themselves apart.

She shouldn't have looked back down the bluffs but she did.

In the river, Sharon looked up breathlessly, her body swirling like a leaf. The body whirled around and around, spinning, and dizziness swept over Daphne. She closed her eyes and shuddered at the thousand-mile an hour spin of planet Earth. Loose soil gave way underfoot and her reflexes pulled her back as her stomach churned, around and around, like Sharon, far below. She opened her eyes and wished Sharon alive. She wished she hadn't killed her. If only she could press the Undo button, like on a computer and make it all reverse. Daphne hugged herself and held back the tears. If Sharon hadn't been such a freak, if she had only been able to control herself and keep her mouth shut, she would still be part of the Secret Circle. Daphne felt rotten, and for a moment, she wanted to let herself go, crash on the rocks and float in the eddy. The whirlpool had become a black hole in her soul, dragging her into despair.

Then lightning cracked. In three counts came thunder, even closer than before, and beneath the gathering thunderhead she spotted a string of rosary beads – Sharon's. They must have slipped from her pocket. Daphne's breathing quickened as she went for them and the movement of her body snapped her out of her trance.

However long she'd been there, she had stayed too long. She couldn't look at Sharon again, or the river. One only had to be within hearing distance of thunder to be within striking distance of lightning. Time to save herself.

Daphne's jacket, candles and cards still lay on the ground, so she scurried to pick them up. Zipping everything into her backpack, she walked to the steps perched on the cliff. No wonder she could smell the sweat on her skin. She was drenched in it.

'Terrible shame,' she rehearsed as she grabbed the railing. 'Sharon was so mad and blue about her boyfriend Cornell after he'd dumped her for Christina. She said she was going up to the trail to clear her head and figure out how to get him back.' That would wind things up.

Through the woods abutting the Sunken Garden, catmint squished underfoot as she trudged. It marked the air with its scent like a cat marking its territory, and she told herself that she had become a mouser cat, killing where needed to safeguard the grounds and ward off the pests. What she'd done was awful but it was for the greater good. It helped to remember that she was more potent and smarter than anyone, like Daphne, the Goddess anointed from beyond. The electricity in the air invigorated her, and she didn't know how she'd ever gotten so low. Right now was the best time of her life. She had never been so free and in control. She could probably make anyone do anything if she put her mind to it. She would never have to kill again. It was all in the past; she had to live in the present tense, no matter how painful her remorse.

Rain sheeted down as she pushed through the locker room door. Her mouth was pasty. A shot of tequila would have helped her relax, but her head throbbed too much. Maybe some water and a shower would rinse off the day.

Indoors, where the smell of eucalyptus leaked out of the sauna, she tried to think back. Had she left anything behind to incriminate herself? Somehow she couldn't remember gathering her things, just the experience of vertigo and looking down at Sharon's spinning body. She tried not to think of the cliffs or the river at the water cooler, but the bubbles glugged as she filled her cup and she got a sinking feeling. The sound of water made her wonder. Did God really care about a bunch of stupid kids? She drank as she walked to her locker, and the cool spring water tasted sweet on her tongue. If He did, then wouldn't He in His wisdom understand why she had to get rid of Sharon, if there even was a God, which she seriously doubted? Of course He would forgive her, baptized or not, because she was sorry and He only helped those who helped themselves. She had heard that somewhere and hoped it was true. She had to get rid of the rosary, maybe pick Sharon's locker or stuff it into the vent.

Daphne set the cup on the bench next to her so she could open her own locker door. The smell of cedar filled her nose as she stowed her backpack inside and ignored Christina's locker in the same row, two down. It was sad, but Christina had brought it on herself, driving them all crazy; she was pathologically pretty on top of being a man thief. As for Sharon, the nitwit had to be silenced so the Circle could continue – for senior year at least, when she and Piper would host the games to restore harmony in school. The whole game had been for the greater good of her classmates. They had never set out to actually kill anyone. Slipping her dress over her head, she took off her bra and wrapped a towel around her chest. She was taking off her panties when she heard a bubbly freshman call to her.

'Daphne?' The girl scanned the room, her eyes flicking right and left as she bounded toward her in shorts and a tank of lapis blue. 'You don't know me but we need to talk.' Daphne's seat shook as the girl plopped next to her with the energy of a chihuahua, and she looked like one, too, with skinny legs and arms and mouse-ear ponytails.

Daphne closed the locker and pinned the key to her towel. 'Not to be rude, but I'm in a hurry.'

'This is life or death.' Tucking a hundred dollar bill into Daphne's hand, the girl sighed and leaned in. 'I'm serious. I have everything to lose.'

'Shush.' Daphne felt refreshed as she sensed a flare of excitement deep inside her body. 'Keep it down. Someone might hear.'

The girl whispered and cocked her head like a puppy. She smelled like strawberry flavouring. 'Madeleine used to be my best friend, but she totally just stabbed me in the back. She's been stealing my clothes and turning my friends against me, gossiping. Not to call a spade a spade, but I swear she wants to take my life from me. She's even sleeping with my boyfriend.' The girl squinted and stunned Daphne by patting her on the thigh. 'Your brother said to ask you about the Secret Circle.' She hesitated before shooting out the words. 'Will you invite me? You know. Liquor up front and poker in the rear?'

Piper had revealed the code. The surge returned. In that instant, the current of omnipotence fed her veins. A warm force surged through her body; she could do anything. She knew the craving and the alchemy. All she had to do was keep playing the game. 'So, go ahead. Ask.'

'OK. I've got more for you if you trust me.' The girl opened her purse. Inside was a bottle of Cuervo. 'Are you really the Mistress of Poker and Shooter?'

♠

The Monks of the Abbey Victoria

Rupert Holmes

H EADS HAD BEEN KNOWN to roll in the RCA building like cabbages in a coleslaw factory. The maroon carpet on the twenty-first floor often doubled as conveyor belt to the waiting express elevator, which was always eager to facilitate an executive's plummet back down to the street. I'd hardly been at the network a month when I found my own fair-haired cranium poised fetchingly on the chopping block. But at least I didn't lack for company.

'This memo in my hand.'

Ken Compton, Vice-President of Programming but second to no network chieftain in his wrath, flourished the document for the four of us to see. The four of us were attorney Shepard Spitz of Practices and Standards, Matty Dancer from Variety and Specials, Harv Braverman in Public Relations, and myself, Dale Winslow, from the catch-all hopper dubbed 'Broadcasting'. As department heads, we formed the quartet that reported directly to Compton, with News, Sports and Original Programming having their own hierarchy within both the network and the building. I'd been brought on board to achieve the goal of broadcasting in compatible colour from sign-on right up through 'Sermonette'. Even the National Anthem and the test pattern were going to be in colour.

'This memo in my hand,' reiterated Compton. 'It's worth more to our enemy up the block than the sum total of your lifetime incomes, including retirement benefits. I say that without even fact-oring in the possibility that one of you won't be working here tomorrow.'

We sat across his desk, four boarding school students caught smoking behind the sports equipment shed.

'Let me tell you how ultra hush-hush this memo was.' He leaned forward as if betraying troop locations in Korea. 'I typed it myself.'

There could be no clearer proof of how seriously Ken Compton feared intra-network espionage than that he would endure the humiliation of sitting at his secretary's desk to hunt and peck on her electric typewriter. He'd had this fixation since Ted Thissel, my immediate predecessor, had been suspected of selling the previous season's Fall schedule to CBS, forcing Compton to relocate some audience favourites to unfamiliar time slots, a last-minute move which many thought had cost us dearly in the ratings.

'Do you know where I found this memo?' he asked. 'Let me tell you where I found this memo. Propped behind a bottle of Vitalis above the sink in the executive washroom. If I hadn't been the next one in there, this document could have been filched by the clean-ing lady and sold to those vipers at CBS.'

The image of our Mrs Dawkins sitting patiently in William Paley's outer office, bucket and mop at her side, was the only thing amusing about the moment.

'Spitz, I gave it to you first. Who had it last?'

I knew the answer to this question and sorely wished I didn't. The memo – which listed by title the films we'd acquired from Paramount which we planned to run as specials against our rivals' strongest shows – had been addressed to the four of us only, and Compton had intentionally made no carbons or photostats. We were each to read the memo, check off our own name, and give it by hand to one of the others. The last of the four to read it was to return it personally to Compton.

Harv Braverman's name was the only one that hadn't been checked when I'd given the memo to him, but now it was as ticked off as Compton was with us. I looked at Harv, who was peering about the office as if the identity of this incredibly careless executive was an enthralling enigma to him. I turned back to discover the others staring at me. I was, after all, the new fellow at the Rock, a refugee from Ogilvey and Mather. The others were lifetime NBC men. Their blood ran peacock blue.

Spitz said, correctly, that there was no way for him to know. Matty Dancer said he couldn't remember as did the blameworthy Braverman, who then turned my way with raised eyebrows.

I could have tried to exonerate myself but, being ridiculously new at the network, I thought it politic not to state my case at Braverman's expense. I hadn't even been assigned a secretary yet and my office still contained the embarrassing scent of fresh paint.

'I have to be honest,' I said, which I thought was as good a way as any to begin a lie. 'I've been dispatching so many memos since coming aboard that I can't recall where I was in this particular sequence of events. If it's any help, I'm strictly a Brylcreem guy.'

Our uniform dim-wittedness left Compton with nothing to tango or tangle with. 'Honour among thieves. Fine. Then I'll deal with you like I'm Ali Baba. Here's our Fall schedule.'

He tossed it onto his desk blotter. We hadn't expected to see it for at least two more weeks. Reflexively, Dancer reached for it, and Compton slapped at his hand. You heard me. He slapped at his hand.

Compton transferred the memo to a lower drawer and locked it with a little key. 'So here's how it works. If you want to consult the schedule, you come in this room, you ask me for the specific information you want, I will look it up and tell you. Until then, no one sees it, holds it, or gets a copy of it. Not my secretary, and not you four.'

I got the feeling we were being listed in order of trust.

'Mighty white of you, Winslow,' mumbled Braverman in the hall as he tucked neat pinches of Cherry Blend tobacco into his briar pipe. The stem made little clacking noises as it rolled against his side teeth. 'Not everyone in your position would have kept mum. As new man here, suspicion was likely to fall on you first.'

I said something about the time I'd sent a line drive through Mr Overmeyer's window and been finked on by Ricky Yatto when it would have cost him nothing to cover for me.

Braverman offered in stumbling fashion, 'This Saturday. A little shindig me and the missus throw each year. Cocktails, canapés, more cocktails, sit-down barbecue. Been meaning to invite you. You're married, I've heard?'

'Fourteen years, three months, two weeks,' I joked, a stock line of mine that I updated every now and then.

It evoked an understanding laugh from Braverman. 'Ever get time off for good behaviour?' 'Not a chance,' I smiled.

'Donna at Reception will be sad to hear that,' he said.

This statement instantly made Braverman one of the most interesting people I'd ever met. 'What do you mean?' I asked, trying to sound casual about Donna at Reception, who bore a passing resemblance to starlet Joi Lansing in every department. This bears repeating. Every department.

'Didn't you know?' he asked. 'She's been waving semaphore signals at you since you started here.'

I smiled. 'She'll lose her enthusiasm when she finds out I'm married.'

Braverman lowered his voice. 'I already broke the news to her, buddy boy, and her reaction was, "What else is new?"'

I couldn't help looking down the hallway, where Donna at Reception was stationed behind a low-cut reception desk. She smiled my way, then arched her back and stretched her arms above her head. I expected the Sweater Police to be on the scene any moment to charge her with assaulting an angora.

'I just invited her to my party,' added Braverman. 'You know what she said?'

'What.'

'She said she'd come stag and asked if you'd be there, too.'

'Joanie,' I said to my wife as she changed for the party early that Saturday evening, 'if you're really feeling under the weather, I'll understand if you want to stay home.'

She was wearing a navy blue strapless cocktail dress and applying roll-on deodorant that I hoped would not gleam so much by the time we got to the party. 'I didn't say I was feeling under the weather,' she corrected. 'I said I was exhausted from shopping. It's Saturday night, I wouldn't think of you going without me.'

Braverman was a HiFi buff and had built himself a great rig. He was putting it through its paces with one of those stereo demonstration discs, *Provocative Percussion* or *Persistent Percussion* or something. Braverman centred me and kept pointing from the right to the left as bongos or claves would ping-pong to either speaker, while an accordion throbbed 'Miserlou' straight down the middle.

He and his wife Linda were serving Gimlets, with the colour and taste of a Charms lime lollipop but one hell of a kick. Braverman revealed himself to be some kind of barbecue nut, complete with one of those aprons that proclaimed 'I'm the chef!' With his straight briar pipe clenched between his teeth, the only thing he said to anyone for an hour was, 'Too rare for you?'

Donna from Reception was wearing a tight canary yellow dress that had undoubtedly brought a pleased smile to her lips when she first saw it in the changing room mirror at Saks. Every time I looked her way, she was already looking at me. She made impatient little arcs with her eyes, urging me to step out onto Harv's patio to chat with her for pity's sake, but Joanie intercepted one of Donna's glances and instantly asked to be introduced to my closest associates at NBC. I was sure she didn't consider Donna to be one of my closest associates, nor did I want her to.

Harv, Sanford Spitz, and Matty Dancer couldn't have been more gracious to my wife, clearly going out of their way to make her feel accepted within the NBC community. Her merest quip regaled them, and she flushed with pleasure at their attention and approval.

While Braverman was otherwise doubled up with laughter at what I thought was a fairly commonplace observation on Joanie's part, he managed to catch my eye and redirect my attention to the sight of Donna leaving the party. She had apparently phoned for Rye Taxi to take her back to Manhattan. As she left, she gave me the most eloquent shrug, causing her cleavage to speak volumes.

Round about ten-thirty, Harv signalled to me from the doorway of his den. It was a room I would have treasured, centred around my idea of rustic: a wide stack of hickory logs ablaze in a natural stone fireplace with an Emmy on the mantle above it.

Braverman smoothly locked the door from the inside. Turning, I discovered that Dancer and Spitz were already seated, holding big-fisted scotches on the rocks. There was the stilled air of ceremony in the room.

'We've been impressed with you, Dale, virtually since the moment you started,' said Dancer. 'And we've agreed to extend you an offer.' Spitz used his best attorney voice. 'Braverman has nominated you into the Order of the Monks of the Abbey Victoria.'

Dancer chimed in, 'We think it's a whale of an idea and we've made it unanimous.'

'I have no idea what to say,' I said appropriately, since I had no idea what they were talking about. I thought it wise to add, 'I'm very honoured, of course.'

Harv Braverman smiled and began to fill his pipe. 'You of course have never heard of our Order, and we like it that way. Membership is only offered to those who have displayed discretion and proven themselves trustworthy. One unexpected demise and another member's retirement had brought our membership down to four. Then Thissel got the boot, and we three were all that was left. Until you showed us this week that you have what it takes.'

Dancer handed me a Scotch identical to his own. 'Look, we'll explain it all to you at the initiation ceremony. Can you get free and clear of your wife this coming Monday night?'

They saw the hesitation on my face.

'Tell her we've asked you to join our weekly poker game,' Spitz advised. 'You won't be lying.'

'American men still possess certain inalienable rights, even as we depart the Fabulous Fifties,' asserted Dancer. 'Our wives have their Mah-jong nights, bridge clubs and canasta. In return, an unwritten law has been left on the books that married men like ourselves are allowed to play poker one night a week, excluding Friday through Sunday.'

Dancer advised, 'You might let her know the stakes are penny ante. Nickel a chip.'

'Joanie, the guys want me to get together with them for their weekly poker night,' I said as I hung my suit on the overnight valet in our bedroom.

To my surprise, Joanie wasn't taken aback. 'Oh yes. Linda Spitz was telling me about it. Molly Dancer, too.' She was in the bathroom, shedding her strapless cocktail dress in an efficient manner, clearly transmitting that tonight was not the night. 'It's on Mondays?'

'I'm lousy at poker,' I said.

'They might be insulted if you turn them down,' Joanie cautioned. 'I know you don't like playing office politics, Dale, but it's NBC, after all.'

The Abbey Victoria was that dowdy one-star Michelin hotel you'd find in Chartres or Rouen, where you were expected to leave your passport with the front desk and the restaurant would close by nine. Except that somehow this prim, bourgeois hotel had drifted off to sea and foundered upon the corner of Seventh and 51st in midtown Manhattan. You'd hardly notice it alongside the gleaming Americana (which to me had always looked like the UN with a coat of whitewash). The Shabby Abbey, as some called it, was crammed full of little rooms with little twin beds that had been purchased in a time when everyone was shorter and two businessmen found nothing odd about sharing a room to halve their expenses.

A number of the Abbey's bedrooms had adjoining parlours so that they could be rented as suites. But if the Abbey wasn't full (and these days it never was), you could book the drawing room alone. Apparently, parlour room 622, situated between bedrooms 620 and 624, was regularly reserved on Monday nights by the Order of the Monks of the Abbey Victoria.

The door swung open and Dancer greeted me. He'd changed since work into a blue turtleneck and tan chinos. He looked at his watch.

'Seven-oh-six,' he noted. Dancer had never struck me as the punctilious type, but my time of arrival seemed to please him. 'You're the first, other than me, of course.'

A table from room service had been wheeled into 622, its two hinged leaves locked in the up position. A green felt cloth served as cover to the now-circular table. Presumably, we were not the first poker game ever to have been played at the Abbey. Alongside a few red-backed Bicycle decks, still sealed, were coloured plastic chips neatly nested in a circular caddy, the kind you'd see in a Sears and Roebuck catalogue.

'What beer do you like?' Dancer indicated a pewter bucket filled with crushed ice and a modest supply of bottled beer. Pilsner glasses were inverted alongside the bucket. He inventoried the supply. 'We have Piels, Schlitz, Knickerbocker, and Miller.'

I wasn't much for beer but when in Rome. 'Miller,' I opted.

'The Champagne of Bottle Beer,' he affirmed. So far the conversation was scintillating. There was a knock at the door and he again looked at his watch. 'Seven-ten and my money says that will be Shep.'

If there was anyone who did not resemble a 'Shep', it was the fellow in the doorway, attorney Shepard Spitz, still in his three-piece suit. He entered, giving no indication he might remove his jacket or loosen his tie.

'I want you to know I turned down ringside seats at the Garden to do *this*,' he complained without preamble. 'Where's Harv?'

'Right here,' said Braverman, entering right behind him. 'Don't make it sound like such a chore to be here, Shepard. This is a big night for Dale. For all of us.'

Spitz sat himself at the circular table. 'Sorry, Winslow. Welcome to the fold.'

'And fold-wise,' said Braverman, using his best ad agency parlance, 'let's hope you have the decency to fold once or twice when there's a big pot, right? Who's dealing?'

'Host is always dealer,' said Dancer, sliding into a vacant chair. 'You know that full well, Harv, and I note that whenever you've been host, you win more hands. Just a comment.' He broke the seal of the blue tax stamp on a Bicycle deck. 'The game is straight poker, brethren. No improvements, wrinkles, exceptions, or exclusions, and nothing is wild. I will now accept a five dollar offertory from all members of the congregation in return for chips.'

We each tossed a bill his way and received our allotment. As he slid our chips toward us, he cautioned, 'For the benefit of Brother Dale, let me remind you that the Monks of the Abbey Victoria observe a vow of silence about the following matters: current work and current events, including sports, motion pictures, TV shows and hit records. Our purpose is to shrug away the world that is too much with us, to speak only of our experiences in the past and the lessons we may have learned from these experiences. Ante up, fellow Monks.'

It seemed an odd set of restrictions on conversation. And considering that the purported reason for our get-together was to have a pleasant time, the evening passed fitfully, as if we were all fulfilling some sort of obligation. Surely life was too short to spend every Monday night this way.

'Don't you think you've had enough?' asked Spitz as I tried to improve my spirits by reaching for a second beer.

I looked at him in bewilderment. 'I've only had the one.'

Spitz nodded to the other's glasses, from which only a few token sips had been taken. 'Best to keep your wits about you. Poker requires a clear head, especially when the stakes are high.'

I took a glance at the current pot, which totalled about eighty cents and was unlikely to achieve a dollar, but the others nodded silent assent. I forsook the beer.

'Hey, did you see the outfit Donna was wearing today?' ventured Harv.

'Not permitted,' said Dancer quietly. He seemed to take his role as chairman seriously.

'Sorry,' muttered Harv. 'Can I talk about her in general?'

Dancer raised the pot another nickel as he pondered the question. 'For the moment, I'll allow some general discussion,' he ruled.

'Sometimes I could swear she's not wearing a bra.'

'Of course she wears a bra,' said Spitz. 'Call.'

'But today, when she was leaning over, in that peasant blouse—'

'Not permitted,' said Dancer. 'Specific to time. Let's move off this general topic, anyway. It's fraught with difficulty. Anyone hungry?'

I hadn't had dinner and said as much. The others agreed that food was in order. I walked to the phone. 'I assume room service is still open? It's not even ten.'

Dancer shook his head. 'We don't like the room service here, except for beer and peanuts. Food's lousy. And the kitchen's had citations from the Department of Health. Who wants Chinese?'

There was some grousing about which Chinese restaurant in the immediate neighbourhood was best. Harv was big on Bill Hong's, whereas Spitz said he'd been going to the New Bamboo Palace, a place I didn't know myself, since the night of his high school prom in Amityville. Matty Dancer insisted Ho-Ho was the finest and Canton Village the cheapest, at least in Midtown. I suggested the one I considered classiest: China Song at 54th and Broadway.

The discussion stopped dead. 'We can't go to China Song, Dale,' said Braverman quietly. 'That's CBS territory. It's wedged in between Studio 50 and Studio 52. They've got paintings of Gary Moore and Durward Kirby hanging over the bar, for chrissake. If Ken Compton sees any of us at China Song, he'll think we've gone over to the other side. We *can't* go to China Song, Dale. Even for take-out.'

Apparently, the Abbey Victoria had a policy against food deliveries from the outside but they allowed guests to walk food in. So Spitz took down our order and volunteered to pick it up at the New Bamboo Palace for us. Braverman said he'd accompany him, which left Dancer and me alone.

It was strange to find myself sitting late at night in a frilly little hotel room with Matty Dancer, a man I barely knew. 'It's nice to have you for company, Dale,' he commented and started to tidy up, cleaning out the four little blue glass Abbey-Victoria ashtrays that rested by our packs of cigarettes and Braverman's pipe. 'We alternate as hosts each week, but it seems as if every time it's my turn, the others go out for food, leaving me to mind the roost. Of course, I'm the neat one.'

I nodded slowly, hoping this was as far as Dancer was going to bare his breast to me. He was married, of course, and his wife Molly was lovely. Still, it's a funny world.

'How long have *you* been married, Dale?' he asked, and I gave him the same stock answer I'd given Braverman, adding a few days to the total. He nodded solemnly. 'These Monday nights are very important to *my* marriage, I have to tell you. They provide me with a much-needed... interruption. The same way our viewers sometimes look forward to a commercial, so they can get some ice cream from the freezer, or see if the kids have turned out their lights, or take a leak. Even Shakespeare had intermissions, for God's sake. So should marriage. Any good, healthy, sound marriage. You know?'

The phone rang, a long 'hotel ring' via the switchboard, and he picked it up. 'Yeah. OK, I'll ask him.' He turned to me. 'It's Harv, he's calling from the New Bamboo Palace. He can't remember if you wanted Almond Gai Ding or Moo Goo Gai Pan.'

I had opted for the former and said so.

In theory, I agreed with the case Dancer was making for a once-weekly break from connubial 'togetherness', as was the newly-coined term for marital constancy. But if the offered respite was four sullen men playing dreary nickel-and-dime poker and taking little sips on ever-flattening beer while eating one from Column A, I did not see this as the ideal alternative.

Spitz and Braverman returned with two brown paper bags. We made no shared feast, but ate our individual orders, each from his own white cardboard box, maintaining the relative silence of those who find the food more interesting than the conversation.

Blessedly, midnight at last arrived. Harv commuted from Rye by car and both Spitz and Dancer lived in Manhattan, but I relied on the New York Central to get me home. So I had no problem rising to my feet and saying, 'Well, guys, it's been a great night, but I have to catch the 12:35 to Pelham.'

'Sit down, Dale,' said Spitz gravely. 'You've not been installed or initiated.'

I could feel the temperature in the room drop by a good ten degrees.

Spitz looked at the others. 'Are we ready?'

Dancer and Braverman nodded assent and turned their chairs to face me. Spitz, who had courtroom experience, opened: 'Dale. Tell us what we did tonight.'

I looked around the room. 'Uh… we played poker.'

Spitz shook his head slowly. 'No, Dale, don't disappoint me. I want you to give us a detailed account of what we did tonight. For example, what time did you get here?'

I remembered Dancer's greeting when I'd first walked in. Perhaps he'd been so specific about my arrival time for the very purpose of this oral exam. 'Seven-oh-six.'

'Who came next?'

'You. Followed by Harv.'

'What brand of beer did each of us drink?'

I pride myself on having above-average recall and rarely came up empty-handed during the interrogation. I accurately synopsized the run at the table, with Dancer playing aggressively and (I said in all candour) foolishly. Spitz had been conservative, folding his hand often; thus, when he did stay in, we assumed he had the goods. This ultimately cost him, as we didn't allow big pots to build when he stood by his cards. I'd played inconsistently, pushing a few weak hands farther than I should have and not riding a trio of sixes as far as I might. The most impressive winning hand had been Braverman's, who had broken up a pair of eights in successful search of an inside straight. He'd been the big winner for the night, apologizing after each victory, and would be departing nearly ten dollars richer than he'd started.

As for conversation, I had little problem reconstructing the general thrust of our discourse. Past histories had come into play, Spitz recounting his years as a civil defence attorney, Braverman the winning of the Colgate Toothpaste account by some fairly devious means, Dancer his prior career as a producer of off-Broadway revues. We'd recalled college days. Braverman was Princeton orange and black, Spitz had been Fordham law, Dancer boasted of being kicked out of several Ivy League schools, and I tried to make the most of my class standing when I graduated from Michigan State.

As I recounted the serpentine path of our unmemorable exchanges in such detail that it alarmed me (surely there was something more noteworthy to occupy the vacancy between my ears), I noticed knowing glances cast between my associates. I wrapped up with, 'Harv, you accompanied Shepard to his favourite, the New Bamboo Palace, at something like nine-forty-five—'

'Forty-two, but who's counting?' said Braverman.

Increasingly peeved, I rattled off, 'You brought back egg rolls for three, shrimp toast for Harv who also ordered sweet and sour pork, Matty had Lung Har Gai Pan, Shepard had Steak Kew and I had the Almond Gai Ding. Matty and Harv had Pork Fried Rice, I had white, Shepard didn't eat his, now may I *please* ask what this inquisition is in aid of?'

Dancer stood and ceremoniously raised his Pilsner. 'Gentleman, I believe we have ourselves a brother. Welcome, Frère Dale.'

'Frère Dale,' echoed Braverman and Spitz.

Dancer clapped an arm around my shoulders. 'I suppose we

must have you pretty confused. Sorry about that. We'll be delighted to enlighten, but first we need your word as a fellow Monk of the Abbey Victoria not to disclose on pain of death what we are about to tell you. Not to NBC, to your neighbors… not even to your wife.'

'I know how to keep a secret,' I said.

'You showed us that the other day,' acknowledged Braverman.

Dancer nodded. 'So we've had ourselves a pleasant evening' – he looked at the others and grimaced – 'all right, let's say we've had ourselves a harmless evening, consisting of poker, beer, Chinese food, and some of the most tedious conversation any of us have ever endured, most of which you've just now recounted in impressive detail. A typical weekly edition of our informal men's club. And now, Brother Dale, I am informing you that it is very likely we will never assemble like this again.'

Spitz added, 'Until such time as necessity dictates. Hopefully not for months to come.'

'Amen, Brother,' murmured Braverman.

I looked at their serene expressions. 'I don't understand—'

'We won't reconvene until we have a need to,' Dancer explained. 'You see, Dale, the reason we got together tonight was so that all of us, including you, could identically describe exactly what transpired this evening, with – what's the word, Spitz?'

'Verisimilitude.'

'For what purpose?' I asked.

'Freedom,' said Dancer. 'We're all of us married, tethered, seven days a week every week of the year. However, as members of the Order of the Monks of the Abbey Victoria, we get one gorgeous day each week to do whatever we wish.'

Spitz elaborated. 'Meaning, Winslow, that we are the poker club that does not play poker. Or even convene. We go our own way, free from wives, neighbours, and each other, to pursue whatever secret pursuits spring to mind.'

'Not to say,' rushed in Harv, 'that we do something *bad* on that one day a week.'

'Perish the thought,' said Dancer. 'It might be that Spitz here feels like hanging around the Shandon Star all night to watch the Dodgers. On that same evening, maybe I opt to see a Mamie van Doren feature at the Trans-Lux that my wife doesn't approve of, ogling the screen in pleasant solitude.'

Braverman lit his pipe as he added, 'It's the adult version of playing hooky, Dale. Every Monday night from here on in, we all do whatever we like without having to account to anyone, even if it's as harmless a distraction as going back to the old neighbourhood to have a chocolate malt while reading a comic book. Simple, innocent pleasures.'

There was a significant pause. Then Braverman added, 'Or you can do something bad.'

'Very bad,' Dancer instantly affirmed with a wicked grin. 'Very bad indeed.' I had the impression he had specific images in his mind, and I was glad I couldn't see them for myself.

'What does "bad" really mean, after all?' waxed Spitz philosophically. 'A life without experience is a life hardly lived.' Then he glared at the room. 'But what we do on our Mondays is nobody's business, correct, gentleman? Even amongst ourselves.'

'Even amongst ourselves,' repeated Dancer, clearly for my benefit. 'As far as any of us are concerned, we are all here every Monday, playing poker. If anyone significant in our lives happens to ask us how the evening went, we will merely try to do as admirable a job as Brother Dale just did in recounting whatever details, very *real* details to be sure, are needed. Thus, should our wives or others compare our stories, they will jibe harmoniously.'

I tried to understand what they were telling me. 'So we're supplying each other with an…' I couldn't think of another word. 'Alibi?'

Spitz fidgeted. 'The term 'alibi' would imply that one or more of us might need one, because we had done something illegal. Think, rather, of the Monks of the Abbey Victoria as a cover story, and that we spend our Mondays… under cover.'

'So how does it work?' I asked, already wondering how I might occupy myself next Monday evening.

Spitz said, 'We don't meet here again until we have to. The innocuous events of this evening will serve as what transpires here every Monday until one of us is obliged to recount the details to another person, in which case we will reluctantly reconvene to create a different real evening to describe.'

Dancer was moving the used glassware to the ice bucket tray. 'Each week, one of us mans this outpost. Today was my turn, next week is…' he mentally went through the alphabet, '…is Shepard, then you Winslow, then Harv, and then it's back to me.'

'And what do I do when it's my turn?'

'The same thing we all do,' said Matty Dancer. 'You check in for the four of us, order up some beer and a card table, and sit here alone for rest of the night. You watch TV or read a book, but you must stay here. Mid-evening the three remaining members phone in, just like Shepard did from the Chinese restaurant, to make sure the coast is clear. If one of our wives has called the hotel, either because of an emergency, an errand, or simply to check up on us, that week's sentry will tell them their spouse is out getting food for the others. When that husband checks in at mid-evening, the sentry advises him to call his wife as soon as possible. We all check in a second time at midnight, just in case.'

Harv chimed in, 'If anyone presses us about what we did, what we discussed, how the poker game went, we just describe the last time we were together. That's why we never discuss current events, TV, movies, things that might date our evening. Under ideal circumstances, we may not have to meet more than once or twice a year.'

'That's fine with me,' murmured Spitz.

'If you like, I'll help you on your first shift as sentry,' offered Dancer as he and I left Room 622 and walked to the elevators. Braverman and Spitz had already left, staggering our departures to draw less attention to ourselves.

'But won't that mean you'll lose out on one of your Mondays?' I asked.

He looked almost embarrassed, 'Oh, I'm afraid I don't have any really exciting prospects at the present. Not like some of us.' He pushed the elevator button. 'Our receptionist Donna, for example. She likes you, damn your eyes.'

'You work too hard, Mr Winslow,' said Donna that Friday. She'd volunteered to bring me a cup of coffee before she left for the night, and I'd had no problem accepting her gracious offer.

'Call me Dale, please,' I requested. 'After all, I call you Donna.'

'But you don't,' she said.

'Don't what?' I asked.

'Call me.' She set the cup on my desk, accidentally brushing the right side of my body. 'My number's in the book, you know.'

'And what,' I inquired, 'would we talk about?' Oh, I was enjoying this.

'About where you might want to take me for dinner after we go to the Planetarium.'

'You're interested in astronomy?' I asked.

'I'm interested in dark places. On a first date, the Planetarium is as far as I go.'

I was certain if I asked how far she went on a third date, I'd get yet another answer I'd never forget, but my conscience nagged at me almost as much as Joanie does when I'm not helping her around the house. I indicated my wedding ring, which suddenly weighed a ton.

'I'm married,' I heard myself say.

Someone knocked at my office door and opened it without waiting for my response. I would have bitten his head off if he hadn't chosen to be Ken Compton.

'Winslow, am I hallucinating or is there simply no ethical behaviour on this Avenue anymore? You will not believe who was just coming on to me, and I mean coming on strong.'

Reflexively I looked at Donna but Compton answered his own

question. 'Those little worms at CBS. Paley's man Denham. Inquir-ing if I wouldn't be happier with *them*, maybe I could do a little better for myself *there*. Insult to my intelligence and ego. It's the damn schedule they want, that's all. They know we've got them beat this season. If you get any calls from anyone at CBS, I want you to put them directly through to me. That's official, got it?'

A second later Donna and I were alone again. 'Where were we?' she asked.

Compton's exit seemed to trigger her need to fidget with the buttons on her blouse, and I was fighting a similar urge. 'I'm afraid I was reminding you I'm married,' I reprised.

'I know,' she said. 'So many people in this country are. It must be the reason for the skyrocketing divorce rate.'

Give me credit. At least I was no longer a foolhardy kid who couldn't foresee an absolute disaster in the making. At least I now had enough willpower to resist temptation, no matter how appeal-ingly it was offered.

'You doing anything Monday night?' I asked.

Joanie shouted to me through the bathroom door, 'How much longer are you going to be using the shower? My make-up's in there.'

'Help yourself!' I called out cheerfully, being in a better mood than I am most Monday mornings.

As she entered, she turned her head away so as not to see me through the translucent shower curtain. It wasn't as if I were deformed or something. I was just naked.

'Where's my make-up mirror?' she asked.

'Sorry, I was using it,' I apologized. 'I was shaving in the shower. I read somewhere you get a much smoother shave that way.' I turned off the water, wrapped a towel around my waist, handed the magnifying mirror to her, and reached for the bottle of Aqua Velva I'd bought on Sunday, ladling its contents onto my face.

'Take it easy with that stuff,' she said. 'It's expensive.'

'Sorry yet again. I'll try to defray the expense by winning a few big hands tonight.'

'It might be more diplomatic to come home on the losing side,' she counselled. 'These fellows can help you at NBC. There's no need to make them look bad.'

I slapped my cheeks hard as the alcohol pleasurably burned my face. 'OK, honey. I'll try not to get too lucky.'

The Planetarium had a bank of pay phones by the corridor that led into the Museum of Natural History. The last Star Show had ended, as had (for the moment) whatever groping and nuzzling I'd been having with Donna, judging by fact that she was now fixing her makeup. I used this hopefully momentary lull to place my check-in call to the hotel, asking the Abbey's operator for Room 622.

'Hello?' Shepard sounded bored and a little dozy.

'It's Brother Dale,' I informed him. 'Anything I need to know?'

'Nope. No one's called except Dancer and Braverman to ask the same question. But make sure you check in again before you head home. The first time you don't call here will almost certainly be the one time your wife does.'

I thanked him for minding the fort and he assured me I'd be returning the favour next Monday. I kind of hoped he'd ask how my night had been going, so that I could boast a bit about my partial conquest, but he honoured the tenets of the Brotherhood and made no personal inquiries.

Donna was checking her make-up in the reflection of a glass case containing a portion of a meteorite that had landed in a Kentucky farmyard in 1928.

'I'm ready for dinner,' she said. 'Necking makes me hungry. Do you have somewhere nice in mind?'

I suggested we not go where either of us might be recognized by someone from work.

'I appreciate your concern for my professional reputation,' she nodded, her tongue planted as firmly in her own cheek now as it had been in mine just a few minutes earlier.

'Do you know anyone from Queens?' I asked.

She shrugged that well-researched shrug of hers. 'I've never met anyone who went to Queens who ever came back.'

'Good. I took the liberty—'

'You sure did,' she said, not altogether disapprovingly.

'—of reserving us a table at a romantic spot with candlelight dining. We'll just ask them not to light the candles.' I waved for a cab, simultaneously using my arm to hide my face from passers-by in the strong light of the streetlamps.

'Hello, morning star,' I greeted Donna at her reception desk the next morning. 'Did you have pleasant dreams?'

I was a half-hour late, having missed my regular train from Pelham. I'd stayed in bed later than usual, debating if I'd been brilliant or an imbecile not to press my luck with Donna after supper. On consideration, I felt I'd done the wise thing. She'd seemed pleasantly surprised that I hadn't tried to translate our racy dinner conversation into action at her apartment in lower Manhattan. But Donna was someone to be nurtured, brought along slowly. At least until next Monday. (I was already hoping I could convince the supportively-disposed Braverman to trade turns with me, so I'd not lose precious momentum with Donna.)

'I thought about you all the way in to work,' I now told her smoothly.

She gave me an icy look that was not sugar-frosted and, keeping her voice low, spoke as if her words tasted of Acromycin. 'I made myself a big mistake last night, Mister Winslow, and thank God it only went as far as it did. NBC would can me and your wife would brain you if either party found out about our date. So let's not ever talk about it again. In fact, let's not ever talk, 'kay?'

I was horrified, I mean *horrified*. That she despised me was all over her face, and I'm sure her face and the word 'despised' were rarely to be found in the same sentence. I frantically searched all memories of the previous night for what I might have said or done to so completely turn her around. As I unmanfully pleaded for an explanation, I saw Matty Dancer approaching and instantly silenced myself.

Dancer offered a far warmer greeting than had Donna, with whom I'd been necking under the projected heavens less than a dozen hours earlier. He set a manila envelope on the reception desk and asked her to see it was correctly messengered to its intended recipient. Then, under the guise of jovial chitchat, he said to me, 'Hey, Ken Compton wanted to have a brief word with you, Brother Dale.' He lowered his voice and added, 'He's already spoken with the Other Fellows You Were With Last Night, if you catch my drift.'

'Bit of a personal question, Dale,' Compton began in an embarrassed manner. He rose from his desk, and flopped onto the leather couch directly behind me. I swivelled my visitor's chair to face him across his Danish modern coffee table, as he began, 'Forgive me, but do you mind if I ask where you were last night?'

I had no idea what this was about, but felt relieved I had a big, fat, juicy answer to offer.

'Well, I guess there's no shame involved in admitting that Dancer, Spitz, Braverman and I were playing poker. Over at the Abbey Victoria. We have a little poker night in Room 622 each Monday. I think I arrived a few minutes after seven and left a bit after midnight. Give me a moment and I can probably be more precise.'

Compton waved away my offered alibi. 'No, I just wanted to hear it from you. I've already spoken to your friends this morning and they told me about your little poker club.' He leaned forward. 'So will you tell me? Who's the best player among you? My money's on Spitz.'

I smiled. 'Well, he's very conservative and that ultimately works against him. It was Braverman who cleaned up last night, if you can call ten dollars cleaning up.'

He nodded. 'Exactly as I expected. But honestly, I don't know how you guys put up with room service at the Abbey. I've heard their restaurant tends toward Italian by way of the Borgias.'

I explained to him how we have to bring food in. 'Last night Spitz and Braverman fetched us some chow from the New Bamboo Palace. My Almond Gai Ding was quite good.'

'Ah, the old New Bamboo Palace.' Compton laughed as much as I'd ever heard him laugh. Come to think of it, I'd never heard him laugh. 'I remember that place. Used to love the Pu-Pu platter there.'

Although we were clearly alone in his office, he looked about as if to ensure our privacy. 'Dale, may I tell you why I ask about your poker party? Last night, someone broke into my office. Pried open the drawer where I was keeping the Fall schedule. Took it. Stole it. Stole a schedule that CBS would pay somebody a fortune for. Like stealing jewellery. And there were only four people, other than myself, who knew that the schedule already existed and where it was kept.'

'When did this happen?' I asked.

'The night watchman discovered the forced lock on my door when he was making his eleven p.m. rounds. I keep telling RCA they have to make people sign in and sign out around here. Anyone could have taken an elevator to a couple of floors above us, waited somewhere along the fire stairs until later in the evening, then grabbed the schedule from my office, walked down to a lower floor, and taken another elevator from there to the lobby. After that, they could walk out of here free as a bird. Or if they felt like celebrating, head back up to the Rainbow Room and dance the night away.'

I agreed that the scenario he described was plausible. 'But there must be some other explanation. Because the four people who knew where you kept the schedule were otherwise occupied last night, until after the break-in.'

'Well I know that, for gosh sake. You were all having Chinese food from the New Bamboo Palace at the Abbey Victoria.' He flashed me a mirthless grin that showed me more of his teeth than

I'd ever wanted to see. 'It's just a damn shame they closed the New Bamboo Palace three years ago.'

As my brain tried to reason how Spitz and Braverman had brought back food from a restaurant that was no longer in business, Compton discarded his genial manner and taught me how frightened one man can be of another.

'Now let me ask you, sonny: why would you make up a pack of lies unless you had something to hide? I've already asked each of your three associates where they were last night. Their stories were impressively consistent. It seems Spitz bet like a wild man and won over a hundred dollars. They ordered in a pizza with anchovies, since the Abbey Victoria graciously allows deliveries. They arrived at six p.m. and played until two a.m. They talked about their upcoming projects at the network, compared notes on current movies, discussed rumours about Wilt Chamberlain leaving the Globetrotters to sign with the Warriors, and admitted they indulged in some fairly graphic speculation regarding the mores of a girl in the secretarial pool named Rita Truscott. Each man's story was completely consistent with the others. Whereas you, Winslow, are totally at odds with all of them. So the question is, why would you so ignorantly and desperately lie to me if there weren't something you need to hide?'

A window alongside the door to the office looked out upon the hallway. Over Compton's shoulder, I could see Donna standing at the water cooler, having herself a quick laugh with Spitz and Braverman, while Spitz was having himself a quick feel of Donna's derriere. It was a silent movie and I was not a member of the cast. Donna was opening the manila envelope that Dancer had left with her, and withdrawing what looked to me like currency. She wore an expression of pleasure, likely the first genuine one I'd ever seen on her face, including last night at the Planetarium.

I understood now. There had never been a Monks of the Abbey Victoria. Not until I came on the scene. The one meeting I'd attended of 'the Order' had been the only meeting ever convened.

My fellow Brothers must surely have struck a deal with someone at CBS. Perhaps they'd made a similar deal the year before, one for which my predecessor Ted Thissel had taken the fall.

Whatever cash from CBS they were splitting, I was certain a modest percentage of their take could be found in the envelope now in Donna's hands.

I knew. But I couldn't speak, couldn't offer my real alibi, tell anyone with whom I'd been the night before, because Donna would simply deny it, and any such claim on my part would give my wife Joanie abundant grounds for divorce. I was caught in a fool's mate, where my King could only toggle between two squares, either of which placed me lethally in check.

'All right, maybe I got some of my facts wrong,' I rasped from my suddenly dry mouth. I was about to be given the red carpet treatment, my head bouncing down the hall, bound for the express elevator that eagerly awaited my plunge to the street. 'But Compton, how would I know about the poker club, and the name we gave it, even the room number if I hadn't been there?'

He frowned. 'Your associates independently explained that, sympathetic to you being the new man here, they offered you the fellowship of their club, which you attended for the first time last week. They were stunned and insulted that, after reaching out to you in a brotherly way, you were so rude as to simply not show up last night.'

I had no idea how I'd explain to Joanie that I wouldn't be working at NBC. What reason I could give her for my dismissal. How I might earn a living after this. I looked back at Compton as if I were staring into the very sun that was setting on me.

He wasn't quite done. 'A very foolish bluff to try to put over, Winslow. Frankly, your friends are lucky to be rid of you.' He stood without offering his hand. 'You must play one lousy game of poker.'

The Eastvale Ladies' Poker Circle

Peter Robinson

THE MAN WAS VERY DEAD. Even Dr Glendenning, the Home Office pathologist, who hesitated to pronounce death when a victim was chopped into little pieces, admitted that the man was very dead. He also speculated as to time of death, another rarity, which he placed at between seven p.m. and ten p.m. that same evening.

All this took place in the spacious study of the Vancalms' detached eighteenth century manor house on the western fringe of Eastvale's chic Dale Hill area, sometime after midnight. The man lying on the carpet was Victor Vancalm, wealthy local businessman, and a large bloodstain shaped like the Asian subcontinent had spread from his skull and ruined the cream shag carpet.

The stain came from a massive head wound, which had been inflicted with enough force to splinter the cranium and drive several sharp shards of bone into the soft tissue of Victor Vancalm's brain. Blood-spatter on the flocked wallpaper and on other areas of the carpet testified as to the power of the blow. A brass-handled poker lay on the carpet not far from the body, surrounded by a red halo, as if it were giving out heat.

The rest of the study was in just the sort of mess Detective Chief Inspector Alan Banks would have expected after someone had been pulling books from shelves and overturning furniture looking for valuables. From one wall, a gilt-framed painting of the Blessing of the Innocents had been removed and dumped on the floor, exposing a small safe, the door of which hung open. It was empty. Someone had smashed the computer monitor, which sat on a desk by the window, and emptied the contents of the drawers on the floor. The Scenes of Crime Officers had cordoned off the study, from which they jealously repelled all comers, even Banks, who stood at the door gazing in, looking rather forlorn, a child not invited to the party.

In the living-room across the hall, discreetly out of the sightline of her husband's body, Denise Vancalm sat on the sofa sniffling into a soggy tissue. Music played faintly in the background, the andante movement from Schubert's 'Rosamunde' quartet, Banks noted as he returned to the room. Chandeliers blazed in the high-ceilinged hall, and outside in the night, police officers went up and down the street waking up neighbours and questioning them.

The problem was that Hill Crest was one of those expensive streets where the houses were not exactly cheek-by-jowl as in the poorer neighbourhoods, and some of them had high walls and gates. Hardly conducive to keeping an eye on your neighbour. Hill Crest was aptly named, Banks thought. It stood at the crest of a hill and looked out west over the River Swain, along the meandering valley where the hillsides of the dale rose steeper and steeper as far as the eye could see. On a clear day you could see the bare limestone outcrops of Crow Scar, like skeleton's teeth grinning in the distance. The skull beneath the skin.

But this wasn't a clear day. It was a foggy night in November, not long after Bonfire Night, and the police officers outside blew plumes of mist as they came and went. Even inside the house it wasn't that warm, Banks thought, and he hadn't taken his overcoat off.

'I'm very sorry, Mrs Vancalm,' he said, sitting in an armchair opposite her, 'but I do have to go over this with you again. I know you talked to the first officer on the scene, but—'

'I quite understand,' said Denise Vancalm, crumpling her tissue and dropping it on top of the copy of *Card Player* that lay on the glass coffee-table. The magazine looked out of place to Banks, who had been expecting something more along the lines of *Horse and Hound* or *Country Life*. But each to her own. He knew nothing about Victor and Denise Vancalm; he didn't move in those kinds of circles.

'You say you arrived home at what time?' Banks asked.

'Half past eleven. Perhaps a few minutes after.'

'And you found your husband…'

'I found Victor dead on the study floor, just as you saw him when you arrived.'

'Did you touch anything?'

'Good Lord, no.'

'What did you do first?'

A V formed between her eyes. 'I… I slumped against the wall. It was as if all the air had been forced out of me. I might have screamed, cried out, I really can't remember.' She held out her hand. 'I bit my knuckle. See.'

Banks saw. It was a slender, pale hand with tapered fingers. The hands of an artist. She was an attractive woman in her late thirties, with tousled ash-blonde hair falling over her shoulders, framing a heart-shaped face, perfect make-up ravaged by tears and grief. Her clothes were expensive casual, black trousers of some clinging, silky material, a burgundy blouse tucked in at the waist. A waft of delicate and expensive perfume emanated from her whenever she moved. 'And then?'

'I called the police.'

'Not an ambulance?'

She shook her head impatiently. 'I dialled 999. I can't remember what I said. I might have asked for all of them.'

She hadn't, Banks knew. She had asked for the police, said there'd been a murder. He could see what she meant. Even someone who has never watched *Taggart* or *A Touch of Frost* would be hard pushed to miss a murder scene like the one in the study, a body more obviously *dead* than Victor Vancalm's. But people panic and call an ambulance anyway. Denise Vancalm hadn't.

'What did you do next?' Banks asked.

'I don't know. I suppose I just sat down to wait.'

'And then?'

'Nothing. People started to arrive. You must know how long it took. I'm afraid I lost all sense of time.'

It had taken seven minutes from the emergency phone call to the arrival of the first patrol car. A good response time, especially given the weather.

'How many people knew about the wall safe?' Banks asked.

Denise Vancalm shrugged. 'I don't know. Victor always kept the key in his pocket, with all his keys. I suppose Colin must have known. Anyone else who visited the house, really.'

'Colin?'

'Colin Whitman, Victor's business partner.'

Banks paused and made a note. 'Where had you been all evening?' he asked.

'Me? Gabriella Mountjoy's house, on Castle Terrace.'

Banks knew the street. Expensive, in the town centre, it commanded superb views of Eastvale Castle, rumoured, like so many others in the Dales, to have provided a brief home for Mary Queen of Scots. He estimated it was probably a fifteen or twenty minute drive from Hill Crest, depending on the traffic.

'What were you doing there? Book club or something?'

She gave Banks a cool glance. 'The Eastvale Ladies' Poker Circle. It was Gabriella's *turn*.'

'Poker?'

'Yes, hadn't you heard, Chief Inspector? It's become quite popular these days, especially among women. Texas Hold 'Em.'

'I've heard of it,' said Banks, not much of a card player himself.

'Four or five of us get together once a month for dinner, drinks and a few games. As I said, it was Gabriella's turn to host us this time.'

'How many of you were there tonight?'

She raised an eyebrow at the question but said, 'Five. Gabriella, me, Natasha Goldwell, Evangeline White and Heather Murchison. I'll give you their addresses if you like.'

'Please,' said Banks.

Denise Vancalm picked up her handbag and took out a sleek Pilot encased in tan leather. She read out the names and addresses. 'Is that all?' she asked. 'I'm tired. I…'

'Nearly finished,' said Banks. 'What time did you arrive at Mrs Mountjoy's house?'

'I went there straight from the office – well, I met Natasha in the Old Oak after work for a drink first, then I drove her over to Gabriella's. It's not far, I know, but I had the car with me for work anyway.'

The Old Oak was a trendy pub off the market square. Banks knew it but never drank there. 'What kind of car do you drive?' he asked.

'A CLK cabriolet. Red.'

A Mercedes sports car, Banks thought. Hardly inconspicuous. 'Where was your husband?'

'He'd been away on a business meeting. Berlin. He was due back from the airport about half past seven.'

'Did you see him?'

'I haven't seen him since last week. Look, Chief Inspector, I've had a terrible shock and I'm very tired. Do you think…?'

'Of course,' said Banks. He had wanted to get as many of the preliminaries out of the way as possible – and whether she knew it or not, the spouse was usually the first suspect in a domestic murder – but he didn't want to appear as if he were grilling Denise Vancalm. 'Is there someone you can go to, or would you like me to—'

She shook her head. 'There are plenty of people I could go to, but believe it or not, I just want to be by myself.'

'You don't… I mean, are there any children?'

'No.' She paused. 'Thank God.'

'Right. Well, you clearly can't stay here.' It was true. Banks had checked out the house, and whoever had killed Victor Vancalm and ransacked the study had also been through the master bedroom, separating the expensive jewellery from the cheap – not that there was much of the latter – and even going so far as to cut up several of Denise Vancalm's favourite dresses and strew them over the bed. It would take most of the night to process the scene.

'I realize that,' she said. 'There's a small hotel just off the market square, the Jedburgh. My husband often suggests it for clients when they happen to be visiting town.'

'I can take you there,' said Banks.

She regarded him coolly with moist, steady blue eyes. 'Yes,' she said. 'Thank you. I probably shouldn't be driving. May I collect a few things? My nightdress? Toothbrush?'

Banks went in to the hallway and saw Detective Constable Winsome Jackman coming through the front door. 'Winsome,' he said. 'Mrs Vancalm will be spending the night at the Jedburgh Hotel. Will you accompany her while she gathers a few essentials?'

Winsome raised her eyes in a 'Why me?' expression.

Banks whispered, certain he was out of Mrs Vancalm's earshot, 'And make sure there's someone posted outside the Jedburgh all night.'

'Yes, sir,' said Winsome.

A short while later, as Banks followed Denise Vancalm out into the chilly night where his Porsche stood waiting, he again reminded himself why he was taking such precautions and feeling so many reservations in the face of the poor bereaved wife. By the looks of it, Victor Vancalm had disturbed a burglar, who might have been still in the building. Confronted with a dead husband, a wrecked den and a big empty house, most people would have run for the hills screaming, but Denise Vancalm, after the immediate shock had worn off, had dialled 999 and sat down to wait for the police.

*

By late morning the next day, a weak grey sun cut through the early mist and the day turned out the colour of Victor Vancalm's corpse spread out on Dr Glendenning's post mortem table. Banks stood on the steps of Eastvale General Infirmary wishing he still smoked. No matter how many he attended, he could never get used to post-mortems, especially just after a late breakfast. It was something to do with the neatness and precision of the gleaming tools and the scientific process contrasted with the ugly slop of stomach contents and the slithery lump of liver or kidneys. Anyway, as far as stomach contents were concerned, Victor Vancalm's last meal had consisted of currywurst, a German delicacy available from any number of Berlin street vendors.

There had been no surprises. Vancalm had been in general good health and the cause of death, barring any googlies from toxicology, was most certainly the head wound. The only interesting piece of news was that Vancalm's pockets had been emptied. Wallet. Keys. Pen. All gone. In Banks's experience, burglars didn't usually rob the persons of anyone they happened to bump into on a job. They didn't usually bump into people, for that matter; kids on drugs aside, burglars were generally so careful and elusive one might think them quite shy creatures.

Dr Glendenning stuck by his estimate of time of death, too, between seven and ten. If Mrs Vancalm had gone straight from the Old Oak to the poker evening with Natasha Goldwell and had not arrived home until eleven-thirty, she couldn't have done it. He would still check her alibi with the rest of the poker crowd. It was a job for a detective constable, but he found he was curious about this group of wealthy and powerful women who got together once a month to play Texas Hold 'Em. Did they wear shades, smoke cigars and swear? Perhaps more to point, could they look you straight in the eye and lie like a politician?

Banks took a deep breath of fresh air and looked at his watch. It was time to meet DI Annie Cabbot for lunch at the Queen's Arms, though whatever appetite he might have had had quite vanished down the drain of the autopsy table plughole, along with Victor Vancalm's bodily fluids.

It was lunchtime in the Queen's Arms and the place was bustling with clerks and secretaries from the solicitors' and estate agents' offices around the market square, along with the usual retirees at the bar and terminally unemployed kids on the pool tables. The smoke was thick and the language almost as bad. Banks and Annie managed to find themselves a free table wedged between the door to the Gents and the slot machines, where Annie sipped a Britvic Orange and nibbled a cheese roll, while Banks nursed a half of Black Sheep Bitter and worked on his chicken in a basket.

'So how was the redoubtable Gabriella Mountjoy?' Banks asked, when the person playing the slot machine beside them cursed and gave up.

'She seemed very nice, really,' said Annie. 'Not at all what I expected.'

'What did you expect?'

'Oh, you know, some upper-class twit with a braying laugh and horsy teeth.'

'But?'

'Well, her teeth are nice enough. Expensive, like her clothes. But other than that she seems every inch the thoroughly modern woman.'

'What does that mean?'

'Oh, really, Alan, you're seriously out of touch.'

'With the thoroughly modern woman? Tell me about it. It's not for want of trying.'

Annie nudged him. 'First there's the career,' she said. 'Gabriella's a book designer for a big London publisher. Works from home a lot.'

'Impressive,' said Banks.

'And then there's the house. Cottage, really. It's small, but the view must be worth a million quid.'

'Does she live alone?'

'As far as I can gather. There's a boyfriend. A musician. He travels a lot. It suits them both perfectly.'

'Maybe that's my problem with the modern woman,' Banks said. 'I don't travel enough. I'm always there when she needs me. Boring.'

'Tell Sandra that.'

Banks winced. 'Touché.'

'I'm sorry,' said Annie. 'That wasn't very nice of me.'

'It's OK. Still a bit tender, that's all. That'll serve me right for being so flippant. Go on.'

Annie finished her roll first. 'Nothing to add, really. She swears blind that Mrs Vancalm was there all evening. Natasha Goldwell was at the cottage, too, when I called, and she confirmed it. Said they arrived together about seven-thirty after a quick drink and Mrs Vancalm dropped her off at home – it's on her way – sometime after eleven.'

'Well,' said Banks, 'it's not as if we expected otherwise.'

'I just had a word with Winsome,' Annie went on,' and she told me that the other two say exactly the same thing about the poker evening. Denise Vancalm's alibi is watertight.'

'God help me, but I've never liked watertight alibis,' said Banks.

'That's because you're contrary.'

'Is it? I thought it was my suspicious nature, my detective's instinct, my love of a challenge.'

'Pull the other one.'

'Whatever it is, it seems as if we'll have to start looking elsewhere. You've checked out our list of local troublemakers?'

'Winsome has. The only possibility at all is Windows Fennester. He'd know all about wall safes.'

'He's out?'

'Been out three weeks now. Living back on the East Side Estate with Shania Longbottom and her two kids. Things is, according to Winsome, he's got a pretty good alibi, too – in the pub with his mates.'

'And whatever he is, he's not a killer.'

'Not as far as we know.'

'The lads have also been out doing a house to house in Denise Vancalm's neighbourhood,' Banks said.

'And?'

'Someone heard and glimpsed a car near the house after dark. Couldn't say what make. A dark one.'

'Nothing fancy like Mrs Vancalm's red sports car, then?'

'No,' said Banks. 'Your standard Japanese hatchback, by the sound of it. And several witnesses have told us that Mrs Vancalm's cabriolet was parked outside Gabriella Mountjoy's house until after eleven.'

'One woman did tell us that Denise Vancalm had a visitor the day before the murder.'

Banks's ears pricked up. 'A man?'

'No, a woman. During the day.'

'So she wasn't at work. I wonder why?'

'From the description we got, it sounds very much like Natasha Goldwell.'

'Well,' said Banks, disappointed. 'There's nothing odd about that. They're good friends. Must have been a coffee morning or something.'

'Afternoon.'

'Coffee afternoon, then. It still takes us back to square one.' Banks finished his drink. Someone else came to play the slot machine and the noise started up again.

'Look,' said Annie, 'I don't want you to make too much of this, but there was something a bit odd about Natasha Goldwell.'

'Odd?'

'Well, I mean, she was convincing enough. They went to the Old Oak, where Natasha had a gin and tonic and Denise had a Campari and soda, chatted about their husbands briefly – Natasha's is a civil engineer – talked a bit about some online poker game they play regularly.'

'These women are really keen, then?'

'I got the impression that Natasha was. She's the main online player. Gabriella strikes me as someone who more likes the idea of it, you know, cracking a male bastion.'

'Better than cracking other male parts.'

'But Natasha was more into the technical talk. It was way over my head. And the impression I got was that one of them is really involved in tournaments and all that stuff. She's even been to Las Vegas to play.'

'Which one would that be?'

'Evangeline White.'

'Do they play for money?'

'Of course. It's no fun if you don't have a little something riding on it, Gabriella told me. I didn't get the impression that huge fortunes changed hands, but enough to make it interesting.'

'But it was nothing to do with the husbands?'

'No. They were very much excluded.'

'And what about Denise Vancalm herself?'

'I got the impression she was keen, a pretty good player, but perhaps in it more for the social aspects. You know, a chance to get together without the menfolk, have a few drinks and talk girl talk, and perhaps even do a bit of business. I mean, they're all top echelon. Almost all. Natasha runs a computer software solutions company, online security and whatnot, Evangeline White owns an upmarket travel agency – you know, Sahara Desert treks and roughing it in Woolawoola – and Heather Murchison... well, you know her.'

Banks did. Heather Murchison was a familiar face and personality on the local television news, and her blonde looks, buxom figure and husky Morningside accent caused many a red-blooded male to be much more informed about local matters than previously.

'And Denise Vancalm herself is a fund-raiser and organizer of charity events,' Annie went on. 'She does a lot of work for hospitals and children's charities in particular.'

'Five successful, attractive women,' said Banks, 'all in their late thirties or early forties, all, or most of them, married to or hooked up with successful, attractive men. Sounds like a recipe for disaster. Any hints of clandestine goings on? You know, musical beds, wife-swapping, that sort of thing.'

'Wife-swapping?' said Annie, laughing. 'You really must leave the sixties behind.'

'I'm sure people still do it. There was that film by Kubrick. Must have been the nineties at least.'

'*Eyes Wide Shut*,' said Annie. 'Even **Tom** Cruise couldn't save that one. Yes, it was the nineties, orgies and such like. But wife-swapping...' She shook her head and laughed again.

'OK, I get your point,' said Banks. 'No need to hammer it home. What I'm saying is that there might have been rivalries among these women or their husbands, liaisons – if that's not too outdated a word – affairs. Jealousy can be a powerful motive.'

'Why look beyond the facts here?' said Annie. 'Victor Vancalm came home and surprised a burglar, one who was somehow familiar with the layout of his house, the safe. Perhaps he decided to take the burglar on, and for his efforts he got bashed on the head with a poker. I mean, the side window had been broken from the outside.'

'Yes, but what about the security system?'

'Turned off.'

'So our would-be burglar would have to know how to do that, too?'

'Any burglar worth his salt can find his way around a domestic security system.'

'True enough, but when you add it all up... a little inside knowledge goes a long way. Anyway, you said there was something odd about Natasha Goldwell?'

'Yes. It was nothing, really, but there was just something a bit... offhand... about her responses. I mean, I know it was very recent, so she'd hardly have to wrack her brains to remember, but it all seemed just a bit too handy, a bit too pat.'

'As if she'd learned it by rote?'

'Maybe. It's something to bear in mind, at any rate.' Annie reached for her glass. 'You know,' she said, 'it's not a bad idea, this ladies' poker circle. I wouldn't mind being involved in something like that, myself.'

'Start one, then.'

'Maybe I will. Winsome might be interested. We could get a police ladies' poker circle together.'

'I can't see the chief constable approving. You know what he feels about gambling and the road to corruption.'

'Still,' said Annie, 'I think it's sort of cool. Anyway, what next?'

'We'll have another word with Natasha Goldwell, see what she was doing at Denise Vancalm's the day before the murder, but first, I think we'll go and have a little chat with Colin Whitman, Mr Vancalm's business partner.' He looked at his watch. 'Their office is in Harrogate, so it shouldn't take us more than an hour or so.'

It took only forty-five minutes in minimal traffic. The offices of the Vancalm-Whitman public relations company were above a wine shop on a sidestreet off the main hill. Banks parked up by The Stray, and he and Annie walked down past Betty's Tea Rooms towards the spa. 'If the timing's right,' Banks said, 'I'll take you to Betty's for a pot of tea and something sinfully sweet after the interview.'

'You're on,' said Annie.

A receptionist greeted them in the first office. The entire floor looked as if it had been renovated recently, the bare brick look with a few contemporary paintings stuck up here and there to liven the monotony. There was also a smell of freshly-cut wood. The phone kept ringing, and between calls, the receptionist, who bore the nametag 'Megan', pointed along a corridor and told them Mr Whitman would see them. They knocked on the door and entered the spacious room, which looked over the street. It wasn't much of a view. The street was so narrow you could practically shake hands with the bloke sitting at the desk in the window of the building opposite. But if you glanced a bit to the left, you could see beyond the slate roofs to the hint of green countryside beyond.

'I wasn't sure what to do when I heard the news,' said Whitman after they had all made themselves comfortable. 'Open the office, close for the day. In the end I decided this is what Victor would have wanted, so we're soldiering on.' He managed a grim smile. Grey-haired, perhaps in his late forties, Colin Whitman looked fit and slender, as if he put in plenty of time on the tennis court, and perhaps even at the gym. He seemed relaxed at first, his movements precise, not an ounce of effort wasted. He had a red complexion, the kind that grey hair sets so much in relief.

'I understand Mr Vancalm was away in Berlin on business until yesterday?' Banks began.

'Yes, that's right.'

'Where were you yesterday evening between the hours and of seven and ten?'

'Me?'

'Yes,' said Annie, leaning forward. 'We're just trying to eliminate all the people closest to Mr Vancalm from our inquiry. I'm sure you understand.'

'Yes, of course.' Whitman scratched the side of his nose. 'Well, I'm afraid I can't be much help there. I mean I was at home.'

'Alone?'

'Yes. I'm not married.'

'What were you doing?' Banks asked.

'Watching television, mostly. I watched *Emmerdale, Coronation Street* and *A Touch of Frost* and warmed up some take-away Chinese food for dinner. Not very exciting.'

'Drink much?' Banks asked.

Whitman shifted his gaze from Annie to Banks and frowned. 'Just a couple of beers, that's all.'

'Good, was it, *A Touch of Frost*? I didn't see it.'

Whitman laughed. 'I wouldn't have thought a real policeman

would have been very interested in something like that, but I enjoyed it.'

'What was it about?'

'A hostage-taking.'

Anyone could have looked it up in the paper and come up with that vague description, Banks thought, but that was so often what constituted an alibi, and unless someone else had seen Whitman elsewhere, it would be a damned hard one to break, too. Whitman was clearly becoming unnerved by the interview. He had developed a nervous tic above his left eye and he kept tapping on the desk with a chewed yellow pencil. He wanted to get this over with, wanted the box ticked, wanted Banks and Annie to get to the point and leave.

'Did you go out at all?' Annie asked.

'No. I'd no need to. It was miserable out there.'

'So nobody saw you all evening?'

'I'm afraid not. But that's often the case, isn't it? How many people see you after you go home?'

'Where do you live?'

'Harewood. Look, are you almost finished, because Victor's death has thrown everything into upheaval. There are a lot of clients I have to inform, and I'm not looking forward to it.'

'I can understand that, sir,' said Annie, 'and we won't keep you much longer. Perhaps you could tell us a little bit about Mr Vancalm?'

'Victor? Not much to tell, really. He was a good man, good at his job, loved his wife.'

'Was he the kind of man who played around with other women?' Banks asked.

Whitman looked shocked. 'Not that I knew of. I shouldn't think so. I mean, he seemed…'

'Would he have told you if he did?'

'Probably not. Our relationship was purely business. We hardly socialized unless it was with a client.'

'What about Mrs Vancalm?' Annie asked.

'Denise? What about her?'

'Did she have other men?'

'Now look here, I don't know what you're getting at, but the Vancalms' marriage was perfectly normal.'

'What does that mean?' Banks asked.

'Normal?'

'Yes. You already told us you're not married yourself, so how would you know?'

'I'm just going b-by what I saw, what I heard, that's all. Look, dammit, they were a happily married couple. Can't you just leave it at that?'

Banks glanced at Anne and gave her the signal to leave. 'I suppose we'll have to,' he said. 'For now. Thanks very much for your time, Mr Whitman.'

Outside in the warm grey air, Banks looked at his watch. 'Betty's? Something sinfully sweet and sticky.'

'Ooh,' said Annie, 'you do know how to charm a woman. I can hardly wait.'

It was after eight and pitch black when Banks got back to his recently renovated Gratly cottage. After the fire had destroyed most of the place a couple of years ago, he had had the interior reconstructed and an extension added down one side with a conservatory at the back. He had turned the extension into an entertainment room, with large widescreen TV, comfortable cinema-style armchairs, surround sound and a drinks cabinet. Mostly he sat and watched DVDs or listened to CDs there by himself, but sometimes Annie dropped by, or one of his children, and it was good to have company.

Tonight he was alone, and that didn't make him much different from Colin Whitman, he realized. He was eating yesterday's chicken vindaloo warmed-up and drinking Tetley's bitter from a can, cruising the TV channels with the aptly-named remote, because he was finding nothing of the remotest interest.

Then Banks remembered that he had set his recorder for *A Touch of Frost*. He always enjoyed spotting the mistakes, but perhaps even more he enjoyed David Jason's performance. Realistic or not, there was no denying the entertainment value to be got from Frost's relationship with Mullet and with his various sidekicks.

He put the vindaloo containers in the rubbish bin and settled down for Frost. But it was not to be. When he pressed the button, what played instead was an old episode of *Inspector Morse*.

At first, Banks wondered if he had set up the recorder wrongly. It wouldn't have surprised him if he had; technology had never been his strong point. But his son Brian had given him a lesson, and he had been pleased that he had been able to use it a few times without messing up. He didn't have to worry about setting times or anything, just key in a number.

He played around with the remote and made sure that this was indeed the programme he had recorded last night. Not that he had anything against Morse, but he had been expecting Frost. When he got back right to the beginning of his recording again, he found that it started towards the end of an explanation and apology.

From what he could make out, *A Touch of Frost* had been postponed and replaced by an episode of *Inspector Morse* because of its controversial subject matter: a kidnapped and murdered police officer. Over the past couple of days, the news had been full of stories of a police officer who had been abducted while trying to prevent a robbery. Only yesterday his body had been found dumped in a bin bag near Southwark. He had been shot. The TV executives clearly thought the Frost story mirrored the real one too much and would be disturbing to people, so at the last minute they had pulled it.

Banks would have happily settled down to finish his beer and watch Morse solve yet another case of inter-collegiate Oxford politics but for one thing. Colin Whitman had swore blind that he had watched *A Touch of Frost* and it hadn't been on. Banks phoned the station and asked the duty officer to see that Whitman was brought up from Harewood to Eastvale, then he rang Annie, turned off the TV and headed for the door.

'Look, it's late,' said Whitman. 'You drag me from my home and make me sit in this disgusting cell for hours. What on earth's going on? What do you think you're doing?'

'Sorry about the melodrama,' said Banks. 'I suppose we could have waited till morning. I don't suppose you were going to make a run for it, were you? Why should you? You probably thought you'd got us all fooled.'

'I don't know what you're talking about.'

The tape recorders made a faint whirring sound in the background, but other than that it was quiet in interview room three of Western Area Headquarters. Banks and Annie sat at the scarred wooden table opposite Whitman, and a uniformed guard stood by the door. Whitman hadn't asked for a solicitor yet, so no one else was present.

'Mr Whitman,' Annie said. 'When DCI Banks and I talked to you this afternoon, you told us you spent yesterday evening at home watching *A Touch of Frost*.'

'It's true. I did. What's wrong with that?'

'Nothing at all,' said Annie, 'except that *A Touch of Frost* was pulled from the air because of a real live hostage-taking. ITV showed *Inspector Morse* instead.'

Whitman's mouth flapped open and shut like a dying fish's. 'I… they… I…'

'It's an easy mistake,' Annie went on. 'Happens sometimes, but not often. Just unlucky, this time.'

'But I…'

'Yes, Mr Whitman?' said Banks, leaning towards him. 'You want to confess? The murder of Victor Vancalm. What were you looking for? Did he have something on you? Something incriminating? Or was it something else entirely? Mrs Vancalm, for example. Had you been having an affair? Did you plan this together?'

'No!'

'No to which question, Colin?' Annie asked.

'All of them. I told you. I was at home all evening.'

'But you were lying,' said Banks. 'At least you were lying about *A Touch of Frost*, and if you were lying about that… well, there goes your alibi.'

'Look, I didn't know I'd need an alibi, did I?'

'Not unless you murdered Mr Vancalm you didn't.'

'I didn't murder anybody!'

'You say you didn't, but yet when we asked you where you were around the time he died, you gave us a pack of lies. Why?'

'I… it just sounded so weak.'

'What did?'

'That I just stopped in by myself.'

'Hang on a minute,' said Banks. 'You're telling us that you thought it sounded weak saying you stopped in by yourself and ate leftover Chinese take-away, but it somehow sounded more believable that you did this while watching *A Touch of Frost*?'

'Well, I must admit, put like that it sounds rather silly, but yes.'

Banks looked at Annie, who rolled her eyes.

'What?' said Whitman.

'I really think we'd better start at the beginning,' said Annie. 'And the truth this time.'

'But it was the truth.'

'Apart from *A Touch of Frost*?'

'Yes. I didn't watch television.'

'What did you do?' Banks asked.

'I just sat there thinking, did a little work. I often have work to take home with me.'

Banks shook his head. 'I still don't get it. Why lie to us about watching television?'

'Like I said, it sounds silly now, I realize.'

'Not really,' said Banks. 'I don't think it's silly at all. Do you Annie?'

'Not at all,' Annie agreed.

'I think it was very clever of you,' Banks went on. 'You came home, got changed, went out and waited for Mr Vancalm, then you killed him. You knew he was away and when he'd be coming back. You also knew the layout of his study, and, I would imagine, the ins and outs of the security system and the wall safe. You didn't want too elaborate an alibi because you knew we'd be suspicious. Let's face it, most people when questioned by the police don't have alibis any better than yours was. It makes perfect sense to me. You were just unlucky, that's all. It only took a simple twist of fate.'

Annie gave Banks a questioning look.

'Dylan,' he said.

Whitman banged both fists on the table. 'But I didn't do it!'

Banks folded his arms and leaned back. 'Sure you weren't having an affair with Mrs Vancalm? She's a very attractive woman.'

'She's my partner's wife, for crying out loud.'

'That wouldn't stop most people.'

'I'm not most people.'

Banks paused. 'No, you're not, are you, Colin? In fact, I'm not sure what sort of person you are.' He glanced at Annie and smiled back at Whitman. 'I can't see that we're getting anywhere here, though, and DI Cabbot and I are both tired, so I think we'll call it a day, if that's all right with you.'

Whitman sat up straight and beamed. 'All right?' he echoed. 'That's the most sensible thing I've heard all evening.'

Banks and Annie stood up. 'Right,' said Banks to the officer at the door. 'Take Mr Whitman here down to custody, make sure it's all done by the book, and find a nice cell for him for the night. A nice cell, mind you, Smithers. Not one of those vomit-filled cages you usually put people in.'

Smithers could hardly keep back the laughter. 'Yes, sir,' he said, and took Whitman by the arm.

'What's this?' Whitman said. 'What's going on?'

'We're detaining you until we're happy with your story,' said Banks.

'But… but you can't do that. I've answered your questions. You have to let me go.'

'Oh, dear,' said Banks, looking at Annie. 'You can tell this fellow doesn't watch his Frost and Morse closely enough, can't you, DI Cabbot?'

Annie smiled. 'Indeed you can,' she said.

Banks turned to Whitman. 'As a matter of fact, Colin, we can keep you for twenty-four hours without a charge – longer if we wanted to go the terrorist route, but I don't think we'll be bothering with that tonight – so that should give you plenty of time to think.' And Smithers dragged Whitman, complaining and protesting all the way, along the corridor and down the stairs to the custody suite.

'Thanks for agreeing to meet me, Mrs Goldwell,' said Banks. The food court of the Swainsdale Centre wasn't the ideal place for an interview, but it was Wednesday morning, so things were relatively quiet. Whitman was still sulking in his cell, saying nothing, and DCs Jackman and Phelps were trawling through his life.

'Please,' she said, 'call me Natasha. Is that wise?'

She was looking at Banks's Egg McMuffin. 'Tastes all right,' said Banks. 'I reckon they're quite manageable if you only eat about five or six a year.'

Natasha Goldwell smiled. It was a nice smile, pearly teeth behind the red lips. In fact Natasha was a nice package all the way from her shaggy blonde hair and winter tan to her shiny, pointed black shoes. She wrinkled her nose. 'If you say so. I suppose it's hard to eat regularly the hours you work.'

Banks raised his eyebrows. Some hadn't seen enough cops on telly, others had seen too many. 'Not really,' he said. 'Mostly in Major Crimes we work regular hours. Unless there's a major crime, that is. Which murder definitely is.'

Natasha put her hand to her mouth. 'Oh, God, yes. I'm sorry. So thoughtless of me.'

'Not to worry.' Banks sipped some coffee. It was hot and bitter.

'What was it you wanted to see me about?'

'It's nothing, really,' said Banks. 'I mean, you vouched for Mrs Vancalm and that seems to check out OK. It's just… did you know Mr Vancalm?'

'Victor? I'd met him, of course, but I wouldn't say I knew him. I got together with Denise and the others for the poker circle, of course, but outside of that we didn't live in one another's pockets.'

'It's an odd hobby, poker, isn't it?'

'For a woman, you mean?'

'Well, that wasn't what I meant, but I suppose now you mention it, yes.'

'Because you usually associate it with men in cowboy boots and six-guns on their hips?'

'Well, not these days so much, but certainly not with a group of professional women.'

'And why not? If we were playing bridge or gin rummy, would it make a difference?'

'OK, I take your point.'

Natasha smiled. 'Anyway, we enjoy it, and it does no harm. It's not as if the stakes are beyond anyone's means.'

'What about the online playing? The tournaments?'

'You've heard about those? They're not for everyone. Only Evangeline from our group goes in for them. But the online stuff…' She shrugged. 'It's fun. Better than computer dating or chat rooms. Safer, too.'

'I suppose so,' said Banks, whose online experience was limited to amazon.com. 'What kind of person would you say Victor Vancalm was?'

'As I told you, I scarcely knew him.' She chewed on her lower lip, then said, 'But from what I did know, I'd say he was used to getting his own way, a bit bossy perhaps.'

'Abusive?'

'Good God, no! No. Certainly not. As far as I ever knew, Denise was perfectly happy with him.'

She didn't look Banks in the eye as she said this, which immediately raised his suspicions. 'What were you doing at Denise Vancalm's house the day before the murder?' he asked.

A couple of women sat down at the table beside them, paper bags crinkling and crackling, chatting about some rude shop girl they'd just had to deal with. 'And did you see her hair?' one of them asked, aghast. 'What sort of colour would you call that? And there was enough metal in her face to start a foundry.'

It gave Natasha the breathing space she seemed to need. When she answered Banks's question, she was all poise again. 'No reason in particular,' she said. 'We often got together for a coffee. Denise happened to be working from home that day and I had a spare hour between clients. One of the perks of running your own business is that you can play truant occasionally.' She wrinkled her nose.

'What did you talk about?'

'Oh, this and that,' said Natasha. 'You know, girly talk.'

'She didn't have any problems, any worries?'

'Mr Banks, it was her husband who was murdered, not Denise.'

'Just trying to find a reason for what happened.'

'I would have thought that was obvious. He interrupted a burglar.'

Banks scratched the scar by his right eye. 'Yes, it does rather look that way, doesn't it? Do you know if either of them had any enemies, any problems that were getting them down. Debt, for example?'

'Debt?'

'Well, there was the poker... and Mr Vancalm's trips.'

'Victor made business trips, it's true, and Denise plays a little online poker, but debt...? I don't think so. Are you suggesting it was some sort of debt collector come to break his legs or something and it got out of hand? This is Eastvale, Mr Banks, not Las Vegas.'

Banks shrugged. 'Stranger things have happened. Anything else you can tell me?'

'About what?'

'About what happened that night?'

'I finished work at six-thirty. Denise met me at the office. We went to the Old Oak for a drink. She drove me to Gabriella's. We played poker all evening, then she dropped me off on her way home sometime after eleven. That's it.'

She did sound a bit as if she were speaking by rote, Banks thought, but she had already been asked to describe the evening several times. 'Who won?' he asked.

'Pardon?'

'The poker circle. Who won?'

'As a matter of fact,' Natasha said, 'Denise did.'

'It's just a minor blip on the radar, really, sir,' said Winsome. She was sitting at her computer, leaning back in the chair, long legs crossed at the ankles, hands linked behind her head.

'Tell me about it, anyway,' said Banks, grabbing a chair and sitting so that he could rest his arms on the back.

'Well,' Winsome went on in her Jamaican-tinged Yorkshire, 'you know that big operation a couple of years back, the one that netted Pete Townshend?'

Banks nodded. He had never believed for a moment that Pete Townshend was connected with child pornography in any way other than research, and was glad when The Who's guitarist was completely vindicated. A bit silly, perhaps, but not criminal.

'That's when Colin Whitman's name came up,' Winsome said. 'The usual. Credit card online.'

'You'd think people would know better.'

'They do now, sir,' said Winsome. 'The pros have pretty much gone back to hard copy. It's safer and less likely to be detected, especially the way the borders are throughout Europe these days.'

'Everyone's too busy looking for terrorists.'

'Right, sir. But there's still a lot of activity over the internet. Anyway, as I said, it almost went under the radar, just a blip, but there it is.'

'Did you check Victor Vancalm's name, too?'

'Yes. Nothing.'

'Was Whitman interviewed?'

'No, sir. They just put his name in a pending file. There were hundreds of them.'

'I remember.'

'It might not mean anything.'

'But then again,' said Banks, 'it might. Think we can use it to get a search warrant?'

'I don't see why not, sir. Want me to get onto it?'

'Immediately.' Banks looked at his watch. 'We've got the pleasure of Mr Whitman's custody until this evening.'

'About bloody time,' said Colin Whitman when Banks had him brought up to his office at six o'clock that evening. Banks stood with his back to the door, looking out of his window. Outside in the market square all was quiet apart from a few people heading home across the cobbles from the pubs.

'I suppose you'll be wanting to go home?' he said, turning.

'Naturally.'

'In a while. Please, sit.'

Whitman stared and stood his ground as Banks sat behind his desk. Then he slowly pulled out the hard-back chair and sat opposite. 'Is this an apology?'

'Not exactly,' Banks said. The radio was playing one of Beethoven's 'Razumovsky' quartets softly in the background, so softly you had to know it was there.

'What, then?'

'Our men are still at your house, but their preliminary findings have already given us enough to hold you for a while longer. Superintendent Gervaise has already authorized the further detention. She takes as dim a view of what you've been up to as I do. I don't think you're going to find a lot of sympathizers here.'

Whitman had turned pale, which told Banks he knew exactly what was going on. 'I want my solicitor,' he said.

'Thought you might. You can put a call in, of course, that's your right, and if you don't have a solicitor we have a duty to get one for you.'

'I'll have my own, thank you very much.' Whitman reached for the phone and Banks let him call. By the sound of it, he got an answering machine.

'Probably out at some function or other,' said Banks.

'I'm not saying a word until he gets here.'

'Your privilege, sir,' said Banks, and while I'm not exactly cautioning you – yet – it might be well worth your knowing that what you don't say can mean just as much in court these days as what you do say.'

Whitman folded his arms. 'I'm still not saying anything.'

'Better let me do the talking, then,' said Banks. 'I'll start by saying I'm not sure why you did it. Perhaps Victor Vancalm got on to your little game and you had to get rid of him. Or maybe there was some other reason, some business reason. But you did it. Your alibi's crap and you've lied to us through your teeth. You're also a pervert. It may be the one group that doesn't have a charter of rights yet, child molesters.'

'I am not a child molester.'

'Fine distinction. I know things like that are important to you lot, how you define yourself. But let's be honest about it. Maybe you don't hang about schoolyards and playgrounds waiting for opportunities to come along, but you do diddle little kids and you do like to look at pictures of other people diddling them. In fact you had quite a collection on those DVDs we found and under those loose floorboards in the spare room.'

'They're not mine. I was keeping them for someone. I didn't know what was on them.'

'Bollocks,' said Banks. There was a tap at the door and a young uniformed officer stuck his head around. 'You sent for me, sir?'

'Yes,' said Banks. 'Could you rustle up a pot of tea. One as it comes and one… how do you take your tea, Colin? It's not a trick question.'

'Milk, two sugars.'

'Got that, constable?' said Banks.

'Yes, sir.'

When the constable had gone, Banks turned back to Whitman. 'Are you going to tell me what happened, Colin?' he said. 'Or are we just going to sit here and drink tea and listen to Beethoven until your brief arrives? I don't mind. The result will probably be the same in the long run.'

'I told you. I'm not saying anything until my solicitor gets here.'

'Right. So we already know you did it. You knew when Victor Vancalm was due to arrive home from Berlin. You probably had a key to the house, but you wanted to make it look like a burglary so you broke that side window and got in that way. Did you smash up the room before or after you killed Victor?'

Whitman said nothing. His jaw was set so tightly that Banks could see the muscles tense, the lips whitening. At this rate he'd have an aneurism or something before his solicitor arrived.

'No matter,' Banks went on. 'And you've no doubt got rid of whatever you stole by now, if you've got any sense. I don't know how long you'd been planning this, but it smells of premeditation to me. At any rate, you won't be out for a long, long time. Now, correct me if I'm wrong, but I'm assuming the most obvious scenario. Victor Vancalm found out about your odd proclivities and he didn't like them?'

A curious and most unpleasant smile crept over Whitman's features. 'You think you're so bloody clever, don't you?' he said.

Banks said nothing.

Whitman leaned forward. 'Well, what would you think, Mr clever detective, if I told you those discs your men found were Victor's?'

'I'd think you were lying to save your own neck,' said Banks, who wasn't too sure. He could already hear the faint alarm bells ringing in the back of his mind, sense the disparate observations and inchoate imaginings suddenly taking shape and forming recognizable images.

Whitman laughed. 'All right, you've got me. Or you think you've got me. We'll see about that when my solicitor gets here. But don't assume Victor Vancalm was the innocent in all this.'

'Do you mean what I think you mean?'

'Even PC Plod could figure this one out,' Whitman went on. He was clearly enjoying his new found sense of superiority, and Banks was not going to disabuse him of the notion.

'You'll have to be a bit clearer than that,' he said.

'I don't think I'd be incriminating myself if I told you that Victor Vancalm was an aficionado of the kind of thing you mentioned earlier.'

'You mean Vancalm was into child pornography?'

'It looks as if I do have to spell it out for you. Yes. That's what I'm saying.' He folded his arms again. 'And you won't get another word out of me until my solicitor arrives. This time I mean it.'

Banks nodded. He didn't really need another word from Colin Whitman. Not just yet, at any rate.

'Have you found anything out yet, Mr Banks?' asked Denise Vancalm. They were sitting in the same room as they had sat two days ago, at Banks's request, though the police hadn't quite finished with the house yet, and Mrs Vancalm was still staying at the Jedburgh Hotel. When Banks suggested the house as a venue, she had readily agreed as she said she had some more clothes she wanted to pick up. DI Annie Cabbot was there, too, notebook open, pen in her hand.

'Quite a bit,' said Banks. 'Mr Whitman is under arrest.'

'Colin? My God. Did Colin…? I mean, I can't believe it. Why?'

'Don't worry, Mrs Vancalm. Colin Whitman didn't kill your husband.'

'Then I don't understand.' She clutched at the gold pendant around her neck. 'Why? Who?'

'You killed your husband,' Banks said.

'Me…?' She pointed at her own chest. 'But that's absurd. I was at the poker circle. You know I was.'

'You told me that was where you were.'

'But Natasha, Gabriella, Evangeline, Heather… they all corroborated my story.'

'Indeed they did,' said Banks. 'And that caused me no end of problems.'

'What do you mean?'

'I just couldn't think at first what would make four law-abiding professional women alibi a friend for the murder of her husband. It didn't make sense. In almost every scenario I could think of, someone would have spoken out against it, suggested another course of action, refused to be involved.'

'Of course,' said Denise Vancalm. 'That's why it's true.'

Banks shook his head. 'No, it's not. I said I couldn't think of anything, and at first I couldn't. Perhaps spousal abuse came close, but even then there was certain to be a voice of reason, a dissenting voice. Maybe if he were a serial killer… but that clearly wasn't the case. Only when Mr Whitman told me the truth did I understand it.'

'I don't know what you're talking about.'

'Of course you do. Your husband was a child pornographer. All these trips. Amsterdam. Berlin. Brussels. Oh, he did business, of course, but then there was the *other* business, wasn't there? The secret meetings, the swaps, the children, often smuggled in from Eastern Europe, bought and paid for.'

'This is absurd. I want my solicitor.'

'All in good time,' said Banks, who was getting sick and tired of hearing that request. 'Somehow,' Banks went on, 'you found out about it. Perhaps he let something slip on the computer, or maybe it was something else, but you found out. You were shocked, horrified, of course. You didn't know what to do. Horror turned to disgust. It sickened you. You had to do something about it, but you didn't know what. All you knew was that you couldn't go on living with a man like that, and that he couldn't be allowed to keep on doing what he was doing. Am I right so far?'

Denise Vancalm said nothing, but her expression spoke volumes. 'Do go on, Chief Inspector,' she said softly. 'It's a fascinating story.'

'No doubt your first thought, as an honest citizen, was to report him to the authorities. But you couldn't do that, could you?'

'Why not?' she asked.

'I think there were two reasons. First, you couldn't live with it, with the shame of knowing who, or what, you had been married to for fifteen years. It would have been an admission of weakness, of defeat.'

'Very good,' said Denise. 'And the other reason?'

'Professional. Your business is important to you. You're a fund-raiser and event organizer for charities, predominantly *children's* charities. Imagine how it would go down with your colleagues that you were married to a child pornographer and you didn't even know it. Oh, there would be sympathy enough at first. Poor Denise, they'd say. But there'd always be those important little questions at the backs of their minds. *Did* she know? How could she *not* have known? It would have meant the end for you. You couldn't have lived with that. But the widow of a murder victim? There you get all the sympathy without the vexing questions. *As long as you have a watertight alibi.* And with Gabriella Mountjoy, Natasha Goldwell, Evangeline White and Heather Murchison all swearing you were with them all evening, the old surprising a burglar routine should have worked very well.'

'But how could I have done it?'

'Very easily. After you got to Gabriella's, you left your car there. There's nothing much more distinctive than a red sports car, and you didn't want anyone to see that around your home that evening. You borrowed one of the others' cars, probably Evangeline White's.

She wasn't particularly a *Top Gear* type. All she wanted was a nice little runner that would get her from A to B. Nondescript. You drove back home shortly before your husband was due to arrive, parked out of the way. You broke in through the side window to make it look as if a burglar had gained entry, and then you waited for him. I don't know if there was any discussion when he arrived, any questioning, any chance to offer an explanation, or whether you simply executed the sentence the moment he walked into his study.'

'All this is very clever,' Denise said, 'but it assumes you have evidence that my husband was what you say he was, and that I knew about it.'

'Friends can only be relied on up to a point,' said Banks. 'Natasha Goldwell values her freedom, and when she found it under threat she decided that it might be best to make a clean breast of things. It doesn't get her off without punishment completely, of course, but I think we can be certain a judge will view her with a certain amount of lenience.'

Pale and trembling, Denise Vancalm reached in her handbag for a tissue and blew her nose. 'And what did Natasha have to say?' she asked, trying to sound casual.

'That not only did she and the others provide you with an alibi because they were as horrified as you were about your husband's activities, but that she went over to your house the day before – remember, when I asked you about that, and you told me it was just for coffee and girly talk – well that's when she cleaned off your husband's computer. She's good at it. It's her job. Computer software design, specializing in security. Our experts found traces when she told them where to look. Not a lot, but enough to show what was there and to give us a few more leads to chase down. You also cleaned out the safe. No doubt there were discs and photographs there, too.'

'It was the computer,' Denise said, her voice no more than a whisper.

'What?' Banks asked.

'The computer. Victor was away in Berlin and my web service was on the blink. We have different services. Sounds silly, I know, but there it is. I wanted to look up a company online. I started the email browser by mistake and a couple of emails came in. I was curious. I'm sure you know what it's like. Oh, there were no photographs of naked children or anything like that, but it was pretty obvious what the sender was referring to. At first I thought it might have been some sick sort of spam, but I checked his folders. There were more. There were... pictures, too. I didn't find those until Natasha... they were well hidden, secured.'

'Is that why you smashed the computer screen?'

'Yes. I wasn't thinking. I just lashed out.'

'He took a tremendous risk in keeping them.'

'Don't they all? But he needed them. Obviously the compulsion overcomes all the risks. Maybe it's even a part of the excitement, the possibility of being caught. I don't know. I really don't know.'

'So you decided to kill him.'

She nodded and sighed. 'You're right. What's the point in lying any more? I don't blame Natasha. She was never really comfortable with the plan from the start. She was appalled by what she saw on the screen, of course, and she went along with it, but of all of them she had the most reservations. As I say, I don't blame her. If I could only have come up with some other way...'

'You could have reported him.'

'No. You were right about that. And there'd have been a trial. I couldn't have stood that. Everyone knowing.'

The irony, Banks thought, was that even now it had come out and Denise Vancalm would certainly go to trial, she would probably get more public sympathy as the murderess of a child pornographer than she would have as the wife of a live one. As for her alibi, the Eastvale ladies' poker circle, Banks didn't know what would happen. Their fate lay in the hands of the Crown Prosecution Service and the courts, not in his, thank God. As he and Annie walked Denise Vancalm out to the waiting police car, Banks found himself thinking that they would probably not have to look very far to find a poker game in prison.

♠

The Uncertainty Principle
Eric Van Lustbader

MY DAD IS A CARD SHARP. Like all card sharps he wanted a son but, instead, he got me. He says he doesn't mind, though, since my brain is filled with numbers. It's filled with equations, really – it's how I see the world, the only way the world makes sense to me – but to him it's the same thing.

Numbers are everything to him. He's spent practically all his life trying to memorize them. I don't have to memorize numbers. They're just there in my head. That's why he loves me just as much as if I was his son, not a girl of eighteen with cornflower-blue eyes, long red hair and the tits of a Penthouse Pet.

I get all that from my mother. Daddy wanted to call me Teddy, but my mother said over her dead body. She named me Charlotte. Daddy got the last laugh, though. He called me Charlie right from the get-go, and it stuck. Which pissed my mother off no end.

Daddy and my mother don't live together any more. She accused him of gambling their savings away; he accused her of lying on her back all the time. That's exactly what he said. I should know. I was standing right there when he said it.

Of course, I didn't know what that meant until I was older. No point in judging either of them. They were doing what came natural to them; they couldn't do any different.

Daddy trained as a dealer. That was right here in Reno, which is where he met my mother. Not at the dealer's school or at the poker tables, where he liked to spend time as soon as school was out for the day. He met her at Maxine's Royal Flush, a high-class chicken ranch, off Rte. 395. By design, the front gate was a stone's throw from Julio's Diner, a popular truck stop. That Maxine was smarter than your average whore.

She'd designed the front gate herself to look like all the working ranches around those parts, which I suppose was a kind of joke. The Royal Flush is where Daddy liked to spend his nights, and his money. He set up a poker game there, fleeced the truckers after they had been well fucked. Maxine didn't mind; he gave her a fat cut. Plus, he got to hang out with all her girls.

My mother was the most beautiful of the bunch. She liked to say that she hated his guts until he taught her how to play poker. He taught her how to smoke a cigar, too, but that's another story. My mother had a talent for playing poker. Soon enough, she graduated herself from turning tricks to fleecing them. In fact, she got to be better at it than Daddy.

He always told me he liked that – he liked all the money she raked in. But now I think he was lying. I think deep down he resented it, and it got to gnawing at him, like a starving rat gnaws at wood. Love turns to hate so easy, doesn't it?

When they split, they left it up to me where I was to go. I chose to live with Daddy. My mother didn't mind. She didn't want me with her, anyways. She said she didn't live the kind of lifestyle that was suitable for a child my age. When she left I told myself it'd just take some time to wrap my mind around that one. I was wrong. I never did understand how she could just abandon me like that.

She even told me 'a secret' that last day: she told me she wasn't my real mother. She said she couldn't have a child, so she and Daddy adopted me. After that first splash of fear and confusion, I recovered pretty good. I laughed in her face.

'I only have to look in the mirror,' I told her, 'to see what a liar you are.'

And that's how we left it, she and I.

Where she is now, God only knows.

Nowadays, I help my Daddy. You'd think I'd still be in school, but right off the bat he signed me up for home schooling. That's just like him. What a scam. They only send a bunch of test papers around once a year to make sure you're learning what you're supposed to learn. Right off I got into the habit of giving the test papers to my friend Seth. At first he didn't want to do me the favour. But then I did a favour for him and it changed his mind, sort of. He still didn't want to take the test for me but, even then, Seth was so ga-ga over me he'd do just about anything to get a favour from me. Nowadays, Seth keeps saying I should quit this life my Daddy and I have. Even though he's two years older, I pay him no mind. Why should I? Daddy and I have it good.

Daddy runs a high-stakes poker game that attracts the real big boys: politicians, mobsters and, once in a while, a celebrity or two who think they know what they're doing. Daddy takes them in, of course. They've got money to burn, and man do they like to burn it. Throwing it around in that company makes them feel – I don't know – I think it validates them, is the word I'm thinking of. (I'm not stupid. I read the dictionary all the time. Also, the encyclopedia. That was Seth's idea. I do it to keep him – what's the right word? – mollified. Now that I'm eighteen, and the home schooling is over and done with, you'd think I'd have blown Seth off. But I haven't. I don't know why, really. Maybe I just like having him around, like an old chair that's too comfortable for words. He's slim and tall, with thick dark hair and pale grey eyes that are hard to look away from. He has a big smile, which is nice, too.)

More often than not Daddy sits in on the games. That's the point, really. That's where we make the big bucks. And that's where I come in, me with my head full of equations. I stand behind him while he's playing, my hands on the ladder back of his chair. Nobody minds. I'm only a girl. Plus, a lot of the men like to look at me. Daddy doesn't mind that; he says it distracts them and, seeing the look on their faces, I believe him. It's always the same look, no matter who the man is. They're filled with a greedy urgency, as if they're chained to their seat, just out of reach of the trough that's been set out in front of them. Soo-wee!

Anyway, there I am standing behind Daddy, watching the cards. Even when the discards are dead and covered with other discards they stay in my mind, their faces making equations that keep rebalancing as each hand goes on. In this case, the equations translate into odds, and I use my fingers tapping on Daddy's back to translate the odds to him. I give him a tremendous edge. We have to be careful, though, so he doesn't win all the time and cause a ruckus. Some of the men at the table are soulless. A human life to them is no more than the flip of a card. Face up you live, face down you die.

You might think I'm making this up or, at the very least, exaggerating. I'm not, believe me. Once, one of those men – Roddy Shone – felt the day's celebrity was cheating on him. In fact, he was, but that's another story. Roddy bit down on his twenty-dollar Havana, stood up, brushed imaginary flecks of ash off his shiny shantung silk suit. Then he walked over to where the celebrity was sitting.

Roddy is slightly bandy-legged, so he sways back and forth when he walks. Some think he swaggers, and hate him for it, but they're wrong. They hate him cause he can make them wet their pants just by clenching his fist.

On his way over, his suit jacket swings open and I see the butt of the .45 semi-automatic snug in its grey chamois holster beneath his left armpit. (I suppose now you're wondering how I know the first thing about guns. I worked on and off for two years at a pawn shop over by Mountain View Cemetery right after Daddy made me quit the bail jumper gig cause he thought it was too dangerous. Truth be told, it was. But in those days I was kinda wild. Of course, for a girl like me Reno is fairly buzzing with career opportunities: dealer, hostess, showgirl, pole dancer – just stop. Don't make me go all the way to the bottom.)

Anyway, back to Roddy Shone. I like Roddy. He doesn't take himself too seriously, except with the politicos, who he has a lot of muscle with. Roddy understands the concept of face, which I picked up from watching all those very cool Kurosawa DVDs I got from Netflix.

The minute I saw Roddy's right hand move up toward the butt I knew we were in for trouble. Trouble is one thing Daddy's card game can't stand. Trouble means the game will fold like a Frenchman on the firing line. Worse, with a rep like that, it will never start up again, and then where would Daddy and I be? We could move to Vegas, I guess, but our hustle is Reno. We know it inside out. That's the hustler's secret, his true edge. No, Vegas was a no-go.

So Roddy is halfway to the celeb who, I might add, is frozen like a hare in the headlights, when I detach myself from Daddy's chair.

'How about a drink, Roddy?' I say.

Roddy's gaze glowers past me. 'Get out of my way, kiddo.' Man, he was pissed. He only calls me 'kiddo' when he's all het up. 'Man beats me fair 'n' square, that's all right. I take my medicine, just like the next man. Who wouldn't? You puts your money down, you takes your chance with Lady Luck. But when I'm cheated out of a pot, that's fucking war, that is.'

'Can't argue with that,' I tell him, my heart throbbing in my throat. 'But wars are won a lotta different ways.'

Something about my voice, or maybe what I said makes him look down at me. 'Where the fuck did you hear that, kiddo?'

'Kurosawa,' I say.

'And who the fuck is Kurosawa?'

'A Japanese film director.'

'Never heard of the bastard.'

'You heard of *The Magnificent Seven*?'

'Are you kidding? With Yul Brynner and Steve McQueen.'

'Then you heard of Kurosawa,' I said. Which isn't, strictly speaking, true, but in Roddy Shone's case it's close enough.

Anyway, while this is going on, Daddy takes the opportunity to hustle the celeb out of the room. As they reach the door, we can all hear him say, 'And don't fucking come back, if you value your skin.'

It was a corny, totally over-the-top movie line but, what the hell, he was talking to a movie star, wasn't he? And it impressed the hell out of Roddy, which was kinda the point.

I take Roddy over to the bar sideboard, fix him a stiff bourbon and water. He laughs a little, shattering the tension like a crystal vase hitting the floor.

'My man, Steve fucking McQueen,' Roddy says, with bourbon shining his lips. 'Him and a Jap, go figure.' He shakes his head, ruffles my hair, which I hate, but I bite my lip rather than tell him that. 'Damn, Charlie. For a girl, you've got a curious mind.'

He should only know how curious. I just smile up at him blandly, like I'm the kid he thinks I am.

Seth says I'm fearless. I don't know about that. Plus, he says it like it's a disease I caught or, more likely, was born with. Seth says a lot of things that piss me off. He says even more things that ought to piss me off, but for some reason don't. Maybe it's because he's the only man I ever met –except Daddy, of course – who doesn't look at me as if I'm stark naked.

Seth says things like, What am I doing with my life? When am I going to have time for him? I'm as soulless as the marks in Daddy's card game. Well, now, that does piss me off. But in response, I say, 'I'm heartless, Seth, not soulless.'

And he, the constant big mouth (but only with me, it seems), comes back with, 'What's the difference?'

And then we're off on some heady discussion about God and Christ and the soul and death. These kinds of talks are Seth's meat. He's like a hungry lion pulling apart red meat with his teeth and claws. Seth likes to get to the bottom of things. And when we do I always say to him, 'OK, now what?'

You don't think it ends there, do you? Oh, no. Mr Big Mouth

comes back with, 'Now we have more knowledge. We know something we didn't know before. We've progressed.'

'Progressed where, Seth?'

His big grey eyes stand out like beacons in almost any light, but most specially when the sun's in them. 'Life is progression; they're one and the same,' he tells me. 'Death puts an end to all that. Death is stillness; it's the opposite of progression.'

Seth is a writer. I don't pretend to understand what he writes, but I know it's good. How do I know it's good? Because once I start reading it, I can't put it down. Actually, Seth claims I *do* understand what he writes. In fact, he says I understand it better than anyone else.

'It's the numbers,' he says. 'The numbers inside your head. Writing sentences is like balancing equations. When sentences aren't in balance, you have to erase them and start over. But the mistake is where the learning comes from. Knowing what *not* to do leads to knowing what *to* do.'

That kind of talk should give me a headache, I think. But it doesn't. I understand it absolutely. Because (and here Seth's right) of the numbers in my head.

Seth wasn't always a writer. Or maybe he was, but he just didn't know it. He went to school to become a doctor – that was his mother's big dream for him. A wish above all others. Seth's dad was a day labourer, working at one of the casinos. His mother hated that, but Seth would say to me, 'What's wrong with what my father does? Look. Look how happy he is.' And Seth was right. His dad was a happy man until the day he died with tubes and blood coming everywhere out of him like some kind of lab experiment.

So at one point Seth was pre-med in college. Then came quantum mechanics and physics. Right away I knew he was no good at it. He struggled and struggled. I tried to help him. I so much wanted to, the way he'd helped me, but when I offered to, he shook his head. (I can tell what you're thinking. How could I help him? Me, who couldn't even pass the yearly home school tests. Well,

God knows I can't write a decent sentence, as I'm sure you can tell, but as for quantum mechanics and physics, I understand them from the ground up. How do I do that? I don't rightly know. I just do. It's the equations inside my head, the things that makes sense of the world around me.)

'You don't think I can help you, do you,' I pouted.

'That's just it. I *know* you can help me, Charlie.'

'Then why won't you let me?'

He closed the thick textbook. 'Because,' he sighed, 'you've got to know when to hold 'em, you've got to know when to fold 'em.'

The next day, he brought all his texts back to the book store, traded them in for books written by Hegel, Kant, Locke, Spinosa, Sartre. Unexpectedly, he bought a book for me. *Sein und Zeit* (*Being and Time*), by Martin Heidegger. In it, Heidegger explains Being and *Dassein*, literally 'existence'. He talks about the concept of 'being there', of time and matter both being a function of mathematics. In other words, what existence boils down to is numbers.

'But I already know that,' I say.

'Read it again,' Seth says. 'This time without my help.'

I do, but it leaves me feeling like I've eaten half my breakfast. That day, I get up early, walk down to the college bookstore. Talking to the clerks there leads me to Schrödinger, whose famous theoretical cat experiment was meant to prove the conflict between what we can see with our eyes and what quantum mechanics tells us goes on at a microscopic level.

Schrödinger, in turn, leads me to Werner Heisenberg, one of the fathers of quantum mechanics. Basically, what Heisenberg discovered was that the relationship between momentum and position is like the relationship between energy and time. It's the Uncertainty Principle. In other words, a single particle can be in a number of places at once. Does that sound like gobbledegook to you? Not me. I totally get it. How we experience things in the world – from motion to time – is a function of numbers. In fact, looking at things that way, motion is time. That's why I could almost always win at poker – or craps, or roulette or… well, you name it. I can see through what everyone else sees to the underlying building blocks on which *everything* is based. What it all boils down to is this: I speak a different language than you do.

Because the poker games take place at night, Daddy and I live an upside-down life. Well, it doesn't seem upside-down to us, but it does to Seth who, like most people in Reno not attached to the gaming industry, live their lives just like anyone else in the country.

For Daddy and me, it's day for night. We get up at five in the afternoon. I get up first, by a half-hour or so, and fix him breakfast. That is, I used to, until Seth started coming around. He eats my breakfast as his dinner. I asked him, once, why he was doing that. He said it didn't make any difference to him. Maybe he's telling the truth, I don't know. Seth says he doesn't lie, but I don't know. Can that be true of anybody? It's not true of Daddy, and it sure as hell wasn't true of my mother.

Tonight, Daddy feeling ill, he cancels the game. I tell him not to. I tell him I've watched him run it long enough, I can handle it myself. He just laughs and goes back to watching porno on the TV and coughing from his phlegmy chest. He'd work with a temperature of 103°, my Daddy, but a cough? Uh uh. You don't want to get the suckers sick, do you?

So I have a night off. Seth is delirious. After a proper dinner, *not* at one of the casino restaurants, we climb into his big cream-coloured vintage Caddy and go to the Luna Drive-In. It's the last outdoor movie theatre in town, a relic from another age that some poker millionaire who loves movies bought and turned into a tourist attraction. The Luna plays only old films like *Dracula* and *Gidget Goes Hawaiian*. Tonight they're playing *Sleeping Beauty*, which is beautiful, sad and happy. Seth buys us Crackerjacks and Red Hots. Only old-time candy at the concession stand.

Afterwards, we drive out into the hills, further than we've ever been. There's a bit of a wind, chill and somehow comforting. The sky is like an iceberg with candles in its hollowed-out centre. That's how many stars shine down on us.

We sit side by side, staring up at the sky.

'Where would you like to go, Charlie?'

'What?' I'm startled. What the hell kind of question is that?

'I mean if you could go anywhere in the world.'

I shrug. 'Why would I want to leave Reno?'

He laughs, not unkindly. Seth doesn't know how to be unkind. 'It's a big world,' he says. 'There's so much to see, so much to learn. So much knowledge waiting.'

'Waiting for what?'

'For us to come find it.'

I turn to him, put my lips over his. We start to kiss, and that feels like the stars are showering down on us. After a while, Seth disentangles himself. He opens the big, heavy Caddy door and steps out. I figure he's got to pee, but instead he turns to me, gets down on one knee. I look down. In the centre of his palm is a diamond ring, which he holds out to me.

'Charlotte Bliss, will you marry me?'

Jesus. I laugh. Honestly, I don't know what else to do. If Seth had hit me over the head with his shoe I couldn't be more surprised. My fault, right? I should've read the signs. I should've seen it coming. You did, I suppose.

The laugh is bad enough, but then I follow it up with, 'I don't think so, Seth.'

'Why not?'

'Marriage? The numbers just don't add up.'

'I know what's going on. Your father doesn't want you to leave him.'

'You've got it ass backwards. It's *me* who doesn't want to leave *him.*'

'That's plain crazy.' He frowns, shakes his head. 'You're saying that because your mother and father didn't make it.'

He's right, of course. Daddy's all I have. Seth is so much smarter than me. Which is yet another reason not to marry him. He'll tire of me in the end, won't he?

'Anyway,' he goes on, 'love has nothing to do with numbers.'

'Of course it does,' I say. '*Everything* has to do with numbers. I know it, and so did Heidegger and Heisenberg.'

'In this one instance,' he insists, 'they're wrong.'

'A principle is a principle. It can't be erased randomly when it suits you.'

He sighs, rises up, gets back behind the wheel. But then he presses the ring into my hand. 'Take it, Charlie,' he says as I try to give it back to him. 'Just… you don't have to put it on. Just keep it, at least for a little while.'

I put the ring in my pocket.

'Let's go home,' he says, slamming the Caddy's door.

'No. Seth.' I take his hand, put it on my breast. 'Let's stay out all night, like I would have if I'd had a prom.'

He can't resist me. He gets an old striped blanket out of the Caddy's trunk, spreads it on the ground. We lie down on it, side by side. It smells of him and of summer, and I love that. For a time we just hold hands, stare up at the milky sky. Then he rolls over on top of me. I can feel how hard he is, like he's bursting with energy. I rise up toward him, meeting his energy with mine. And time is rocked by the force of our momentum.

So today has dawned just like any other day, red and hot, and dry as a prayer meeting. Unlike every other day, I see the dawn. But just for a bit. My arms and legs are wrapped around Seth. I fall back asleep to the soft beating of his heart.

It's noon by the time we both open our eyes again. We go have a bite to eat at the diner and talk about everything, except the one thing Seth is dying to talk about. I feel the diamond ring in my pocket. In secret, my fingers go to it, turning it around and around. I want to say something, erase the sad look on his face but, honestly, I don't know what to say.

It's four-thirty by the time Seth drives me home. Two blocks away, I see the red and white lights flicking on and off. We turn the corner and I see the cop cars, three of them, all nosed in towards the front door of the ranch house I share with Daddy.

I'm out of the car, tearing down the street even before Seth's Caddy rocks to a stop on its pillow shocks. The clutch of uniforms standing around turn toward me as I race at them. One reaches out to stop me. Then I hear Seth's raised voice:

'That's Tommy Bliss's daughter.'

Between that and the fact that I know one of the uniforms, Bill Penny, they let me through. Penny hurries after me.

'Charlie,' he says. 'Charlie…'

I hear the urgency in his voice. It makes me want to vomit. My heart hammers in my throat. Through the living room, past the kitchen with its familiar breakfast smells of toast and bacon. Down the hall.

'Daddy,' I call. 'Daddy!'

There's a tall, slim man slouched at the open doorway to Daddy's bedroom. Not a uniform. A suit with latex gloves stretched over his hands.

'This is Detective Ralphs,' Penny says from behind me, like a prompter at a play. It's all so unreal. I feel like an actor who's forgotten her lines.

'It's OK,' I hear Penny say. 'This is Charlotte Bliss. The deceased's daughter.'

Oh, God. No.

I stand in the doorway for I don't know how long, staring in at what looks like a set piece from *CSI*. Daddy's sprawled on the bed face up. There's blood everywhere. A cadaver bends over him, taking flash photos from every angle. The sharp smell of cordite hits me.

'Who shot him?' My voice seems to come from far, far away.

The detective takes a toothpick out of the corner of his mouth. 'I'm sorry for your loss, Ms Bliss.'

I'd like to plant my fist in his face. Instead, I repeat my question.

The detective tells me. Someone Daddy kicked out of his game. A flat-broke busted nobody who's sure as hell somebody now.

'We have him out in one of the squad cars,' Penny says.

He puts a hand on my arm. I shrug it off.

'We got him, Charlie,' Penny says. 'We got him.'

His words seem like the only sound in the world. The camera flashes one more time, then the cadaver slides past me. I can hear Penny's words following the cadaver as he navigates the hallway on crepe-soled shoes.

Time and energy seem to collide inside me, cancelling each other out, creating the form of stillness Seth would call death. Only I'm not dead. Daddy is.

Then what the hell am I?

Seth doesn't say anything, doesn't hold me. He knows I don't want that. Not now, anyway. He does all the calling – the mortuary, all that. Me? I just stand, looking in at Daddy. He's so still that I think Seth must be right. Does everything come to a rest some time? I wish I could ask Heisenberg, because I don't know the answer. The equations in my head seem to add up to zero today, no matter which way I configure them.

Seth tracks down my mother, how I don't know. Maybe she wasn't all that hard to find, after all. Maybe I just didn't try. You want to know why?

'Mrs Bliss. Faith?' Seth says into the receiver. 'Oh, sorry, Ms Horner.' Typical. She's regressed to the name she used when Daddy met her at Royal Flush. 'I'm sorry to tell you that your ex-husband passed away today.' He waits, his face so twisted up I can imagine the tongue-lashing the poor lamb's got to put up with. 'OK, OK, I understand that you hate him, Ms Horner, but there's your daughter to think of. Charlotte's all alone and—'

He stops abruptly, a look of disgust overcoming his handsome features. 'I understand,' he says finally. 'I mean, I don't under—'

He looks at the receiver before he puts it back in its cradle. 'She hung up on me,' he says softly, as if to himself. Then to me: 'She doesn't want to see you, Charlie. She—'

'Yeah, I know,' I say, cutting him off before he can finish. I don't want him to finish. I don't want to know what else she said. Whatever it was, after the first bit, it doesn't matter now, does it?

'Charlie, I'm so sorry.'

Dry-eyed, I pad down the hallway to the pink and mulberry tiled bathroom, shutting the door firmly behind me. I avoid the mirror. I don't want to see myself now, because I'll see her, and right now that would be too much even for me.

Instead, I sit on the edge of the porcelain tub, turn on the taps, let the hot water run over my feet and ankles. I did this when I was a little girl. It was comforting. It blocked out the pain their screaming brought me.

Once the tears come, I can't stop them. I'm hunched over, face in my cupped hands, sobbing until I can't catch my breath. How could you do this to me, Daddy? I silently wail. Damn you, why did you leave me all alone?

I sit there for the longest time, immobile again, in Seth's death-like state. Until he knocks on the door, calls my name, comes hesitantly in.

'Charlie,' he says. 'Are you all right?'

I don't answer him. What could I possibly say?

He takes a step across the mulberry tiles. 'Charlie, the detective needs to talk to you.'

I nod and get up. Without wiping my feet I brush past him, walk towards the uniforms, standing around thinking of donuts and their aching backs.

After they've left, after the coroner has taken Daddy's body away, after Seth has taken Daddy's black suit out of his closet, after he and I sit in the deathly atmosphere of the mortuary and make decisions that have no bearing on my Daddy, or on me, it's all over.

But it isn't.

On the way back home, Seth says, 'Charlie, the game is scheduled for tonight. I can find your father's book. I'll call all the players, OK?'

For a time, I stare out the side, see fixed lights and passing traffic as part of the same blur. But they're not the same, are they? Seth, wanting to get me home as quick as he can, accelerates, matches the speed of a car on our left. For a moment the blur vanishes. It looks as if we're not moving at all, as if both cars have entered a world within the larger world, where time has slowed and motion has stopped altogether. Then, Seth's Caddy continues to accelerate, and the blur returns. The world is as it was. But it's not, is it? Daddy's no longer in it.

Or is that true? The game is his. If the game continues, does Daddy continue, too? It sounds funny, even to me. But only at first.

When I come to think of it as a principle, a truth of its own, I turn to Seth and, with the wind blowing my flaming hair, say, 'No. Don't call anyone.'

'Charlie, I really don't think you're up to doing it yourself.' Not surprising, he doesn't understand.

'I'm not calling anyone, Seth. *I'll* be running the game tonight.'

Of course he tells me not to do it. You'd think I'd be angry at him for trying to stop me, but I'm not. You'd think I'd be angry at him being so predictable, but I'm not. What I am is in a mind-set where the equations have started rolling again. Zero is not an option. As I go about the preparations, I can hear Daddy's voice in my head, clear as a bell. He wants to make sure I don't forget anything.

I don't, which is good, because here they come, right on time. Three local politicos, Tony Danko and Roddy Shone, a Hollywood celeb who I can tell at a glance is from the Vince Vaughn school of Texas Hold 'Em. He's gonna get a good fleecing tonight. If not from me, then for sure from Roddy.

Speaking of Roddy, the minute he steps through the door, he takes my elbow, pulls me aside.

'We've all heard about your Daddy,' he says in a low voice. It seems everyone but the celeb, who's new in town and doesn't know any better, has gone to see Daddy tricked out in his best black suit at the mortuary. 'We're here tonight to pay tribute to him and to say goodbye to you.'

'Say goodbye?' I stare up at him. 'What on earth do you mean?'

'The game's over, Charlie. The fat lady's sung. Finito.'

'No, it's not,' I say defiantly. 'The game's going on.'

Roddy cocks his bald head. 'How's that?'

'I'm running it. I'm taking Daddy's place.'

Now he seems shocked. Imagine. Roddy Shone.

'Don't kid a kidder, Charlie,' he says sternly. 'The game's no place for you.'

'The game's all I have. Don't shut me down.'

He's about to answer me when his mouth snaps shut. He's clearly thinking about what I've said. Roddy's a loner, too, apart from his revolving-door girls. All they do is suck his cock. When he tires of their technique he kicks them out. I hear he's got a kid he's never seen – daughter or son, I don't know. That's damn sad, if you ask me.

'OK,' he says at last. 'Let's try it, see how it goes.'

I heave a sigh of relief. The world starts spinning again. 'I'll take Daddy's place at the table.'

His brows knit together. 'Now you're going too fucking far, kiddo.'

'Let's try it,' I say. 'See how it goes.'

He laughs to hear his own words so easily thrown back at him. 'Like I said, you've got a damn curious mind.' He nods. 'But no crying now when I take your profits in a showdown pot.'

We all take our places at the table. Still and all, Roddy insists on a moment of silence. Then they all agree to tell a story about Daddy – all except the celeb, of course, who's on his cell until Roddy slaps it out of his hand.

'No cellphones, PDAs or pagers allowed at the game,' I say to the celeb, to keep things from escalating. 'House rules.'

'Plus,' Roddy says, his eyebrows pulled into the centre of his face, 'it's disrespectful to Charlie here, and her Daddy, God rest his soul.'

'You're very kind, Mr Shone,' I say, even though I've always ever called him Roddy. Today's a new day, and I'm a new person. I'm the big kahuna here. The sooner everyone around the table knows that, the better.

The story I tell? The day my mother left, Daddy took me down to Louie's for one of their giganto hot fudge sundaes. He stayed with me all day, talking to me about how good our life would be from now on. No more shouting matches, no more coffee mugs thrown across the kitchen. I knew he had work to do, stuff that had to be done to get ready for the game. But there was no game that night. That night Daddy took me to the movies and put his arm around me while I cried my goddamn eyes out.

I will say that at the get-go the other players have a bit of a problem with me sitting in. In fact, one of the politicos says, 'You're playing, Charlie? Really? Isn't that illegal?' We all have a big chuckle over that, especially Roddy who has this piece of crap firmly in his back pocket. Photos somewhere, I think, and a nicely lit video with a little boy in a (very) supporting role. Yuck! Politicians make my skin crawl. Next to this one, Roddy is a goddamned choir boy.

Anyway, it all gets ironed out and we start to play. At first, I keep my skill in check. I win every third or fourth hand. Then the stakes go up and Roddy goes on a winning streak. Right away I see that he's gunning for the celeb, but for one reason or another I get caught in the backwash. All of a sudden, I'm down a thou and Roddy's grinning at me across the table, as if to say, I warned you, kiddo. Get out now before I hurt you bad.

No way I'm getting out. In fact, I've just begun. Now I bear down, put Daddy out of my mind, concentrate solely on the equations, which are running through my head like a river of quicksilver. I win three hands in a row. I let Roddy win the next one, just so he won't get suspicious.

The deal comes to me. I'm about to ask Tony Danko, who's on

my left, to cut the deck when the door opens and Seth comes in. I stare at him. What's he doing here? He's never come to a game before.

Tony Danko looks at Seth, along with the others. 'What the hell's this?' he says. 'No fucking observers allowed.'

'He's helping me,' I say. 'He stays, if he wants.'

Tony Danko looks at me for a minute, then grunts in what I take to be disgust.

Seth's eyes meet mine. I don't need the numbers to tell me what he's thinking. I can see it in the slight downward curve of his lips, I can see it in his pale grey eyes. He doesn't think I should be here. He wants to marry me, take me away from all this. His thirst for knowledge makes me dizzy, and for a moment I can't think.

Then Tony Danko's big hairy ape hand has cut the cards and it's go time. I deal the cards. I've got a so-so hand, a pair of eights. The politico on my right opens and we all place our bets. Right away, Roddy raises. One of the politicos folds. I ask for cards. Naturally, I take three. Roddy slides one card from his hand, places it face down on the table. That's all he wants? One card? His eyes meet mine as I deal him one card. I know what he's thinking. He wants to teach me a lesson. He wants to squash me like a bug. He wants me to know that the game is no place for a girl, even if I am my Daddy's daughter. He's so fucking sure he knows what's good for me.

Over by the door, Seth leans against the wall, arms folded. It seems like I can hear everyone's else's thoughts, but not mine.

I fan out my cards, take a look at my hand. Good deal. I've picked up an eight. The bidding starts again. Another politico bites the dust. Again, Roddy raises. The third politico turns over his cards. Now I raise, doubling Roddy's raise. Maybe it's a bit reckless, I don't know. The numbers are adding up, though.

There's over ten grand in the pot now. This last round is too rich for Tony Danko. That leaves me, Roddy and the idiot celeb, who for sure doesn't know when to fold. For the one and only time, Roddy and I are in league. Two rounds of raises later, we run the celeb out, after he's ponied up the big bucks.

Almost seventeen big ones are piled up on the table. There's just me and Roddy now. Winner take all. Does he have a straight, a flush? Did I deal him four of a kind at the beginning of the hand? Is Lady Luck that cruel? But it's Roddy who believes in Lady Luck. Me, I'm all about the numbers.

'Now we separate the men from the girls,' Roddy says, as he puts five grand on top of the pot.

I risk a glance over at Seth. Don't ask me why. He's got an odd look on. If I didn't know better, I'd say it's a poker face. Now I can't tell what he's thinking. Is he terrified for me? Does he feel what I feel? The sudden rush of adrenaline. Daddy used to talk about that. 'Damn, there's nothing better than being in a high-stakes poker game, Charlie,' he'd say. 'Not even sex.'

So OK, here it is. The moment it seems I've waited for my whole life. I can either call Roddy or I can raise him one more time, go for broke. I look at my three eights. What's he holding? I run the numbers one more time. The equations line up, like yellow metal ducks in a shooting gallery. I know what I have to do. I know how to win.

Seth is watching me with hooded eyes. Is that a tiny smile playing around the corners of his mouth? Is he proud of me, proud of what I can do? He alone of everyone on the face of the earth knows what I can do. More than that, he can appreciate it.

I search his face. What does he want me to do? I run the numbers, but the equations have gone all fuzzy, so blurred for once in my life I can't read them. I don't know what they add up to.

I continue to look at Seth. Is this what he meant when he said 'love has nothing to do with numbers'? And what did I answer? 'A principle is a principle. It can't be erased randomly when it suits you.'

But what if the principle is false? Didn't Heisenberg say that Schrödinger's theory was crap?

Unconsciously, my hand goes into my pocket. I feel the ring, its diamond hard and sharp against my fingertips. It feels warm, the ring, and I clutch it tight.

What if my principle is false? But how could it be? I *know* that existence is based on mathematics. The numbers. Equations. But what if something exists *outside* of *Dassein*, outside of existence. Something that isn't governed by the numbers? What would that thing be? Would it be love?

So now here I am at that moment. Call or raise? But there is another choice. It exists outside of everything that's in my head, everything that makes up this room, this table, these cards. It's standing over by the door, arms folded, looking at me with hooded eyes.

Am I calling Roddy's hand or am I raising another round? But it's more than that, I see now. Am I sitting at the table, across from Roddy Shone, about to play this last hand with the ginormous stakes? Am I walking out the door with Seth? Or am I doing both?

I want to ask Heisenberg: Where am I?

Once again, momentum and time rush towards each other, and here I go.

♠

Hardly Knew Her

Laura Lippman

S OFIA WAS A LEAN, HIPLESS GIRL, the type that older men
still called a tomboy in 1975, although her only hoydenish
quality was a love of football. In the vacant lot behind the neighbourhood tavern, the boys welcomed her into their games. This
was in part because she was quick, with sure hands. And even touch
football sometimes ended in pile-ups, where it was possible to steal
a touch or two and claim it was accidental. She tolerated this feeble
groping most of the time, punching the occasional boy who
pressed too hard too long, which put the others on notice for a
while. Then they forgot, and it happened again – they touched, she
punched. It was a price she was more than willing to pay for the
exhilaration she felt when she passed the yewberry bushes that
marked the end zone, a gaggle of boys breathless in her wake.

But for all the afternoons she spent at the vacant lot, she never
made peace with the tricky plays – the faked hand-offs, the double
pumps, the gimmicky laterals. It seemed cowardly to her, a way for
less-gifted players to punish those with natural talent. It was one
thing to spin and feint down the field, eluding grasping hands with
a swivel of her hips. But to pretend the ball was somewhere it
wasn't struck her as cheating, and no one could ever persuade her
otherwise.

She figured it was the same with her father and cards. He knew the game was steeped in bluffing and lying, but he could never resign himself to the fact. He depended on good cards and good luck to get him through, and even Sofia understood that was no way to win at poker. But the only person her father could lie to with any success was himself.

'That your dad?' Joe, one of the regular quarterbacks, asked one Friday afternoon as they sprawled in the grass, game over, their side victorious again.

Sofia looked up to see her father slipping through the back door of the tavern, which people called Gordon's, despite the fact that the owner's name was Peter Papadakis. Perhaps someone named Gordon had owned it long ago, but it had been Mr Papadakis's place as far back as Sofia could remember.

'Yeah.'

'What's he doing, going through the back door?' That was a scrawny boy, Bob, one of the grabby ones.

Sofia shredded grass in her fingers, ignoring him. Joe said, 'Poker.'

'Poker? *Poker?* I hardly knew her.' Bob was so pleased with his wit that he rolled back and forth, clutching his stomach, and some of the other boys laughed as they had never heard this old joke before. Sofia didn't laugh. She hated watching her father disappear in the back room of the tavern, from which he would not emerge until early Saturday. But it was better than running into him on the sidewalk between here and home. He always pretended surprise at seeing her, proclaiming it the *darnedest* coincidence, Sofia on Brighton Avenue, same as him. On those occasions, he would stop and make polite inquiries into her life, but he would be restless all the while, shifting his weight from one foot to another, anxious as a little kid on the way to his own birthday party.

'How's it going, Fee?' That was her family nickname, and she was just beginning to hate it.

'S'all right, I guess.'

'School OK?'

'Not bad. I hate algebra.'

'It'll come in handy one day.'

'How?'

'If you get through high school, maybe go on to community college, you won't be stuck here in Dundalk, breathing air you can see.'

'I like it here.' She did. The water was nearby and although it wasn't the kind you could swim in – if you fell in, you were supposed to tell your mom so she could take you for a tetanus shot, but no one ever told – the view from the water's edge made the world feel big, yet comprehensible. Dundalk wasn't Baltimore, although the map said it was. Dundalk was country unto itself, the Republic of Bethlehem Steel. And in 1975, Beth Steel was like the Soviet Union. You couldn't imagine either one not being there. So the families of Dundalk breathed the reddish air, collected their regular paychecks, and comforted one another when a man was hurt or killed, accepting those accidents as the inevitable price for a secure job. It was only later, when the slow poison of asbestosis began moving from household to household that the Beth Steel families began to question the deal they had made. Later still, the all-but-dead company was sold for its parts and the new owner simply ended it all – pensions, health care, every promise ever made. But in 1975, in Dundalk, a Beth Steel family was still the best thing to be, and the children looked down on those whose fathers had to work for any other company.

'Go home and do your homework,' her father told Sofia.

'No homework on Fridays,' she said. 'But I want to eat supper and wash the dishes before *Donny and Marie* comes on.'

They never spoke of his plans for the evening, much less the stakes involved, but after such encounters Sofia went home and hid whatever she could. She longed to advise her mother to do the same, but it was understood that they never spoke of her father's winning and losing, much less the consequences for the household.

'I bought it for you, didn't I?' her father had told her younger brother, Brad, wheeling the ten-speed bicycle with the banana seat out of the garage. Brad had owned the shiny Schwinn for all of a month. 'Why'd I ever think we needed fancy candlesticks like these?' her father grumbled, taking the grape-bedecked silver stems from the sideboard, as if his only problem was a sudden distaste for their ornate style. One Saturday morning, he came into Sofia's room and tried to grab her guitar, purchased a year earlier after a particularly good Friday, but something in her expression made him put it back.

Instead he sold the family dog, a purebred Collie, or so her father had said when he brought the puppy home three months ago. It turned out that Shemp had the wrong kind of papers, some initials other than AKC. The man who agreed to buy Shemp from them had lectured her father, accusing him of being taken in by the Mennonite puppy mills over the state line. He gave her father twenty-five dollars, saying: 'People who can't be bothered to do the most basic research probably shouldn't have a dog, anyway.'

Sofia, sitting in the passenger seat of her father's car – she had insisted on accompanying him, thinking it would shame her father, but in the end she was the one who was ashamed that she had chosen her guitar over Shemp – chewed over this fact. Her father was so gullible that he could be duped by Mennonites. She imagined them ringed around a poker table, solemn bearded faces regarding their cards. Mennonites would probably be good at poker if God let them play it.

Her father spoke of his fortune as if it were the weather, a matter of temperature outside his control. 'I was hot,' her father crowed coming through the door Saturday morning, carrying a box of doughnuts. 'I've never seen a colder deck,' he'd say, heading out Saturday afternoon after a long morning nap on the sofa. 'I couldn't catch a break.'

You just can't bluff, Sofia thought. But then, neither could she. Perhaps it was in her genes. That was why she had to out-run the boys on the other team. *Go long and I'll hit you,* Joe told her and that's what she did, play after play. She outran her competition or she didn't, but she never tried to fool the other players, or faulted anyone else when she failed to catch a ball that was thrown right at her. She didn't think of herself as hot or cold, or try to blame the ball for what she failed to do. A level playing field was not a figure of speech to Sofia. It was all she knew. She made a point of learning every square inch of the vacant lot – the slight depressions where you could turn an ankle if you came down wrong, the sections that stayed mushy long after the rain, the slope in one of their improvised end zones that made it tricky to set up for the pass. With just a little homework, Sofia believed, you could control for every possibility.

Sofia's stubborn devotion to football probably led to the onslaught of oh-so-girly gifts on her next birthday – a pink dress, perfume, and a silver necklace with purplish jewels that her mother said were amethysts. 'Semi-precious,' she added. There were three of them, one large oval guarded by two small ones, set in a reddish gold. The necklace was the most beautiful thing that Sofia had ever, seen.

'Maybe you'll go to the winter dance up at school, Fee,' her mother suggested hopefully, fastening the necklace around her neck.

'Someone has to ask you first,' Sofia said, pretending not to be impressed by her own reflection.

'Oh, it's OK to go with a group of girls, too,' her mother said.

Sofia didn't know any girls, actually. She was friendly with most of them, but not friends. The girls at school seemed split about her: some thought her love of football was genuine if odd, while others proclaimed it an awfully creative way to be a tramp. This second group of girls whispered that Sofia was fast, fast in the bad way, that football wasn't the only game she played with all those boys in the vacant lot behind Gordon's Tavern. What would they say if she actually danced with one, much less let him walk her home?

'I'd be scared to wear this out of the house,' she said, placing a tentative finger on the large amethyst. 'Something might happen to it.'

'Your aunt would want you to wear it and enjoy it,' her mother said. 'It's an heirloom. It belonged to Aunt Polly, and her aunt before her, and their grandmother before that. But Tammy didn't have any girls, so she gave it to me a few years ago, said to put it away for a special birthday. This one's as special as any, I think.'

'What if I lost it?'

'You can't,' her mother said. 'It has a special catch – see?'

But Sofia wasn't worried about the catch. Or, rather, she was worried about the other catch, the hidden rules that were always changing. She was trying to figure out if the necklace qualified as a real gift, one that her father couldn't reclaim. It hadn't been purchased in a store. It had come from her father's side of the family. And although it was a birthday gift, it hadn't been wrapped up in paper and ribbons. She put it back in its box, a velvety once-black rectangle that was all the more beautiful for having faded to grey. Where would her father never look for it?

Three weeks later, Sofia awoke one Saturday to find her father standing over her guitar. Her father must not have known how guitar strings were attached because he cut them with a pocket knife, sliced them right down the middle and reached into the hole to extract the velvet box, which had been anchored in a tea towel at the bottom, so it wouldn't make an obvious swishing noise if someone picked up the guitar and shook it. How had he known it was there? Perhaps he had reached for the guitar again, and felt the extra weight. Perhaps he simply knew Sofia too well, a far more disturbing thought. At any rate, he held the velvet box in his hand.

'I'll buy you new ones,' he said.

He meant the strings, of course, not the necklace or the amethysts.

'But you can't sell it,' she said, groping for the word her mother had invoked so lovingly. 'It's a hair-loom.'

'Oh, Fee, it's nothing special. I'll buy you something much better when my luck changes.'

'Take something else, anything else. Take the guitar.'

'Strings cut,' he said, as if he had found it that way and believed it beyond repair. 'Besides, I told this fellow about it and he said he'll take it in lieu of… in lieu of debts owed, if he finds it satisfactory. I don't even have to go to the trouble of pawning it.'

'But if you don't pawn it, we can't ever get it back.'

'Honey, when did we ever redeem a pawnshop ticket?'

This was true, but at least the pawnshop held open the promise of recovering things. If the necklace went to a person, it would be gone as Shemp. Sofia imagined it on the neck of a smug girl, like one of the ones who whispered about her up at school. A girl who would say: *Oh, my father bought me this at the pawnshop. It's an antique. My father said the people who owned it probably didn't know it was valuable.* But Sofia did and her mother did. It was only her father who didn't value it, except as a way to cover his losses.

'Please don't take it,' she said. She tried to make her face do whatever it had done the day he had backed down before, but it was dim in her room and her father was resolved. He pocketed the beautiful box and left.

But he didn't leave the house right away. He never did, not on the glum Saturdays that followed his bad nights, the ones that came and went without doughnuts. He went down to the breakfast table and wolfed down a plate of fried eggs. Sofia followed him down to the table, staring at him silently, but he refused to meet her gaze. Her mother might intervene if she told her, but Sofia didn't feel that she had earned anyone's help. She had sat by while the candlesticks left, turned her back when Brad cried over his bicycle. She was on her own.

Her father took a long nap on the sofa, opening his eyes from time to time to comment on whatever television programme was drifting by. 'Super Bowl's going to be a snorer this year.' 'Wrestling's fixed, everyone knows that.' It was going on three by the time he left the house and Sofia followed behind, shadowing him in the alleys that ran parallel to Brighton Avenue. She thought she might show up at the last minute, shaming her father, then remembered that hadn't worked with Shemp. Instead, she crouched behind a row of yewberry bushes at the end of the property that bordered the vacant lot. She had retrieved many a misthrown football from these bushes, so she knew how thick and full they were. She also knew that the red berries were poison, a piece of vital information that had been passed from child to child as long as anyone in the neighbourhood could remember. *Don't eat them little red berries. They look like cherries, but one bite will kill you.* When she was little, when she was still OK with being Fee, she had gathered berries from the bushes and used them in her Hi-Ho, Cherry-O game at home. For some reason it had been far more satisfying, watching these real-if-inedible berries tumble out of the little plastic bucket. She was always careful to make sure that Brad didn't put any in his mouth, schooling him as she had been schooled.

A man was waiting for her father behind Gordon's place. He held himself as if he thought he was good looking, and maybe he was. He wore a leather jacket with the collar turned up, and didn't seem to notice that the day was too cold for such a light jacket. When he opened the velvet box, he nodded and pocketed it with a shrug. But he clearly didn't appreciate the thing of beauty before him and that bothered Sofia more than anything. At least Shemp had gone to a man who thought he was a good dog deserving of a good home. This man wasn't worthy of her necklace.

She watched him get into a red car, a Corvette that Joe and the other boys had commented on enviously whenever it appeared in Gordon's parking lot. He wasn't an every-weeker, not like her dad, but he came around quite a bit. Now that she was paying attention, it seemed to her that she had seen the car all over the neighbourhood – up and down Brighton Avenue, outside the snowball stand in spring and summer, in the parking lot over to Costas Inn, at the swim club. He came around a lot. Maybe Joe knew his name, or his people.

Three months later

The clocks had been turned forward and the days were milder. There was another dance at school and Sofia was going this time. Things had changed. She had changed.

'Why isn't Joe picking you up?' her mother asked.

'We're meeting there,' Sofia said. 'He's not a *boyfriend*-boyfriend.'

'I thought he was. You've been going to the movies together on weekends, almost every Saturday since St Patrick's Day.'

'Just matinees. Things are different now. We're just friends. This isn't a date. But he'll walk me home, so you don't have to worry. OK?'

'What time does the dance end?'

'Eleven.'

'And you'll come straight home.' A command, not a question.

'Sure.'

Sofia shouldn't have agreed so readily; it made her mother suspicious. She studied her daughter's face, trying to figure out the exact nature of the lie. Reluctantly, she let Sofia go, yanking her dress down in the back as if she could extend the cloth. Sofia had grown some since her birthday and the pink dress was a little short, but short was the fashion of the day, as were the platform shoes she clattered along in. She had practised in them off and on for two weeks, and they still felt like those Dutch shoes, big as boats around her skinny ankles, Olive Oyl sandals. Thank God they had ankle straps or she would have fallen out of them in less than a block.

Two blocks down, where she should have crossed the boulevard to go up to the school, she turned right instead, heading for the tavern. She didn't go in, of course, but waited by the back door, which was just a back door on Saturday nights, nothing more. Within five minutes, a red Corvette pulled into the parking lot.

'Hey,' said the man in the driver's seat, a man she now knew as Brian. He wore his leather jacket with the collar turned up, although the night was a little warm for it.

'Hey,' she said, getting into the car and pulling her dress so it didn't bunch up around her.

'Never seen you in a skirt before, Gino.' That was his joke, calling her 'Gino' after Gino Marchetti.

'And I've never seen you in anything but that leather jacket.'

'Well, technically, this is our first date. There's a lot we don't know about each other, isn't there?'

Sofia smiled in what she hoped was a mysterious and alluring way.

'Maybe we should get to know each other better. What do you think?'

She nodded.

'My place OK?'

She nodded again. It had taken her three months to get to this point – three months of careful conversation in Gordon's parking lot, which began when she threw the ball at the red Corvette, presumably in a fit of celebration upon scoring a touchdown. Brian, who had just pulled up, got out and started screaming, but he settled down fast when Sofia apologized, prettily and tearfully. Plus, she hadn't damaged the car, not a bit. After that afternoon, he would stand in the lot for a few minutes, watching them play. Watching her play, she was sure of it. He brought sodas for everyone. He asked if they wanted to go for ice cream. He took them, one at a time, in rides around the block. Sofia always went last. The rides were short, no more than five minutes, but a lot can happen in five minutes. He told her that he managed a Merry-Go-Round clothing store, offered to get a discount. She told him she was bored with school and thinking about dropping out. He said he had been married for a while, but he was single now. 'I'm single, too,' Sofia said, and he laughed as if it were the funniest thing in the world.

'Maybe we should go out sometimes, us both being single and all,' he said. That had been yesterday.

The date made, it was understood that he would not come to her house, shake hands with her father and make small talk with her mother while Sofia turned a round brush in her hair, trying to feather her bangs. Other things were understood, too. That it would not be a movie date or a restaurant date. Sofia knew what she was signing up for. Her only concern was that he might want to drive some place, stay in the Corvette, when she wanted to see where he lived.

So she said as much, when he asked what she wanted to do. 'Why don't we just go to your place?'

His eyebrows shot up. 'Why not?' He passed her a brown bag that he had held between his legs as he drove and she took a careful sip. It wasn't her first drink, but she recognized that this was something sweet, liquor overlaid with a peppermint flavour, a girly drink for someone assumed to be inexperienced. Thoughtful of him.

Brian lived out Essex way, in some new apartments advertising move-in specials and a swimming pool. She hoped it wouldn't take too long because she only had so much time, but she was surprised at just how fast it happened. One minute they were kissing, and it wasn't too bad. She almost liked it. Then all of a sudden he was hovering above her, asking if she was fixed up, a question she didn't understand right away. When she did, she shook her head, and he said 'Shit,' but pulled a rubber over himself, rammed into her and yelled at her to come, as if he were a coach or a gym teacher, exhorting her to do something difficult but not impossible.

'I... don't... do that,' she panted out.

He took that as permission to do what he needed. Once finished, he pulled away quickly, if apologetically.

'Sorry, but if you're not on the Pill, I can't afford to hang around, you know? One little sperm gets out and my life is over. I've already got one kid to pay for.'

That detail had not come up in their rides around the block.

'Uh huh.'

'You ready to go back?'

'Can't we watch some television, maybe try again?'

'Didn't get the feeling that you cared for it.'

'I'm just… quiet. I liked it.' She placed a tentative hand on his chest, which was narrow and a little sunken once out of the leather jacket. 'I liked it a lot.'

He chose the wrestling matches on Channel 45, then arranged the covers over them and put his arm around her.

'You know, wrestling's fixed,' she said.

'Who says?'

'Everybody.' She didn't want to mention her father.

'So? It's the only decent thing on.'

'Just seems like cheating,' she said. 'I don't like games like that. Like, for example… poker.'

'Poker? I hardly knew her.' He gave her rump a friendly pat and laughed. She tried to laugh, too.

'Still,' she said, gesturing at the television. 'It doesn't seem right. Pretending.'

'Well, I guess that's why you don't do it.'

'Wrestle?'

'Fake it. You know, it wouldn't hurt you to act like you liked it, just a little. If you're frigid, you're frigid, but why should a guy be left feeling like he didn't do right by you?'

'I'll try,' she said. 'I can do better. Maybe if there could be more kissing first.'

He tried, she had to give him that. He slowed down, kissed her a lot, and she could see how it might be better. She still didn't feel moved, but she took the man's advice, shuddering and moaning like the women in the movies, the R-rated ones she and Joe had been sneaking into this spring. At any rate, whatever she did wore him out, and he fell asleep.

She didn't bother to put on her clothes, although she did carry her purse with her as she moved from room to room. When she didn't find the velvet box right away, she found herself taking other things in her panic and anger – a Baltimore Orioles ashtray, a pair of purple candles, a set of coasters, a Bachman-Turner Overdrive eight-track, an unused bar of Ivory soap in the bathroom. Her clunky sandals off, she was quiet and light on her feet, and he didn't stir at all until she tried a small drawer in his dresser. The drawer stuck a little and Sofia gave it a wrenching pull to force it open. He whimpered in his sleep and she froze, certain she was about to be caught, but he didn't do anything but roll over. It was the velvet box that had made the drawer stick, wedged against the top like peanut butter on the roof of someone's mouth. But when she snapped it open, the box was empty. In her grief and frustration, she gave a little cry.

'What the—'

He was out of bed in an instant, grabbing her wrist and pushing her face into the pea-green carpet, crunchy with dirt and food and other things.

'Put it back, you thievin' whore or I'll—'

She grabbed one of her shoes and hit him with it, landing a solid blow on his ear. He roared and fell back, but only for a minute, grabbing her ankle as she tried to crawl away and gather her clothes.

'Look,' she said, 'I'm thirteen.'

He didn't let go of her ankle, but his grip loosened. 'Bullshit. You told me you were in high school.'

'I'm thirteen,' she repeated. 'Call the police. They'll believe me, I'm pretty sure. I'm thirteen and you just raped me. I never had sex before tonight.'

'No way I'm your first. You didn't bleed, not even a little.'

'Not everybody does. I play a lot of football. And maybe you're not big enough to make a girl bleed.'

He slapped her for that and she returned his open-hand smack with her shoe, hitting him across the head so hard that he fell back and didn't get back up. Still, she kept hitting him, her frustration over the long-gone necklace driving her. She struck him for every-thing that had been lost, for every gift that had come and gone and couldn't be retrieved. For Brad's bicycle, for her mother's candlesticks, for Shemp. She pounded the shoe against his head again and again, as if she were a child throwing a tantrum and, in a way, she was. Eventually, she fell back, her breath ragged in her chest. It was only then that she realized how still Brian was.

She put her ear to his chest. She was pretty sure his heart was still beating, that he was still breathing. Pretty sure. She put on her clothes and grabbed her macramé purse, still full of the trophies she had taken. She checked her watch, a confirmation gift. There was no way she could get home in time without a ride. She helped herself to money from Brian's wallet, and it turned out he had quite a bit. 'I'll meet you outside,' she told the taxi dispatcher in a whisper, although Brian didn't appear to be conscious.

It was almost midnight when she came up the walk and both parents were waiting for her.

'Where were you?'

'At the dance.'

'Don't lie to us.'

'I was at the dance,' she repeated.

'Where's Joe? Why did you come home alone, in a cab?'

'He came with another girl, a real date. Another boy, someone I didn't know, offered to walk me home. He got... fresh.' She pointed to the red mark on her face.

'Who was he?' her father demanded, grabbing her by the arm. 'Where does he live?'

'All I know is that his name was Steve and when I wouldn't...' she shrugged, declining to put a name to the thing she wouldn't do. 'At any rate, he put me out of the car on Holabird Avenue and I had to hail a cab. I'm sorry. I know it was wrong of me. I won't ever take a ride with a stranger again.'

'You could have been killed,' her mother said, clutching her to her chest. Sofia's father simply stared at her. When she went up to her room, he followed her.

'You telling the truth?' he asked.

'*Yes.*' It seemed to Sofia that her father's eyes were boring into her macramé bag, as if he could see the stolen treasures inside, including Brian's cash. Even after the cab ride all the way from Essex, there was quite a bit left over. But maybe all he was seeing was another object that he would raid, the next time he was caught short.

'Daddy?'

'What?'

'Don't take any more of my stuff, OK?'

'You don't have any stuff, missy. Everything in this house belongs to me.'

'You take any more of my stuff, I'll run away. I'll go to California and do drugs and be a hippie.' This was about the worst fate that any parent could imagine for a child, back in Dundalk in 1975. True, the Summer of Love was long past, but time moved slowly in Dundalk, and they were still worried about hippies and LSD.

'You wouldn't.'

'I would.'

'I'll drag you home and make you sorry.'

'I'll make you sorrier.'

'The hell you say.'

'I'll go to police and tell them about the game at Gordon's, in the back room.'

'You wouldn't.'

'I would. I'll do it this very Friday night. But if you promise to leave me and my stuff alone, I'll leave you alone. Deal?'

He didn't shake on it, or even nod his head. But when her father left her room that night, Sofia knew he would never enter it again.

That was the spring that Sofia learned to bluff and, once she started, she found it hard to stop. She would never have called the cops on her father because it would have killed her mother. She was sixteen, not thirteen, but she knew that she could pass for thirteen. All of a sudden, Sofia could bluff, pretend, plan, plot, trick, cheat, cajole, threaten, blackmail. Even steal if she chose, for while the necklace belonged to her and she would have been within her rights to take it back if she had found it, she had no claim on the other things she had grabbed. Brian hadn't stolen from her, after all. He knew nothing about the necklace or who owned it or what it was worth, except in the most literal terms. He had probably pawned it soon after accepting it for payment, or given it to another girl who went for rides in that red Corvette. For several days, Sofia checked the paper worriedly, reading deep into the local section to see if a man had been found dead from a beating in an Essex apartment. She even considered getting rid of her shoes, but decided that was a greater sacrifice than she needed to make. Whatever happened to Brian, his red Corvette was no longer seen up and down Brighton Avenue.

She used part of his money to buy a padlock for her bedroom door, a fancy one with a key. She used the balance to buy a lava lamp from Spenser's Gifts at East Point Mall. At night, her homework done, she watched the reddish-orange blobs break apart and rearrange themselves. Even within that narrow glass, there seemed to be no limit to the forms they could take. Her father stewed and steamed about the lock, saying she had no right to lock a room in his house. He also criticized the lava lamp, saying it proved she was on drugs because what sober, right-minded person could be entertained by such a thing.

But for all he complained, he never tried to breach the lock, although it would have been a simple thing to pry it off with a hammer, not much harder than slicing through a set of guitar strings. He was scared of her now, just a little, and incapable of concealing that fear no matter how he might try.

It was a new sensation, having someone scared of her. Sofia liked it.

♠

A Friendly Little Game

John Lescroart

I AM A COP. I don't believe in repressed memory.
Or I could say that because I'm a cop, automatically I don't
believe in repressed memory. It comes with the territory. Certainly
it could never happen to me.

Then I started having the dreams – really, the one dream.

I'm enclosed in some small, dark place. I'm young, under
ten. There's a strong cigar smell. Don't let 'em tell you there's no
smells in dreams. The smell is so strong and so real that I wake up
and, wide awake, put my nose in the sheets that are crumpled all
around me.

Then there's the sounds – all this awful disco music playing
behind men's tight laughter and a kind of staccato rhythm of
monosyllabic words: check, in, fuck, out, fold, raise. They get
louder as the dream goes on. (Jen tells me I scream them out, too,
sometimes.)

Suddenly it's hot, now, where I am. When the noise and the heat
get to be too much, I push on the wall next to me. The wall burns
my hand, but it opens anyway, and for the rest of the dream I'm
aware that my hand is burnt and it hurts. But as soon as the closet
opens, everything goes quiet, though it's still hot.

My dad, my Pop, is sitting alone at a table. He's not moving, just
staring out in front of him. I go up to him and he still doesn't move,

so I touch his arm. He's much bigger than he was in real life, towering over me. Or maybe I'm crawling on the floor. Anyway, he turns on his own and then falls onto me. Dead and cold.

And I wake up, sometimes crying, always gasping for air, smelling cigar smoke. The last couple of times I had the dream, I told myself (in the dream) to try and wake up before I got to Pop. But that never worked out.

I want to be clear. This was an actual dream every time, not a daydream. It was always in the middle of a real sleep at night. I wasn't in some semi-hypnotic state trying to recover some memory, or to get to something I had unknowingly buried in my subconscious, which I don't believe people can really do. No, the dream just came at me, night after the one particular night when it first showed up, and it wouldn't let me be until I figured out what it might mean.

It started a night or two after a training weekend we had in Las Vegas, where a bunch of us decided to sit in at a table of Texas Hold 'Em. I lost my $100 buy-in before my seat got warm, then I went up to my room and barfed and I thought that was the end of it.

But, as it turned out, it wasn't.

As a general rule, and for a few good reasons, I don't gamble with cards. First, there's the old saying, 'Lucky at cards, unlucky at love,' and early on, just out of the Academy, I placed my big bet where it mattered most and got lucky with Jen. (That's six years ago. Now we've got two kids – Kyle and Larry, and she's big with the girl we wanted.) If it meant even the tinest chance of losing her, I didn't *want* to get lucky at cards.

Second, call me rigid, but in spite of the internet and ESPN, private poker games remain illegal almost everywhere, including San Mateo, where I live. How am I supposed to enforce laws that I break myself? What kind of an example does that set for my kids?

Third, money is an issue, and my Mom always told me never to gamble with what I couldn't afford to lose.

Finally, and maybe most important, I really just don't have much of a temperament for the game – in college, I'd sit in on a poker game once in a while, but I'd get literally sick with tension if I found myself in a big pot – big in those days being maybe twenty dollars. I'd barf back then, too. Here's a free life lesson: something makes you barf, avoid it.

I had the dream for the first time the night after I got back from Vegas. About six weeks later, after maybe a dozen terrified wake-ups, Jen and I went downstairs and wound up sitting hip to hip on the couch with our hot chocolates. 'It's got to be something about your dad,' she said.

'Except that I barely knew my dad.'

Aaron Sr was killed in a home robbery when I was nine years old. I was staying at my neighbour's down the street and my Mom had gone away to her sister's to help with the birth of what turned out to be my cousin Emmy, and evidently whoever had cased the house for the burglary thought it was going to be empty. When they broke in, Pop tried to stop them, and paid with his life.

It's probably one of the main reasons I decided to go into police work – take bastards like that off the street.

Since we'd had the kids, Jen had come to have some faith in what I'll call non-verbal communication. It wasn't quite ESP – it didn't involve anything supernatural or religious. It was more like a preternatural awareness of those closest to us. Mostly her with the kids, specifically, but I can't deny my own feelings of hyper-awareness, both with her and the kids, that sometimes felt like mind-reading. I think it's just what 'tuned-in' to your kids means, but Jen had come to believe it extended out to a slightly larger radius. Now, she said, 'Your dad's trying to tell you some-thing.'

'I don't think so, hon. We've got about five thousand years of history and no verified sign that anybody's ever come back and delivered a message from the dead. I can't believe Pop would be the first.'

'All right, then,' she said. 'You're trying to tell yourself something.

But it's about him. Doesn't that make sense? You owe it to yourself to find out what it is.'

'And how do I do that?'

She shrugged. 'I don't know. Maybe talk to somebody?'

'A shrink? There's no way I need to see a shrink.'

'I didn't say anything about needing one. But you started with these dreams…'

'This dream.'

'OK, this dream. You started with this dream the day after you got back from Vegas, where you got sick after playing about five hands of poker…'

'Maybe I'd had too much to drink.'

'Two beers?' She held up a hand. 'Now you're waking up yelling, 'Fold', or 'Call', or 'Raise'. Clearly, whatever's going on, it's something about your dad, and somehow poker's part of it, too.' She reached across the table and took my hand. 'Aaron, look, you're a cop. All I'm saying is investigate it. That's what you do. This thing's eating you up. If you ever want a good night's sleep again, you've got to get to the bottom of it.'

Suddenly, her permission – more than that, her suggestion – made it seem less weird. I wasn't going out trying to interpret a dream. I wasn't buying into a repressed memory. I was merely investigating because that's what cops do.

My mother, Abby, had remarried and for almost twenty years now had been with my step-dad, Neal Farber. Because of the ghosts, after the marriage they'd moved into Neal's place a couple of blocks from where Pop had gotten shot, and they still lived there. Early on the morning after Jen and I had our talk, I showed up in uniform, my hat in my hand, at their place to talk to my Mom – already up and dressed for school where she taught fifth grade. What a class act, I thought, as I often did. Diamond earrings and tailored suit, hair done and face made up – a sign of respect to her 'kids'. She'd often say, 'Respect them and they respect you back.' I love the woman.

'Well, this is a pleasant surprise,' Mom said. She held me by the shoulders and came up to kiss me. 'How's my handsome baby this morning?'

'Mostly, your baby's thirty years old, Mom, and feeling every year of it.'

'Lucky you,' she said. 'You think thirty's tired, try fifty-two.'

My Mom, by the way, still qualifies as a babe. Blond, great figure, flawless face. Jen, who is no slag-heap herself, thinks it's unfair. Like the rest of the world, it probably is. I smiled down at her and kissed her back. 'It looks like you're holding up.'

'Actually, I'm fit as a fiddle, knock wood,' she said. 'Do you have time for a cup?'

'I thought you'd never ask.'

After years of making what was quite possibly the worst brewed coffee in the universe, Mom had suddenly become an espresso junkie, proud owner of one of those new-fangled machines like you see in Starbucks that can make a couple of cups at a time. In a flash, we were sitting across from one another, sipping a really delicious cup from cat-themed mugs. Nero, her black cat, was stretched out on the kitchen counter between us.

'Now,' she said, 'to what do I owe the pleasure of your company?' She reached over and gave me a tap on the cheek. 'And it is a pleasure. I don't get to see enough of you and my grandchildren.'

'We're only two blocks away, Mom. The door is always open.'

This was true, though somehow Mom and Neal didn't seem to find the time to visit too often. I attributed it mostly to some unnamed tension between Jen and my mother, although it might equally well have been the similarly-unspoken disconnect between Neal and me. I didn't think he was that bad a guy, really, but he just wasn't Pop and he never could be. I didn't really blame him if he didn't try too hard to get closer to me anymore after the hard time I gave him in the early years. He knew it wasn't going to happen, no matter what. We were where we were with each other – in orbit around my mother, never close, sometimes far apart.

But I wasn't there to fix the family dynamic, so I pressed right on. 'Actually, I've got a question that I don't know who else could answer. About Pop.'

Immediately, her pretty face fell into a frown. 'Your father? What about him?'

'I've been having this dream.' I gave her the short version – the cigar smell, the phrases from poker games, my burning hand, Pop's death. 'I just wonder if any of that sings to you?'

Slowly, she put down her mug. 'What are you doing with this, Aaron? Are you re-opening his case?'

'Not really. Certainly, nothing formal. I'm trying to figure out what the dream means at this point. If that leads me to something, I'll try to follow it. But right now, it's just something that keeps waking me up.'

She twirled the cup slowly on the counter, her eyes somewhere far away. 'It's so funny you should mention that,' she finally admitted. 'I mean, in connection with his death. I don't think I ever thought about it in that context.'

'What?'

'The cigar smell.' Suddenly, her eyes were back with me. 'But it was very much there.'

'Where? What do you mean?'

'Home. I mean the day I came home after, well, after… when I first walked into the house. The smell was still overpowering. You know that stale two- or three-day old cigar stench. I've always hated that smell.'

'Me, too. But you didn't think it had anything to do with Pop's death?'

'No. Why would I think that? Do you?'

'No. My only connection to it is in the dream. So what did you think it was?'

'I thought since I was away… he knew I hated that smell in the house, but while I wasn't there, he must have got up a game. He always smoked cigars when he played poker.'

'I never realized he even played poker.'

She shrugged. 'And almost never at home, at least after the first time when we reached an understanding. But he had an irregular group he played with once in a while. He loved the game. And when he got invited, he'd go, even though it meant no kissing when he got home.' She smiled at what must have been a tender memory. 'One of my stupid rules I've come to regret. I should have kissed him every chance I got.' Shaking herself from the reverie, she seemed to remember her coffee, and picked up the mug. 'But I never thought the cigar smell had anything to do with the break-in. Do you think it does?'

'I've got no idea, Mom. I'm working with a dream here. It's a little nebulous.'

'Well, at the time I just realized that he must have had a game there, but I didn't think any more about it. Other than that if I'd known, I promised myself I wouldn't have gotten mad at him.' She touched a fingertip to the bottom of each of her eyes, blinked away the sudden glassiness. 'It's funny,' she said after a sharp inhale and exhale of breath, 'now I'd let him play every day if it would bring him back. Cigars or no cigars. No offense to Neal, I mean.'

'No. Of course not,' I said. 'None taken.'

'I mean, Neal can be a fine man, too, when he tries to be. You know that. And it's just that your father was... he was very special. And us never getting a chance to say goodbye. It's not something you really get over.'

'No. I can see that.' I let her recover for a minute before I talked again. 'So, Mom, who do you think Pop would have invited over to play?'

The question brought her up short. 'Oh, God, Aaron. I don't know. You're talking over twenty years ago.'

'I know. You and Pop had friends, though, right? Who were they back then?'

But Mom was shaking her head. 'Social friends, Aaron. Couples. We were in the couples with kids crowd.'

'Maybe some of the other dads liked to play poker. Or maybe Neal?'

'No. Neal doesn't play at all. He lost a fortune once and learned his lesson.' Sighing, she seemed lost for a moment. Suddenly the tragic but clean and uncomplicated death of her first husband had become problematic. She looked up at the wall clock and back at me. 'I've got to get to work, Aaron. How about if I think about this today and give you a list tonight? It's a little upsetting.'

'It is, I know. Tonight would be fine, Mom.'

She was getting up, automatically grabbing both mugs, moving toward the sink. 'Meanwhile, you could ask the Tompkins and Cortipassos. Oh, and the Waylens. One of them might remember something.' She turned around to face me, her face now drawn with worry. 'You don't really think one of them might have had something to do with your father's death, do you?'

'I don't know, Mom. I just don't know. Somebody did, and whoever it was, they never caught him.'

Terry Anders was the inspector who'd worked the case. Retired now, he was working in his home garden on the flats behind the Hillsdale Mall when I caught up to him on my lunch break. It was late May, the day had grown warm, and Terry was a sight in work boots, Giants cap, khaki shorts and a tank-top T-shirt. With his protruding stomach, it might have more accurately been called a basketball-top T-shirt. He had about twelve rows of young corn and stood facing me, leaning on his hoe, immune to the sun beating down on us. 'Yeah,' he said, 'I wondered when that one was going to get to you.'

'It got to me right away, Terry, but there didn't seem to be any mystery. Now there might be.' I saw no point in mentioning the dream to a fellow cop. I knew what my own reaction to that would have been in other circumstances, and didn't want to even start to have to explain. Spur of the moment, I decided to lay it off on my mother who, I told Terry, had suddenly asked me about the cigar smoke and poker. 'Granted, it's slim and none. But hey, it's my Mom. I've got to ask.'

'Sure. No sweat. Speaking of which.' He wiped the perspiration from his forehead with his baseball cap. 'Let's go find us some shade.'

On a small covered patio by the back door, we sat in lawn chairs. Terry filled up a couple of Mason jars with cold hose water and that's what we were drinking. 'So,' he began, 'what do you want to know?'

'Just what you eventually got.'

He drank and shook his head. 'You know, I'm ashamed to say, not much. It was a pretty cut and dried B & E. You check the file yet? The pictures?'

'No. Records can't dig it out for another day or two. So I thought I'd come to the horse's mouth first.'

Terry laughed. 'Horse's ass is more like it. OK, give me a minute.' Sitting back, Anders did a darn fine Nero Wolfe impression – eyes closed, lips puckering in and out, huge gut rising and falling. 'The shooting was on the stairs, your dad maybe coming down from the bedroom. He was wearing pyjama bottoms. The bed was unmade, so maybe he'd already gotten into bed, then heard something. There was a metal softball bat on the stairway, too – maybe the nearest weapon he could grab. The shots were through a pillow to kill the sounds.'

'What got stolen?'

His eyes still closed, Terry nodded. 'Wallet, watch. Your mother reported some jewellery. That's about it.'

'Jesus. And Pop gets himself killed over that?'

'Hey,' Terry said, 'all the guy needed was his next fix. He probably got it.'

'You think that was it?'

Terry cocked his head. 'You don't?'

'I don't know. It's damn slim pickin's if the guy went in thinking the house was empty, which is the explanation I'd always heard.'

'It could have been that, true. But it could just as easily have been a junkie hitting a dark house at random. And either way, your dad being there put a crimp in the plan. The guy took what he could as fast as he could and lit out.'

I lived with that for a second before asking, 'You see any sign of a poker game?'

He closed his eyes again, riffling through his brain, until he finally opened them again and shook his head. 'I can't say I remember anything. If he had one, he'd cleaned it up pretty good.'

'So that's it?' I asked.

Terry tapped his head. 'That's all I could pull out of here. You get the file, I'd be glad to come down and go through it with you.'

I stood up, shook the man's hand. 'Thanks, Terry, appreciate it.'

I was around the side of the house, almost to my car parked at kerbside, when I heard his voice behind me calling my name. I turned and waited for him. 'This is probably nothing. I mean, really probably nothing,' he said, 'but it just came back to me. One of the burners on the stove was on.'

'The stove?'

He nodded. 'Big old electric stove in the kitchen. Your dad probably just forgot to turn it off after cooking something. But one of the burners was on low. As I say, it's probably nothing, but you never know.'

I didn't trust myself to say much more than thanks again to Terry. Driving away, I looked at my hand, the one that's hot in my dream. No scar, no trace of a burn. But I had felt a definite something in that hand when Terry had mentioned the stove, a sense memory barely more than a twitch. Opening and closing my fist a few times, I turned the nearest corner and pulled up at the kerb again. I had the sweats and it wasn't from the heat.

Suddenly I had remembered how I got the burn. I'd been with my best friend Danny O'Keefe, who was spending that night at my house – the next night, when Pop got killed, I was sleeping over at his place. It was summertime and Danny and I had been trading sleepovers on summer nights since we'd been about six or seven. This night, we watched our usual TV until it was time for bed, and then went upstairs.

But with the poker game – the poker game! – going on downstairs and Pop paying no attention to the kids, Danny saw an opportunity to sneak out. His high-school-age sister and her crowd were hanging out at another neighbour's house and skinny-dipping in their pool – the mother there let them, and sometimes, so the rumour had it, even went in herself. Future cop that I was, I didn't want to disobey my pop's standing orders, and the thought of seeing naked teenagers and even adults scared me to death, but Danny shamed me into going along with him.

The problem was that the poker game was going on in the living room, so the front door wouldn't work. To get out of the house, we had to sneak down the stairs, then around through the kitchen and out the side door. And, of course, not make a sound.

While Danny was trying to open the door, I don't know why or how, I inadvertently put my hand out and laid it down on the burning stove element. The pain had been immediate and severe, and blisters in concentric circles formed on my palm as I stared down at it. I know I didn't turn it off then, and Pop must not have either.

But I couldn't yell out. After all, I wasn't the kind of kid who snuck out at night. Both of my parents trusted me, and how was I going to explain my being here in the kitchen, dressed to go out? I was in agony, but couldn't do anything about it. And I certainly had no more interest in checking out the skinny dipping. I was staying home, and that was that.

But Danny was going. He didn't care. The men would be playing for at least a couple more hours, and he wasn't going to waste an opportunity like this one.

So for the next two hours, while I silently prayed for Danny to get back before the game ended so my father wouldn't ever know what we'd planned, I sat hidden behind the stair's banister, my hand throbbing, hoping I wouldn't be discovered there and have to explain Danny's absence and my own burn, listening to the men swearing and laughing as they placed their bets.

It had been a long and terrible night. How had I forgotten about it for all of this time? If not that the next night's violent trauma had washed my memory clean.

But at least I now had all the elements of my dream.

Except for one.

Pop being dead.

We had a family dinner that night and then Jen and I read stories to the boys and had them in bed by their usual bedtime of seven-thirty. After that, I made some calls to my mom's old neighbour-hood social network and got a bite on my third and last try with Vic Cortipasso. He himself hadn't ever played any poker with my father, but thought that his wife's brother, Ben Steiger, might have been a regular at several of the local games. Unfortunately, Ben had died six months ago of a heart attack, but Vic had a suggestion. 'Maybe you could talk to his ex-wife Ruth. I've got her number. She might remember something.'

Except poker for Ruth Steiger didn't appear to be one of the happier memories of her late husband. 'I wish he'd never heard of the game, to tell you the truth. He was a mostly good and a sweet man, God rest his soul, but poker almost broke us up at least half a dozen times. I finally made him stop for good after he lost our entire vacation money seven or eight years ago. Can you believe?'

'I don't play myself,' I said, 'so no. It's a little hard to imagine.'

'Smart man. So what do you want to know?'

'Just if you remember your husband mentioning any games he might have played with my father, Aaron Lowens. This would have been something like twenty years ago.'

'Twenty years ago?'

'Yes, ma'am.'

'Well, twenty years is a long time ago. I don't believe I ever knew your father, and I don't think Ben did, either. Have you tried Larry Menchino?'

'The barber?'

'That's him. He still plays, I believe. But he and Ben used to go to games together. Maybe he'd have some memory.'

After Vic Cortipasso sent me to Ben Steiger and Ben's wife passed me on to Larry Menchino, I started to talk to other men and eventually even got lists of names of friends and acquaintances. Over the next few weeks, I ran through a veritable rogues' gallery of local gamblers, some of them quite serious about their games, others more recreational. San Mateo is a town of about ninety-five thousand people in the heart of the San Francisco peninsula, bound by other densely-populated bedroom communities. Pop's last poker game probably had no more than six players, and finding any one of them – if, indeed, any of them were still alive – was going to take perseverance and luck. Still, I kept at it, putting the word out, dropping Pop's name, leaving my phone number, hoping for a chain letter effect.

Until finally, on a Monday night in early June, at least a dozen generations of poker players beyond Larry Menchino the barber, I knocked at the door of a mansion in Hillsborough, the town just north of San Mateo. To say that Hillsborough is a high-end community is to say that Catherine Zeta-Jones is mildly attractive. I couldn't help but think that the resident here was an unlikely past friend of my blue-collar carpenter of a father. But I'd left my message on the machine here without knowing anything about the house or the man who lived in it, Charles Baden. In the endless round robin I'd been playing, I'd gotten his name from one of the paramutuel clerks at Bay Meadows, the town's racetrack. Mr Baden called me back, saying he used to play sometimes with a man named Aaron, but he wasn't sure of the last name. In any case, he'd be happy to talk to me.

Once I'd gone through the first ring of connected friends who might have known me as a cop anyway, I'd found that my uniform didn't serve me particularly well in these meetings, so I was in my non-threatening yuppy civvies – khaki chinos, Lacoste shirt, docksiders without socks. When Baden opened the door, he was wearing the same uniform, except that his pants were blue. After we shook hands, he invited me in, introduced me to his wife Carla and their two well-behaved teenaged children – all as healthy-looking, robust and attractive as the man of the house himself – and then led me to a small backyard deck that overlooked the black-bottomed pool.

'So,' he began after we'd gotten settled, 'how can I help you?'

'As I said on the phone, I'm trying to locate anybody who might have played poker with my father about twenty years ago.'

'Right. And why do you want to do that?'

'Well, the short answer is that my dad was murdered.'

The word seemed to verify something for him. He sat back in the patio chair and looked off into the distance for a second before coming back to me. 'Not murdered at a poker game, though?'

'No. The connection of his killing to the poker game, if any, isn't really established. The theory is he was killed during a burglary attempt at our house. That's the official story anyway.'

'But you don't believe it? After all this time?'

'It's not a matter of believing it. It's true on the face of it. Somebody did break in to our house and took a bunch of stuff and killed my father.'

'And you think this has something to do with a poker game?'

'I don't know.' This was as close as I'd come to what might be a witness, and I decided to be honest with him. 'Look, Mr Baden…'

'Charles, please.'

'All right. Charles. I'm a cop myself. In San Mateo. A month ago, I started having a dream about poker and cigars that ended with my father dead. That's about as far as the connection goes, but I feel like I need to follow it until the trail ends.'

'A dream,' he said.

'If it was someone telling it to me, I might laugh it off, too.'

He looked sharply over at me. 'I'm not laughing. It's not a laughing matter.' That settled, he came forward rubbing his hands together. 'Do you have a picture of your father?'

'Sure.' I gave him the snapshot I'd been carrying, which was pretty much the only picture of Pop I had from my childhood. And actually, it was more a picture of my stunning and regal-looking mother, her hair up in a swirl, who happened to be standing next to him. They were both beaming and showing off her 25th birthday present which up until that time was the most expensive and special gift she'd ever received – a pair of diamond earrings of about a half carat each. (Alas, they got stolen in the robbery.) But Pop was in the picture, too, his arm around her, proud and protective.

It didn't take Mr Baden very long. After five or six seconds, he looked up at me and nodded. 'Yep. That's the Aaron I knew.'

'Did you play poker with him often?'

A shrug. 'Maybe a couple of dozen times.' He looked back down at the picture. 'Beautiful woman. Your mother?'

'That's her.' But I wasn't there to talk about Mom. 'Did you ever play at his house?'

'That I don't really remember. Where was it?'

I gave him the address in San Mateo, but he just shook his head. 'Maybe. It doesn't really ring a bell, but I could have. We had a kind of a floating game for a couple of years there.'

'Do you remember names of any of the other players?'

Again, maddeningly, he shook his head. 'Last names, I can't say that I do. Lennie' – the Bay Meadows clerk who'd made my connection to Charles Baden – 'mentioned that you were looking for an Aaron, and the name's unusual enough, but I remembered the murder. I mean, that kind of thing, it sticks. But the other guys… I don't know. Just guys. None of them were really friends.'

'What were the games like?'

'What do you mean?'

'I mean, what were the stakes? Were they friendly games?'

Baden chuckled. 'The proverbial friendly little game, huh?' He scratched at the side of his face. 'I guess the buy-in, trying to remember now, was probably low hundreds. And we played table stakes. You know what that is?'

'No limit, right? Everything in on any given hand.'

'Essentially, correct. So no, I wouldn't say it was exactly casual. A good night, the big winner could net a grand or two.'

'That's a lot of dough.'

He laughed. 'It was a ton of dough back then, believe me.'

'But my dad didn't have that kind of money back then.'

'Yeah, he did. If he was in these games. He must have been good, and kept his winnings separate from the day job. Lot of guys did that. I know I did.'

I looked down at the picture that was still on my lap and again noticed the diamond earrings. It suddenly didn't seem possible that he made enough to buy them building cabinets.

Baden asked, 'I'm not going to get in trouble telling you all this, am I?'

'Why would you?'

'You know, poker. It was different back then. We all knew we were breaking the law, we could get busted. That's why we moved the games around, broke up the rhythm.'

'No. You're safe from me, anyway.' A blue jay flew to the edge of the pool below us and proceeded to take a bath. I realized I didn't have any more questions. The trail, marginal to begin with, had petered out again. Sighing, I uncrossed my legs and started to stand up.

'But you know,' Baden said, 'maybe I do remember something. Maybe it's nothing. At the time, it was just… odd, I thought. Weird. It freaked a few of the guys out, I know, enough that they stopped playing with any of us.'

I settled into my chair and gave him time to bring it back. 'What?'

'Well, there were probably about fifteen or twenty of us, but as I said, the games floated. We'd get six guys one time, four the next, sometimes ten or more, which meant we'd have to go to two tables. Some guy would show up one week and then disappear for two months.'

'OK.'

'OK, so the news kind of leaked slowly, kind of as a rumour, before it got out to everybody. I think your dad was the first, and he was the only one who was murdered, of course, but two other guys who were in the general group wound up dying within like a week or two.'

I felt a chill run down my back. 'Two guys? Do you know who they were?'

'The names? Jeez.' He rubbed the back of his neck. 'God. OK wait. Maybe Brian or Byron. I'd say Byron. The other? I'm going to say Chet, or Chick, but I could be wrong.'

'How did they die?'

'One got hit by a car, I remember. And the other, I think… I'm going to say maybe he killed himself. But if it's the same guy I'm thinking of, he was pretty strung-out, doing a lot of weed, maybe more than that, probably dealing to get his buy-in, I'd guess. Pretty loose with his game. Anyway, suicide made sense to me when I heard it, I remember that. Anyway, as I said, not too many of us were really friends who saw each other outside of the games, so this all came out in dribs and drabs over a matter of weeks, although the deaths might have actually happened pretty close to the same time. There wasn't any real sense that they were connected in any way. It was just one of those weird coincidences.'

'Yeah, except for one thing.'

'What's that?'

'In the cop business,' I told him, 'coincidences don't happen.'

I started with the obituary page of the *San Mateo Times* from the day of Pop's death. Two days after that, a 34-year-old father of three named Brady Wirth was the victim of a hit-and-run accident on the suburban street in front of his home in Belmont. Brady was close enough to Brian or Byron, and I figured I'd possibly located my second murder victim, but none of the Wirths listed in the phone book in any of the local directories, and there were plenty of them, had any knowledge or memory of a Brady. The wife had probably remarried, changed her name, and moved away. Going back to the Belmont police, I learned that there had been a serious investigation at the time but the case, like most hit and runs, had never been solved.

Which left Chick, or Chet. Unfortunately, no names that were close surfaced in the *Times* for the two-week period I was checking. Next I was going to check the *San Francisco Chronicle*, but because the *Redwood City Tribune* was both smaller and closer to home, I thought I'd eliminate that first. Good thing I did.

On the third day after Pop's murder, one day after the hit-and-run that had killed Brady Wirth, I ran across the name Chester Mobley, 'Chet', age twenty-five, who'd shot himself in the temple with a nail gun one day at the end of his construction shift. There was a small story on the second page with a few details: he'd been alone at the time at the construction site, he had a minor criminal record for narcotics violations, he had one baggie with two ounces of marijuana and another with a gram of cocaine in his pockets. His girlfriend had broken up with him a few weeks before. No hint that it was other than a suicide.

His mother Laraine still lived in the same house that Chet had grown up in, the most unkempt yard in an otherwise nice residential neighbourhood up by Foothill College in Redwood City. Although it was still shy of eight o'clock on a warm and still-light summer evening, Laraine Mobley answered the door in a cloud of tobacco smoke, wearing a frayed and faded quilted housecoat and slippers. She was smoking a cigarette and holding a glass of amber-coloured liquid in her other hand as she pushed open the screen door. With a weary welcoming smile, she told me in her husky voice to come on in and take any seat.

A rerun of the Flintstones was playing on the television, muted.

Before I'd even sat down, she said, 'Chet didn't kill himself, you know. If that's what this is really about.' She'd told me the same thing on the telephone when I'd called her an hour earlier. And for this interview, I was in uniform. 'That's what I told you guys when it happened.'

'It wasn't "us guys", ma'am. I'm up in San Mateo.'

As if that mattered to her. Her hand brushed the comment away. 'I mean, how could they ignore the dope connection. He was selling it, everybody knew that. I think the guy he bought it from paid you guys off to go away. I still think that. Chet wasn't an unhappy boy. He was straightening himself out, too. I mean, the job. OK, maybe he was buying and selling, too, but he was working at a real job. That's trying, isn't it?'

'Yes, ma'am. It sounds like it to me. Was that his first real job?'

She took a deep drag and let it out, talking through the smoke. 'Full-time, yeah. Except for McDonald's in high school. And he and Shelly were done, anyway. That didn't even bother him.'

'Shelly?'

She nodded. 'His girlfriend. They all made such a big deal about how they just broke up, but he'd been talking about breaking up with her when she went and beat him to the punch. But you know, they find dope on you, you're a known stoner, they don't look as hard or as much as they look with other people. It's a known fact.'

'So you think somebody killed Chet?'

'Absolutely. I've always thought that.'

'Why?'

'Because of the dope, somehow. He was trying to get out of the business, but they don't let you just quit something like that. Whoever he was buying his stuff from. I told all of you guys back then, but nobody listened.'

'I'm listening now, Mrs Mobley. Do you know who was selling him his dope? Do you have any names?'

Stubbing out her cigarette, she hesitated, sipped from her drink, and shook her head. 'No. He wouldn't ever talk about that, except to say that they were scary guys. You didn't want to cross them.'

'I'm sure that's true. Do you think he might have done that?'

'Well, that's just the thing. I know he wouldn't. He was trying to get out and just kind of slip away from it all. I mean, getting the real job, making new friends, all of that.'

'So it really doesn't make sense to you that he would have double-crossed his dope partners, does it?'

'I know he wouldn't have done that. It was the one thing he was really scared of.'

'But didn't the police investigate those connections back then?'

'They said they did. But you know how that goes. Chet wasn't nobody important. He had some weed on him, big deal. Somebody paid off the cops to go away.'

'I don't think so, ma'am. Not in a murder case. That's not how it happens.'

'Well, sure, that's what you'd say. You're one of them.'

'I am one of them. But I'm also interested in finding out who killed your son. Maybe the police couldn't find anybody among his dope connections because they didn't do it. Have you thought of that?'

'Well, who else, then? He wasn't real like involved in nothing else.'

'How about poker? Didn't he play poker?'

In the middle of lighting up, she stopped the match inches before it reached the cigarette, then finally moved it to the tobacco and inhaled deeply. 'What makes you say that?'

'Because I'm pretty sure that poker is what killed my own father. Was Chet a poker player? Did he have a regular game?'

'It was the one thing he had a real passion for,' she said. 'How could you know that?'

'Never mind that. Do you know if Chet got in a game in the last couple of days before he died?'

Sinking back into her chair, Mrs Mobley seemed to shrink before my eyes, the enormity of this new theory settling over her, weighing her down. Silently, she began to cry. Tears broke over the rim of her eyes and began to course her cheeks. 'I knew he wouldn't leave me,' she said. 'He would never have left me like that.'

I came forward and spoke softly. 'Do you remember the names of anyone he used to play with, Mrs Mobley? If I knew who was in that last game, I believe it could get us to the bottom of all of this at last.'

Staring into the middle distance between us, tears continued to fall off her chin and onto her housecoat. 'I'm afraid there's only one I remember,' she said. 'One of the boys from Chet's new job. I know they played together a few times. A sweet kid, which was a nice change from the usual stoners, you know. I remember he came to the funeral.'

'And who was that, Mrs Mobley? Do you remember his name?'

She told me.

'What's so important, Aaron? You sounded so upset on the phone.' My mother, well turned out as always, stood in the doorway, concern etched in her fine features. It was eight-thirty in the evening on the day after I'd spoken to Laraine Mobley. 'Are the kids all right? Jen?'

'The kids are fine, Mom. Come on in. Jen's in the kitchen.' Leading her back into the house, I asked, 'What did you tell Neal?'

'Just what you said. That you and Jen were having a fight and you needed me to come and reason with her about something.'

'Right. Good.'

'Aaron. What's this about?' Then, seeing my wife – pale, drawn, red-eyed at the table. 'Jen, dear. What's the matter?' Back to me. 'What's going on?'

'Sit down, Mom,' I said. 'We've got to talk.'

Pulling out a chair, carefully lowering herself into it, she looked at me expectantly. I sat down opposite her and pulled out the photograph of her and Pop that I'd been carrying around for the past couple of weeks. 'Do you remember this picture, Mom?' I asked.

'Of course I do.'

'It's the day Pop gave you the earrings, right?'

Her hand went to her ears, where a set of earrings still glittered. 'Yes.'

'But those earrings got stolen along with your other jewellery during the burglary, didn't they?'

'Yes, of course. What are you getting at?'

'I'm getting at the earrings you're wearing right now, Mom. Where did you get those?'

She hesitated, cocking her head questioningly. 'From Neal. He knew the originals were one of my favourite things I'd ever got from your father, and on our second anniversary, mine and Neal's that is, he bought me a pair that matched it. It's why I never take them off, because the first time I did, I lost them.'

While I stood up and crossed over to the phone, Jen reached across the table and put her hand over my mother's. 'Abby,' she said, 'that's not a matching pair. Those are the same earrings.'

'What? Don't be ridiculous. We looked at that picture and Neal matched them as well as he could. What are you both saying? How could Neal have the original…?'

I missed the rest of it. I was telling my colleagues in San Mateo homicide that I had my last piece of the puzzle, and that they should move in and take Neal into custody.

Among the insurance papers that had settled my Pop's estate and that Mom and I had stored in the Safety Deposit box we still rented at our local Bayshore Savings, the earrings had been appraised and described in minute detail, down to the distinctive flaws that made each of the diamonds unique.

It's always preferable in a murder case to have foundational hard evidence linking the suspect to the crime. And it doesn't get much harder than diamonds. Without them, Charles Baden's testimony that he'd played poker regularly with Neal wouldn't have been enough to convict, or to force Neal to confess. And neither would Laraine Mobley's information that Neal worked at the same construction site at the same time as her son. He might have even stood up against the evidence of the diamonds themselves, but he finally could not withstand the look of loss, despair, and hatred in my mother's eyes. You want my opinion, that's what finally broke him.

So this was the way it had gone down.

There had only been four players at that last game – Pop, Brady, Chet, and the man who was to kill all of the others over the next three days. These were my Pop, because Neal needed the money back, and he had to take the jewels to make it look like a burglary. Brady and Chet had to go because they very well might have figured it out. Chet, Neal said, was even a likely blackmail threat – he was feeling out the possibility when Neal put a quick stop to it with a nail upside his head.

They'd played table stakes, with a several hundred dollar buy-in per player, and Pop had been the big winner, cleaning out the other three. It was a big enough financial hit for all of them, but for Neal, the money loss was world-shattering. He'd almost saved the down payment and had made an offer for his first house which was just a bit more money than he had in hand. He thought he was close enough to win the difference with one good game.

Instead, he'd been wiped out.

By a good friend—

Whose beautiful wife had fed him dinner several times over the past couple of years, and whom he coveted deeply.

And whose son the future cop had buried as an impossible secret, a repressed memory, the significance and identity of the man he'd seen all those years ago, and every year since – sitting in as the fourth player at his father's table at a friendly little game of poker.

♠

Missing the Morning Bus
Lorenzo Carcaterra

I LIFTED THE LID ON my hold cards and smiled. I leaned back against three shaky slats of an old worn chair, wood legs mangled by the gnawing of a tired collie now asleep in a corner of the stuffy room, and stared over at the six faces huddled around the long dining room table, thick mahogany wood shining under the glare of an overhead chandelier, each player studying his hand, deciding on his play, mentally considering his odds of success, in what was now the fifth year of a weekly Thursday night ritual. I stared at the face of each of the men I had known for the better part of a decade and paused to wonder which of these friends would be the one. I was curious as to which of the six I would be forced to confront before this night, unlike any other, would come to its end.

I wanted so desperately to know who sitting around that table was responsible for the death of the woman I loved. And I would want that answer before the last draw of the evening was called.

I tried to read their faces much the same as they would the cards in their hand. There was Jerry, wide smile as always plastered across his face, a forty-year-old straight and single man free of the weight of day-to-day worries, a millionaire many times over due to a five thousand dollar investment in a small computer start-up outfit working out of a city he had never heard of, let alone visited. Jerry McReynolds never missed a Thursday night game, boasting of his streak as if he were a ball player about to make a move on Cal Ripkin's long-standing record of consecutive games played. He came outfitted in the same casual manner in which he approached the cards dealt his way, catalogue-ordered shirts and jeans, nothing fancy, nothing wild. I could count on him to come in with two high-end bottles of Italian reds and quickly ease into the steady flow of cards and chatter that filled our weekly five hour sessions. Jerry was the guardian of the chips and kept a small pad and a pen by his side, starting off the game with a fifty dollar feed and dispensing out whites and blues to any player running low or chasing empty. Jerry kept his cards close, doing a quick fold if he felt his hand weak, playing the table as he did his life, on the up and up and without a hint of bluff. In five years of play, I could never recall a time when Jerry left the room with less in his pockets than he had at the start.

I sat back, rubbed the stiffness from the nape of my neck and tried to recall how I came to know Jerry in the first place and couldn't quite place it, my cloudy memory confining it to one of the holiday receptions my wife used to host on a semi-regular basis back in the days when our marriage still had the scent of salvation. God, how I hated every one of those parties, forced to make small talk in a room packed with mostly her friends since the few I had were seldom invited nor welcomed into her cloistered world. I took a long gulp from a glass of scotch and looked back on those long and tedious nights and did a quick flash of Jerry being dragged by the hand in my direction, a glass of white wine in one hand, my wife's in the other. 'You two will be good friends in no time at all,' she said as she made a quick U-turn back into party traffic, her short and tight black skirt giving strong hints of the curvy body that rested beneath, long red hair hanging just off the edge of her shoulders. She was about forty-two then, give or take, and looked at least ten years younger, the quick smile and easy laugh a sweet antidote to the onslaught of age. I wasn't quite sure how Dottie and Jerry came to know one another and I never did bother to ask, but there was always more to their friendship than they were willing to let on. There was that look between them. You know the kind I mean? As if someone was in front of them telling a joke and they were the only two in on the punch line.

'Five card draw, jacks or better to open,' Steve said, giving the deck one more shuffle before the deal, waiting for us all to ante.

'I need a re-fill,' I said, tossing my one dollar chip into the centre of the table, pushing my chair back and walking over to a crowded counter top, filled with half-empty bottles of scotch, bourbon, gin and wine. I spun open the top of a Dewar's bottle and stared over at Steve as he meticulously doled out the cards, eyebrows thick as awnings shading his eyes. I had known Steve since forever started, both of us only children raised in the same Bronx neighbourhood and going to the same Catholic schools up straight through till college. And even then, while he froze his ass off studying economics and law at Michigan and I was smoking and doping my way through four years of English, a language I already had a leg up on, at Williams, we never drifted that far apart. We saw each other during breaks and vacations, hustling over to the same parties and looking to score with the same girls. I guess if I had to pick one, I'd point to Little Stevie Giraldo as my best friend, the fast-talker with a good line of shit and a born-with-it ability to talk the unwilling to tag along on any outing he thought was worth the time and money. As he got older and life started dealing him a tougher set of cards, Steve's youthful edge took a sharp nose dive and by the time he hit his forties he was a man adrift, moving from one mid-tier job to the next, in debt to credit cards and street loaners, a decade into a loser's marriage and with two kids who cost him ten for every five he earned. I was the only one in the room who knew he tried to do a final check-out about eighteen months back, but even there his bad luck stayed that way. He chugged enough pills and booze to knock off Walter Hudson, that guy was so fat they had to bury his ass inside a piano, and all it got him was a long night at a crowded hospital, his stomach pumping out everything he had managed to shove in. I was the one waited for him, rushing over from a nearby bar where I was nursing a few, soon as I got the word from Mackey, a mutual pal working the wood that night. Dottie came by at sun-up, driving the old Nissan she would never let me sell, and took us both back to our place where she made some coffee and let him sleep the rest of the OD off in the back bedroom. She didn't say all that much about it and I said even less. But I couldn't help but catch the look of concern on her face, odd since she never much cared for Stevie one way or the other. Made me wonder what kind of look I would have earned if it was me instead of him lying in that bed, one pill removed from the long nap.

'Are you in or not, Ike?' Joe asked. 'I mean, you going to pony and play or you just looking to mix drinks all night?'

'I'm in for a dollar,' I said, dropping two cubes into my tumbler and glaring over at Joe, decked out as he always was in a battered New York Yankee baseball cap, Detroit Red Wings sweatshirt and San Diego Chargers workout pants. A walking billboard of sports franchises. Joe was a trash-talking, ball-buster of a work-from-home bonds tradesman who only left his Upper West Side apartment for poker games or sporting events. Other than on those semi-regular occasions, he shopped, ordered food, chatted with friends and read for both leisure and business on his laptop. His two-bedroom condo, bought with the inheritance he scored off the double death of his mother and a great aunt three days apart in 1995, was a smoothie blend of Ikea, sports and movie memorabilia furniture and utensils. Dottie disliked Joe with an intensity that bordered on the fanatical which, if he knew how she felt, he would ironically appreciate, able to compare it to his rabid feelings towards both the Boston Red Sox and the New York Islanders. I guess I liked him for the same reasons she didn't. Joe was filled with passion and was never shy to let anyone with ears know how he felt about his teams, his favourite movie or TV show. Hell, he would even get into a beef and a brawl over the athleticism of pro wrestling. Funny though, in all the years I've known Joe, and I've been doing his taxes now going on ten years this next April, he's never once asked me what my favourite sport was or which team I liked. For all he knows, I can't stand the sight of any sport, let alone follow one close enough to dip into my savings for season tickets and wear the team colours to my best friend's wedding or wake. But Joe did know that Dottie liked basketball and that she never missed a New York Knicks game on television during the season and, on rare occasions, the playoffs. I only know that because he mentioned it once during a poker game, after the Knicks by some miracle had beaten the Miami Heat the night before, how happy Dottie must have been to see that happen. How the hell could he have any idea that she was a fan or was even at home to watch the game?

I was back at my seat looking down at a pair of tens and a queen high, the fresh drink by my side. I glanced to my left and caught Tony's eye and was given a warm smile as a reward. 'Everything good with you?' he asked.

'Good enough,' I said, trying to keep the conversation light and not veer it towards the personal which is the road Tony always seemed to prefer.

It made sense that he would, of course, what with him being a shrink and all. Tony enjoyed doing hit and run probes into the lives of the men around the table, treating the entire night as if it were a casual group session with cards, chips and money added to the mix. He would keep it all very chatty like, never giving the impression he was picking and pawing or even the least bit curious about any one of us but always leaving the table owning a lot more information than he had when he first walked in. When he wasn't busy jabbing at our collective scabs as casually as he would a platter of potato salad, Tony regaled us with tales of his sexual conquests, most of them arriving courtesy of his practically all female practice. It was difficult not to envy any man who in a given week would bed as many as five different women, so you can imagine how well his tales travelled around a poker table filled with either those that had gone without for longer than they would dare to remember or the few that felt strangled by double-decades' worth of marital gloom. 'This is one you won't believe,' he said, dropping his cards on the table in a fold and sitting back, wide grin flashed across a face that looked far too young for a man one month shy of his fifty-second birthday. 'I have this new patient, right? Drop dead blonde with stallion legs and a killer smile. Only on her second visit, asks if it's OK for her to call me at home. You know, just to shoot it whenever the urge hits.'

'You ever see any ugly patients?' I asked. I really didn't want to believe every woman who paid to tell Tony sad tales of an unful-filled life was poster girl material even though, deep in my heart, it figured probably to be indeed true.

'Only on referrals,' Tony said. 'Anyway, I'm supposed to say no to such a request, I suppose. I mean if I'm going to do a line by line with the rule book.'

'But you never have before,' I said. 'No sense finding religion now, especially when it's a different promised land you're looking to find.'

'So, I give her my home number and go about the rest of my day,' Tony said. 'I had no doubt she would make use of it down the road a bit, maybe get a few more sessions under her garters before she made the move.'

'Let me take a stab at a guess here,' Joe said. 'She dialled your private line right about the start of the second period of the Rangers game. Right or not?'

'If that's about eight or so, then yes, you win the stuffed bear,' Tony said. 'She was very upset, needed to talk and couldn't make it wait. I offered to do a free phone consult, but she wanted a face to face. An hour later we were down a half bottle of red and doing a wild roll on the water bed.'

'I didn't think anybody still had a water bed,' Steve said. 'Or that they even made them. You don't have a lava lamp too, do you?'

I brushed Steve's question aside with one of my own. 'This woman,' I asked, 'was she married or single?'

Tony stared at me for several seconds before he answered. 'Would it make a difference either way?' he asked.

'It might,' I said, 'to her husband.'

'She is married,' Tony said with more a sneer than a smile. 'Truth be told, most of the women who come to me for help are bound to the ring. If they weren't then maybe they wouldn't be so damn unhappy and I wouldn't be pulling down seven figures to dole out my pearls of acquired wisdom.'

'Does any of that cause you concern?' I asked. 'I mean forget about the doctor–patient mumbo crap. I'm talking here as a man. Does it bother you one inch to be taking another man's wife into your bed?'

'It never has,' Tony said, staring right at me as if his measured words were meant for my ears alone. 'And it never will.'

'Is there any more pie?' Jeffrey asked. 'I don't know what it is lately, but I can't seem ever to get enough to eat.'

'That may well be because you're celibate,' Tony said. 'You need something to replace what the body most needs. If you took my advice, which I rarely offer for free, you would switch gears and reach for a warm body instead of a warm plate.'

Jeffrey hated to talk about sex or at least that's the impression he wanted to convey. He was a Jesuit priest when I first met him, waiting in line to see Nathan Lane go for laughs in a Neil Simon play – an original not a revival. It was a cold and rainy Wednesday and the matinee crowd was crammed as it usually was with the bused in and the walk-ins. We both should have been somewhere else, doing what I was paid to do and, in Jeffrey's case, what he was called to do. We made a valiant attempt at small talk as we snaked our way up toward a half-price ticket window and were surprised when we scored adjoining orchestra seats. 'Now if the show is only half as funny as the critics claim,' Jeffrey said, 'we will have gotten our money's worth.'

We stopped by Joe Allen's for drinks after the show and I had just ordered my second shaken-not-stirred martini of the afternoon when I invited Father Jeffrey to join the poker game, eager to fill the void left by Sal Gregorio's spur of the moment move to Chicago to tend to his father's meat packing plant. Even back then, Jeffrey seemed to me a troubled man, grappling with the type of demons I would never be able to visualize in the worst of my black dog moments. I did come away with the sense that he had reached the top of the well when it came to his chosen vocation, not sure whether it was the paedophile scandal rocking the church that did it or just the very fact that he was a modern man forced to live a sixteenth century life. 'Do you miss it?' I had asked him that day.

'What,' he asked, 'the women?'

'We can start with that,' I said, trying my best to make light of what would have to be considered a serious deal-breaker in *any* contract talks that brought into play a lifetime commitment.

'There are moments,' Jeffrey said, 'when I *don't* think about it. It is, by a wide margin, the biggest obstacle a priest must overcome. At least it has been for me. But hidden beneath the cover of misery, a silver cloud often lies.'

'What's yours?' I asked, maybe crossing deeper into the holy water than I should.

'That it's young women who draw my eye and not innocent boys,' Jeffrey said, the words tinged with anger and not regret.

'Are you one of those rebels in a collar who think Christ and Mary Magdalene were more than just pen pals?' I asked, doing what I could to steer the conversation away from the uncomfortable.

'I am one of those rebels in a collar who think Christ was too much of a man *not* to be in love with a woman as beautiful and as loyal as Mary was to him,' Jeffrey said.

One year later, just about to the day, Father Jeffrey turned his back on his vows, handed in his collar and walked out of the church life for good. Yet, in the time from that eventful day to this, he stayed celibate or, at least, so he claimed, though not from a lack of effort but more from a lack of experience. Now, of all the guys in the poker group, he was the only one Dottie liked, the one she didn't roll her eyes or mumble beneath her breath if we ran into on the street or in a local restaurant. She even mentioned once that she went to church to see him serve mass and listen to one of his sermons. 'How was he?' I asked her that day.

'He looked like he belonged up there,' Dottie said about Jeffrey in the same natural tone I would have reserved for Frank Sinatra or Johnny Cash. 'But then again, it's not like it was his first time.'

'Full house, kings high,' Jerry said, resting his hand flat on the table and reaching over to drag a small mountain of different coloured chips his way.

'Was that deck even shuffled?' Adam asked, shaking his head, thick hair covering one side of his thin face. 'I mean, really, just look at all the face cards that are out. I don't think it was shuffled.'

'You only ask that when I win a hand,' Jerry said. 'There a reason for that?'

'That's because the only hands you ever win usually come off a deck that hasn't been shuffled,' Adam said.

Adam and Jerry hated one another and I never understood why one, if not both, didn't just walk from the game. It wasn't as if the city was lacking weekly poker gatherings and God knows most of them served better food and had a nicer selection of wines to choose from than what I offered and set out. Adam was a doctor and a noted one, often cited in medical journals and in the Science section of *The New York Times* as the gold standard in regards to matters pertaining to women and their bodies. He was handsome with an easy smile and a scalpel sharp sense of humour, except of course when he found himself sitting across a table from Jerry, cards in hand and a stack of poker chips resting between them. And while I could never quite put a finger to the pulse that got the feud started in the first place, in many ways I felt myself to be the one responsible. After all, as with the rest of the group, I was the one who brought Adam into the game. And I would just as soon bring the weekly sessions to an end than to see it go on without Adam holding his usual place at the far end of my table.

Dr Adam Rothberg had saved my wife's life.

Three years ago, after a long bout with a flu that wouldn't quite surrender the fight, Dottie, fresh off a five day siege of heavy-duty antibiotics mixed with cough syrup and aspirin collapsed on the floor of our tiny barely walk into-it-and-move-around kitchen. She was doubled up and clutching her stomach, foam thick as ocean spray flowed out of her mouth and her body shook as if it were resting on top of a high-speed motor boat. I was about to jump for the phone and dial 911 when I remembered that the new face that had moved in down the hall during the last week belonged to a doctor. I rushed out of the apartment and ran out into the narrow hall, banging at a door two removed from mine. I felt like a boy sitting under a tree crammed with packages on Christmas morning when I saw Adam's face as he swung open his apartment door.

He saved Dottie's life that day and we have been friends ever since.

In that span of time, Adam's practice flourished and his stature rose, while mine pretty much hovered at the same level it had been for years. I don't hate the work I do really, it's just that I don't love it either. I look around this table and don't see anyone happier at their chosen work than I am, except maybe for Adam who truly loves putting on the white coat and playing God twelve hours a day. I am good at what I do, bringing a financial balance to the lives of my clients, despite the fact I can't seem to accomplish those same goals for myself. I could never get it to where I was a step ahead, with all the bills paid and some money set aside. And I could never figure out where the hell it all went, especially since we didn't have the financial burden of kids and had lived in the same apartment for more or less the same rent since we were first married and except for a two-week splurge in Italy during our first year together seldom took long or expensive vacations.

It bothered Dottie, I knew that. Not that I was an accountant.

But that I was one without money and minus the drive or the talent to earn it. Women like Dottie go into a marriage and expect more out of it than they first let on, not wanting to be the kind of woman who lives her middle age years in a financial and emotional rut. And the truth of that, the belief that I had let her down in some way, ate at me more than I would let on. I had failed her, and over time it chipped away at the love she felt for me. I could see it, sense it, her eyes vacant and drawn when she looked my way, her manner indifferent at best, her kisses directed more to the cheek than the lips, as if she were greeting a distant relative with whom she would prefer to have very little contact. It was so different from when we first met. Back then, I was sure we would love each other forever.

I first saw Dorothy Blakemore at a counter on the second floor of a department store on the Upper East Side. It was a week before Christmas and the place was mad crazy with shoppers with a hunger for gifts, credit cards clutched in their hands. She was staring down at a counter filled with men's gloves and kept shaking her head each time a tall, thin and harried sales clerk made the slightest attempt at a suggestion. 'I don't even know his size,' were the first words I heard her say, her voice a sultry mix of Southern warmth mixed with a North-east education.

'If I had an idea as to his height and weight, then perhaps I can narrow down your choices,' he said to her, his tone more condescending than consoling.

Dottie paused for a brief second and then glanced in my direction. When she turned and our eyes met, I knew that I was in the middle of a movie moment, standing a mere distance from a woman as beautiful and striking as any I would ever be lucky enough to see in my lifetime. 'He's about the size of this man,' she said to the sales clerk as she walked toward me.

I helped her pick out a pair of black leather gloves for her brother who lived in some town in Maine whose name I could never remember. I wasn't the type to move fast when it came to women, but I knew in my heart if I didn't connect with Dottie on that day, then I would for sure never see her again. There have been few moments in my life when I've been able to manage to put the pieces together and not muck up the works and that early afternoon was top-of-the-list one of them. I offered to buy her a cup of coffee at a nearby lunch shop that, if it were anywhere else other than on the Upper East Side of Manhattan would be called a diner, and she smiled and nodded. I fell in love that day and have been ever since.

'Cards don't look to be falling your way tonight, Ike,' Steve said, dropping a three of hearts next to my six of spades. 'But then, why should tonight be different from any other game?'

'I used up my run of luck looking for love; there wasn't any left over for cards,' I said with a slight shrug, my words sounding much meeker than I intended.

'So things between you and Dottie are good now?' Tony asked.

'Did I ever give you a hint that they weren't?' I asked, not bothering to disguise my annoyance at the question.

'How about we just play the hand?' Joe advised. 'You want to talk about unhappy marriages let's talk about Isaiah Thomas and Stephon Marbury. Not only are they mucking it up with each other, they're destroying any remote chance the Knicks have at ever sneaking into the playoffs.'

'Dottie and I are not unhappy,' I said with as much vigour as I could muster. 'And if I did or said anything to give you that impression, it was wrong and unintentional.'

'And there it shall end,' Jeffrey said with a nod and a smile. 'To be quite honest, I never realized how much men loved to gossip until I started playing poker. Unless it's just this particular group that happens to be so chatty.'

'I can only imagine what you and your crew talked about back in your rectory days,' Steve said. 'I would bet a full load it covered nastier terrain than who was swigging too much of the communion wine.'

I sat back, smiled and listened as the kidding and ribbing continued around me, holding my anger in check, knowing that the moment was at hand, the killer soon to be revealed. It was all very easy in some way to piece it together, deciding who in the group sitting around my table would bear the responsibility that had led to my Dottie's sudden and unexpected death.

It was his fingers that were wrapped around the thick black handle of the carving knife as much as mine. It was his hand along with mine that plunged that blade into Dottie's frail and tender body again and again and again until she fell to the floor of the back bedroom, her head slumped to one side, blood oozing out of the deep and severe wounds and staining the thick Persian rug she had bought with the proceeds from my first and only Christmas bonus back during that first year of wedded bliss.

I was a 44-year-old man, alone and in debt, out-of-shape and mentally drained, my hair thinner than it had any right to be and my stomach rounder than anyone my age would prefer. I had a past that was filled mostly with dark and gloomy days and empty nights, touched only on rare occasions by the light and tender glare of happiness. I had a future that promised to be even bleaker, doomed to live out what was left of my time alone and in a constant struggle to survive.

So I needed to keep my focus on the present.

In one room, staring up at a chipped and stained white ceiling, an overhead fan on low, circulated warm air in gusts, was the body of a woman who had shared twenty-two years of my life.

And in this room, surrounded by poker chips, two decks of playing cards, near-empty bowls of nuts and salsa, drinks waiting to be finished, sat the man who had forced my hand and directed it toward murder.

'Looks like it's your deal, Ike,' Adam said. 'And your call. What's it going to be?'

'Let's make this the final hand,' I said.

'It's not even ten,' Joe said, 'we usually go to eleven, sometimes an hour or two later. Why make it such an early call?'

'If it's the last one, can we at least make it interesting?' Steve asked.

'I intend to,' I said. 'Midnight baseball, no peak, threes and nines are wild, you draw a four and you can buy yourself an extra card.'

'How about we double the ante, then?' Joe asked. 'And let's put no limits on the raises. That square with everybody?'

'You go that route and the pot can start to get a little steep,' Jerry said. 'It's always been a friendly game. This will take it out of that ballpark, no doubt.'

'What, you afraid of losing something off the heavy pile of dough you got stashed?' Joe asked.

'I'm afraid of sitting here and watching you lose money I *know* you don't have,' Jerry said. 'Nothing more.'

'You should all be afraid,' I said. 'This is the one hand none of you can hide from and not one of you can afford to lose.'

'What the hell are you talking about?' Adam asked. 'Just deal the cards and let's get this over with. These weekly games are starting to wear a bit thin. It might just be time for me to move on.'

I shuffled the deck one final time and pushed it over to my left, waiting for Tony to cut the cards and turned to Adam. 'And if luck singles you out, then you may well get your wish, doctor,' I said.

I had their attention now, each staring at me not sure whether I was drunk or tired or had totally spun my wheels off the rails. I slowly and with great care doled out seven cards to each player, myself included. 'This isn't at all like you, Ike,' Jeffrey said, more than slightly annoyed. 'Maybe Adam is on the right track. We may all need to call it for tonight. You look like you could do with a good night's rest.'

'You might be right on that score, Padre,' I said. 'I might just need a few solid hours of shut eye. But before I push back and trot off to bed, I need to bring our little game to a fitting end. I think that's something we all would want. So how about you sit back and sit tight? This won't take very long.'

I caught the glances racing across the table from one set of eyes to another, the looks a mixture of confusion, anger, concern and indifference and it made me smile. I had them now, these six friends of mine, men I had trusted and confided in, to some had even bared secrets I would never want spoken outside this room. They were for a long stretch of time in my troubled life the raft that I could wrap my arms around and ward off, however briefly, the arching waves, dark clouds and approaching storm of an existence that seemed destined to end with my drowning death. But they all carried with them the Judas coin and the blood of a good woman was now smeared across it.

We all turned our first card over. Steve was high with a jack and casually tossed a one dollar chip onto the centre of the table. I stared at him and waited for him to return my look. 'She cared about you,' I told him, 'and took good care of you after your minor mishap a while back. It was her idea to put you in bed, *our* bed, and leave you there until you were well enough to walk out on your own. But even after all that, you seemed to act as if you didn't even notice when she was around. Or was that a charade meant only for my eyes?'

Steve looked around at the others, embarrassed that his suicidal secret was now open for discussion, before he turned to me. 'I don't know what you're getting at, Ike,' he said. 'You're a bit out of control and not just tonight, but for a while. We've all picked up on it and let it slide, figuring you needed to work a few things out, is all. But now it's reached a sharp point and maybe we should bring it all to a stop right here and right now.'

'It's only a game, Ike,' Jeffrey said. 'It would be madness to let friendships be cast aside over some silly game.'

'What's only a game, Padre?' I asked, turning my attention to Jeffrey. 'The hand you've just been dealt or the deal between you and Dottie?'

'What are implying?' Jeffrey asked. 'I have never had an improper moment with Dottie. Not one, not ever. And for you to even think something like that borders on madness.'

'If it wasn't you, Padre,' I asked, 'then who did have their moments with Dottie, improper or otherwise? Maybe it was you, Jerry. Dottie always did do a fast spin toward a man with money and you have more than most. Or maybe you, Joe, Mr Reebok himself. After all, how many games can one man go to without wanting to play in one of his very own? Of course, there's always Adam, the good doctor and the one who once rushed in to rescue her in a time of need. What woman wouldn't want to show how grateful she was for a second chance at an unfinished life? Or maybe it was the one obvious choice in the room. That would be you, Tony, the shrink with the black book Rolodex. Dottie's main complaint about me was that she talked but I never listened. And who better to listen and be receptive to her problems than someone like you? A man who has devoted his life to soothing and comforting women in need.'

'Is that what all this is about?' Joe asked. 'You think one of us is having an affair with your wife?'

'You're a fool, Ike,' Tony said, his voice crammed with pure hatred. 'And you may live under the same ceilings as Dottie but you don't know the first thing about her or you would know she is willing to do anything to help salvage the shambles you've made of your marriage.'

'You're right about one thing, though,' Steve said. 'We haven't been on the square with you about our relationship with Dottie. We've all been seeing her, everyone sitting at this table. She insisted on it.'

'All of you?' I said, not bothering to mask either the shock or the surprise. 'You've *all* been with her?'

'Yes,' Jeffrey said, 'but not for the reason that's currently racing through your mind. Her visits with us were not of a sexual nature.'

'Then what the hell were you seeing her for?' I shouted, pounding a closed right fist onto the table, knocking over Steve's wine glass, the red liquid flowing over a stack of chips. 'Why was she spending time with any of you? And if it all was on the up and up like you're trying to sell me, then why didn't she tell me about it?'

'She couldn't, at least not yet,' Adam said, his words weighed down with a certain edge of sadness. 'There were a few more items she needed to clear up first.'

'Dottie was sick,' Jeffrey said, 'very sick. That bout with the stomach that Adam helped clear her of was merely the first indication of how deep her illness ran and how serious a final outcome it would lead to. That was what brought her to us, individually at first and then later in small groups.'

'What did she want from you?' I asked, the words forcing their way from my mouth. My throat burned and I felt my heart doing a Keith Moon pounding against my chest. I held onto the edges of the table as if it were a life vest, doing all I could not to scream out in agony.

'She asked us to take care of you, look after you after she was gone,' Steve said. 'Each in a way she knew we could. Adam would make sure you took care of your health. Jerry would pull you out of debt with whatever was left of the insurance money coming your way, working to set your finances in order. Me? I had been your closest friend and she asked that I stay that way, no matter how much of an ass you turned into.'

'I would take you to as many games as you could stand,' Joe said. 'Dottie told me how often you wished you had a chance to see one team or the other play and she felt going with a friend would help take your mind off your loss. Tony could show how good a therapist he really is and would see you free of charge only you wouldn't know it since all your bills would be going to Jerry anyway.'

'And Adam and I were asked to simply look after anything else that fell through the cracks,' Jeffrey said, 'either spiritually or physically. Dottie covered every base by simply turning to the only friends she knew you had. The men at this table.'

'It was also important to her that the game keep going,' Jerry said. 'She felt the weekly poker nights served as an anchor against all the other crap that was going on in your life. She thought you needed it. But after tonight, I'm not all that sure she was right on that count.'

'Your suspicions were right,' Steve said, 'only they were headed in the wrong direction. We were all involved with Dottie. And Dottie was involved with all of us. We each had a mutual interest and that was you.'

'Feel better now?' Adam asked.

I looked at them, scanning their tired and worn faces, and nodded. 'I'm sorry,' I said, my mouth as hot and as dry as an August afternoon. 'I wasn't thinking straight. I most likely said a lot of the wrong things. And I did something horrible which I know can never be undone.'

'We might be pissed at you, Ike,' Joe said. 'But, trust me, we'll get over it. Dottie is right. We're friends here. Even Adam and Jerry, whether they want to admit it or not. And that gives us all quite a bit of leeway. By the time the next game rolls around what happened tonight will be only a memory.'

'I hope that's true,' I said. 'You don't know how much I want that to be true.'

'It will be,' Jeffrey said in a soft voice. 'There's no reason for it not.'

'How much time did, excuse me, *does* Dottie have left?' I asked, directing my question mainly to Adam.

'It's a fast-moving disease,' Adam said, 'and it was caught very late. Based on her most recent tests, I would say a month at best, two if she's at all lucky.'

'And is there any chance she might beat it?' I asked.

'No,' Adam said. 'I can't lie to you about that. There's no chance at all. What Dottie has is terminal.'

'And did you all agree to help me?' I asked. 'To do all the things she asked you to do for me?'

'What kind of friend would say no to something like that?' Jerry said. 'We would do anything Dottie asked. And to be honest, we would have done it even if she hadn't come to ask.'

'We're all you have,' Joe said. 'We're all what each of us has. The poker game is just a good excuse to get together. We're family. This is it, all of it, right here in this very room, no matter how crazy or stupid some of us get at times, we are all here and will always be here for each other.'

'Dottie was right,' I said. 'You are my friends and my family. She always could see that in a much clearer light.'

'She told me if we could keep it all together then none of us would ever be alone,' Tony said. 'And there's no reason why we should ever not let it be so.'

'Would you help me then with Dottie?' I asked. 'See that she gets buried proper, with respect and with care.'

'You know we will,' Jeffrey said. 'You don't even need to ask.'

'Dottie's in the bedroom,' I told them. 'I'm going to take a few minutes alone with her. Once we're ready, I'll call for you. I will need your help then.'

'We'll be here for you,' Steve said. 'Count on it.'

'I will,' I told them. I eased out of my chair and began to make my way toward the back bedroom and the bleeding and ruined body of my wife Dottie.

'Believe me, I will.'

SCOTTISH BORDERS COUNCIL

LIBRARY &
INFORMATION SERVICES